"This fantasy series installment maintains excitement through charming protagonists and ever evolving challenges."
—*Kirkus Reviews*

"C. A. Pack is a great storyteller with a unique gift for plot. The author writes characters that are compelling and sets them out on a breathtaking, magical adventure."
—*Readers' Favorite*

FIFTH CHRONICLES OF ILLUMINATION

Frenemies

BOOKS IN THE LIBRARY OF ILLUMINATION SERIES

Becoming Johanna
A Library of Illumination Prequel

Chronicles: The Library of Illumination
Book One: The Library of Illumination
Book Two: Doubloons
Book Three: The Orb
Book Four: Casanova
Book Five: Portals

Second Chronicles of Illumination
First Book of the Knowledge is Power Trilogy
Book Five: Portals
Book Six: The Overseers
Book Seven: Myrddin's Memoir

Third Chronicles of Illumination
Second Book of the Knowledge is Power Trilogy
Book Eight: Games

Fourth Chronicles of Illumination
Third Book of the Knowledge is Power Trilogy
Book Nine: Endgame

A Library of Illumination Christmas
Book Ten

Fifth Chronicles of Illumination
Book Eleven: Frenemies

FIFTH CHRONICLES OF ILLUMINATION

Frenemies

Library of Illumination: Book Eleven

by

C. A. PACK

Artiqua Press

www.artiquapress.com

ARTIQUA PRESS
info@artiquapress.com
Westbury, NY 11590

TRADE PAPERBACK

November 24, 2020

FIFTH CHRONICLES OF ILLUMINATION
Frenemies
Library of Illumination - Book Eleven

Copyright © 2020 C. A. Pack
All rights reserved.

ISBN-13: 978-1-970028-05-8

Library of Congress Control Number: 2020914378

"It is a riddle, wrapped in a mystery, inside an enigma."

—*Winston Churchill*

WHEN LAST WE LEFT OUR INTREPID HEROES...

JOHANNA CHARETTE AND Jackson Roth had just helped win the war waged by the multi-tentacled Terrorians. The sneaky aggressors thought they could take over all the Libraries of Illumination by force, but learned in the end—it's hard for evil to triumph over good, especially if the "good" includes our plucky curators. Overseer Pru Tellerence lost an arm during the battle and could have lost her life. However, quick-thinking Johanna grabbed the overseer while tossing a precious diamond to the bad guys as they tried to make a quick get-a-way in a stolen time machine. Can you spell K-A-B-O-O-M? Only on Lumina do diamonds explode when you try to remove them from the realm.

AFTERWARD, THE ADVENTURANS fitted Pru Tellerence with a prosthetic arm that she claims feels just like her own.

HOWEVER, THE BIGGEST turn of events occurred after the dust settled and everyone was on their way home. That's when an innocent question about a statue led to the discovery that Johanna is not an orphan but the daughter of overseers Pru Tellerence and Ryden Simmdry. Talk about a pedigree. Oh, forbidden love!

ONE

Johanna Charette, co-curator of the Library of Illumination, felt her nerves dance as if a small electric current suddenly flowed throughout her body. She had just caught sight of the famous prognosticator, Nostradamus, heading toward the front door. It had been left open by a UPS driver, who was now checking labels on the parcels Johanna had just handed her.

Chris Roth, who worked at the library part-time, quickly closed the gap between himself and the French astrologer in an effort to head Nostradamus off before he escaped into the real world. Johanna pushed a package toward the UPS driver to keep her from turning around and asked, "Does this address look right to you?"

Chris grabbed Nostradamus by the arm with one hand and put his finger to his lips with the other—signaling the famous seer to not speak—and led him back into the far reaches of the library.

The UPS driver finally gathered the outgoing packages and left. Johanna closed the front door, leaned against it, and sighed before searching for Chris. She called out, "Where is he?"

"Back in the 16th century. I was flipping through a translation of *The Prophecies* when he escaped. I closed the book after I caught up with him."

Few people were aware that books inside the Library of Illumination came to life.

"You should have closed the book immediately, instead of chasing him. What if anyone had seen him?"

"I would have said he's an actor getting ready for a surprise party. Most people would have accepted that rather than believe the real Nostradamus was here. Don't worry. I can be just as resourceful as Jackson."

Jackson, Chris's older brother and Johanna's co-curator, had decided to take two courses on the same day at Cranford University, so he'd only have to go to school one day a week during the summer. He'd suggested that he and Johanna hire his younger brother to work around the library, cleaning up and shelving books. Jackson's entire family had temporarily lived in the library the previous spring and had sworn to keep the library's secrets in order to prevent it from being plundered by people with defective moral compasses.

Now that the Terrorian threat had ended, the Roth family had moved back to their house on the other side of town. Johanna missed their camaraderie. The Roths had taken care of library business during much of the spring when Johanna and Jackson had their hands full because of one rogue curator's plan to take over all the libraries in the Illumini System. The twelve Libraries of Illumination were enchanted, and each one contained an identical wealth of knowledge, although the books that appeared in the main reading room at one library, might be tucked away in a rarely-visited sublevel of a library on another realm.

The books' properties differed as well. They sprang to life in only four facilities. In other libraries, books might automatically rearrange themselves in order of importance for that particular day; or a genie could pop out of a book to determine a reader's true intention. Then there were the libraries in which people could become a character *inside* a book. Those libraries proved to be popular vacation destinations on those realms. Unfortunately, it could also be a hazard, like it had been on Juvenilia, when the curator of that library entered a literary world and the book accidently closed, trapping him inside.

In Johanna and Jackson's library, the characters and sometimes entire scenes came to life inside the library, which could be a curse or a blessing. Having Casanova appear but not disappear when his memoir closed, caused a rift in the teens' growing relationship. However, if they needed someone to guard the portals when everyone else was busy, it was always good to be able to open a book and ask Thor, or Wild Bill Hickok, to lend a hand.

Johanna thought Jackson might appear before the end of the day. He had hinted at continuing to live at the hotel suite inside the library, even though the rest of his family had moved out. *It would be a good compromise,* she thought. Jackson would be nearby, but in separate quarters. *And we could always order room service for dinner!*

He would probably want to discuss it further after he finished his classes for the day.

*

Jackson fumbled through his wallet, looking for cash while juggling books in the Cranford University book store. He had just completed his English Literature and Information Technologies classes and had stopped to buy textbooks and supplies.

He stared at the man who informed him he couldn't download the IT textbook onto his tablet. "You mean I have to buy the actual book?"

"Yes."

"I can understand that for English lit, but my IT book is all about emerging technologies. Shouldn't the university try *embracing* technology by allowing students to download the book?"

"No."

Jackson shook his head, picked up the heavy books, and the five sweatshirts he'd purchased—one for each member of his family plus Johanna—and headed toward the car. He wanted to talk to Johanna about living at the library, and hoped the sweatshirt might soften her up. *Maybe that and a nice dinner from room service,* he thought, if she hadn't already closed the travel guide that allowed the hotel suite to materialize inside the library.

"Jackson!"

He stopped when he heard his name and looked around. Cameron Thorne was walking toward the bookstore, and Jackson stood right in his path.

"Dean Thorne." Jackson nodded.

"I think you can call me Cameron. We've both faced Terrorians, although you had a much bigger role to play than I did. I believe we have enough shared history, however fleeting it might be so far, to be on a first name basis."

Jackson shifted his books and the bag of sweatshirts and shook the dean's hand. "In case you can't tell, it was my first day."

"How did it go for you?"

"Not bad, but it's been a long day. I thought two classes would be a piece of cake. But two *four-hour* classes— not so much."

"You'll thank yourself when the fall semester starts. You'll already have two classes under your belt, and can take a lighter load than your classmates."

"I planned to do that anyway. I want to have enough time to do well in college, but still be able to pull my weight at the library."

"I have Johanna in one of my classes on Thursday," the dean said.

"Really?" Jackson's voice sounded an octave higher than he wanted it to.

"Yes. Shakespeare 101. She told me she's looking forward to it."

"Oh."

Cameron saw one of his students heading toward them, calling out his name. "I've got to go. It's good to see you," he said before abruptly rushing off.

Jackson's left eyebrow rose in surprise when Cameron walked away from the young woman calling to him. His pursuer, who appeared to be in her mid-twenties, was pretty in a very put-together kind of way; as if she tried really hard to look perfect. She wore very precise makeup, and her skirt was short and tight, but not in an overly slutty way. Still, he had no trouble imagining the view a professor would get if she crossed her legs in class. His eyes opened even wider. *Maybe she's a teacher, and it's her students who get the view.*

He felt himself blush. *I have too much imagination to be thinking these things.* He packed up the car and headed for the library.

BY THE TIME the summer semester officially started at Graydon Ransom University News Tonight—affectionately known as GRUNT—Logan Elliott had already proven himself to be an able reporter. He had automatically become one of the organization's top choices to cover important stories because he already had experience, owned his own camera equipment, and he happened to be enrolled during the pathetically understaffed summer semester when fewer students took courses because financial aid was not available. Logan volunteered to go in every day, rather than the single day required of students, thus endearing himself to the people in charge. In return, he received plum assignments over students who had already taken part in the internship for several semesters.

It didn't hurt that he was rich, good-looking, and drove a nice car. Girls flocked to him like moths to a flame. But in his opinion, none of them could hold a candle to Emily Brent. She could pass for a model, and he already had history with her.

Unfortunately, Emily didn't remember their history. She only knew him as her recently-deceased best friend's grieving boyfriend. She did whatever she could to ease his pain but as far as she was concerned, she was still dating his best buddy, Jackson Roth, from the Library of Illumination.

That has to change, Logan thought. Jackson was a great friend when we were kids. Having him around was like owning a puppy. *Jax* had a good sense of humor, was always outgoing and friendly, and the guy was a chick-magnet. But Logan didn't need Jackson anymore. *I've outgrown him.* He wanted Emily, and to do that he would have to besmirch Jackson's reputation. He already had a lot of the tools he needed to pull that off, and it would only take a few more weeks before Jackson, the Library of Illumination, and its unusual secrets all became headline news on *The Elliott Report.* Sure, he was honing his skills and making connections as a member of the GRUNT news team, but he preferred to put his own interests first, and would be able to do that as president, producer, anchor, and star of his own show, *The Elliott Report.*

He smiled. *It won't be long now. I'll use the summer to prepare, wield my axe in the fall, and by winter the most famous name on the planet will be mine.*

LOGAN RUSHED INTO Max & Jareds, ready to start his shift. He feared he might be late, but he'd made it just in time. Working after putting in a full day at GRUNT was a pain, but it gave him the extra cash he needed to get *The Elliott Report* up and running. A woman got his attention and pointed to her son, who looked perplexed sorting through a table display of jeans. "He doesn't like the weight of the denim. Do you have anything heavier?"

Logan morphed into salesman mode as he walked over to the son. "These are the latest style," he said, pointing to the stacks of jeans. "They're a little more European and the hottest style on trend, right now. We have our plainer, heavier-weight jeans in the bins against the back wall." He pointed them out. "They're great, don't get me wrong, but they're really *last year.* It's like the difference between a new Porsche and an older model Chevy. Which would you rather be?"

The teen looked at the jeans in the back and sighed. Then he handed his mother a pair of jeans from the table display. "I'll take these."

The woman shoved them in Logan's hands. "You heard him. Ring them up."

As Logan keyed in the price of the new jeans, which cost twice as much as the ones along the back wall, he smiled. But then he felt the hairs on the back of his neck prickle. He looked around and then stared out the front window. It felt like someone was watching him.

"Could you hurry, please. We don't have all day." The woman's words jarred him to attention.

"Of course," Logan said, as he placed the jeans in a bag. He handed them over. "Have a nice day." As the woman and her son left the store, he looked out the window, again, but didn't see anyone watching him. Still, it left him feeling uneasy.

TWO

AVA ROTH THREW a shopping bag on her bed. She had been saving her allowance for months, but it wasn't until Johanna and Jackson gave her a healthy *bonus* for helping out at the library while they were busy battling Terrorians that she had enough money for some serious purchasing power. She had just blown most of it on clothing for school. Sure, the new semester was still six weeks away, but she knew she would need a whole new wardrobe for "high" school. *This isn't the little league,* she mused. She had plenty of friends from middle school, but moving up to tenth grade meant she'd be playing in the big leagues. She tried everything on, *again,* before putting her new clothes away in her closet. She sighed. As recently as last year, she had started every school year with just one new outfit—something from one of the local outlet stores. It was all her mother could afford. She had to make do with whatever else she could pick up for herself using babysitting money and her allowance. This was the first year she'd had some major money.

She studied herself in the mirror. *Maybe a new hairdo. Or color. And makeup.* She hadn't been allowed to wear makeup in middle school, but her mother had always promised she could when she reached high school. *I'll ask Johanna.*

That evening at dinner with her mother and her brother, Chris, she mentioned seeing Logan at the mall.

"Logan's a world-class shopper," Chris said between forkfuls of meatloaf and mashed potatoes. "I'm not surprised you saw him."

"He wasn't shopping," Ava said. "He was ringing up a sale in a clothing store."

Chris's fork clattered when he dropped it on his plate. "Logan's working in a clothing store? Why would he have to? His father's loaded."

Niamh Roth shook her head in disapproval. "You have to get your priorities straight, Christopher. I think it's admirable that Logan is developing a good work ethic. Cassie's suicide must have torn him apart. He's been through a lot, but he's pulling his life back together by using his time to do something to help himself."

"If he's torn apart," Chris replied, "he sure doesn't show it. I saw him leering at Emily Brent in Piccolo Italia the other night. She is," he made air quotes, "supposed to be Jackson's girlfriend. And Logan is supposed to be his best friend. But it didn't stop Logan from *Don Juaning* her."

Ava's face reddened as she threw her napkin on the table. "Emily is not Jackson's girlfriend. He's with Johanna again. At least, they're trying to patch things up. He's just trying to let Emily down easy, so she won't go blabbing about what happened in the library on prom night."

"I thought the overseers already took care of that," Chris said, shoving half a dinner roll in his mouth.

"Maybe they did," Ava said in a huff, "but it never hurts to be too careful. Where is Jackson, anyway?"

Chris smeared butter on the remaining half roll. "He was walking into the library when I left and asked me to wish him luck. I think he's trying to convince Johanna to allow him to continue living there."

JACKSON SHOVED A heavy trestle table against the wall in the Antiquities section of the library. "'Now what?" He looked at Johanna with eager anticipation.

She paced out the floor and marked the space with masking tape. "I think we can fit six bookshelves here."

Jackson wrinkled his nose. "I don't think so—"

"Three across, back to back," Johanna continued.

"Back to back. Right. Will that be enough?"

"Yes. If we put the larger collections here, and we display magazines and newspapers on moveable racks in the reading room, we'll be good."

Jackson cocked his head. "Who reads paper newspapers anymore?"

"Some of our old school patrons. Don't forget, this is a library with special properties."

"The newspapers come to life?"

"Yes. But you actually have to run your fingers across the words to have the story pop off the page. That's why I always ask you to wear cotton gloves when you change out the newspapers."

"Huh. I always thought that's because you didn't want me to get them dirty."

"That, too."

Together, they moved empty shelves out of the Periodicals section and into Antiquities.

Johanna started arranging magazine sleeves in order of date.

Jackson pointed to piles of old books that had previously been stacked on a trestle table and now sat on the floor. "What should I do with these, put them back on the table?"

"No." Johanna studied the shelves in the corner of the room. "There's plenty of space here. Each shelf is only half full. If you move up the books to fill every upper shelf, the ones on the floor should fit nicely on the lower ones."

Jackson pulled out a few books, and sneezed. "They're dusty."

"You know where the rags are."

"You should have had Chris do this while he was here."

"We didn't have the discussion about you living here full-time until after Chris left. If the George V Hotel suite is going to become a permanent fixture at the library, we have to move the periodicals. That's what we're doing. You're getting your wish. Now get a dust cloth and some wax."

Jackson worked on the Antiquities shelves for the next half hour, singing to himself. Not too far away, Johanna worked just as industriously, putting the periodicals in order.

Suddenly, the singing stopped. "There's something weird about this shelf. There's something along the back of it that I can't remove. It doesn't feel like it should be there."

Johanna walked over to investigate. She found Jackson sitting on his heels staring at the bottom shelf.

She sat next to him on the floor and ran her hands over the back of the shelf. "We need more light. Go grab the flashlight out of the drawer behind the information desk."

It took Jackson less than a minute to return. He switched on the light and aimed it in the dark corner. Johanna reached in and tugged at an odd piece of wood that was sticking out. It started to give, and soon Jackson reached in as well and helped her pull out what appeared to be a primitive drawer. "What's in there?" he asked.

Johanna removed a blackened column made of several well-fitted pieces of heavily-carved wood. She rolled it around in her hands. "It looks like it could be an old puzzle."

"Cool," Jackson said. "What do you think those markings mean?"

"I don't know." She sat there studying the box for a while.

"May I?" Jackson asked.

She handed it to him.

He pushed at the individual pieces of wood, looking for a way to take the puzzle apart.

"Do you think that's wise?" Johanna asked.

Jackson stopped and turned toward her. "You don't think it's cursed, do you?"

"I hadn't even considered that. But now that you mention it, it's a possibility."

"Where do you think we can find a book about what these marks mean?"

She smiled. "Well, we are in a library..." Her eyes widened as a new thought occurred to her. She placed the puzzle down on the floor in front of her and moved her hands above the object as she chanted. The air above the wooden column took on a bluish tint and light shot out of the carvings as they appeared to float off the surface, rearranging themselves into words.

Jackson leaned in to read the new clues. "What does this all mean?"

"I don't know. I used a translation charm, but it seems to have converted the markings into a language I don't recognize."

"I'd have thunk the translation charm would have taken care of that?"

"Thunk?"

"Yeah. Like think, thank, thunk."

"Thank?"

"Alright. Forget it. I would have thought the translation charm would have translated the markings."

"It did," she replied. "Just not into anything we understand. Maybe we should take a short trip."

"Where do you want to go?"

She stood up and he followed suit. She held the puzzle against her as she linked her arm through his. A moment later, they found themselves inside the Library of Origination in Lumi.

Jackson looked around. "Your magic still works."

"It not only works, it continues to grow stronger."

"I thought it would all go away after the Terrorian mess."

"No." She sighed. "As the child of two overseers, I seem to have developed their gifts, tenfold."

⌘*More like a thousand-fold.*

They turned at the sound of Ryden Simmdry's voice in their heads.

Johanna smiled. "Father." She gave him a hug.

Jackson stepped forward and shook the overseer's hand.

⌘ *What brings you here? Not that I'm not glad to see you both.*

Johanna unhooked her arm from Jackson's and handed Ryden Simmdry the puzzle box. "We found this in the library. It was hidden behind a shelf in Antiquities. We're having a difficult time trying to figure out what the symbols mean. I used a translation charm on it, but we didn't understand the words conjured by the charm."

The master of the overseers tried a similar charm. ⌘ *This is indeed ancient. This looks like the First Language.*

Jackson leaned in. "The First Language? Like the very first language, ever?"

⌘ *Yes.*

"Can you translate it?" Johanna asked.

⌘ *No. It is a dead language, now obsolete. That is probably why your translation charm didn't work. It predates the Libraries of Illumination.*

Jackson ran his hands through his hair while he sifted through his thoughts. "Is there a 'First' book, or something, that we could open, so the guy can come to life and talk to us?"

⌘ *There is, but even then, we may not be able to understand his language.*

"I think Jackson has a good idea," Johanna said. "Maybe if we hear him speak out loud, a translation charm will work."

⌘ *It will take me time to locate such a book. Return home, and I will come as soon as I have found one.*

"We could wait," Jackson offered.

⌘ *Like I said, it will take some time to locate it. And*

then remove the protections guarding it. If it's a first book, then it is indeed ancient, and it may be quite fragile. Moving it may be difficult. But I will persevere. Once I have located one, I will transport it to Fantasia. Your mother will probably want to accompany me. Right now, she's visiting Bel on Romantica. But we should get everything sorted out within two- or three-day's time. I will see you then.

LOGAN RUSHED HOME after working at the mall all day. He had only agreed to work because someone had called in sick. What he really wanted to do was work on *The Elliott Report.* He locked himself in his bedroom and looked over his notes. On the previous day, he had finished shooting the video he thought he needed to round out his big story.

He took a deep breath and rubbed the palms of his hands together. *It's now or never.*

He attached some clip-on lights and aimed them toward where he would be sitting, before setting up his camera. He turned it on and sat at his desk, then introduced himself.

Logan jumped out of his seat and reviewed the few seconds of video he had shot. His voice sounded tinny and a shadow darkened half of his face. He adjusted one of the lights before hooking up the microphone.

Teleprompter. He hooked up a tiny, portable teleprompter he could attach to his phone and cued up his script.

Take two. He started the camera again, and sat down. He introduced himself a second time, and read the first few lines off the teleprompter. He jumped out of his chair again and checked his video. He grinned. *Much better.* He made one more minor adjustment to the light before sitting down. *This is it.*

Take three. Logan looked down at some notes on his desk. He counted to three before looking into the camera and began.

> "Welcome to the Elliott Report. I'm Logan Elliott. For some time now, our village has played host to a very unusual library, not well known among local residents. I'm not talking about the Exeter Memorial Library on Piedmont Street. That library has served the general public well. I'm referring to the private Library of Illumination, located on a small square that, apparently, I can't seem to find on any maps. But it's there. Believe me. My best friend works there and we had our prom pictures taken there."

I'd better edit pictures taken by Jackson's mom over this narration.

> "The outside looks like many other well-kept, old buildings you'll find around town. In fact, this one is even more picturesque—with its many narrow, leaded windows and its copper dome with gabled, octagonal windows breaking up the rich patina. However, this heritage-like site hides a dark secret. One that endangers the people who work inside as well as local residents. I know this because I am an eye-witness to one of the most chilling stories you'll ever hear."

Logan paused. He had already created a package painting a picture of the Terrorian incursion into the library on prom night. He had refrained from giving specific facts, knowing he could use that information to embellish the content of future reports. For now, he only wanted to create interest surrounding what had happened; shake up some memories. He looked into the camera.

"In case you're wondering, the previous incident was not reported to the police. The people in charge of the library are much too afraid of what will happen if word ever gets out about what goes on inside those ancient walls."

He looked down at his notes. He had another package he had completed earlier in the week about the latest gadgets introduced at a high-tech exhibition at the Gainesford Convention Center. He looked up again.

"In other news, I got a chance to try out some of the coolest new electronics at the annual high-tech show in Gainesford this year, from the smallest, wireless earbuds you'll ever find, to the best new gear for your home entertainment system. Check this out."

He paused one last time before wrapping up.

"And that's it for this inaugural edition of *The Elliott Report*. I'm Logan Elliott. Thanks for watching. Until next time."

He winked at the camera before looking down at his notes. After a minute, he popped out of his chair and checked his video. *Perfect.*

THE ONE THING neither Logan nor most other people realized, was that copies of his newscast had just material-ized on shelves inside the various Libraries of Illumination. Would anyone know it was there? Probably not, at least, not for some time. It was also possible that no one would ever notice its existence, or if they did, would know what to do with it.

THREE

It DIDN'T TAKE Ryden Simmdry as long as expected to find an early book written in the first language. The ancient text was encased in a sealed, diamond box resting in a niche on the lowest level of the Library of Origination.

He brought the box up to his residence to study it. He ran his long, slender fingers over the seams of the case and found they were perfectly smooth, as if no seams existed at all. The master's concentration was so intense, he had failed to hear the entrance of Pru Tellerence. Until recently, overseers had been banned from having families or intimate relationships. The ancients believed it would cloud their judgement when making life or death decisions. However, the College of Overseers—upon hearing Pru Tellerence had long ago given birth to Ryden Simmdry's child—decreed that the joining of two overseers reinforced their strength rather than violated the Ultimium Codi. The two overseers now lived together, although no ceremony had been performed consecrating their union.

★ *What have you there?*

⌘ *Pruelle. I did not hear you come in.*

★ *Whatever it is, it looks antediluvian.*

⌘ *It is a first book,* he said, without looking up.

★ *I didn't think any still existed. I thought they were all destroyed by the Titan Conflagration, and that was why the Libraries of Illumination were created.*

Ryden Simmdry smiled as he finally glanced up at her. ⌘ *I see you know your history.*

★ *I was enthralled by the history of the first people and the reason for the creation of the libraries. Where did you find it?*

⌘ *On the lowest level of the library, tucked into a niche.*

She wrinkled her nose. ★ *What were you doing down there?*

⌘ *Looking for this! It seems our daughter has uncovered an enigma that dates back to ancient times.*

★ *How is Johanna?*

⌘ *Fine. I'm going to visit her. You may accompany me if you'd like.*

★ *I had hoped to have an opportunity to bathe and change first. It seems Bel is in a sticky stage and likes to touch everyone within reach.*

⌘ *There is no rush. I must first determine the best way to unseal the book without damaging it.*

She kissed his cheek. ★ *You have no secret incantations up your sleeve?*

⌘ *I have several but none that will help me here. I would hate to open the case and immediately have the book disintegrate.* He rubbed his cheek. ⌘ *Your lips are sticky.*

★*Bel would be happy to hear that she's able to share her treats with her 'Pip-pip.'*

⌘*Pip-pip?*

★*I think that is Dame Erato's doing. Bel needs to call us something. So, you are Pip-pip, and I am Mimo.*

⌘*How thoughtful of her,* he said in a voice that belied his words.

RYDEN SIMMDRY AND Pru Tellerence appeared in the Fantasian library where they found Jackson putting the finishing touches on velvet cords he had strung across the two former entrances to Periodicals. They were a lush green color and had a brass plaque affixed to them that said *Private.*

⌘*You are making part of the library private?*

Jackson jerked up, startled. "Uh, yeah. Hi. I didn't see you there."

Pru Tellerence touched the velvet cords. ★*They're very handsome.*

Jackson's face reddened. "Johanna got them." He called out to her. "Johanna."

Johanna rounded a corner and greeted her parents with a hug. She backed away from Pru Tellerence and touched the new prosthetic arm the Adventurans had created for her. Johanna looked down to her mother's hand and felt the fingers. As the curator worked her hands up the prosthetic arm, her smile grew. "It feels real!"

★*The Adventurans are quite clever. They used synthetic skin and muscle-like tissue to make it feel like flesh. She lifted the sleeve of her robe. They even tinted the material they used as a covering to match my own coloring. If you look at it closely, it even has very fine hair growing on it.*

"That's amazing," Johanna said. "How does it feel?"

★*It's taking me a while to get used to it. I'm much better at picking up small objects now than I was at the start. And there are sensors built into it that correspond with a chip behind my ear, telling my brain what I am feeling. According to Prophet IAN c. I should feel like it's my own arm in just a few more weeks.*

★*I like your new decorations.* Pru Tellerence pointed to the velvet ropes.

Jackson stiffened. "We didn't steal them."

The overseer blinked. ★*I didn't think you did.*

"They look nice, don't they?" Johanna said. "We borrowed one from a European palace for a few minutes, so I could replicate it. Jackson feels guilty even though we returned the one we borrowed before they had a chance to miss it."

⌘*Do you think that was wise?*

Johanna grimaced. "It wasn't done maliciously. We only wanted to copy it." She suddenly noticed the crystal-like box in her father's hands. "What is that?"

⌘*A first book, probably the earliest in existence. I'm afraid of what might happen to it when I unseal the box. The book, as you can imagine, is millions of millennia old.*

Jackson tapped the diamond box. "Is there any way to create a sealed room to keep it from reacting to the air?"

"May I?" Johanna reached for the box and stared inside. "This book predates the paper, ink, and bindings that are used today. If it's on animal hide, like parchment, it would be more durable, and I may be wrong, but it looks thick, like it's fan folded. The bigger problem may be the pages sticking together, rather than disintegrating."

★*My brilliant daughter.*

⌘ *Obviously takes after her father.*

Johanna smiled. "I'm sure I inherited my best traits from both of you." She paused. "Still, I think we have to be very careful when unsealing and touching this document."

Jackson grabbed a pad and pen. "So, what do you think we need?"

"It will need to be both low-moisture and low-light."

Jackson started scribbling. "Got it. Dark and dry."

"And we've got to protect it from coming in contact with acids, or the oils from our fingers."

"So, we'll need cotton gloves," he repeated as he wrote.

"Even breathing too closely to it may cause an unanticipated reaction. So, I think you're right. We need an environmentally-safe room that will do the least damage."

Jackson narrowed his eyes. "Are we still going to be able to breathe if you pump all the oxygen out of the room?"

"I think we'll be fine. Although, we should wear masks."

Jackson's face lit up. "Like James Bond wore in *Thunderball!*"

"That might be overkill. Besides, they may have only been props that don't really exist."

"Too bad the time machine exploded. We could travel ahead to the 23rd century and see if they have something like it."

⌘ *I think that can be remedied.*

LOGAN TOOK HIS time editing the first installment of *The Elliott Report.* He wanted it to be flawless. He added graphics and some jazzy, industrial music at the beginning and end of the newscast and to the individual stories. The wee hours of the morning arrived by the time he actually uploaded the finished show. He spent the next hour drumming up buzz on social media.

His stomach growled. *You're just going to have to wait.* He jumped into the shower.

On the way to his internship, he stopped at a drive through for coffee and an egg sandwich. He arrived with one minute to spare, and didn't feel guilty about eating at his workspace while he read the morning paper.

The assignment manager listed the day's shoots on a large whiteboard. "Logan," Jennifer O' Loughlin said, "I'm sending you out to cover the governor today. He's announcing the budget for additional improvements to the local railway system. It's at the new depot that opened last week. It should be visual. But don't let that steer you. Concentrate on where the money is coming from and what it will be going toward." She handed him whatever information she had on the story as he called the governor's press office to confirm the time.

He grabbed his gear and stopped at Jennifer's desk on his way out, handing her one of his business cards. "I started my own online show. *The Elliott Report.* If you get a chance, can you check it out and give me some feedback? I'd really appreciate it."

She took his card. "Okay, sure. I'll let you know what I think when you get back."

He left with a huge smile on his face. *Nothing like coming back to the newsroom after a hard day of work, to adulation and positive feedback from my assignment manager.*

*

RYDEN SIMMDRY LINKED arms with Johanna and Jackson. *⌘Johanna, think of where you want to go.*

She imagined a place that would outfit divers with oxygen masks in the 23rd century. In a nanosecond, they were whisked to a place that catered not only to divers but to aviators as well. Apparently small oxygen masks were big money in a future where personal flying devices were all the rage.

Aeropods looked like short, missile-shaped fuselages with fins, thrusters, and a diminutive windshield. It reminded Johanna of an old film she had once seen about kids' soapbox cars. The aeropods on display were slightly bigger—made to fit a single adult—and were required to fly under a two-thousand-foot ceiling. They used solid fuel rods that could take them as far as a thousand miles before they had to be refueled. Besides the miniscule oxygen masks, fuel rods and aeropods were sold at the place her mind had taken them to.

Jackson pointed out things like a kid in a toy shop. Apparently, this particular emporium also sold individual *aquapods,* similar to the ones designed for the open sky, except aquapods facilitated ocean diving. "How much do you think these are?"

"Too much," Johanna answered. "We're just here for oxygen masks."

The proprietor showed them several different types of masks with what Johanna thought were unbelievably inflated prices. Living in the 23rd century apparently required a huge bank account, at least to people not naturally born during that time period.

When they heard the grand total, Ryden Simmdry implanted a thought in the proprietor's head, and he adjusted the bill to reflect a ridiculously reasonable price.

Jackson marveled at the low cost when they returned home. "I can't believe that guy gave us such a good deal."

Johanna looked at Ryden Simmdry. "I think he may have had a little outside influence from someone."

⌘*Adjusting for cost of living and inflation, I had him charge us what a purveyor of such items would charge for something of equal value in this time period.*

"Gee," Jackson mused, "If I had known you were going to do that, I would have gotten myself a personal aeropod."

⌘ *Even in today's dollars, an aeropod would have been expensive.*

Jackson shrugged. "A guy can dream, can't he?"

THANK GOD THE *morning rush ended.* Jennifer got up from her desk and went to the cafeteria for a latté. It wasn't as good as what she might get at a coffee shop, but it cost a third of the price and was better than the swill the school usually served up. She bought a black and white cookie to go with it and brought it back to her desk.

After her first sip, she keyed in the URL for *The Elliott Report.*

She smiled when she saw the opening graphics and heard the music. She nodded at Logan's apparent ease as he introduced his first story. She blanched when she heard his unsubstantiated allegations. It sounded like something out of a comic book. All she could think of was how his report might reflect on *her* newsroom.

She walked into the equipment room, searching for program manager, Luke Harris. "You've got to take a look at something Logan did. I have no idea what to do about it."

Luke watched a replay of Logan's newscast on Jen's computer. "The kid's got initiative."

She rolled her eyes. "Well, that's one positive thing we can say."

"And the report on the new tech wasn't bad; equal to anything he might have done here."

"There is that," she agreed.

"What was all that stuff about a man with tentacles attacking some girl and almost dropping her off the balcony of some library that people can't find?"

"That's the part that worries me."

Luke grinned. "Because you believe it?"

"Because it's so far-fetched, that if anyone I send him to interview has seen this report, they may not call us in the future to cover their stories. The last thing we need is to be compared to some schlock newscast."

"What are you going to do about it?"

Jen sat back in her chair and sighed. "I haven't figured that out yet."

FOUR

JOHANNA STOOD BY the conference table in the Executive Board Room and stared at a picture of protective cleanroom overalls. She did her best to conjure some up, but the best she could do was a small scrap of fabric.

Pru Tellerence looked over her shoulder. ★*It's not an easy task.*

"But you were able to do it when the *militairres* and Furst needed uniforms."

★*Not exactly. I started with a completed uniform that someone custom made for me. I used the replicator to increase the number of garments. The only magic I used involved casting a spell to transport them all and using a charm to fit each garment to its owner.*

"I'll be right back." Johanna evaporated, causing a light breeze as molecules raced to fill in the space she had occupied. Ten minutes later, she reappeared with several packages that, when unwrapped, appeared to be four flimsy snowsuits with hoods along with fabric booties and clear goggles.

★*I see you have your own tricks.*

"Going directly to the manufacturer is the easiest way I could think of to acquire them. I just have to remember to send the company a check." She laid out the suits alongside oxygen masks and cotton gloves.

⌘*We need to step out of the room.*

Jackson laid the diamond box on the table. "Why?"

⌘*I need to remove the existing air in the room and replace it with something more conducive to examining old documents.*

The teen nodded. "Which is why we need the oxygen masks. So we can breathe."

⌘*You would be able to breathe, regardless.*

Jackson waved the mask in the air. "Then why did we get these?"

⌘*So you don't inhale ancient mold spores from the parchment that might very possibly kill you.*

"Good answer."

⌘*A First Book is priceless. But no more priceless than a human life. Nor less.*

Jackson led Johanna and Pru Tellerence out of the room. "Do your thing," he said as he closed the door.

Ryden Simmdry emerged a moment later.

Johanna looked at her father. "That was fast!"

⌘*It was a bit premature. We are going to need to be in the room while I perform the spell if we don't want to introduce substandard air when we re-enter the chamber. And we should already be wearing all this paraphernalia,* he waved his arm at the clean room suits and masks, ⌘*before I begin.*

Jackson picked up an oxygen mask. "How are you

going to say whatever incantation it is that cleans the room, while holding one of these in your mouth?"

⌘ *Like I said before, we'd be able to breath regardless. I'll slip mine on after I say what is necessary.*

They all suited up, causing Jackson to smile as he watched the overseers put their miters on top of their hoods. As soon as they appeared ready, Ryden Simmdry performed the necessary spell and slipped on his oxygen mask.

Johanna felt her skin pucker as the spell sucked the air from the room, before immediately replacing it with a more suitable atmosphere for their purposes.

The Master pulled the diamond case with the First Book directly in front of him and laid his hands gently on top. He couldn't chant out loud wearing the oxygen mask, but he could hum; it was apparently sufficient to suit his needs. The air sparkled as the box disintegrated into a pile of diamond dust, exposing the First Book. Ryden Simmdry gently lifted the heavy cover. The end of the parchment had been inelegantly tied to the cover with slender strands of animal hide. He gently coaxed the rigid fanfold open, revealing a faded frontispiece next to the title page. ⌘ *Someone took great care in preserving this book. The parchment is stiff, yet miraculously supple enough to prevent cracking.*

Realizing she couldn't speak with the oxygen mask in her mouth, Johanna concentrated on using telepathy to transfer her thoughts. *Can you read it?*

⌘ *Barely. The ink has faded considerably. Light did its damage before any attempts of conservancy took place.* He continued to open pages as much as he dared, trying not to damage them. He lingered over one page for an extremely long time, committing what he saw to memory. ⌘*I do believe we have found the answer.*

Jackson looked from Ryden Simmdry to Johanna. *Now what do we do?* Jackson didn't possess the power to transfer his thoughts to the others, but Johanna read his mind and made them known.

⌘*I did not think it advisable to have the wooden puzzle box and First Book in close proximity. They are both organic but they hail from different eras and may contain conflicting pathogens that could affect each other, possibly disastrously. Instead, we will use the knowledge I have committed to memory to solve the enigma of the puzzle box.*

Ryden Simmdry cupped his hands and moved them around the book in the shape of a dome. The individual specks of diamond powder rose and swirled around the *First Book,* once again encasing it. The Master picked it up and inspected it. Then he hummed once more and Johanna felt her skin pucker again. Ryden Simmdry nodded to the others. ⌘*You can open the door. We are done here.*

LOGAN RUSHED INTO the newsroom much later than expected. "The governor was an hour late but don't worry," he told Jennifer, "I've got everything in hand. This story will make tonight's show."

He played the video of the press conference while he organized his thoughts, and jotted down the soundbites he thought he'd need as he heard them. A half hour later he approached Jennifer's desk and read his story to her, paraphrasing the soundbites.

She made a few changes before saying, "Okay, go. You don't have much time."

The remainder of the afternoon flew and before he

knew it, it was showtime. Logan's story headed the first block. While the show aired, he sat in an editing cubicle, copying his story and *B-roll*, so he could recut it for *The Elliott Report*. He got so caught up in saving footage from another reporter's story about packs of wild dogs menacing local beaches that he didn't notice Jennifer O'Laughlin leaving.

OUTSIDE, JENNIFER HURRIED to her car. She did not want to confront Logan, at least, not until she'd had some time to think about his internet show. *If I'm critical, and it's all a joke, I'll feel like a fool. But if I let it slide, and it affects GRUNT, I could come under fire for not doing anything about it.* She sighed. On her way home, she stopped to pick up her favorite comfort food, spaghetti and meatballs. While she waited for it to be prepared, she ducked into the store next door and bought a bottle of chianti. *Maybe the wine will loosen me up and help me think.*

LOGAN FELT HIS energy slump when he realized Jennifer had departed without discussing *The Elliott Report*. He really wanted to hear what she had to say. *She probably thinks I'm a rock star. After all, I am blowing the whistle on a tightly contained web of deceit that the public is probably funding.* He didn't allow himself to dwell on his disappointment. Instead, he rushed home to put together another internet report. He already knew what he wanted to add to his ongoing report about the Library of Illumination. However, he needed time to look over the footage from the other story and edit it into a usable piece.

*

Ryden Simmdry took hold of the puzzle and ceremoniously handed it to Johanna. ⌘ *If you will do the honors, I will try my best to translate what I read in the First Book into something more useful.*

"I think we need to start here." She pointed to a specific symbol. "It's the only one that's raised."

Jackson leaned over to see what Johanna meant. "That makes sense," he said. "When I see a circle with an arrow in it, I assume it means *press to start*."

Ryden Simmdry pulled out an ancient pair of spectacles and placed them on the bridge of his nose before studying the puzzle. ⌘ *That is not an arrow in a circle. It is alpha and omega; the beginning and the end.*

Jackson grinned. "That's my point. Wouldn't you start at the 'beginning?'"

Johanna pressed the symbol. Nothing happened. She shook her head.

Ryden Simmdry studied the other symbols carved into the slender column. He slowly turned it in his hand. ⌘ *This is directly opposite the alpha and omega.*

Johanna felt the raised impression with her fingertip. "What does it mean?"

⌘ *It's a triskelion. An ancient symbol, indeed. I believe there is one on the entrance stone at Newgrange.*

Jackson perked up. "What's 'Newgrange?'"

"It's a prehistoric site in Ireland," Johanna answered. "It's believed to be older than Stonehenge."

⌘ *It dates as far back as...* Ryden Simmdry lost focus for a second, *...3200 BC.*

"So, if this is at the entrance," Jackson pointed to the symbol, "it must mean *this way in?*"

⌘ *Perhaps.*

Johanna took the cylinder and studied it. She held it to her forehead and closed her eyes. A moment later, her eyes sprang open. "Cup your hands," she told Jackson. She placed the container on his palms and pressed the triskelion. At the same time, she twisted the alpha and omega symbol. It clicked, and the puzzle separated. A distinct *ping* rang out as a piece of metal hit the floor.

Jackson swooped down to pick it up. He held out his hand with the object resting on it. "Look at that! Isn't that the symbol of the library?" On Jackson's palm rested an old key, rusted despite the residue of oil that had apparently been rubbed into it.

Ryden Simmdry picked it up, a smile playing on his lips. ⌘ *This is the work of Dean Kelius Forthringer, a former overseer and rather artistic metallurgist. When this object was created, keys were, at their best, simple and rudimentary.*

*

THE PHONE RANG several times before Luke heard Jennifer answer. "Hey, what took you so long? You're usually glued to your cell phone and answer on the first ring."

Jennifer rubbed her forehead as she spoke. "I must have fallen asleep. I had wine with dinner. It gave me a headache and made me tired."

"I can tell you've been drinking. You're slurring your words."

"Am not."

"Are too. But that's beside the point. I'm calling because I just took another look at the stories on Logan's website, and he added a new twist to it tonight. Last night's story was vague. But tonight's version included two names: Emily Brent and Jackson Roth. I Googled them and they apparently both graduated last month from Exeter High School. They're real people. Either they're in on this with him, or they're lawsuits waiting to happen. Logan claims Emily was nearly killed by a beast with tentacles for arms, while Jackson tried to cover up the story because he works at the library where it allegedly happened. I don't see this going away any time soon, unless we take steps to nip it in the bud."

"What do you think we can do?"

"Are you whining? I've never heard you whine before. This is a new side of Jennifer O'Laughlin that I've never experienced."

"You said we should 'take steps.' What steps should we take?"

"You need to tell him he's compromising his position at GRUNT. And if he doesn't remove the video that he's already released on the internet and recant the story, we'll be forced to expel him."

"Did you talk to Ben about it?"

"No. You have a better working relationship with Castleton than I do. I'll leave it to you to deal with our illustrious executive producer. But you'd better talk to Logan first. If we can be proactive, maybe Castleton won't need to be involved."

"Are you sure you don't want to talk to Logan? The two of you get along pretty well."

"Maybe, but you're the one he respects; the one he wants to impress. I think this is best coming from you."

"Maybe we should both do it."

"Nope. That would look like we're ganging up on him."

"Aren't we?"

"We're just trying to resolve a problem before it gets out of hand. Gotta go. G'night."

Jen disconnected the call. The buzz from the wine had worn off entirely. The headache had not.

JOHANNA STUDIED THE key from the puzzle. She and Jackson, along with her parents, had searched the library the previous evening, looking for anything the key might fit, without luck. *Perhaps a display case,* she thought. She tried it on the display cases on the main floor of the library, but it was the wrong size.

"What are you doing?" Jackson asked, as he entered the library, dragging a trunk.

Johanna stared at the box. "Have you got a body in there?"

"No. It's just my stuff. It's the only thing we have left that belonged to my father. His parents had purchased it for him to pack his stuff in when he went away to college.

But then, my mom got pregnant and college went out the window. When he left, he took everything with him except the trunk. I guess that's why I always thought he'd come back." He scratched his head. "In retrospect, it must have been an unpleasant reminder of how quickly his life changed course."

"How do you feel about using it?"

"It's just a chest that made transporting all my stuff easier." He shrugged. "That's it."

"Do you need help moving in?"

"Nah. It'll only take a minute for me to dump everything in my room." Jackson smirked. "My room. I don't have to share with Chris anymore."

"Not just your room." She smiled. "Your suite."

"Yeah. I like it!"

Ten minutes later, Jackson returned, dragging the trunk behind him. "Do you think it would be all right if I stashed this downstairs?"

"Sure. Come on." Johanna led Jackson down to the lower level and searched for an out-of-the-way place to store the luggage.

Jackson shoved it into an opening between a broken book press and a wobbly tripod with a damaged armillary on top. "Do you think we should keep all this junk?" Jackson asked, shaking the tripod. While he did, snippets of deep space flashed before their eyes.

"I think we have to if they have magic in them. And this one definitely has special properties."

"Can't we decommission them or something?"

"I don't know. That's a question for my father. If anyone knows, he will."

"Maybe we should look around while we're down

here. You know, look for something with an opening for the key we found."

Johanna's shoulders slumped. "I know you're right, but it looks like a daunting task."

Jackson slipped his arm around her shoulder. "Yep. But we have to start somewhere."

"So, we're going to work our way down more than thirteen-hundred levels?"

He winced. "What if it's not even on our realm?"

"That would be disappointing," she said with an enigmatic smile.

FIVE

LOGAN DRAGGED HIMSELF out of bed and thought about blowing off his internship for the day. He had been up late editing a secondary package for *The Elliott Report* and working on the ongoing script about the goings-on at the library. He had rewritten it several times, before giving up. The next edition of *The Elliott Report* would be a day late. He blamed it on Jennifer. He wanted to get her feedback before proceeding. So, he hit the shower and picked up a double-espresso on the way to the newsroom.

By the time he walked in, Jennifer was already handing out assignments to other reporters. He cursed to himself because he knew someone else probably got the lead story. But in its own way, it was also a blessing because it would give him time to talk to her.

After the third crew left, he dragged a chair over to Jennifer's desk. "Did you get a chance to look at *The Elliott Report*?"

Jennifer took a deep breath before answering. "Yes, I did, and I have to ask you to take it down."

Logan jerked back as if he had been physically assaulted. "Take it down! Why?"

"It's irresponsible reporting. There is no hard evidence to back up what you're saying. And, quite frankly, your accusations against the library sound preposterous. 'A beast with tentacles for arms?' Really?"

"You don't know anything about it," he said a little louder than he'd planned.

"All I know is what I saw on the internet. And I'm afraid if any of the high-profile business executives or politicians we send you to interview see that report, it will affect the reputation of this newscast and the university as a whole."

Luke approached from the back room. "Everything okay here?"

"No. It's not," Logan said, shoving the chair he had been sitting on so hard, that it flipped over and clattered against the floor.

"Calm down, Logan," Luke said.

"Are you in on this, too? Did you already know what she was going to say to me?"

"Yes. And I agree with Jennifer completely."

"Have neither of you ever heard of freedom of speech?"

Luke leaned his hip against Jennifer's desk and crossed his arms. "This is more than freedom of speech. The story about the library borders on slander. Do the two students you named in the report know you implicated them?"

"It doesn't matter. What I said is true."

Luke unfolded his arms. "Fine. Show us the evidence."

Logan looked away. "I can't."

"Then I suggest taking down your report on the library before it lands you in trouble. The rest of the show is fine. I like your initiative. But you can't go around making outlandish claims against people and institutions unless you have hard evidence."

Logan picked up his coffee and newspaper. "The way I see it, I've already put in seventeen days this semester. Since the term only requires fourteen appearances, I'd say I'm done here. Have a nice life."

Luke and Jennifer remained silent for at least a minute after Logan bee-lined it out of the newsroom. Finally, Luke looked at the assignment manager. "Do you think he'll come back?"

"I think he has too much ego for that."

"Are you going to fail him?"

"And have his faulty reporting blow up in our faces? Nope. Like he said, he's already put in enough time to constitute an entire semester. He gets a *pass* and that's the end of it."

"Here's hoping you're right."

JOHANNA AND JACKSON searched through the detritus that had accumulated on sub-level six, looking for an object that their mysterious key might fit. While there were plenty of items that looked promising at first sight, no tiny locks needed opening.

Jackson ran his fingers through his hair, making several strands stick out. "You know, what if we're looking at this all wrong. What if the key opens a lock in the wall as opposed to an item?"

"I've been checking for that, as well. Haven't you?"

Jackson grimaced. "No."

"Then you may want to go back and check again."

He stood quietly, neither moving nor answering, as he contemplated going through the many spaces he had already examined, all over again. His stomach growled, disturbing the peace. "I think maybe we should take a break first." His stomach growled again.

Johanna smiled. "Room service? Or pizza take-out?"

"Meatball parmigiana hero from Piccolo Italia."

"Make it two."

JACKSON RELAXED INTO a newfound feeling of contentment as he sat in Johanna's office, sharing lunch. Even more than that, he felt the already-strong bond between the two of them growing. He leaned over and placed his hand on her thigh. Johanna raised her eyebrows as she stared at him, not saying anything. He removed his hand, dragged his chair closer to her, and then placed it back on her thigh. He stared into her eyes, leaning in, and suddenly choked when Ryden Simmdry appeared on the other side of Johanna.

⌘*Am I interrupting something?*

Jackson jerked his hand away from Johanna's leg. "I didn't expect to see you there. You startled me."

⌘*I've had a revelation of sorts and thought I would share it with you.*

Johanna rose and kissed her father on the cheek. "What is it?"

⌘ *The key you found looked vaguely familiar. When I returned to the Library of Origination, I consulted the oracle, and the words Re Transfigurator crept into my consciousness.*

Jackson glanced at Johanna, then back at her father. "What does that mean?"

⌘*A Re Transfigurator is a device that transforms reality into something it is not.*

Johanna smiled. "And since it took form in your mind, you can describe it, so we'll know what we're looking for."

⌘*Not exactly.*

Jackson eyed his half-eaten meatball hero, wishing he could go back to it without seeming rude. "What do you mean by, 'not exactly?'"

⌘*One of the things it can transform into something it's not, is its own form. Although, I believe it would probably still look similar to an automaton.*

"And that is…" Jackson made circles with his hands as if to say *continue*.

⌘*It is usually a mechanical device that performs a pre-determined sequence of actions, however, this automaton may be a magical machine, and as such, might be able to self-adjust in unpredictable ways.*

Jackson grabbed an iPad off Johanna's desk and looked up *automaton* in their card catalogue. "I'll be right back. I need a book to help me understand what we're talking about." The teen disappeared out the door.

⌘*The two of you looked scandalized when I appeared in your office today. Is there a problem I should know about?*

"Well, Dad," Johanna took Ryden Simmdry's arm, "while it's very convenient that you can just think about me and appear, sometimes it might prove… inconvenient. Like if I'm bathing. Or perhaps, involved in an amorous entanglement."

Ryden Simmdry had the good grace to blush. ⌘*I*

see. However, neither appeared to be going on.

"I believe we were working up to that point. And although, this time, we had barely started, getting caught *in flagrante delicto* is not desirable."

⌘ *Of course. Perhaps I should just project my intention to visit, before actually appearing.*

"That would help. And if it's a bad time, I'll simply project the word, "later," and I'll get back to you when it's more convenient."

⌘ *Having a child is new ground for me. Especially a grown daughter who knows her own mind.*

"Found one," Jackson called out as he rushed back into the room. He placed a large book on the table and paged through it. "Look, it's a monkey dressed like an 19th century gentleman, and it smokes a cigar." He scrunched up his face. "What would be the point of that?"

⌘ *Novelty. Entertainment. If it's the only one of its kind it might appeal to a collector.*

"Look at this," Jackson's eyes crinkled as his voice went up an octave. "It's a mechanical duck that will take a seed from your hand, eat it, and then poop. How cool is that?"

⌘ *As you can see, automatons can be quite... interesting.*

"Yeah," Jackson said, sliding the book toward Johanna, "but how are they made? This stuff is supposedly hundreds of years old."

⌘ *That would depend on the maker. Many were made during the 18th and 19th centuries and were created using the same types of gears and levers you might find in a well-made clock or timepiece. But automatons date back to well before that time period. I do believe on this realm, a device called the*

Antikythera Mechanism *dates back to ancient Greece. It was used to forecast astronomy and the position of the planets, their moons, and the stars.*

That piqued Jackson's attention. "How ancient are we talking about?"

⌘*Perhaps as far back as the second century BC.*

The teen shook his head. "I'm not buying it. How could they have the knowledge to make something like that so far back in history?"

Johanna tilted her head. "The Ancients?"

⌘*I wouldn't be surprised.*

Jackson leaned back in his chair. "Aren't the Ancients from time before we know it?"

⌘*Yes. And the Ancients believed in magic as well as science. So, it is very probable that an automaton, even one as apparently advanced as this one, can be quite old.*

THERE WAS NO one at home in the Elliott house to hear Logan slam his bedroom door. *Where does that bitch get off telling me my report was irresponsible? I'll show her. The Elliott Report will go on and this story will make national headlines.* He paused. *Maybe I should have more proof. But I'm not going to get it from Johanna or Jackson. Or Emily. I need footage inside the library. And I need someone to talk about what happened.* He tapped a pen against his desk, thinking about his next course of action.

For the better part of an hour, his mind pinged like a pinball, flashing from prom night to the high school to the Roth family to the GRUNT newsroom. Finally, a slow smile developed. *This is perfect. I'll have to be careful, but I think this will work out just fine.* For the first time, Logan was glad he was younger than Jackson. It would make the gap between his age and his intended victim appear to be less of an issue. Now, he only had to figure out how to make everything seem organic and casual.

Ryden Simmdry stood perfectly still with his eyes closed and his arms held out before him with his palms facing up. It looked like he was inviting knowledge into his being. And he was. He chanted quietly and allowed his mind to roam throughout the library in search of the Re Transfigurator.

After more than an hour, his eyes popped open. He sighed. ⌘*It is not here.*

"What does that mean exactly?" Johanna asked.

⌘*The automaton is not located within the library proper.*

Jackson's eyes bugged out. "You mean it could be anywhere? Anywhere on Earth?"

Johanna corrected him. "Anywhere on Fantasia."

⌘*It is highly doubtful something this sophisticated would have been secreted outside of a library.*

Jackson paced the length of Johanna's office. "How can you be so sure?"

⌘*Because someone made a point of hiding the key in an out of the way place to, most probably, protect the device.*

"Or the library," Johanna stated. "If the Re Transfigurator is magical, maybe it was separated from its key to protect the people in the library in case someone was after the device and broke in to steal it."

⌘*That is a possibility. However, the oracle didn't allude to that. I still believe it is inside a library.*

"Okay. That narrows down the possibilities. Now, we only have to search eleven other Libraries of Illumination," Jackson said. "I can't wait to see what the

Terrorians think about that, considering we're responsible for the death of Nero 51."

⌘*Nero 51 caused his own death. If he had remained a trustworthy curator who wasn't greedy for power, he would still be alive today. I will make sure you have* carte blanche *to visit the other realms and search their libraries.*

"Maybe my mother moved back home too soon," Jackson reasoned. "This is going to take a while."

⌘*Perhaps it would go more quickly if I taught Johanna how to scan the libraries for the device.*

"That would help," she replied. "Then, instead of taking us twelve months to go through all the libraries, we might be able to do it in twelve days."

"Yeah. That would be a plus," Jackson added.

"But like you said, some curators may not like the idea of us poking around in their libraries."

SIX

LOGAN ARRIVED AT Piccolo Italia early and staked out a booth with a clear view of the counter. He ordered lasagna knowing they wouldn't chase him out too quickly, especially if he ate really slowly. And he would. He wanted to see who would visit the popular hangout and what time they would arrive. He had his notes and camera with him, just in case he ran into someone he could interview. As luck would have it, he didn't need to wait long, but the last person he wanted to bump into was Jackson, and that's just who walked in a few minutes later.

Jackson ordered at the counter before turning around to scope out the dining area. "Logan! It's been a while." Jackson walked over to the booth and slid in on the opposite side. "How are you doing? I guess your internship has you running around a lot."

That's as good an excuse as any, Logan thought, as he tried to muster a smile for Jackson. "You got that right. I happen to be working on a story right now, even though I'm on a lunch break." He pointed to his notebook and camera.

"News 24/7, huh?"

"Yeah. It's exciting. I meet a lot of the movers and shakers in the community. I keep people informed about what's happening and alert them to possible threats to their safety. It's very rewarding. And the chicks love me."

Jackson gave him a half-smile, revealing a single dimple. "The chicks have always loved you."

"No," Logan said, narrowing his eyes. "They loved *you*. They only wanted to be with me because my old man is loaded."

"You're exaggerating. Cassie wasn't interested in you for your money."

"No. To her, I was husband material, even though I repeatedly told her I had no plans to settle down before turning thirty."

"Well, I guess…" Jackson prevented himself—just in time—from saying what he was thinking. *I guess he won't have to worry about Cassie's marriage plans anymore.* Jackson clearly remembered how Logan had treated Cassie on the night of the senior prom. *It's a good thing the overseers erased everybody's memories, or Logan wouldn't be able to show his face around here.*

"Thanks for waiting for me." Ava's tone was anything but pleasant and directed at her brother.

"What?" Jackson asked.

"I told you to wait for me when you stopped in to see Mom, and you left without me."

"I didn't even hear you, Ava. I'm in the middle of a project with Johanna, and she's waiting for me to pick up lunch. I guess I was so worried that Mom was going to talk my ear off that I ignored everything else in my rush to get out of there." Jackson shrugged. "Sorry."

One of the servers shouted, "Jax, your heroes are ready."

"I'd better go. Good to see you Logan. We should get together some time when you're not so busy. You too, Ava." He gave his sister a one-armed hug, grabbed his lunch, and left.

"Want to sit down?" Logan asked, now that Jackson was gone.

"Do you mind? I could sit somewhere else. There are still plenty of booths. I'm just waiting for a couple of friends to meet me here."

"I haven't really had a chance to talk to any of my friends all summer, so it would be nice to catch up with you. Have a seat." He lowered his voice and said in a persuasive manner, "I'll treat you to whatever you want."

A waitress stopped next to Logan's booth and placed his lasagna and a side salad on the table.

Ava slid into the booth. "Okay. But I want what you're having."

Logan smile at the waitress. "Another order of lasagna for my friend, please."

"Whatcha drinking with that, honey?" the waitress asked Ava.

"Diet Coke."

"And the dressing on your salad?"

"Italian."

"It'll be up in a minute."

Logan leaned his fork against the edge of the plate and casually leaned back. "So how have you been, Ava?"

"Busy. Shopping for high school stuff." She sat up a little straighter when she said the words 'high school.' "And I'm still working at the library, so that keeps me hopping."

Finally, the right party on the right topic. "How is everything going at the library?"

"Fine."

"Yeah? No repercussions from prom night?"

"What's so special about prom night?"

They got to her, too? Logan hid his surprise that Ava had forgotten about prom night, but it plagued his mind. *How did they manage to do that?*

"Oh, you know, the usual. Scary beasts from another planet running around the library, threatening people."

Ava scrunched up her face. "You mean the Terrorians?"

"Is that what they're called? Big beasts with tentacles for arms?"

Ava wasn't sure she should answer. Then she remembered Jackson saying that Logan wanted to work at the library. *I guess they made him take the oath.* "Yeah," she whispered. "We shouldn't talk about them here."

He had to think quickly. "You're right, of course. But there's something I need to ask you. What if we were to talk somewhere more privately?"

"Like where?"

"How about we take a ride to the Dunes after lunch and walk along the beach. If we park on the east end, it shouldn't be too busy."

"Okay. Meanwhile, Jackson says you're training to be a reporter."

"I am. And I'm not 'training'. I'm 'doing.'" Logan

launched into descriptions of the stories he had covered as they ate lunch.

"I can't believe none of my friends showed up," Ava complained. "They were supposed to meet me at noon. I even tried to make it later but this one girl, Keli, who I don't even like, said it had to be noon because she has something else she has to do this afternoon."

"Friends," Logan quipped, "you can't live without them; you can't kill them." They walked out to Logan's car and he pulled open the door for Ava.

That's when her friends turned the corner. "Hey, Ava," Keli Gaughren called out, "where are you going?"

A small smile played on Ava's lips. "Logan and I have some catching up to do. See you around." And with that, she slid into the car and Logan shut the door behind her."

Logan smiled at the group of girls, saluted them, and then got into the car and drove away.

Ava looked in the sideview mirror and laughed when she saw the group of girls staring open-mouthed at the car from the sidewalk.

RYDEN SIMMDRY SAT across from Johanna, teaching her the words she would need to chant continuously to telepathically search each individual Library of Illumination.

⌘ *You must remember, there are three keys to being successful. First, you must eliminate all extraneous thought. Your mind must be an open vessel to receive any hint of where the Re Transfigurator may be. Second, you must continuously chant the words I am teaching you to keep the connection open. Third, you need to understand that you may not recognize an image or clue and eliminate it by mistake. That means you must be willing to linger in certain instances to determine the value of what you "see."*

"How am I supposed to keep my mind free of 'all extraneous thought' and yet still be able to consider the value of what I 'see?'"

⌘ *Part of the spell you are chanting keeps the gateway open so you can search the far reaches of a library from a single given point. An addendum to the spell allows you to visualize any magical components within. Do not be concerned with anything non-magical. You must continuously chant to keep the connection open, and you must keep your mind clear, so it can receive the images that appear. As long as you continuously chant, you can call on another part of your brain to study the image. You just have to be careful to keep the image you are examining fixed in your mind, so you don't lose it.*

"I'm not really sure how to use one part of my brain to remember the chant, and another part of my brain to study whatever image appears, while keeping my mind free of extraneous thought. It sounds daunting. I would say *impossible*, but it clearly isn't because I know you can do it." Her shoulders sagged. "I'm just not sure I can."

⌘ *That is why we are here. Learning the chant is child's play. Being able to employ it to its fullest potential takes skill. And skill is improved by practice. Do you know the words by heart?*

"Yes."

Ryden Simmdry waved his hand, telekinetically locking the door to Johanna's office.

⌘ *Then let us begin. Clear your mind. I will give you a few moments and then will touch your arm with my hand. When you feel my touch, do not think about it. Just begin chanting. As soon as an image of something magical enters your mind, try to lock it in place so you can study it. Go ahead.*

Johanna took a deep breath and let herself relax. As soon as she felt pressure on her arm, she began chanting.

⌘ *Stop.*

Johanna's eyes flew open.

⌘ *The correct pronunciation is MA-jee-chees. Not ma-JIK-is. Say it aloud.*

"MA-jee-chees. Ma-jee-chees."

⌘ *Good. Begin again.*

Johanna cleared her mind once more and began chanting. It was difficult keeping her mind clear but she worked at it. After several minutes, a blue orb took shape in her mind. She tried to study it, but as soon as she did, the orb disappeared. She stopped chanting.

⌘ *What happened?*

"The power generator appeared in my mind, but when I tried isolating it so I could examine it, it faded."

⌘ *Try again.*

For the next hour and a half, Johanna chanted in fits and starts, not quite perfecting the skill. She could feel her stomach rumbling and wanted to stop for lunch.

⌘ *Just give it a little more time.*

For what seemed like the millionth time, she began chanted and allowing magical images to appear until a vision of the replicator entered her brain. She tried to fix it in place and used her mind to replicate a grilled cheese sandwich. She could almost taste it, then she let it go, and opened her mind to receive the next image. Her concentration was broken by a knock on the door.

Ryden Simmdry waved his hand and the door opened.

"Hey," Jackson said. "I don't know if this means

anything, but there was a humming sound coming from the staircase, and I followed it downstairs to see what was going on. I found this warm cheese sandwich sitting in the duplicloner. But the door to the room was locked and no one was in there, and the top of the machine was empty. So, I don't know where this came from." He thrust out the sandwich in front of him. "Spooky, huh? Do you think we're being infiltrated through the duplicloner?"

Johanna broke into a big grin.

⌘*Is that your doing?*

"I'm really hungry, and I tried to compartmentalize the duplicloner while independently thinking about what I would make in it." Her voice went up in pitch. "And it worked!"

Jackson's brow furrowed while his jaw dropped. "You did that? From here? Without using another sandwich?"

She nodded.

"You gonna eat this?"

She grabbed the sandwich and took a bite. "Umm. I wish I had thought about some hot tomato soup to go with it."

⌘*It looks like my work here is done.*

"I promise I'll practice all afternoon, but right now, I need lunch." She gave Ryden Simmdry a kiss on the cheek, and he nodded at Jackson before disappearing.

"Does this mean I can have your meatball parm hero?" Jackson asked.

"Didn't you order one for yourself?"

"Yeah, but I'm a growing… man. And I could use the extra protein. Besides, I don't want it to go to waste while you eat a pseudo-sandwich."

"This is a very real sandwich," she answered, waving

it in his face.

"Made with magic. Does it even have any flavor?"

"Yeah, it tastes just like grilled cheese. However, just to show how magnanimous I am, I'll split my meatball parm with you, so I can grow less hungry, and you can grow less annoying."

NIAMH ROTH FINISHED folding the laundry and was about to put it away, when she thought better of it. Some of it belonged to her son Jackson, and she thought she might drop it off at the library in case he needed it. Some belonged to her other children, Chris and Ava, and they were old enough to take on the responsibility to put their own things away. The remainder was hers, and while she knew she should place it in her dresser drawer, something was telling her she shouldn't. She looked at the suitcase she had emptied earlier. She didn't know why, but she felt compelled to place her clean clothing back in it. *Well, at least it will make it easier to move them to my bedroom.*

She looked around the small house. Not a thing was out of place. When she had arrived home, she had thrown open the windows and cleaned it top to bottom. Since she and her family had been living at the Library of Illumination for the past few months, there wasn't much out of place, so cleaning had been easy. At first, she had been happy to be home. But now, she felt a compelling urge to go back to the library. *Jackson would hate that. He just got the hotel suite to himself.* Still, until the urge dissipated, it wouldn't hurt to keep her clothing in the suitcase, ready to go at a moment's notice.

*

Johanna spent the remainder of her Saturday afternoon practicing isolating the images in her mind, and studying them. She grew more comfortable going through the process, probably because the chant was now so ingrained in her mind, she could repeat it without thinking about the words. That made everything else easier.

Jackson knocked, before walking into her unlocked office. "I'm not disturbing you, am I?"

"No. I think I'm getting the hang of this. I'll practice more tomorrow, but we should plan to start traveling off-world on Monday."

Jackson grimaced. "Do you think Chris will be able to handle the library on his own?"

Johanna closed her eyes for a moment. "You know, I'm so used to having your family here to look after things, I didn't even realize the library would be unmanned when we travel off-world to search for the Re Transfigurator. Will your mother hate me if I ask her to come back for a couple more weeks?"

"I'll hate you. I just moved into the master bedroom, and I'll have to move back into the smaller bedroom I shared with Chris."

"Aren't all the bedrooms the same size?"

"The master is part of the suite. Ava's room, too. But my room is an adjoining room that could be added to the suite, or not. It definitely isn't the same level of luxury."

"You poor thing."

"Should I call my mom? Or better yet, do you want to call my mom?"

Johanna reached for the phone on the desk. "I'll do it." She dialed. Niamh picked up almost immediately. "Hi, Mrs. Roth. It's Johanna."

"Is everything all right? I didn't unpack in case you need me."

"You never took your clothes out of your suitcase?"

"I did. I had to wash them but then I folded them and put them right back. I don't know why. I just did."

"Well, either you have some magical powers of your own, or my father planted a long-distance thought in your head because you're right about us needing you. Jackson and I have to travel off-world for a couple of weeks to find something."

"What are you looking for?"

"We're not sure. It's called a Re Transfigurator, but we have no idea what it looks like. Anyway, we would hate to leave Chris alone in the library to fend for himself."

"I understand completely. When do you need me?"

"We're not leaving until Monday morning. But if you return tomorrow night, we can all have dinner together before we go."

Niamh hesitated before replying. "Is your trip going to be dangerous?"

"I don't see why it should be, but you can never tell with library business. We have to be ready for anything."

SEVEN

Ava couldn't believe Logan wanted to talk with her. She had seriously crushed on him ever since her twelfth birthday, when she saw him helping Jackson blow up balloons for her party. *Some party. It was only my family, Logan, and my friends Mackenzie and Hailey.* Her mother had baked a chocolate cake and she'd received a new blouse from *the family.* Her friends had given her a beaded necklace and bracelet that they had made in a craft class, and Logan had given her *The Secret of the Old Clock,* a Nancy Drew mystery book. She slept with it under her pillow for a year until a boy in her English class threw her a kiss from across the room. Nancy Drew was immediately moved to Ava's bookshelf and Noah Petrovitch became her new crush. Noah moved to Chicago with his family a year later, leaving Ava bereft. Now she was sitting in close proximity to Logan, who wanted to talk with her privately. She felt her nerves tingle with anticipation until she suddenly remembered that Logan's girlfriend, Cassie, had recently killed herself. She pushed that thought right out of her mind. Instead of questioning why Cassie ended her own life, she wondered if Logan was lonely and was reaching out to her for companionship. Or more. *What if this grows into something bigger than friendship?*

LOGAN PULLED INTO the last available space in the east parking lot of the Dunes.

"I can't believe how busy it is," Ava said. "*Everyone* is here. There goes any chance for privacy."

"We'll still be able to talk privately. Everyone at this end is migrating west toward the main pavilion because that's where the restrooms and concession stands are. If we walk east, we'll be out of the crowd in a minute. C'mon." Logan opened the door for her and led her onto the sand. They took off their shoes and walked where the tide kissed the shoreline, moving further from the crowd. "I'm really glad you're able to spend some time with me this afternoon. I've been trying to stay busy with school and work, so I don't think too much about how sad I am about losing Cassie. She was my best friend and confidant, and now I have no one to talk with about, you know, life. I mean, your brother is my friend and I can always talk with him. But he's really busy, too, with school and the library. We've hardly seen each other since graduation. Besides, he can't give me the female perspective on life like you can." He reached for her hand.

Ava did not pull her hand away. Instead she tried to suppress the happiness, exploding inside of her. "I can do that."

"It's really crazy, you know?" Logan playfully

bumped his shoulder into hers. "Oh. Let me check my phone. I think I just received a text." He played with his phone a second before putting it back in his pocket. "As I was saying, I've hardly had time to talk to your brother, especially since the—what did you call them—Terrorians, showed up in the library. They're ugly suckers. Did you ever take a picture of one?"

"Ew. Who would want a picture of a Terrorian? Besides, we've been too busy trying to keep them from invading our world to spend time snapping photos."

Logan felt the hairs on the back of his neck react to Ava's statement. "How do you keep them from invading?"

"We have a special weapon the overseers gave us that turns Terrorians, or anything really, into dust."

"Have you shot one of them?"

"I've shot *at* them. But I've never killed one. Not like Johanna and Jackson."

"Jackson has actually killed one of those creatures?"

"He's killed a lot of them. Not as many as Johanna, but Johanna has magical powers. Jackson doesn't."

"What do you mean, 'magical powers?'"

"Do you know about the overseers, the old guys who are in charge of the libraries?"

"Yeah," Logan lied.

"Well, both of Johanna's parents are overseers. Her father was actually Merlin the Magician at one point in time."

Logan stopped walking, pulling Ava to a halt. "Now you're just pulling my leg."

"No, I'm not. Overseers have some kind of enchantment placed on them that allows them to live for thousands of years. They only age one year for every thousand. Johanna and Jackson have a longevity blessing too, but theirs isn't nearly as good. They age one year for every ten years that pass. So, Jackson may technically be three years older than me, but when I turn fifty-five, he'll really only be twenty-two. Isn't that crazy?"

"Unbelievable, actually."

"But I'm not pulling your leg. It's really true."

"And when did Jackson get this special 'blessing?'"

"When he became Johanna's co-curator. In the beginning, he was just her assistant. But after the Terrorians invaded the library and killed one of the overseers, Johanna and Jackson had to go to Lumina for the funeral and that's when they got their blessing."

"Where is Lumina, exactly?"

"I don't know." Ava waved her arm toward the sky. "Somewhere out there."

"C'mon, Ava. You don't really expect me to believe that?"

"You believe in Terrorians, don't you?"

Logan's heart began to race. "Yeah."

"Well. Do they look *earthly* to you? I bet not. They're from somewhere out there, too."

"They're from Lumina?"

"No. They're from Terroria. And those are just two of the places where there are Libraries of Illumination. Jackson said one realm is made up entirely of kids under the age of sixteen, and he said they were really good at getting the upper hand on the Terrorians because they were fearless and really creative in how they fought back. I don't remember the name of that realm, but I know each one has a different kind of people. One even has robots with human hearts and brains. It's really interesting, like a sci-fi or fantasy novel."

"But how did Jackson and Johanna meet all these… aliens?"

Ava smiled. "By using the portals in the library."

LOGAN KNEW HE would be taking a chance with Ava, but he had to try or else *The Elliott Report* would die in its tracks. They were far along the beach, away from everyone else. He turned Ava to face him. "You really are something, you know?" He pulled her toward him and kissed her. Nothing too aggressive. He didn't want to scare her away. Just a gentle, lingering kiss. When he pulled away from her, she stood still for a second before slowly opening her eyes. "I hope you don't mind that I kissed you. I really should have asked your permission first."

Ava blushed. "You don't ever have to ask me permission to kiss me."

Logan smiled at her. "We should start heading back."

"I guess."

"You know, considering the Library of Illumination is… well… a library, do you think it would have a picture of Terrorians in one of its books?"

"I'm sure of it. We just have to be careful about which book we choose."

"Why is that?"

"Because we don't want them to suddenly overrun the library. But if we choose a level zero or level one book, we should be okay."

"What does that mean? Level zero? Level one?"

"Each book has a special property classification. *Zeros* don't do anything. They're like regular print books.

Ones actually come to life in front of you, but it all should disappear when we close the cover. The higher the classification, the harder it is to control the outcome. So, we'll have to be really, really careful."

"I didn't realize the library was so complex. No wonder Jackson doesn't want anyone knowing about it."

"Johanna says she realized the importance of secrecy after Jackson opened a copy of *Treasure Island* and the pirates left gold doubloons behind. The book was closed. The pirates were gone. But the doubloons were very real—authentic 17th century gold pieces worth a lot of money. Imagine if people broke into the library so they could open books to strike it rich. It would be a disaster. The library would be ruined. Financial markets might be affected. And what if they opened a book about the bombing of Hiroshima to the page where the actual detonation occurred? The affect could be devastating. That's why *what happens in the library stays in the library.*

Logan's mind raced. The library was so much more powerful than he originally thought. He could respect that. But even more, he could imagine the power that the holder of the keys to such an institution could wield. *I want in.*

LATER THAT AFTERNOON, Ava dumped her pocketbook on her bed. "Mom," she called out. "Why is my suitcase on the bed with my clothes still in it?"

Her mother's footsteps grew louder before Niamh appeared at Ava's bedroom door. "Because Johanna and Jackson have asked us to move back to the library, temporarily, while they're out of town."

"We just got back."

"I know."

"And you're smiling. You miss the library, don't you?" Her voice took on a teasing tone. "You miss Christophe! You miss Christophe!"

Niamh blushed. "Stop. This is not about me. We promised your brother and Johanna that we would take care of the library if they needed us. And they need us."

Ava thought about Logan. "Do you really think they need me too? I could always stay here and watch the house."

"You will do no such thing. You know how crazy it can get at the library. Besides, think of all the wonderful things you can order from room service."

"True." *But it would be even nicer to invite Logan over and have some privacy.* "When are we going?"

"Tomorrow evening. Johanna said it would be nice if we could all have dinner together before they leave."

"I'm ordering steak. And those super-creamy cheesy potatoes."

"Potatoes au gratin."

"And dessert. But I don't know if I want chocolate soufflé or ice cream. Or maybe we can ask Christophe to bring in some Paris Brest pastries. I have to think about it.

"You do that," her mother said. "And while you're thinking about it, look through your suitcase to see what's there—it's all clean—and pack whatever else you'll need for a two-week stay."

JOHANNA SAT IN front of her computer, holding her head in her hands.

Jackson walked in with a pizza box and a paper bag filled with disposable utensils. "What's wrong?"

"I've been trying to research *Re Transfigurator,* but

all I get are religious websites about the transfiguration of Jesus."

Jackson's jaw dropped, along with the pizza box, which plopped onto Johanna's desk. "You don't think we're going to meet Jesus, do you?"

"What? No, of course not. From what I gleaned from my father, the Re Transfigurator predates Jesus."

"Good. Because I don't know if I'm prepared to meet him. Do you think he can read minds? He's supposed to know what everyone is thinking. At least, God is. I don't think I could handle that."

"I can read your mind. Can you handle that?"

"Yeah, but that's different. You're my girlfriend, my best friend, and my co-curator. You know me better than anyone else. Even my mother, although I think she would disagree with that."

"Keeping secrets from Mom?"

"No. Stop it. Don't go making me crazy. And don't go probing my brain looking for secrets you can tell my mother. I don't want to have to wear one of those aluminum foil hats whenever I'm around you. Which is a lot."

Johanna's shoulders shook as she laughed at the idea of Jackson's head wrapped in foil.

"I made you laugh. That means I get to choose the first slice." He opened the pizza box, but before he finished looking over the contents, Johanna licked her finger and stuck it into the juiciest slice. He narrowed his eyes. "That's so gross."

"Perhaps, but it marked the slice I wanted."

He reluctantly took a different slice and sat down across from her. "So, whatever this Re Transfigurator thing is, at least we know it's mechanical because it needs a key."

"Not necessarily. It could be encased in some kind of container that needs a key to open."

"How are we ever going to know one box from another?"

"I haven't figured that out yet. But I think we may be able to come up with a spell that will absorb some of the properties of the key and give us a little vapor trail that we can see when it gets close to the corresponding object."

"You can do that?"

"I may need a little help from my father."

RYDEN SIMMDRY COULD hear his daughter calling him telepathically. A moment later he appeared in front of her in the Fantasian library.

⌘*Are you having a problem?*

"I'd like to brainstorm. I'm wondering if there is an existing spell or a way I can—while holding the key—call on some of its properties to give me a physical clue when my mind encounters the Re Transfigurator?"

⌘ *What an intriguing idea. Where is the key now?*

Johanna removed a chain from beneath her blouse. It held a locket and the key she and Jackson had found in the puzzle box. She took it off the chain and handed it to her father.

⌘ *Give me your hand.* He grasped Johanna's hand with one of his own, while holding the key in the palm of his other hand. He cleared his mind and envisioned the key.

Johanna could see the key in her mind as well. She could feel her father's concentration and concentrated in the same manner.

Ryden Simmdry began chanting.

Johanna chanted as well, using the same words as her father. As their chanting increased in volume and speed, the key grew brighter, glowing more with each passing second. It also grew hot as the intensity increased, until it glowed red and sparks flew from it—the heat so strong—Ryden Simmdry felt forced to flip his hand over, dropping the key. Just before he did, a white flash illuminated his and Johanna's minds. The Master took a deep breath when he heard the key hit the floor. ⌘ *It is done.*

Johanna stooped, picking up the key. "I can't believe it. It feels cool to the touch."

⌘ *That should make your task easier.*

She smiled. "I wouldn't be able to do it without you."

The father and daughter hugged, and as suddenly as Ryden Simmdry had appeared, he disappeared.

EIGHT

IT WAS THE perfect time for Ava to sneak Logan into the Library of Illumination. Her mother was out shopping, Chris had taken his girlfriend on a picnic, and Johanna and Jackson were away doing whatever it was they did.

"If no one is here but us, why did you ask me to come up the ally and sneak in the back door?" Logan asked.

"Just in case," Ava answered. "Besides, it has nothing to do with you. I thought it would be better for me if no one saw me letting you in. You know my mother. She would have a hissy fit even though you're Jackson's best friend."

Logan pasted on a smile. "You know, I've

never seen a book come alive. Can you show me one?"

"Okay. But we'll have to be careful. I don't want to unleash King Kong on an unsuspecting public."

"I didn't know that was originally a book. I always thought of it as a movie."

"It wasn't a book to start out, but it was turned into a novel right after the movie was filmed. And the book actually came out before the movie was released."

"Wow. You learned that here?"

"Nope. I found out about it in my Popular Culture class with Mr. Simmons."

Logan rubbed his hands together. "So, let's open a book."

Ava walked over to the shelf containing popular novels. Logan trailed behind her.

"This looks good," Logan said, pulling out George R. R. Martin's book, A Storm of Swords. He opened it to a random page. Suddenly, chaos erupted around him and he felt the splatter of warm blood hit his face. A moment later, his mouth shot open as a sword pierced his back and he saw the blade come out of his stomach. He crumpled to the floor.

"Logan," Ava screamed. He felt her push his hair off his forehead. He opened his eyes for one last time, but everything remained dark.

I'm dying, he thought, *so why is my main concern about how much I need to pee?*

Logan's phone began to flash as the *Crazy Frog* ring-tone played. He turned his head and realized no trace of the massacre at the Red Wedding remained, and he was in his room. He pulled himself into a sitting position. *A dream. It was only a dream.* The phone stopped ringing. He checked to see who had called, but didn't recognize the number.

He took a quick shower before going down to breakfast. The house was quiet. *I guess I have to fend for myself.* He pulled out a frying pan to make eggs but changed his mind. *It's easier to eat out.* He considered inviting Ava to join him but remembered she usually went to church with her mother on Sunday mornings. He thought about inviting Jackson. *I shouldn't cut ties with him right now. I'll let him do it when he discovers I infiltrated the library and broadcast all its secrets.* He smiled momentarily. *If Jackson sees* The Elliott Report, *he might shut me out. Maybe I should take it down until I have more hard evidence against the library.*

He called Jackson to ask if he wanted to go out for breakfast, however, Jackson said he and Johanna had a ton of work to do, and really couldn't. Not that Logan cared. He didn't mind eating alone. However, he did want to stay on Jackson's friendly side. *For now.*

Before he left the house, he adjusted his website so viewers would see an *Under Construction* page instead of *The Elliott Report.* That should take care of spilling the beans ahead of time. He'd just bide his time until he could get some hard evidence, using Ava as his key into the library.

*

Johanna swallowed her last piece of buttery brioche before saying to Jackson, "That was quick. Who was on the phone?"

"Logan. He asked me if I wanted to go out to breakfast."

"Are you going?"

"No. We just finished eating. And I'm pretty full."

"Considering the way you attacked everything on your plate, it's no wonder."

"He hasn't called me in weeks, and now he suddenly wants to go out to breakfast. Why?"

"Well, assuming the mind eraser worked on him, he probably doesn't remember the prom and still thinks you're besties."

"So, why hasn't he reached out to me before this?"

"Because you're both busy earning summer college credits? And didn't Ava say he has a job at the mall? Maybe he's just been really swamped until now."

"You think I should call him back and say I'll go?"

"Only if you want to. If you don't want to, leave it be. There's probably no harm done."

Jackson looked down at his shoes for nearly a minute. "If I hadn't seen what he did to Cassie on prom night, I probably would have gone with him. But he acted like such a jerk."

"There *is* that."

"So, even though we have a lot of history and may still technically be friends, I don't think 'besties' applies."

She walked over to him and rubbed his back. "I understand. Besides, you can't be besties with Logan if you're besties with me. I won't stand for it."

"We're more than besties," Jackson said, slipping

his arms around Johanna's waist and pulling her close. "We are amalgamated."

"Like the Amalgamated Bank?"

"Like combined, united, inseparable, one. You're my shebang."

"Excuse me?"

"You know, like 'the whole shebang.' You're everything to me."

"I'm glad we got that straightened out. The words 'she' and 'bang' have a whole 'nother connotation."

"I only said that because you questioned amalgamated." He lightly touched her face with his fingertips.

Johanna brushed his lips with her own. She felt a surge of heat radiate inside of her. "Okay." She leaned into him, kissing him several more times as the morning wore away. *Amalgamated.*

LOGAN TOOK HIS camera equipment on the road, looking for stories he could use on his show. He saw a bunch of teenage girls coming out of *Pink Bliss*, a clothing store for young women and pulled up to the curb, opening his window. "Ladies, I'm a reporter for a local online news show. Can I interview you on-camera about the hot new trends for back-to-school?"

The girls giggled. One of them, whose ombré hair ranged in color from pale blue to dark purple, said, "I'm game."

"Stay right there." Logan grabbed the equipment and got out of the car. Within seconds, he had the tripod set up and a minute later, the camera and mic were on and ready.

"So, what's hot for fall?" he asked.

The girls gave him a full rundown of all the things they hoped to buy before going back to school, whether they could afford them or not. They all seemed to know the latest trends, and one even had her own style blog. They showed him everything they bought and he shot video of them holding up their new purchases.

"So, how much do you think you'll be spending for school clothes this year, and who's footing the bill, you or your parents?"

One of the girl's said she was earning her own money working at Yonnie's Yogurt Yurt. Another said her grandmother always slipped her money to buy what she really wanted because her mother was kind of strict about what she purchased. The other girls said their parents would foot the bill, "…to a point," and then they all giggled again.

He made sure he got all their names and grades before saying, "One last question?"

"Sure," they answered in unison.

"What do you know about the Library of Illumination?"

Most of them looked at him blankly. One girl's eyebrows raised. "My father talks about that place sometimes. I asked him to pick up a book I needed for a report due in one of my classes, but he said it's not that kind of library. He said it's special. It's not even open to the public. That's weird, right? Whoever heard of a library that's not open to the public?"

"You're right about that. The Library of Illumination is definitely weird," Logan replied. "Has your father told you any stories about it?"

"No. I asked him about it, but he said if he told me,

he would have to kill me. Then he started laughing, like it's a big joke." She blushed, looking down at her feet, then tried to save face. "He's strange like that. He's a scientist. I think the chemical fumes have gotten to his brain." Her friends all giggled.

Logan figured he'd quit while he was ahead. "I'd like to thank you all for your help. You've been great." He quickly put everything in the back of his car before jumping in the driver's seat."

"Hey," one of the girls called out. "Where can we see this?"

"On *The Elliott Report*, he said, before peeling away. *The new, improved version.*

Jennifer couldn't stop thinking about her confrontation with Logan. *If he goes to the administration, I'm going to have a lot of explaining to do.* She looked for the card he had handed her for *The Elliott Report*. She wanted to put together a plan to address the problem if Logan made a stink. She logged onto the website and was shocked to see a page saying *Under Construction.* She switched browsers on her computer and tried again. She got the same message.

She picked up the phone and dialed Luke's number.

"How are you?" he asked when he answered the phone.

"I've been miserable all weekend, until I just tried to log onto *The Elliott Report* and saw a message saying the site is under construction."

"Do you think he's adding more questionable content?"

Jennifer paused before answering. "It looked pretty pulled together, except for the unsubstantiated reporting in that one story. The site was already 'constructed.' I think, maybe, we got through to him. I think he took the site down."

"Just to play devil's advocate, let's say he did take it down. What, if anything, do you think *we* should be doing about it?"

"You mean should we welcome him back into the program?"

"That's exactly what I mean."

"I don't know. I'd have to talk to him first and ask why he took the site down."

"It's summer, you know?"

"Yes, I know."

"We don't have a lot of people, especially people who know what they're doing. It would be helpful if he came back."

"I know, but we can't take him back unless his priorities are in the right place."

"So, what are we, and by 'we' I mean you, going to do about it?"

"I'll check again tomorrow to make sure the site is still down, and if it is, I'll call him. If he sounds reasonable and sincere about why he removed it, I'll invite him back. He can decide what he wants to do. If he comes back we'll send him out on stories, just like old times. If not, be prepared to do a lot more shooting and editing this summer."

Luke sighed loud enough to be heard by Jennifer over the phone. "That's what I was afraid of."

THE ROTHS RETURNED to the library that evening, and it was as if they had never left.

Jackson had already moved his stuff back into the room he had shared with Chris, and everyone else unpacked quickly because they all looked forward to dinner from George V.

Mrs. Roth called in their room service order. She'd dreamed about grilled scallops ever since she learned they were returning. Meanwhile Johanna and Ava preferred the truffle spaghetti and the boys wanted "Black Market" beef.

Chris was the last one to sit down at the table and the first to dive into his meal. "So where are you guys going first tomorrow?"

Jackson looked at Johanna before speaking. She nodded. "First, we're going to Lumi to see if Ryden Simmdry wants to accompany us."

"He doesn't have to," Johanna clarified, "but we thought it would be nice to ask, in case he's really interested."

"And what do you need to do, exactly?" Mrs. Roth asked.

"We're just going to each of the libraries," Jackson said, "to look for a kind of mechanical thing."

His mother held his gaze. "A mechanical thing."

"Not like a weapon or anything. More like a toy or a jewelry box. Ryden Simmdry thinks it will fit the key we found in the puzzle box."

Chris's head jerked up. "What puzzle box?"

"You know," Jackson said, "that round thing that's been sitting on the Information Desk all week."

"That's a puzzle box? Why didn't you tell me?" Chris whined. "I would have tried to open it."

Jackson nudged him with his elbow. "We already opened it and removed the key that was inside. So, even if you could open it, which I doubt, there would have been nothing inside."

"Maybe not," Chris said, "but just the words 'puzzle box' are so cool."

"Is danger involved?" Mrs. Roth asked.

"I don't think so," Johanna answered. "We only found the box by chance. And it looked like it had been hidden away for a very long time. No one, besides my parents, and now, all of you, knows we found it. So, it's not like anyone is looking for it. It's just a little enigma that we want to solve."

Ava put her fork down. "Define 'enigma?'"

"It's a mystery, or something puzzling. So, we're going to find out what it is. Maybe, we can do a program about what we find—here at the library this Fall."

"If you need help, I can come with you," Chris offered.

"No," his mother replied. "I need you here, with me."

Chris's shoulders slumped. "Figures."

"Actually, Chris, it will probably be very boring,' Johanna said, trying to ease the frustration of his mother's command.

"Until it's not," Jackson replied, nudging Johanna with his elbow and smiling.

NINE

JOHANNA AND JACKSON had perfected their ability to pack everything they needed into backpacks, and were ready to leave early Monday morning. Mrs. Roth insisted they eat breakfast before they left, so they called on room service once again to supply an array of food.

"Who pays for all this stuff?" Ava asked. "The prices looked pretty high when I ordered it for mom, so I did a euro to dollar conversion. This meal costs a small fortune. Are we paying for it?"

Jackson wiped his mouth on a napkin. "Not exactly."

"Well who does?"

Chris put down his fork. "I've got this." He looked at his sister and smiled. "Mr. Oswald-Fitzpatrick of New York."

Ava narrowed her eyes. "Who is that?"

"He's the registered guest in this room, and the

hotel hasn't once said he's reneged on the bill. So, we're squeaky."

Niamh stared at her younger son.

"Clean, Mom. Our reputation is squeaky clean."

"It's not a problem," Johanna added.

"How can you be so sure?" Niamh asked, looking concerned.

"Because I made sure the hotel has our Library of Illumination credit card on record for this room. The library handles Mr. Oswald-Fitzpatrick's bills."

"No," Chris wailed. "Now you've ruined it. Why did you have to go and give them a credit card when we could eat for free?"

"You are eating for free. The library is footing the bill." She turned to look at Jackson. "It's time to go."

Niamh placed her teacup back in its saucer. "Do you know when you'll be back?"

"Less than two weeks," Jackson said, kissing his mother on the forehead. "Hold down the fort, but don't worry if you need to leave one of our many fictional characters in charge if you want to go out. We're no longer fighting the Terrorians, so everything should be copacetic."

THE TEEN CO-CURATORS materialized inside the main lobby of the Library of Origination just as Mal emerged from the door leading to a stone stairway.

"Hey!" Mal opened his arms, inviting a hug.

Johanna broke into a huge smile. "I haven't seen you in a while. It's been too long."

After Johanna stepped away, Jackson grabbed Mal's hand and pulled him into a bro hug. "How's everything going?"

"I'm trying to train myself to go almost completely telepathic but it's going to take me some time. Spending time here at the College of Overseers is like hanging out with a very nice fraternity, without the hazing."

Jackson grinned. "Just a bunch of good ol' boys, huh?"

Johanna nudged her co-curator. "I don't think my mother would like to be referred to as a 'good ol boy.'"

"No disrespect to Pru Tellerence, but you know what I mean. It's like the best kind of club."

"That it is," Mal agreed. "So, what brings you two here?"

"We stopped by," Johanna answered, "to see if my father wants to come with us on our quest."

Mal perked up a bit. "A quest? Now you've piqued my interest—even more."

"It could have been your quest, after all, the puzzle box was placed in the library long before Jackson and I ever became curators."

'Where did you find a puzzle box?" Mal asked.

"In the new periodical section," Jackson answered. "Or, as you would know it, the former antiquities section."

"You combined periodicals with antiquities? How unusual—the new and ephemeral with the old and time-proven."

Johanna's mouth fell open in mock horror. "You make it sound terrible. Antiquities had a lot of partially filled shelves, as did Periodicals. We just condensed antiquities onto half as many shelves and did the same with periodicals. Plus, we moved the most current newspapers and magazines to the main reading room."

Mal scratched his head. "And what are you going to

do with all this newly found space?"

"We're keeping it as the George V suite," Jackson said. "That way, I can live in the library and help protect it."

Mal laughed. "And eat as many French pastries as you want?"

"There are perks," Jackson agreed. "You'll have to drop by for dinner."

"And considering Jackson's home has room service and housekeeping, feel free to visit often," Johanna said, rubbing Mal's arm.

He smiled. "I'm surprised you're willing to leave it to go on a quest."

"We won't be gone that long," Jackson said. "Besides, my family moved back in to watch over the library while we're gone."

"Oh," Mal raised an eyebrow. "I didn't know they'd left."

Johanna laughed. "Just long enough to miss room service. Jackson's mom says it was the perfect amount of time for her to go home and clean, before she started to miss being pampered.

"But we'll have to put off the rest of our catching up until later. Do you know where my father is?"

Mal closed his eye for barely a second. "Your parents are in their chamber, but now that they know you're here, they're coming down."

A moment later, Ryden Simmdry and Pru Tellerence entered the lobby.

★*My darling daughter.* Pru Tellerence hugged Johanna a little longer than usual. She had only learned Johanna was her daughter a few months prior, when Mal recounted how Johanna had first arrived at the Library of Illumination in the arms of a woman named Josefina Charo, the same Josefina Charo that Pru Tellerence had left her infant daughter in the care of, shortly after giving birth. She'd lost her connection to her daughter when Josefina disappeared—never to be heard from again.

⌘ *Johanna.* Ryden Simmdry kissed his daughter on the cheek.

Johanna linked her arm in his. "We were wondering if you would like to accompany us on our first visit to one of the other realms? As an observer, of course. Although it wouldn't be bad to have you with us on this particular visit."

⌘ *Terroria.*

Pru Tellerence stiffened. ★ *You're starting with Terroria?*

Johanna nodded. "I thought we might as well get it out of the way, so we could forget about it, rather than putting it off and having our anxiety grow."

★ *Did you consider that if you postponed that realm until last, you might find the Re Transfigurator before then and not have to visit Terroria at all?*

"Now you're talking my language," Jackson said. "Because, as far as I'm concerned, revisiting Terroria isn't high on my to-do list."

"Don't listen to him," Johanna said. "I think it's important for us all to go there to show we are neither afraid of the Terrorians, nor do we discount their importance as part of the Illumini System.

A smile teased the corners of Ryden Simmdry's mouth. ⌘ *Every time I hear your reasoning for handling an obstacle in a specific way, I can see more and more that you are truly my daughter. We are so very alike.*

Johanna patted her father's arm. "So, you'll go with us?"

⌘ *Yes. I believe I will.*

"Mother?"

★ *Your father can help you with this. I must admit, I have no desire to return to Terroria right now.*

Ryden Simmdry's gaze softened as he glanced at the woman he loved. ⌘ *It is an irrational fear.*

Pru Tellerence subconsciously rubbed her prosthetic arm. ★ *I know. My injury happened right outside, not on Terroria. Yet I do not wish to see* any *Terrorians. I'm sure I will get over it in time. But not today.* She kissed Ryden Simmdry goodbye. ★ *Stay safe. Protect Johanna and Jackson as well.*

He smiled at her. ⌘ *It will be my first and foremost concern.*

LOGAN GROANED WHEN his cell phone woke him. He had been up late the previous night, putting together the story for back-to-school trends, and logging the interview by the girl whose father used the Library of Illumination. *'He said if he told me, he would have to kill me.'* That one line made Logan smile. That's just what he needed. He could use the rest of what she said, but that fragment, used alone at the end of the piece, would be a great way to close the next report.

His eyes popped open when he saw the call on his phone was from GRUNT and all vestiges of fatigue drained away. The ring-tone stopped. *Why are they calling me? Probably to beg me to come back. I was a one-man wrecking crew for them.* He smirked. *Let them stew.*

He hopped into the shower. While the water beat

down on his head, he wracked his brain, trying to figure out who else might know something about the library. He had plenty of information that Ava had given him, but it was only audio, and it was muffled because his phone had been in his pocket. *I need video of Ava.*

As he dried off, he formulated a plan he hoped would work. It required Ava being independent enough to come over to his house, alone, for dinner; and he needed to be proficient enough in the kitchen to cook her a meal she would enjoy. He could grill steaks, but *that* reminded him of Cassie and a night that had ended disastrously.

Pasta can't be that difficult. You just had to boil it, right? He'd buy some fancy sauce and throw it in a pot and make it look like he made it. And maybe make a salad. *Chicks love salad.* He grinned. *And something chocolate for dessert.*

He texted Ava.

FAM AWAY. COOKING DINNER. JOIN ME?

It didn't take long for Ava to answer back.

WHERE?

He texted his address and wrote 6:00 pm. *It's kind of early for dinner, but if I make it later, it might be harder for her to get out of the house.*

CU THEN.

Logan spent the rest of the day readjusting the nanny cam his parents had installed when he was little. They didn't bother with it anymore, and the batteries were dead. He replaced them and tested the device but the technology was a decade old. It was okay, but not the best quality. In the end, he went out and bought a new system that claimed to be "professional grade" and would record video and audio on an SD card. He tested it several times before he was happy with the placement of the camera. *Anything Ava says will be recorded. This is it.*

LOGAN YAWNED. HE had prepared everything for dinner with Ava, and now all he could do was wait. He turned on the TV and sunk back into his favorite chair. It didn't take very long for his eyelids to drift southward.

RING! His parents' landline shattered the peace. *That better not be Ava calling to cancel.* He jumped out of his chair and answered. "Logan Elliott."

"Hi Logan, it's Jennifer O'Loughlin. Do you have time to talk?"

His eyes narrowed, not that anyone could see him. "Yeah."

"Good. We noticed that you took down your website, and I can't begin to tell you how relieved I am that you are doing the responsible thing. It shows your maturity and your respect for others' opinions. And we'd like to invite you back. It's really quiet here without you, Logan. I didn't realize until today what a major role you played in this newsroom. What do you say?"

One side of Logan's face raised in a crooked smile. "Sure, Jen, I'd like to come back."

"So, we'll see you tomorrow?"

"Gee, I can't do tomorrow. I already have a commitment." *I'll be editing tonight's conversation with Ava.*

"Wednesday, then."

"I would if I could, but I already promised to work on Wednesday."

"Thursday?"

"Sure, Jen, I think I can do Thursday. I'll see you then."

"Okay, Logan. It's good talking with you."

"Yeah, Jen. You, too."

JENNIFER LOOKED FOR Luke after hanging up. She found him helping a student edit. She caught Luke's eye and motioned her head toward his office. He finished what he was doing and eventually followed her back there. "I just called Logan."

"How did it go?"

"He was very formal, but he agreed to come back."

"Tomorrow? Thank god. I didn't want to schlep to the Transit Authority's press conference on rebuilding the train station. It's supposed to be in the 90s tomorrow. And humid. And we usually have only one other student on Tuesdays."

"Thursday."

"What do you mean, Thursday?"

"He said he's busy tomorrow and has to work on Wednesday. He's coming back on Thursday."

Luke made a face. "Better late than never."

"I just hope we did the right thing. I hated asking him to take down his website in the first place. And I hated making today's phone call, asking him if he wanted to come back."

Luke ran his hand through his hair. "Actually, I'm surprised he agreed. He's usually on his best behavior around you, but I've seen him act pretty hot-headed. He comes from a well-to-do family, and it's apparent that he has feelings of entitlement at times. I just hope we don't see any indication of that on Thursday."

TEN

Ryden Simmdry, Johanna, and Jackson materialized on the steps in front of the Terrorian Library of Illumination.

"We should have brought masks. It really stinks in there." Jackson's nose wrinkled as he sniffed the air. "It doesn't smell so good out here, either."

"Suck it up," Johanna replied, as she marched into the library.

"I definitely won't be doing that," Jackson muttered.

Johanna approached the Terrorian standing behind the Information Desk, while whispering the spell for the universal translator. "I'm Johanna Charette, prime curator of the Fantasian Library of Illumination. My co-curator, Jackson Roth and I are searching for a lost artifact. I would like to search your facility."

"You have brought an overseer with you."

"Yes," she replied. "The Master of the Overseers."

"Why are you making the request instead of the overseer?"

"He is here as an observer."

"I do not have time to take you on a tour of my library, nor can I allow you to roam the halls freely on your own. Not even with an overseer who is here in an observatory capacity."

"Would you mind if I quietly stood here in your lobby?"

"You can stand there as long as you want, but as I've already said, I do not have the time to assist you."

"That's quite alright." She led Jackson and Ryden Simmdry to an out-of-the-way place along the front wall. "This is it." Her eyes lost focus as she concentrated on the uppermost level of the library. She searched for anything magical, quickly studied it and let it go. As she continued with her task, it became easier and her speed increased. It was reflected in her eyelashes, which fluttered as she negotiated the floors below sub-level. Her mind lingered when she scanned Nero 51's secret bunker. The most remarkable thing about that space was a picture on the wall that seemed to vibrate with history. *I'll definitely have to come back and study that someday.* Once she got past that chamber, her speed increased and she completed the rest of her mind search within the hour. "There's nothing here," she told her companions. She walked over to the desk where the Terrorian stood watching them, while pretending not to. "Thank you for your cooperation."

"I did nothing to cooperate," he answered.

"Regardless, the object I'm seeking isn't here. Thank you for not interfering with my extrasensory investigation."

She returned to her father and co-curator, and in a

blink, they disappeared, reappearing on Lumina.

⌘*I'm very impressed. I mentally mirrored your search of the library and witnessed your actions. You worked with great precision and speed and handled a non-helpful Terrorian with grace and professionalism. You did not allow yourself to be deterred by Nero 51's secret sanctuary, although, I'd like to be with you if you ever choose to re-investigate the magical portrait. It radiated power and collusion. I believe that was Nero 51's direct ancestor who helped shape your former nemesis' quest for power.*

"Garpa."

⌘*Excuse me?*

"I subconsciously picked up the name *Garpa*, but did not consciously examine it because it would be a distraction."

⌘*Interesting. I didn't realize you had gleaned so much from that interaction.*

"Like you taught me, I compartmentalized it."

Jackson's stomach growled. "I hate to interrupt, but I'm starving. I realize overseers rarely get hungry, but curators like myself are mighty fond of food, and I need some sustenance."

⌘*I could prepare something for you in the replicator.*

"No, thank you," Jackson answered. "Mal once took us to a place called the IllumOrangerie restaurant, that I really enjoyed. I'd like to go back there."

Johanna's face lit up. "I liked it there, too." She turned to her father. "Join us?"

⌘*I want you two to enjoy yourselves. However, I found the search quite wearying and would like to spend the rest of the afternoon in quiet contemplation.*

"Okay. I'd better say goodbye to Mom. We

probably won't be returning until after we find something conclusive. Unless you want to accompany us to the remaining realms?"

Ryden Simmdry smiled when he heard Johanna call Pru Tellerence, 'Mom.'" ⌘ *You have no need for me. You are more than proficient. And you are young and energetic, attributes I can no longer claim for myself. Stay illuminated.* He kissed Johanna, shook Jackson's hand, and watched as they walked away.

AVA HELPED HER mother wrap the books slated for pick-up later that afternoon. "Mom, would it be okay if I went to Madison's for dinner?"

Niamh considered it. Chris had a date that evening, and if Ava went out, she would be left alone. *The war with the Terrorians is over and the work for the day is done. It would be a perfect opportunity for* Mrs. Oswald-Fitzpatrick *to have an in-room massage and a facial.* "I don't see a problem with that. What time will you be home?"

"What time is Chris coming home?"

"What time Chris comes home has nothing to do with you. I'm sure Madison's parents are quite nice but you can't expect them to sacrifice a quiet evening at home."

"Eleven o'clock, okay?" Ava begged. "I'll be home by eleven."

"No. You'll be home by nine."

"But they don't eat until seven-thirty. We probably won't finish eating dessert until nine."

"Ten o'clock, then. And that's it. Not one minute later."

Ava felt her excitement growing. "Okay."

"What time do you want me to drop you off?"

"Can you drop me off in the village in about an hour? I need to find a birthday gift for Keli Gaughren, and I can do that before I head over to Madison's."

"Will Mr. Rizzuto be driving you home?"

"Yes. Madison already told me he would."

"Okay, then. I may as well call the delivery service and tell them I'll drop off the packages, rather than wait for them to come here."

Ava rushed to her room to get ready. She pulled out a new, gauzy blue blouse and belted it over a pair of cropped skinny jeans. She applied her makeup lightly, so her mother wouldn't wonder what was up. She'd stop in the bathroom of one of the stores in the village and touch it up. She picked up earrings, but didn't put them on. On second thought, she took off the belt as well. She would add that later. She didn't want to appear too dressed up for dinner at *a friend's house*. She'd save the finishing touches for just before she met up with Logan.

LOGAN OPENED THE front door. His mouth quirked in a tiny smile. Ava was looking sexier than he remembered. *This is going to be like taking candy from a baby.* "Hi, Ava. I was surprised you didn't want me to pick you up. How did you get here?"

"I was in the village buying a birthday present for a friend. It wasn't that far away, so I walked it. But I would appreciate it if you could give me a ride back to the library, later."

"Sure. No problem." He paused for a moment. "Do you have a key to get in?"

"Something like that. There's a special way to get in that I use."

"Intriguing. I can't wait to hear about it."

"Oh. I don't know if I'm supposed to share it. It's kind of a secret."

"Maybe I should take you home, now. One thing I can't tolerate from someone I'm close to is secrets and lies. If we're going to be… together, there can't be any secrets between us."

Ava's eyes grew wide. "Okay. No secrets."

Lohan smiled as he turned around and led Ava toward the back deck. *Now we're talking.*

Logan had thought about serving wine with dinner, but had changed his mind and picked up something he thought Ava might like better. "Can I interest you in some pink champagne?"

Her eyes sparkled. "I've never had it before."

He popped open the bottle and filled two champagne flutes. "It's a special way to celebrate our new relationship."

Ava's heart fluttered. "Okay."

Logan handed her a glass and clinked his own against it. "To us." He held her gaze while he took a sip.

Ava's face turned as pink as the champagne. "To us," she repeated.

Johanna and Jackson followed their meal with a walk around central Lumi.

"You can't even tell there was a war here," Jackson said. "The place looks just like it did before the battles were fought."

"It must be nice to live among the overseers. The deans have apparently repaired everything." She paused for a moment as she communicated with Pru Tellerence.

"Yes. They did. My mother just told me the people of Lumi were not at fault for the Terrorian incursion. So, repairing the damage was the least they could do. The only loss they could not reverse, was the loss of life." She couldn't hold back the single tear that spilled over her cheek.

Jackson put an arm around her shoulders and pulled her close.

"Jackson, no. They have a law against PDAs."

He didn't let go. "You're as powerful as an overseer. What are they going to do to you?"

"I do not wish to embarrass my parents."

He allowed his arm to drop. "Point taken."

"We'd better head over to the hotel. I'm exhausted. Searching an entire library—even standing in one place— is mentally exhausting. I need sleep, badly. Plus, it would be nice to get an early start in the morning. I'd like to see if I can do two or three libraries a day. I know we were only planning to do one, but it's not really time consuming."

"Yeah, but from what you just said, it sounds like it's *brain* consuming."

"True. But we'll never know unless I try. And tomorrow will be the day."

"Just don't burn out on me. Your parents would never forgive me, and they're pretty powerful. I wouldn't want to be on their bad side."

LOGAN NURSED HIS champagne, all the while encouraging Ava to drink up and enjoy it while topping off her champagne flute. She had the equivalent of two glasses before dinner and downed another two while eating. As the meal progressed, she laughed more and joked about everything. She had a quick wit and was genuinely funny.

She pushed her glass toward Logan with a smile, raising her eyebrows.

He took a deep breath. "I think, maybe, you've had enough."

"I can never have enough of that." She motioned toward the bottle with a nod.

"Okay. We'll have another glass with dessert. But I have to make it first."

She started to get up. "Can I help you?"

"No," he said, more forcefully than he meant to. "You stay right here. I'm only going to be on the other side of the kitchen island. And this is my surprise for you."

He pre-heated the oven and took two small chocolate soufflés out of the freezer. He added cream and sugar to his mother's whipped cream maker before popping the soufflés in the oven. "I should have started these just before we sat down to eat. It's going to take a while."

"I've got all the time in the world," Ava replied.

"Didn't you tell me your mom wants you home by ten?"

"Who cares what my mom wants. I'm old enough to make my own decisions."

He sat down and took Ava's hands in his. "So, tell me about the library. What's the scariest thing you ever encountered?"

"The Terrorians, for sure. They're huge, ugly brutes with tentacles instead of arms. And their tentacles can stretch out really, really far."

"Where do they come from?"

Ava giggled. "From Terroria. That's why they're called Terrorians."

Logan gave her an encouraging smile. "How do they get into the library?"

"Through the portals."

"Right. Tell me about the portals. Where are they?"

"They're on the top level. Jackson discovered them when he found a small hazy window on the inside that wasn't on the outside of the building. It took him and Johanna a while to figure out how to open it, but once they did, there was no going back. Plus, the Terrorian had these weapons called decimators. They could vaporize anything in a split second, including people." Ava's face turned serious.

The champagne is wearing off. Logan picked up the bottle of champagne and filled Ava's glass, topping off his own. "So, tell me about your favorite book."

"It used to be *The Secret of the Old Clock* with Nancy Drew—a present from you." Ava grinned as she poked Logan in the arm. "I also love *The Secret Garden* by Frances Hodgson Burnett. I remember opening it in the library and watching flowers and vines spring up everywhere. The library smelled like a garden for days, even though I closed the book after a couple of minutes. I thought it was pretty, but my mother said it smelled like a funeral parlor." She sighed, leaning back in the chair with a faraway look in her eyes.

The timer for the oven went off and Logan jumped out of his chair. "You're going to love this." He put the hot dessert treats on plates, poked holes in the middle of each one, and dumped in a shot of liqueur. He placed them on the table with the whipped cream dispenser. "We'd better let these cool a minute. Why don't you tell me what Johanna and Jackson do to protect the library?"

"They do stuff like battle aliens, and it really worries my mother. Plus, there's no one to watch over the library when they're away, so when that happens, we move in."

"And you all sleep in Johanna's little apartment? That must get interesting."

"No, silly. We stay in a suite from the George V hotel in Paris. Johanna just opens a travel guide and the suite appears inside the library, that way there's plenty of space for everyone. And room service."

"You're pulling my leg, right?"

"No, it's true. I'll ask my mother if I can invite you over for dinner. Then you can see for yourself."

ELEVEN

Johanna slept later than expected. The process of searching the Terrorian library had been more mentally draining that she'd anticipated. She had hoped to awaken at sunrise, but discovered it was nearly midday as she grabbed her cell phone to text Jackson. She looked at the screen. *No signal.* There were no cell towers in Lumi because Luminans didn't own cell phones. She looked around for a room phone, and then realized she could telepathically say she had overslept and would like to leave as soon as she showered and had something to eat.

Fifteen minutes later she heard the hotel's automated system say, "Jackson Roth is at your door."

"Let him in," she said aloud as she rushed to get dressed. "I'll be right out," she shouted.

"No rush," he replied.

Johanna quickly dressed and pulled her wet hair into a pony tail. "I'm sorry," she said walking out of the bathroom. "Did you oversleep, too?"

"Maybe, a little, until my stomach growled really loud. So, I got up and ordered room service."

"Oh. I didn't eat yet. Do you mind if we stop and get something?"

"Sounds good to me, after all, it's lunchtime… somewhere."

"Your stomach is like a bottomless pit."

"My body is a highly-tuned machine," he answered, "and it takes a lot of fuel to keep it running optimally."

"What did you have for breakfast?"

"Well, I ordered *ponkekz,* which I thought were pancakes. But it wasn't. It was a kind of green soup with what looked like hard-boiled eggs in it. Normally, I would have gagged at the sight, but it smelled good. So, I tasted it and it was pretty good. And there was some kind of imported specialty bread that had flowers baked into it."

"Brichi."

He narrowed his eyes. "Why does that sound familiar?"

Johanna half-exhaled, half-laughed. "Because the last time you gave me flowers, Pru Tellerence baked brichi out of them. And you thought I had ripped apart your flowers because I didn't like you."

"Right. I remember that. You really hurt me."

"I didn't do anything. Except, perhaps, eat them."

"You got rid of the evidence," he said, as they arrived back at the same restaurant where they'd had dinner.

"Come on. Let's eat." She grabbed his hand and pulled him inside.

"PDA," he said quietly.

She let go of him. A moment later, she received

a message from Ryden Simmdry. "We need to go see my father before we leave."

"Why?"

"He apparently just thought of something."

⌘ *I HAVE NO reason to believe that what you're searching for might be located here on Lumina, however, that didn't stop me from searching Lumi telepathically. While I did so, a possibility arose that I hadn't previously considered. Lumi plays host to many dignitaries from many worlds, and it is possible that at some point in the past, one of them may have hidden the Re Transfigurator here.*

Johanna shook her head. "But you said it's not here."

⌘ *Correct. However, if it were abandoned at a hotel or stolen from whoever had it, it may have made its way to a place at the outskirts of Lumi where an irreputable market holds sway. On your realm, I believe it is referred to as the black market. Unfortunately, it is very well protected by what may be a jamming device.*

"Where is it?" Johanna asked. "What is it called? How do we get there?"

⌘ *It is known as Illicitus Arto and it is wedged between Municipal Water & Power and the Lumi Transport Center. It lays behind a formidable fence hidden by trees and bushes. Most casual observers would pass it by if they were not looking for it but it's there.*

Jackson snorted. "I'm surprised the *Land of No* would allow such a thing to exist."

⌘ *It's true the ruling members of this society do not permit much to go on here that it finds distasteful. However, the Illicitus Arto has proved beneficial to certain members of the ruling class who are either looking for rare artifacts, or need to sell such objects without a lot of fanfare. I suggest you take a look there. However, I warn you to be cautious. It is not populated by the savoriest of characters. Keep your wits about you.*

Johanna offered her hand to Jackson. "Shall we?"

"I'm with you."

JOHANNA AND JACKSON materialized in a shadowy corner within the boundaries of Illicitus Arto. Jackson took a step forward, but Johanna grabbed his arm and pulled him back. "First, we study our surroundings," she whispered.

From where they stood, they could see a vast yard piled with heaps of junk, old furniture, other types of household and business furnishings, and a small area that no one seemed interested in. There were about a half dozen people poking through the wares, looking for items of interest.

Johanna nodded toward a fairly small area against the border wall that prevented Lumi residents from falling off the outcrop and plunging into the sea. "What do you think is over there?"

"I don't know," Jackson answered. "Do you want to go look?"

Johanna hesitated. Suddenly, an animal started howling and someone near the entrance shouted, as everyone turned to see what was going on. She grabbed Jackson's hand and they transported to the area Johanna had been interested in.

"Toys," Jackson said.

"Not just toys but items of amusement, including music boxes and musical instruments. Let's look around."

Jackson picked up a musical instrument that looked like a guitar. He plucked a string and the most ungodly squeal made Johanna wince. "Put that down," she said quietly. "We don't want to call undue attention to ourselves."

"Right."

Something caught Johanna's eye. "That looks interesting. She made her way through the countless artifacts strewn about until she reached a highly detailed, richly colored wooden box, sitting in plain sight. The intricate detail on the case appeared to be old, however, unlike everything around it, it was immaculate; no dust had collected in the nooks and crannies of the carving, nor did it appear to be scratched or worn. Yet, here it stood, in a dusty old bazaar, exposed to the elements. Everything else around it looked the worse for wear.

The box appeared to be about a foot and a half tall, perhaps twenty inches wide, and about eight inches deep. Although its shape reminded Johanna of a small suitcase, it contained no handle, yet the sides were hinged. Johanna and Jackson inspected it closely. "Look at this, Jackson. The back looks solid, and there doesn't appear to be a seam on the front, but this carved wooden embellishment may be hiding the seam."

"It doesn't look like anything I'd ever want to own. It must be for girls."

She rolled her eyes. "Look at the colors. Deep crimson. Burnished gold. Cobalt blue. Burnt sienna. Viridian. Not pink and powder blue. These are manly colors. How can you say this is meant for girls?"

"Look at all the scrolly things. Guys aren't into that."

"Maybe not now, but I think this is old. Really old. And if you ever studied the Renaissance, you would know that guys were much more ornamentally predisposed back then."

"So, you think this is from the Renaissance era?"

"No. I think we're looking at something that predates that era by a long shot."

"How do you figure that?"

"We found the key in a box, dating back to a period before the realms were created. The time before time as we know it."

"Maybe somebody found the old puzzle box a lot more recently, and just decided it's a dandy place to hide a key."

"You're like a man stumbling around in a dark room you've never been to before. I'm in there too. And I've seen the floor plan. But you always seem to be the one who inadvertently finds the light switch."

Jackson shook his head ever-so-slightly as if to clear out some cobwebs. "What does that mean?"

"That if you're right, I'm looking at this whole thing the wrong way."

"This calls for a snack. Let's go get a couple of… do you think they have burgers here? I could really use a burger. Or we could go back to the IllumOrangerie Restaurant."

"I'm not leaving this box here."

"What makes you so sure it's what we're looking for?"

"I'm not sure at all, but I think it's old. People don't make things like this anymore."

"It looks brand new, in kind of an old-fashioned way. Maybe it's a reproduction."

"No. I touched it before and it's as smooth as glass. It looked like enameled wood, but it's warm to the touch. Like something other-worldly."

"Duh. We're on another world. That's the way it should feel."

"Maybe, but the key was left on Fantasia for a reason. And the puzzle box looked like it hadn't been opened for a long time. Even the key looked like it hadn't been used in a long time. I think whatever the key opens is meant for the curator of the Fantasian Library of Illumination to find. That's us."

"So, are you saying this box is for us? Or are you saying we're looking for something more Fantasian?"

"I don't know what I'm saying, but my gut tells me we have to take this box with us."

Jackson picked up the case. "Okay, but don't pay the asking price. You gotta bargain with these people." The pair walked back to the main tent. Mo'Aniche, the purveyor, sat slouched on a padded mat. "My girlfriend likes this suitcase," Jackson said. "How much?"

Mo'Aniche stared at the case and then at the teens. "Three million credits."

Jackson leaned toward Johanna. "How much is that?" he asked in a low voice.

She did a quick calculation in her head. "Too much," she whispered. She bent over to look at something else. "Put it back," she said in a louder voice. "It's not worth it."

Jackson narrowed his eyes. "You really want me to put it back?"

She waved him away with her hand. "Yes. I saw a case at the hotel that's much nicer for a lot less. I only wanted that one because I thought it would be cheaper."

Mo'Aniche held up his hands. "You are from off-world. I can see you don't know our ways."

"What *ways* are that?"

"Luminans are willing to pay a pretty price for orbital sweetness."

"Orbital sweetness?" Johanna countered.

"Eye candy," Jackson whispered.

She stood up slowly. "I'll give you two hundred thousand credits."

Mo'Aniche jerked upright. "Are you trying to rob me? That's a ridiculously low amount. Go buy your suitcase at the hotel."

"See. I told you, Jackson. Let's go before the hotel sells the case I like."

They had taken several steps toward the gate when the purveyor's voice rang out, "Eight hundred thousand credits."

Johanna tried to keep herself from smiling. She turned and glared at the man. "Five hundred thousand. That's my final offer."

Johanna and Mo'Aniche stared at each other for more than a minute. "Sold. But you are taking food out of my children's mouths."

"You don't have any children," Johanna said, handing him a card with the credits on it.

"Who told you that? They are lying!"

"I'll tell Master Ryden Simmdry you called him a liar. I'm sure he'll be very interested to hear your opinion of him."

The purveyor shrank back. "That is not necessary. Technically he is correct. I have no children on this world. I'll let it pass."

I bet you will, Johanna thought as she looked at Jackson and nodded toward the gate.

"You're pretty good at this bargaining thing," Jackson said quietly.

"And to think you doubted me."

As soon as the gate closed behind them, Johanna grabbed Jackson's arm and they transported back to the Library of Origination.

THE GATE TO Illicitus Arto reopened a moment later, and two men emerged. Mo'Aniche had instructed them to follow the teens. They looked around, then split up, one walking quickly toward the Avenue > Transportation, and the other toward Avenue > Commerce, each without luck.

"He's not going to like this," one said to the other when they reunited empty-handed.

"There's nothing we can do about it," the other man answered.

TWELVE

RYDEN SIMMDRY STUDIED the case clutched in Jackson's arm. ⌘ *Is that what you're looking for?*

"I don't know," Johanna answered. "It doesn't have a keyhole, if that's what you're asking. But it has a strange hold over me. I couldn't leave without it."

"You mean this might not be the right artifact?" Jackson asked, a little too loudly.

"I'm not sure. But now that we're here, we can take a closer look at it." She ran her hands over the outside, once again, looking for unusual markings or seams. The case almost seemed to vibrate from her touch. As she analyzed the design on the top of the case, her eyes grew wide. She looked at her father. "Did you refer to this type of symbol as a triskelion?"

Ryden Simmdry came closer to take a look. ⌘ *I'm surprised you were able to see that. It's very finely worked into the intricate design of the box.*

She tried pressing the triskelion and when that didn't work, searched for an alpha and omega. There didn't appear to be one. She tried to stick her fingernails under the carved wood embellishment on the front of the box but was unable to pry the box open.

⌘*Perhaps a little magic is called for.*

Johanna took a step back and concentrated on opening the box. Nothing happened. "Would you like to give it a try?" she asked her father.

Ryden Simmdry chanted for a moment, and then waved his hands over the box. It appeared to vibrate more, but did not open.

"Maybe you should both do it together," Jackson said.

Johanna watched her father for a moment and mimicked his movement and his chant. The box shook violently, for several moments, before springing open. The front of the case dropped as the two sides fanned out, revealing an interior that resembled the reading room of a Library of Illumination. Suddenly, a projection shot out of the box, recreating the information desk and the display cases inside the library. *Her* library. Right down to the counter stool from the bar in the George V hotel that her mother had borrowed.

"Jackson took a step back. "This is kind of freaky, don't you think?"

"I'd close it," she replied, "but I'm afraid to touch it. And I'm scared we won't be able to open it again."

"Look at the floor of the library. It has the same symbol that ours has, but, is that a keyhole?"

Johanna took a step forward and looked more closely. "No."

"So, we found this freaky thing that is obviously related to our library, but it's not the freaky thing we're looking for."

"Not as far as I can tell."

Pru Tellerence entered the room, surprised to see Johanna standing there. ★*Johanna, you're still here. I thought you left a while ago.*

⌘*She did, but then I thought she might find the artifact at Illicitus Arto, and she came back with this.*

★*Oh my! I didn't think any of these still existed.*

⌘*You know what this is?*

★*I was very taken with stories and illustrations of them from my childhood. I saw one holographically reproduced and I never forgot it.*

⌘*Well, don't keep us waiting, Pruelle. What is it?*

She leaned closer to it and studied it dreamily. ★*It's a portable portal.*

Jackson sat on his heels and stared at it. "That's a portal?"

★*Yes. I had heard that they were all destroyed after the Two Millennia War to prevent anyone from illegally travelling to other realms. This one seems to have escaped detection.*

⌘*Johanna, I have no right to ask this of you, but I'd like to keep this in our vault, at least temporarily. If it is a portal, it's an extremely dangerous artifact for you to have in your possession.*

"Fine. I'd hate dragging it around with us while we look for the Re Transfigurator, anyway." She carefully closed it and handed it to her father.

"Goodbye, little Fantasian library." Jackson stood up. "So, where are we off to now?"

"Maybe you should say, "Where are we off to, Furst.""

"We're going to Dramatica? Cool. I like Furst. But I doubt you'll find what we're looking for, there."

"Why?"

"Because the place looked like it was straight out of medieval England. A mechanical device would look totally out of place there."

"That should make our job easier."

THEY ARRIVED JUST outside the main entrance to the Dramatican library, in a shadowy area. Johanna surveyed the scene. The overseers had been busy. Like Lumi, this realm showed no signs of having suffered in the war—even though she had heard of the fierce battles fought here.

"I like what they've done with the place." Jackson studied the front door. "This looks like the time lock mechanism to a Swiss bank vault. Not the entrance to Furst's library. I love how you can see brass and steel right through the glass." He put his hand up to touch it, and took a step backward, startled, when the door suddenly opened.

"All of this, the overseers did," Furst said in stilted Dramatican syntax. He swept his arm back, as if to welcome them in, and then leapt, so he could greet them from the new information desk.

"Hey, Furst, good to see you in all your jeweled splendor." Jackson's head swiveled as he viewed all the changes. "This place looks 180 degrees. It's very next generation."

"Of heat, a measurement. Warm, you are?"

"No." Jackson suppressed a grin. "I mean it looks

like it's the complete opposite of what it previously looked like." He picked up a book from the desk. "So instead of looking like the front of this book," he flipped it over, "it looks like the back of this book. I rotated it 180 degrees—" his voice trailed off. "Why does the back of your book look like the front of your book?"

"Easier to identify, it is. More efficient, it is." Furst couldn't help but smile. "180 degrees less work, it is."

Johanna ran her hand across the smooth surface of the counter. "What do the other Dramaticans think?"

"Like it, they do not. Trust it, they do not. Our way, it is not. But, get used to it, they will. Too, I will."

Jackson slapped his hand on the top of the Information Desk. "You're way ahead of your time. And while it may not impress your countrymen, it will impress curators from other realms who visit here."

"And show them your mettle," Johanna added.

"And your metal, because they can see it through the freakin' door. I love that!"

"A direct hit from a decimator, strong enough to withstand, the door is. Unbreakable, its transparent walls are. They deflect any concentrated power aimed at them. Make us feel safe, the overseers wanted to."

"And I love this new uniform my mother created for you. It shows how important you are."

"Your mother, why did you say?"

"Oh," Johanna replied. "I don't know why I thought you knew. But of course, you had returned home by then. After the war on Lumina, we traveled to Romantica where Mal saw a statue of a woman who died at the Fantasian Library of Illumination. My mother recognized the woman. She was the high priestess Pru Tellerence had left her newborn daughter with three millennia ago. At the time, it was illegal for overseers to have children. She tried to keep the baby a secret, but when the priestess, Josefina Charo, began dying, she took the baby to Fantasia where she thought it would be safe. Unfortunately, she died before she could tell Pru Tellerence where she'd taken the baby.

"Selestra, the child is."

"No. Not Selestra. Me."

Furst took a step back. "A child of an overseer, you are?"

"Not just any overseer," Jackson said. "Johanna is the child of Pru Tellerence and Ryden Simmdry. Both her parents are overseers."

Furst scratched his bushy red eyebrows. "Can this be, how?"

"It happened a long time ago," Johanna said. "Three thousand and eighteen years ago to be exact. I did not start aging in normal Fantasian years until I was found at that library. My mother believes Josefina Charo must have cast a spell removing the Longevicus Blessing I was born with, so I wouldn't be detected as being different from the other people living on that realm."

Furst simply nodded.

"While it's wonderful to see you, Jackson and I don't wish to disrupt your daily routine. We are searching for something we believe is hidden on one of the realms. An old artifact. Would it be okay if I searched your library? You don't have to do anything. I can do what I need to do from right here."

"Curious, you have made me. Do that, how can you?"

Jackson shook his head at Furst. "She inherited

Ryden Simmdry and Pru Tellerence's telepathic powers. She searches with her mind."

"Work, does that?"

"I'll be looking for a magical signature, which is actually easy. Just time consuming. And tiring."

"Ahead, go."

Johanna picked the same spot against the wall that she had chosen in the Terrorian library. She leaned against the wall, closed her eyes, and began her investigation."

"You do, what do?"

Jackson walked over to Johanna and stood beside her. "I'm her bodyguard. I'm the *here-and-now* guy, while she's the *there-and-then* babe."

"Babe? Regress, she will?"

"No, forget I said that. It was just a dumb joke."

"Sustenance, do you need?"

"No thanks, Furst. I slept through breakfast, but I had two lunches to make up for it. I may have overdone, it. Or it might have been the stuff I ate on Lumina attacking from within."

"Outhouses, we have."

"You don't have indoor plumbing?" Jackson half-grimaced, half-smiled. "Good to know, Furst. Good to know."

Furst left Jackson alone with Johanna while the Dramatican had his midday meal. By the time he returned, Johanna's eyelashes were fluttering.

"Okay, is she?"

"She coming in for a landing. She does that with her eyes when she's winding down."

"'For a landing, she's coming in,' mean, what does that?"

No air travel, Jackson thought. "Someday, you'll have to visit us on Fantasia, so I can show you."

"Honored, I would be," Furst said, breaking into a huge smile. "Very much, I would like that."

"What would you like?" Johanna asked.

"I invited Furst to come visit us on Fantasia."

Johanna turned toward her fellow curator. "You are welcome to visit us any time, Furst. We would really love for you to see our world."

While Jackson said goodbye to Furst, Johanna took a moment to commune with her father. When it came time to leave she grabbed Jackson's hand. They instantaneously transported to another realm.

Jackson looked around. "We're on Romantica, right?"

Johanna nodded.

"I could tell by the flowers. There's a lot of them. No wonder they use them to bake bread. They have to use them up somehow."

"My mother said there's a new inn right across from the library that the overseers created in case Natalia Dalura is ever locked out of her library again. She said it's quite charming and should be perfect for an overnight stay."

"I'm glad we're staying here instead of Dramatica."

"I thought you liked Dramatica."

"I do, but they don't have indoor plumbing."

"They don't?"

"Nope."

"Well then, I guess I'm glad we're staying here. too."

AVA SLAPPED THE last mailing label on a package of books. "I'm done, and you're still wrapping, which means I get to pick what we're having for lunch."

Niamh's mouth quirked into a half smile. "I didn't realize we were competing for food."

"French food is great. But I really want a burger from Meister Burgerie."

"In Gainesford?"

"You make it sound like it's in another state. It's less than five miles away."

"Room service is less than five feet away."

"Aw, come on, Mom. It will be nice to get out. When I go to college, you're going to miss me."

"That's still three years away. Don't rush your life. Enjoy every day while you're still young."

"It's not always easy being me."

"Why? What's the problem, exactly?"

"I'm interested in a boy. But he just graduated high school and I'm afraid once he goes to college, he'll forget all about me."

"You are way too young for boys who have just graduated high school."

"No, I'm not. I'm in high school and all the other girls date guys who are a few years older than they are."

"You know nothing about him."

"I know plenty about him." Ava lowered her voice. "So do you."

"So do I?" her mother's reply was more of an exclamation than a question.

"It's Logan. And I'd like to invite him to dinner here, tonight."

"Jackson's friend? Well, we do know him, but Ava, I still think he's too old for you."

"Like Jackson's too old to be my brother?"

"Now you're being ridiculous."

"No, I'm not. He's a friend of the family. A really great guy. And I like him a lot. If Jackson asked if he could invite him to dinner, you would say yes right away. But just because I'm the one doing the asking, you're saying no."

Her mother sighed. "I think it's a bad idea, but if you really want to invite him here, go ahead."

Ava jumped up and threw her arms around her mother's neck. "I love you. I love you. I love you. Thanks, Mom. We don't even have to go to Gainesford. We can have lunch right here. Again." Ava ran for the suite.

"I didn't realize you were so hungry for lunch," her mother called out to her.

"I have to decide what to wear," Ava yelled back. "And then we can have lunch."

LOGAN'S PHONE VIBRATED in his pocket. He picked it up and saw *Library of Illumination.* "Hello."

"Hey Logan, it's Ava."

"Ava, what's going on?"

"I'm calling to invite you to dinner at the library tonight."

"Really? Are you sure it will be okay with everyone?"

"I asked my mom. She said it's fine. Chris will be here too."

Logan paused for a moment, waiting to see if she would say anything else. "What about Johanna and Jackson?"

"They're away taking care of library business. We don't expect them back until next week."

She heard him take a deep breath over the phone and she frowned. "Why? Do you want to wait until then?"

"No." The single word came out more emphatically

than Logan would have preferred. "Tonight's fine. I'm excited."

Ava felt her spirits lighten. "Me too. Is seven o'clock okay?"

"Perfect."

"I'll see you then."

THIRTEEN

AVA HUNG UP the phone in Johanna's apartment, leaned against the wall and slid down to the floor. *He said yes.*

She ran down to her room and started rummaging through her clothes. She had only brought a few items with her and nothing suited her.

Her mother's voice called out, "Ava, it's time for lunch."

She nodded to herself. *Lunch. Good. And then I'll run home and find something to wear.* She moaned. *I don't have anything to wear.* She straightened out. *Johanna.* She let herself into Johanna's closet to check out her clothes. *Johanna always looks great.* Ava was surprised by the small selection. *What did she do, take everything with her?* Then she saw a fluttery, white blouse hanging in the corner. It had a high funnel neck, almost like a loose turtle neck, and smooth shoulders attached to full poet sleeves which ended in deep cuffs. The body of the shirt was made up of loosely draped fabric, gathered at the waist, with an almost non-existent peplum that was cropped short. It was modest, yet sexy; edgy, yet sweet. *This is perfect. I can wear it with the new black jeans I bought for school.* Ava grabbed the hanger and went down the curator's staircase, hoping her mother didn't see her. She didn't think Niamh would let her borrow something from Johanna without asking her, but Ava *needed* this shirt. She ran into the hotel suite and stuck the blouse in her closet before her mother could see it. *Okay. That's done.* She smiled.

"Ava?" her mother called again.

"Coming," she yelled as she left her bedroom, thinking about what she could order from room service.

THE ROMANTICAN HOTEL looked like it came straight out of a fairy tale. The sprawling white building with pale lilac plantation shutters sat in the middle of a beautifully-tended garden, with water fountains and statuary. Inside, the lobby courtyard was just as stunning with a beautiful fountain.

Jackson stopped short and pointed at a raised planter. "Is that a garden gnome?"

Johanna shook her head. "It's a cherub."

"It sure looks like a garden gnome to me."

"I'm sure most Romanticans have never even heard of garden gnomes."

"It's got a pointy hat."

"It's a sun hat."

"It's pointy."

"So, what? It's a cherub."

"How can you be so sure?"

"It's naked. Garden gnomes wear pants. And boots. And jackets."

"You got me there. Score one for the prime curator."

A pretty young woman welcomed Johanna, hardly looking at Jackson. "Welcome to the Botanical Inn. I'm Lisanna. Do you prefer a gardenette or an aerie?"

Johanna paused. "What's the difference?"

"A gardenette opens up to a private little retreat in the back garden. An aerie has a retractable transparent ceiling that opens up to the sky."

"Aerie," Jackson said before Johanna had a chance.

Lisanna took a step back, her eyes huge.

"Make that two aeries," Johanna said.

Lisanna addressed her reply to Johanna. "Men are not allowed in the inn. We have an outbuilding for them. I'm sure we can find space out there for…" She pointed at Jackson.

"Excuse me?" Jackson's mouth hung open.

Johanna nodded. "I understand that is the way of life here on Romantica, but we are from another realm. I am the curator of the Library of Illumination on Fantasia, and Jackson," she gestured toward him, "is my co-curator. Perhaps you know Pru Tellerence? She's a Romantican and happens to be my mother. I'm sure she would vouch for Jackson's integrity."

Lisanna appeared flustered. She turned to go, turned back to face Johanna and Jackson, shook her head, then exited out the back door.

"I can't believe she wants to find me space in an outhouse!" Jackson exclaimed.

"An 'outbuilding,'" Johanna corrected.

Jackson slapped his hand against the counter. "Semantics."

Nearly a half-hour passed before Lisanna returned

dragging Natalia Dalura with her. Natalia smiled warmly. "Johanna, Jackson, how nice to see you again." She gave them each a hug. "What seems to be the problem?"

Lisanna's head snapped when she saw Natalia hug Jackson. "The man wants an aerie!"

Natalia continued to smile as she turned to the young woman. "I understand not allowing co-habitation is the way of our world, but these are visiting dignitaries from afar. We must be gracious and offer both of them our full measure of hospitality. If it weren't for them, working along with our militairres, Roma would be reduced to rubble and under Terrorian rule. They are more than curators. They're war heroes. Give them our best aeries, at no charge."

If Lisanna's eyes could open any wider, they would have popped out of their sockets. "Uh… uh… of course, whatever you say." She rushed behind the reception area and selected keys for the two biggest aeries they had.

"Please say you'll join me at the library for your evening meal. I'm sure Dame Erato would join us with Selestra."

"You're going to cook for us?" Jackson asked with a trace of awe in his voice.

"Of course."

"Then, we'll be there. Right?" He turned to Johanna, suddenly realizing she might have other plans.

"We'd love to," Johanna answered.

Ava pulled her hair over to one side and braided it so it hung down over her shoulder. She applied her makeup, just the way she saw her favorite celebrity do it on YouTube and dressed in Johanna's white blouse, black skinny jeans, and black sandals.

When she emerged from the hotel suite, her brother Chris did a double-take. "Who are you, and what have you done with my little sister?"

She cringed at the word *little* but it was better than *baby*. "Maybe I should say that about you. Here you are at the end of the day, pretending to work, while Mom and I went crazy all afternoon, trying to fulfill all the requests for books—by ourselves. Where have *you* been?"

"I've been busy working out in the school gym, building myself up to play football this fall."

"You're trying out for the football team?"

"Exeter girls love to date jocks, especially the ones on the football team."

"So, you're doing it to get dates."

"No," he paused, "well, yeah. I guess…"

"And how is that working out for you?"

Chris narrowed his eyes. "Since when did you get so feisty?"

"Not feisty." She shuddered. "Fierce."

"Is that what you're doing, wearing all that makeup? Trying to look fierce?"

"I always look like this," Ava replied, even though she knew it wasn't true.

"Liar! Mom already told me you asked Logan over for dinner. You've always crushed on Logan. Admit it."

"I like Logan, just like everyone else in the family."

"I think not. I'm pretty sure you like Logan a lot more than everyone else in the family. I remember when you used to sleep with some dumb book that he gave you, under your pillow."

"Did not."

"Did too!"

"Stop arguing this instant," Niamh admonished

her two youngest children. "Chris, you should be done inputting that information by now, and I need you inside, Ava, to help me make the selections for dinner."

Ava took a step back. "It's too early to order dinner, Mom. Logan isn't even here yet."

"I'd like to put in the order now," her mother said, "and ask the wait staff to deliver it at 7:30. Didn't you tell me Logan will be here at 7:00?"

"Yeah," Ava answered with a shrug.

"Fine, I don't want to put everything off until the last moment. This way it will give us all time to visit before we eat."

Ugh, Ava thought. *This is my date. Not everyone else's.* "I just thought I'd show him around while we wait."

"Why?" Chris butted in. "Logan has been here before. It's not like he needs a tour." He changed his voice to mimic his sisters. "Oh, look Logan," he swept his right arm toward the shelves, "these are the books. And over her," he swept his left arm in the opposite direction, "are the other books."

If daggers could have shot out of Ava's eyes, they would have.

"Ava," Mrs. Roth asked, "where did you get that blouse? I don't remember you buying it."

A quick sign of panic flickered in Ava's eyes. "Uh… it's Johanna's. She told me I could borrow it."

Mrs. Roth touched the fabric. "I don't think I've ever seen her wear it. Its beautifully made. Are you sure it's all right?"

Ava tensed. "Yes. It's all right."

Her mother turned toward the hotel suite. "As long as you're sure. Come along. Let's pick out the food so it will arrive precisely at 7:30.

Ava's shoulders slumped. "Fine," she answered quietly.

Logan's frustration mounted. He'd been to the Library of Illumination dozens of time, so why was he having such a hard time finding the place? He drove around the block one more time, and as if by magic, he saw the building that had eluded him for the past half hour. He slid into a nearby parking space and grabbed the large bouquet of flowers he had picked up on the way.

"Logan's here," Chris called out when he spied him on the security camera. "Illumination," the teen said aloud. The front door slid open.

"Hey Chris," Logan said. "I see they've got you working here, too."

"All in the family," Chris replied, before yelling, "Ava," at the top of his lungs.

Logan smirked. "Classy."

"Now what did he do?" Ava asked, overhearing them.

"Nothing, really," Logan answered. "It's just my way of saying hi."

Mrs. Roth emerged from the suite. "Hello, Logan. It's nice to see you again."

"Same, here, Mrs. R." He handed her the huge bouquet of flowers. "For the hostess."

"Then you should probably be handing these to Ava, but I would be happy to place them in water for her." She turned to go back into the suite. "Dinner is in fifteen minutes. Ava, why don't you get Logan something to drink."

Ava's eyes hardened as she looked at her mother,

but she quickly relaxed her face as she turned to Logan. "What can I get you?"

"Nothing for now. Why don't you show me around?"

"Let's start at the top." She led Logan up the cupola stairs but didn't speak until they reached the uppermost level. "This way," she said, leading him into an alcove.

Logan raised his eyebrows. "Trying to get me alone?"

"No. It's just that our voices echo to every corner of the library if we speak in the open area of the cupola. At least here, there's some degree of privacy."

Logan pulled a book off the shelf. "This looks interesting, *The Voynich Manuscript*. Is this like a Dan Brown book?"

"Don't—"

Logan opened it before Ava could stop him and then stiffened when odd looking plants and flowers materialized around him with words in an unfamiliar language floating in the air. Eerie whistling sounds and a peppery odor assaulted his senses. He began coughing and sneezing. Ava grabbed the book away and closed it before the air could become more rancid. But it had affected her, as well, and tears spilled from her reddened eyes, streaming down her cheeks.

In his haste to get away from the offending book, Logan bumped into a freestanding table and knocked *Fantastic Beasts and Where to Find Them* onto the floor. It opened, allowing a hippogriff to escape into the library. The hybrid eagle-horse creature divebombed the teens as it circled the cupola, looking for a way out.

Ava crawled over to the book and closed it, sending

the creature to oblivion. "Do not open," she paused to cough, "any more books."

"I didn't open that one. It opened by itself."

"Ava," Chris screamed, "you better get down here pronto and clean up this mess. I don't know what you have flying around up there, but it just took a dump, and it's HUGE! It splattered when it hit the floor and it's everywhere."

Ava groaned. "Come on."

Logan coughed. "I'll be down in a minute. I need to catch my breath after those flowers nearly poisoned me."

Ava rushed down the staircase, her feet thumping on every tread.

Logan did his best to pull himself together while he grabbed his smart phone and took video of the covers of the two books that had opened. With video still recording, he propped the phone against the bookcase, took a deep breath, and quickly opened the first book, releasing the plants and floating words. He counted to 10 and closed the book before breathing again. *It's a shame I can't open the other one, but Ava will notice that one for sure. I've got to get her to open another book for me while I pretend to get a text. Then I can shoot whatever emerges.*

ALL THROUGH DINNER, Natalia talked about all the rebuilding on Romantica that had happened since the Terrorian incursion. "The library is better fortified than ever before, although if you would have asked me at the beginning of the year, I would have dismissed any need for fortification."

"Now that Nero 51 is dead," Johanna added, "you'd probably be fine thinking that again."

"I don't know," Jackson said, turning toward

Natalia. "There must be a dozen more Terrorians who want to follow in Nero 51's footsteps. Fortifying the library is in your best interests."

Natalia smiled. "When I first met you, you were more like a boy. But now, you speak like a man who has been to war, and as a result, has the experience to understand the motives of other men."

"Yah," three-year old Bel said, sticking a flower she had pulled out of a piece of *brichi* into Jackson's ear.

Jackson pulled the crumpled flower out of his ear, ruffling the hair on Bel's head. "Looks like you've created a flower-strewn path."

A row of flowers and a trail of crumbs snaked across the table where Bel sat.

"I can't keep *brichi* in my cottage when Selestra is visiting, or I'll find a trail of mauled bread just like that," Dame Erato said, pointing to the child's handwork.

Natalia made a face. "Remind me again why you call her Selestra, but Jackson and Johanna call her Bel?"

Johanna laughed. "Her name was Bel when Pru Tellerence adopted her—believing Bel was her daughter. She asked Ingur Aguri to keep her safe, and Ingur insisted on re-naming her Selestra, so any potential enemies wouldn't know she was the child of an overseer."

"And as it turns out," Dame Erato added, "she's not. Johanna is Pru Tellerence's real daughter. However, Ingur is so used to calling the child Selestra, the name has stuck." She put her arm around Bel and hugged her. "So now, she's the girl with two names." She dropped a kiss on Bel's forehead.

"I can see you enjoy being an aunt," Johanna said.

"A *great aunt*. My sister has everyone believing she's the child's grandmother, so I'm a great aunt."

"That couldn't be truer in any sense of the word," Natalia said, clearing the table. "You're so great, I wish you were my aunt."

Natalia's praise made Dame Erato glow. "So, what brings the youngest and first co-curators of a Library of Illumination back to Romantica?"

"I'd like to do a quick search of the library. I'm looking for something magical that fits a key I found on Fantasia. My father and I searched our library, as well as his, but it's not in either one."

"It's not on Dramatica, either," Jackson added.

"That will take a while, Dame Erato said. "May I be of assistance?"

"Thank you, but it's not a physical search. Ryden Simmdry taught me how to do it telepathically. It takes about an hour."

"Do you want to do it now?" Natalia asked, setting dessert on the table.

"It's very tiring, and I already searched one library today. I'd prefer to wait until morning when I'm fresh, if that's okay with you?"

"Of course," Natalia answered. "Now who would like a piece of—what I like to call—gems in a cloud of tulle?"

FOURTEEN

Down on the main level of the Fantasian library, Logan found Ava wiping down books and furniture with paper towels dampened with a mild disinfectant. He wrinkled his nose. "That smell…"

"It will get better after I dump the garbage bag."

Mrs. Roth emerged from the hotel suite. "It's time for dinner. Come in and eat while the food is still warm."

Chris grabbed Logan's arm. "C'mon, let's eat."

Mrs. Roth made a face. "What happened out here?"

"Just a little accident, Mom," Chris said before Ava could reply. "Ava's on top of it and will have it all cleaned up in a few minutes. I'm sure she doesn't expect us to wait for her while the food gets cold." He dragged Logan into the suite while Ava made a face and continued to clean.

"Try not to take too long," her mother told her.

"Right," Ava said, as she rushed to finish cleaning everything up.

Logan's jaw dropped when he entered the suite. "What is this place?"

"It's where we stay when Johanna and Jax need us to babysit the library," Chris said. "This is nothing. Come with me." He dragged Logan out onto the balcony where the Eiffel Tower sparkled like a laser light show in honor of the Tour de France.

"I don't recall seeing that on my way here," Logan said.

"That's because you didn't drive here by way of Paris. That's the Eiffel Tower. This suite is in Paris. But once you walk out the front door, you're back in the library in Exeter."

"I've got to get a picture of this."

"You'd better not. Johanna and Jackson would have a fit."

"Chris," his mother called. "Can you help me for a moment?"

Chris walked out, leaving Logan alone.

Logan shot as much video as he dared, before leaving the balcony.

Chris eyed the phone in Logan's hand.

"A text from my mother," Logan lied. "The woman doesn't know how to leave me alone."

Chris smirked, dropping any signs of suspicion.

"You're here next to me, Logan," Ava said, patting the empty chair beside her.

Logan looked at the vast array of covered dishes sitting on the table. A waiter removed the metal domes that had kept the food warm, and Logan saw a juicy steak on his. Ava had shrimp, Chris had a burger, and Mrs. Roth had a large salad with chicken.

"Is the steak okay? If not, you can have my shrimp. Or Chris's burger."

"Hey, hey, hey, little sister. Don't be giving my dinner away. I'm in a burger mood. Although their steak is really good."

The waiter positioned himself alongside Logan. "Béarnaise sauce?"

Logan nodded. "Yes, please."

The waiter ladled some sauce on the steak and left the bowl with the remaining sauce on the table. "Will there be anything else?"

"No thank you, Lucien," Mrs. Roth answered. "I believe we have everything we need."

He rolled the cart to the front door and exited the suite.

Logan chewed his first mouthful of steak and smiled. "This is delicious. What restaurant did it come from?"

"It's from room service," Chris said, smacking him in the arm. "And they're the best. We can order whatever we want 24/7, and they'll deliver it within a half hour."

"But where's the kitchen?"

Chris broke out in a huge smile. "In Paris."

Logan put his fork down. "That's impossible."

"Not in the Library of Illumination," Chris said.

Logan cut another piece of his steak. "Do you have to pay for this in euros?"

"We don't pay for it. Mr. Oswald-Fitzpatrick of New York gets billed."

Logan stopped eating again. "Who's that?"

"It's a name Jackson made up one night, and now everything gets charged to him and no one says a word."

"Christopher," his mother said, "you make it sound

like we're stealing the hotel's food. The bill is covered by the Library of Illumination."

"I've never seen a bill for this place when I'm opening the mail."

Ava reached for the salt. "It probably goes directly to the overseers."

"On another planet?" Chris challenged her. "I don't think so."

"I'm sure Johanna has everything firmly in hand," Mrs. Roth said, hoping she was right.

Talk around the table turned to summer pursuits.

"I'm teaching myself Morse Code," Ava said nonchalantly, thinking it might pique Logan's interest.

"What good is that?" Chris asked. "Does anybody even use it anymore?"

"It's been replaced by new technology," Logan said, "but people still recognize it, and you never know when it may come in handy." He tapped out a short message on the table.

Ava recognized it and smiled. "Isn't that S-O-S?"

"Save our ship," Logan agreed.

Chris guffawed. "Yeah, you can use it the next time your ship is sinking, little sister."

Ava's face reddened.

Logan felt his phone vibrate in his pocket. He pulled it out and looked at it. It had been recording the conversation all through the meal, but now his battery was dying. He shut it down and shoved the phone back in his pocket.

"Your mother again?" Ava asked quietly.

Logan smiled. "Like I said, the woman never leaves me alone."

*

Johanna's search of the Romantican library the following morning proved to be futile. "Well, we've exhausted all the realms we've previously been to, so from here, it looks like we're making new friends and forging new ground."

"Where to next?" Jackson asked.

"I don't know why we didn't start with the class "L" realms, considering that's the same classification as Fantasia, so it would seem to be more likely that we'd find the Re Transfigurator on one of those. I only started with Lumina and Dramatica because we've been there before, and I knew we'd find friendly faces here on Romantica. But it's time to visit the other class "L" realms."

"Which are…?"

"Educon and Comedia."

"Are the Educons the people with the creepy eyes?"

"They have two irises, yes."

"And Comedia is the one with the girl who rides a pig?"

"Yes."

"Comedia. C'mon, let's go."

"Don't you want to say goodbye to Natalia, first?"

"That goes without saying."

They hugged Natalia, but she wouldn't let them leave. "If Dame Erato heard that you left without saying goodbye, she'd have my head!" The Romantican curator dragged them to Dame Erato's cottage.

It was more than an hour before Johanna and Jackson were able to transport to Comedia, where they found a world that didn't look quite real. The capital city of Comi was oddly situated on the top and face of a sheer cliff with a beach below. The only structure they could see that looked like their idea of a real building was the Library of Illumination, which sat atop the cliff like a monument. However, unlike many of its sister libraries, this one was not located across from a town square because its front door opened onto nothing. Anyone walking out the door would drop straight down to the beach several hundred feet below.

Jackson stared up at the cliff wall. "This place looks like swiss cheese with little balloon gondolas tied up outside the holes. How strange is that?"

"When we transported here, my thought was to transport right outside the front door of the library. And I guess you could say we did."

"But how are we supposed to get up there?"

Johanna grabbed Jackson's hand and a moment later they were standing in front of the Information Desk. Except, it wasn't an information desk. It looked more like Balloon Central with hundreds of multicolor balloons rising above the surface on different length ribbons.

Jackson tried to poke his head through the balloons to see if anyone was under them, but the balloons were too dense. Both teens jumped when a voice behind them asked, "May I be of assistance?"

Johanna turned and quickly studied the man in front of her. "Abbello Abbato?"

"Yes."

She smiled. "I'm Johanna Charette and this is Jackson Roth. We're co-curators of the Fantasian Library of Illumination."

"Yes, of course. We met on Lumi. Or rather, we didn't actually meet but should have. We were both at the same party for the little girl who turned out to be the very first child of an overseer."

Jackson shook his head. "Actually, she's not."

Johanna poked him with her elbow.

Abbello's eyebrows seemed to crawl up his forehead. "She's not?"

Jackson waved his thumb at Johanna. "She is. It turns out my co-curator is the child of Ryden Simmdry and Pru Tellerence."

"I heard that they had a child, but I didn't realize there were two."

"No. The other—" Jackson stopped speaking when Johanna poked him a second time.

"Mr. Abbato. Abbello. That has nothing to do with why we're here. I am looking for a lost artifact that may be hidden in your library and I would like your permission to search for it."

The Comedian's eyes suddenly looked like eggs. "How can I say no to the offspring of Ryden Simmdry and Pru Tellerence?"

Johanna's shoulders sagged. "I'm not here to intimidate you. And I will in no way take you away from your library duties. I just need an undisturbed hour, to telepathically search for the item's signature. And then we'll be out of your hair."

Abbello Abbato rubbed his balding pate. "There's not much hair to get into."

Johanna winced until the Comedian laughed at his own joke. "Of course, you can search the library. Go ahead."

"I'd prefer to wait until morning. Is there a hotel or inn we can stay in overnight?"

"The Cliffside Hotel. I'll get a rafti to take you." He led them out the back door of the library where they saw a large market square. But before they could get a closer look, Abbello signaled a man in a red, yellow, and black peaked cap. "This is your rafti navigator. He'll take you to the hotel."

"This way," the navigator said. They followed him to a small fleet of rafts suspended from balloons that were tied to posts in an undersized field. Each rafti had a single seat in the front followed by two rows with three seats each. "Strap yourselves in, and we'll be on our way." A moment later, he pressed a lever releasing his vehicle, and they floated away over the beach. It only took a few minutes to get to a section of the 'swiss cheese' they had not noticed earlier. The rafti landed on a large ledge they hadn't seen from the beach. Two young men quickly hooked the vehicle to large pins so the passengers could safely disembark.

"That was quite a trip," Jackson remarked.

"I wonder what they do in bad weather?" Johanna asked.

"Good question."

Johanna turned to pay the navigator, but he was already floating away. "Wait!"

He saluted her as he flew back in the direction of the library.

She turned to one of the men who had helped her off the rafti. "I didn't pay him."

"Pay him?" The man laughed out loud. "Who ever heard of paying for a rafti?" His companion laughed as well.

Johanna looked at Jackson, who shrugged.

"Let's get a couple of rooms." He took her arm, leading her inside.

Their jaws dropped when they entered. The inside of the hotel didn't look like the cave they had expected.

Instead, they found a luxurious, upscale hotel where they were immediately greeted by a young woman in uniform. From the neck down she appeared professionally attired, but above the collar, her hair was an assortment of vivid hues that stuck out in all different directions. Her ears sported earrings that looked like masses of large, undulating, multicolor bubbles. "Abbello Abbato told me to expect you. Follow me."

She led them to an elevator shaped like a glass ball inside a pneumatic tube. The globe they stood in moved slowly at first, picking up speed as it traveled in several unexpected directions. Finally, it opened into what looked like an empty closet with a door. The hotel rep led them to the door and waved her hand along the side. "State your name please."

"Johanna Charette."

She turned to Jackson. "And yours."

"Jackson Roth."

She waved her hand again and the door opened. "You only need to say your names to gain entrance. The door will only open for you. No one else."

"This seems really high-tech for a place like Comedia," Jackson muttered.

"Don't allow appearances to deceive you," the woman said. "To outsiders, we may look like we lead simple lives, but we have many advancements here that improve our health and secure our future. Being on the cutting edge is not one of our priorities. We are not covetous people. We don't shun technology; however, we do enjoy the simpler things in life. That said, we like them with a large dose of whimsy."

Johanna merely nodded. The woman turned to

walk away. "Wait. Do you need a credit card or cash for the room? Or do I pay when we leave?"

"We don't take money for our rooms. They are simply here for the people who need them." She disappeared into the elevator and was gone.

The room was sumptuous. Jackson sank onto one of the beds, while Johanna inspected the rest of the space. She emerged from the bathroom with an odd look on her face.

"Please tell me they have real bathrooms," Jackson said.

"Yes. With floor to ceiling windows and transparent fixtures. Everyone can see everything."

"You would think I would have noticed that," Jackson replied, "from outside."

"You would."

"But now that I think about it, I don't remember being able to see inside any of the windows.

Johanna slid off her backpack and dropped it on a chair. "Neither do I."

"I wonder if we could rent one of those rafti things and see if we can see into other peoples' windows?"

"You want us to become peeping Toms?"

"No. I just want to see if anyone can see into our bathroom."

"By looking in theirs."

"Forget it."

LOGAN FINISHED LOGGING the video and audio he had recorded inside the library the previous evening. *It's all coming together.* He smiled. Breaking this story would be his key to fame and fortune. And he planned to rub the truth in the faces of Luke and Jennifer. Their newsroom could have shared in a little of his success, but they chose to distance themselves. *It would serve them right if the college decided to terminate them for missing the boat on this one.*

He searched the internet for unusual occurrences regarding books, but only found *unusual* books. He also wondered if the Library of Illumination was the only one of its kind. *No, it can't be. Johanna and Jackson keep going away on library business. There have to be more.* But finding proof would be difficult.

I think a thank you visit is in order. This time around, the flowers he bought were for Ava and the box of chocolates were for her mom.

Chris opened the library door when he saw Logan approaching. "Look at you, all in white just like a bride. And I see you come bearing gifts."

"I brought a little something for Ava and your mother."

"Yes," Chris wagged his finger at Logan, but what did you bring for me? After all, I'm the guy who let you in."

Logan handed Chris the box of chocolates. "Here, take these. Your mother never has to know they were intended for her."

"Won't know what was intended for me," Mrs. Roth asked out loud as she approached the Information Desk.

"I had such a great time last night, I got you and Chris a box of chocolates to say *thank you*, but Chris wants to hog them for himself."

"Christopher!" his mother exclaimed.

Chris glared at Logan. If he corrected what Logan said, he would lose his claim to the chocolates altogether.

"Sorry, Mom, but I'm so hungry, I could eat the whole box."

Mrs. Roth took the box from his hands. "I'll put these in a safe place. We don't need you ending up at a doctor or dentist's office because of too much chocolate."

"No. We couldn't have that," Chris replied sarcastically.

The front door slid open startling everyone inside.

"Ava," Mrs. Roth said, "I didn't know you were out. Where did you disappear to?"

"I brought the blouse I had on last night to the cleaners."

"Oh. Fine." Mrs. Roth nodded. "That was a thoughtful thing to do."

Ava grabbed the box of chocolate out of her mother's hand. "Chocolate." She looked at Logan, "Is this for me?"

Chris snatched the box away from Ava. "No, it's for me and Mom."

"This is for you." Logan handed Ava the bouquet he had picked up that morning.

Her face lit up. "Thank you." She smelled the flowers and smiled. "I'd better put these in water."

"So, is that the whole reason why you're here?" Chris asked. "To hand out gifts?"

"No. It's really nice out, and I wanted to see if anyone wants to play tennis."

Chris grimaced. "The courts at County Park have potholes."

"I was thinking more along the lines of the Haversham Country Club. My family has a membership there and it has really sweet amenities."

"I'd love to go to Haversham Country Club," Ava said as she re-entered the room.

"Except, you have to work the Information Desk after lunch." Mrs. Roth said. "So, if Chris wants to go, he'll be able to leave in another twenty minutes or so." She turned to Logan, "But not Ava."

"Mom," Ava whined.

"You took an advance against your library paycheck earlier this week. You promised to work this afternoon to pay it back. Case closed."

Ava's shoulders sank.

So, did Logan's spirits. He wanted to pump Ava for more information. He wasn't so sure Chris would be as forthcoming.

FIFTEEN

JOHANNA AND JACKSON returned to the Comi market square to learn more about the culture of Comedia. It looked like a street fair with jugglers and musicians and featured booths where artisans created rich textiles, whimsical statuary, and displayed fanciful artwork. Johanna purchased a locket for her mother, a doll for Bel, and a bracelet for Ava, while Jackson spent his hard-earned money on food and sweets. Over the course of the afternoon, they found the Comedians to be very forthcoming about their realm and its history, and they found the inhabitants' upbeat positivity very appealing.

Jackson popped the last piece of a fudgy confection in his mouth. "I like this place."

"You're certainly eating your way through it. It looks like I'm going to have to eat dinner alone."

"What are you talking about? These are just snacks."

"Regardless, if the hotel has room service, I think

we should eat in tonight. Investigating the libraries may look easy, but it takes a lot out of me."

"That's fine with me." Jackson stopped short in front of a book stall.

"Now what? It's not like there's food for you to buy here."

He picked up a colorful softcover book. As he flipped through the pages, a smile creased his face. "It's a graphic novel about the history of Comedia." He haggled over the price before paying the vendor. "If we're staying in, I think a little light reading may be in order, and this looks like fun."

"I can't believe you bargained down the price. The library will reimburse you whatever the cost."

"It's not about the money. I did it because everyone is doing it."

Johanna looked around her. In every instance where money or goods were about to change hands, people were dickering over the price.

Jackson winked at her. "Never let it be said that I don't observe and assimilate my surroundings to more easily fit in. It makes this job a lot easier."

AT THE TAIL end of dinner, Johanna fought off drowsiness, without much luck.

Jackson tugged on her elbow and led her to one of a pair of comfy chairs facing out of the huge floor-to-ceiling window in their room. The view of the beach was mesmerizing, and considering there wasn't anything remotely like a television, it would have to do.

Johanna sank into the depths of the chair, favorably comparing it to a giant cloud.

Jackson sat across from her, breaking the tranquility of the quiet evening with soft chuckles as he read the graphic novel he had purchased.

Just as he laid the book down on the table separating their chairs, the Comi sky outside their window lit up like the inside of a refrigerator in the middle of the night.

"Whoa!"

Something in the tone of Jackson's voice immediately woke Johanna. "What is it?"

The flash of light had been so quick, Johanna missed it, however Jackson still had the flash etched on his retina. "It was a bright, white flash—like an A-bomb or something. But only for a second."

"Could it have been lightning?"

"It was kind of intense, even for lightning, and was equally bright in all directions."

Johanna jumped out of her chair and grabbed his arm, transporting them to Lumi.

Pru Tellerence appeared startled by their sudden presence. ★*Something is wrong.*

"Maybe," Johanna said.

The entrance to the overseers' chamber opened and Ryden Simmdry rushed in, looking from Pru Tellerence to his daughter. ⌘*You saw it too?*

"I was sleeping. However, Jackson saw an unusually bright light."

⌘*Where were you when you saw it?*

"Comedia," Jackson answered.

⌘*That shouldn't be possible.*

"Why?" Johanna asked. "What was it?"

⌘*If we both saw something several realms apart, it could be a celestial beacon.*

★ *Lighting a path for someone?*

⌘ *Or searching for someone. Or something.*

"Like a Re Transfigurator?" Jackson asked.

⌘ *Either that, or a portable portal. Perhaps finding the puzzle box and the key it held is not a random occurrence. It may be by design. Or the portal may have given off a signal when we opened it.*

"So," Johanna ventured, "opening the puzzle box or the portal may have sparked some type of reaction; cause and effect."

Ryden Simmdry smiled at his daughter. ⌘ *A remarkable observation, perhaps, a brilliant one. Regardless, time is suddenly of the essence, and you must do everything you can to find the Re Transfigurator quickly.*

"But if no one knows about the key but us," Jackson asked, "how is that possible?"

⌘ *The Universe is aware of it and attributes a level of importance to it. Unfortunately, treasure hunters from outside the Illumini Constellation have ways of learning about these types of objects, and if they believe it will command a high price, they will begin searching for it as well, possibly using technology beyond our comprehension.*

CHRIS WAS SURPRISED when Logan pulled into his driveway. "I thought we were going to play tennis?"

"We are. But you're dressed a little too casually for the country club's dress code. You'll never get in the front door wearing camouflage cargo shorts and a T-shirt. However, I have a pair of tennis shorts that should fit you."

"That's ridiculous."

"I couldn't agree with you more, but I didn't write the rules."

Twenty minutes later, Chris stuck a plastic bag containing his clothes behind the passenger seat of the car. "I don't mind the *polo* shirt," he made air quotes with his fingers when he said 'polo,' "but I hate these white shorts."

Logan laughed. "I do, too. That's why I'm wearing a different pair. Those were always a little too short for comfort."

While they waited for a court at the club, Logan casually asked, "So what are Jackson and Johanna up to these days?"

"They're out looking for some artifact that they found a key to. It's supposed to be special; don't ask me why. But it's supposedly hidden in one of the Libraries of Illumination. Since they couldn't find it in ours, they're off to the other realms looking for it."

Logan kept his voice even. "Where are the other realms, exactly?"

Chris waved his arm toward the heavens. "Somewhere, out there. Who knows? The closest I ever got to leaving Exeter is the balcony of our hotel suite at the library."

"So, Jackson's traveling to other worlds when he doesn't even have a passport?"

"Oh, he has a passport. He needed one when he and Johanna traveled to Wales looking for a group of wizards. He's got the passport. The girl. And a salary that I will never be able to match in all probability, even after I've worked half-my life. He really lucked out when Johanna hired him to help out at the library."

"Aren't you 'helping out' at the library now?"

"Yeah, but I'll never be curator. That's their job. And they supposedly received some blessing that slows down their aging so they'll live for hundreds of years."

Logan felt the hairs on the back of his neck prickle. "That's impossible."

"Maybe it is. But that's what Jackson says and Johanna swears to it. To my mother. And I don't think they would try to mislead my mom, do you? Besides, I don't think Johanna knows how to lie."

Ryden Simmdry and Pru Tellerence returned to Comedia with Johanna and Jackson. The master of the overseers took pity on his daughter's exhaustion and performed the telepathic scan of the library. ⌘ *What we seek is not here.*

"Now what?" Jackson asked, yawning.

"We move on to the next library on our list," Johanna answered.

"Tomorrow, right?"

⌘ *That is no longer an option.*

"But we already have all our stuff at the hotel."

⌘ *Then we shall go and collect it, and move on to the next library on your list, which is…?*

"Educon," Johanna answered.

"I sure hope it's there," Jackson added, "because I could use some sleep. I think I may have eaten a little too much, today."

It didn't take long for them to check out of the hotel, and transport to the library on Educon. Ryden Simmdry and Pru Tellerence conversed with Dr. Infinitis while Johanna plunged right into looking for the artifact.

"It's not here," she said finally, looking like she was about to drop.

★ *Then I suggest we move on,* her mother said, making their excuses to the Educonian curator.

Pru Tellerence conducted the search on Mysteriose, giving Johanna and Ryden Simmdry a chance to rest. It took Johanna's mother longer to conduct her search, considering the high number of magical objects that could be found in that realm. She did a thorough job, and stated with certainty that the object wasn't there.

Ryden Simmdry searched Inspiracon without luck, and the foursome traveled to Juvenilia where they were greeted with lots of sticky fingers as soon as word got out that the *chocolate guys* were there.

"I can't believe this place has no residents over the age of sixteen," Jackson said.

"Peer Meap," one of the boys answered in an unusually deep voice. "He's older than dirt."

"Nah," another boy said. "These guys are older. Aren't you?" he asked, pointing to Ryden Simmdry and Pru Tellerence.

⌘*Indeed we are.*

The visitors were mobbed, and their slow trip toward the library, looked like an amoeba erratically propelling itself home.

The curator, Peer Meap, greeted them at the door. "This is a wonderful surprise."

⌘*Johanna would like to do a quick scan of your library.*

"Of course. Okay, everyone, line up single file and march back to Town Hall. Today is a school day."

An aggregate whine went through the young mob, but they lined up as instructed and marched in the direction of Town Hall.

Johanna leaned against the wall and slid to the floor. So did Jackson.

★*Are you two going to be all right?*

"Yes. I'm fine as long as I'm sitting down and leaning against something."

"I'll catch her if she falls over," Jackson added.

And with that, Johanna started searching.

After a half-hour had passed, Jackson's snores interrupted the conversation the overseers were having with Peer Meap. Johanna's eyes were closed as well.

★*Do you think they're asleep?*

⌘ *They very well could be.*

Johanna eyes shot open. "Sublevel 757." She turned to Jackson and tapped his cheek. "Sublevel 757," she repeated.

He jumped up and pulled Johanna to her feet.

"Peer Meap," she asked, "may we search for something on one of your sublevels?"

"Of course," he answered, leading the way.

They entered the elevator, and Johanna was pleased to see it had been updated, so they didn't have to use the hand crank that still held a position of prominence in the cage. Jackson ran his finger over the shiny metal. "How come you kept this? It looks cool, but you don't need it anymore."

"It's for emergencies. In a world overrun with young people, it's always smart to have backup because I can never be sure what they're going to get themselves into. Usually, they're quite inventive and ingenious, but sometimes, their eagerness for innovation can prove to be a challenge. Just ask the Terrorians. I believe they were sorry they ever tried to take over this realm. By the time we were called to Lumi to help with the war there, the Terrorians here were incarcerated with their tentacles glued together.

The Juveniles are very good at taking care of themselves." The curator laughed. "I'm only here to protect their library and provide insight."

The elevator ground to a halt. Johanna walked out first and followed her instincts toward a magical signature. She stopped outside a bulky wooden door. "It's in here."

Peer Meap placed his palm against the door and it clicked open. A dull green-tinted light automatically turned on. The room wasn't as small as Johanna had hoped. It seemed cavernous, although it was difficult to determine the exact dimensions in the dim illumination. Piled inside were broken toys and gadgets of every description.

"I guess we found your junk room," Jackson said, as he picked up a wooden horse with three legs.

"You could call it that. It also helps generate ideas. Sometimes, when one of the children is feeling low, we come down here and select a project to work on. That usually takes their minds off their troubles and gives them something new to play with."

"What kinds of troubles can they have," Jackson asked, "with no adults around? Present company excluded."

"Children can be mean to other children, especially if they believe it will get them something they don't already have, like popularity, power, or possessions. In the balance of life, when someone gains something, someone else loses it."

'Yeah." Jackson sighed. "I guess it's like that all over."

While Jackson chatted, Johanna searched through the pile of discarded playthings, zeroing in on the magical signature. She had reached a section that she felt reluctant to move because it was precariously piled.

Suddenly, the objects in the pile began to rise into the air. She looked behind her and saw her father, palms raised in the air, lifting the toys out of her way. She reached underneath and pulled at a brass and glass object, but it was like pulling the supporting brick from the bottom of a teetering pile. She felt the toys shift and suddenly looked up, to see a rusty, metal robot aiming for her head. It suddenly stopped in mid-air. Johanna turned her head and saw her mother using her powers to hold the avalanche of toys at bay.

Johanna extricated the magical box and stepped out of harm's way, so her parents could allow everything to settle back in place.

Jackson stared at the box. "That's it?"

Johanna nodded. "It's the only object in here that's giving off magic."

"Does the key fit?"

"I don't know. I didn't bring it with me."

"I thought you were wearing it on a chain around your neck?"

"I took it off and left it in the vault. Until I know what we're dealing with, I thought it would be smart to keep the key under lock and… key. Pun intended."

"Except the vault doesn't use a key," Jackson remarked.

"I like to think Merlin is *key-ping* it safe."

Jackson shook his head but the corner of his mouth lifted, hinting at a smile.

They dined with Peer Meap, and before departing, Pru Tellerence conjured up huge baskets of chocolate treats the curator could distribute to the Juvi children.

After saying goodbye, Jackson and Johanna headed to Lumi with her parents. Johanna promised them she would not try to unlock the Re Transfigurator without them, but said she needed a good night's sleep first, so she'd have her wits about her when she did try the key.

★ *You're both exhausted. Why don't you spend the night here on Lumi, that way you'll be assured of getting some sleep? If you return to Fantasia tonight, you'll start talking about your adventure with the Roths and you'll be up half the night.*

Johanna looked at Jackson. "She's right," he said. "My family will grill us like a hamburger. Let's just pop over to the Grand Illumi Hotel and relax."

"I guess that's as good a plan as any," she answered before kissing her parents good night.

THAT EVENING, LOGAN pieced together another news package for *The Elliott Report*. In this one, he meticulously cut video of the magical books with supporting statements by Ava on books with special properties. However, he wasn't ready to put it online. He still wanted to edit another package on the odd Parisian hotel suite in the middle of Exeter. And do a third story on all the other odd bits and pieces about portals to other worlds.

He also needed footage of other events happening in the area, stories he would take possession of courtesy of GRUNT. Those stories would give more gravitas to *The Elliott Report* and in turn, to his exposé of the Library of Illumination.

They'll never know what hit them.

He got into his car and drove around. He wanted to drive past the library and wasted twenty minutes locating it. Then he cursed when a pothole almost made him lose control of his car. *Damn construction.*

*

Logan tossed and turned all night, trying to figure out how to get additional video of the inside of the library. The fewer people inside the library, the better. He yawned. It didn't help that he was aggravated over the damage the pot hole had done to his wheel rim. *I'm lucky I stopped to get it looked at and they fixed it, or I'd be waking up to a flat in the morning.* As he thought about the construction mess, an idea began to take shape. He mulled it over, trying to project all the consequences of different courses of action. By the time he drifted off to sleep, his plan was almost complete.

SIXTEEN

Ava felt like the belle of the ball. She had just been named prom queen over all the seniors—even though it was her first year in high school. She walked out to the center of the stage and the school principal placed a gold and diamond tiara upon her head. "We usually use cheap plastic crowns," he said. "But when I saw your name as the winning contestant, I knew we needed something special." She looked over the crowd, ready to make her acceptance speech. Suddenly, her cell phone rang. She stiffened. "Excuse me," she mumbled, as she tried to silence the phone in her evening bag, but found she could barely move. It felt like her whole body was encased in putty. Her world darkened.

Taking a deep breath, Ava forced eyes open. She was in her bed in the George V suite at the library. *It was a dream.* Disappointment overwhelmed her. But her phone continued to ring. It was charging right next to her on the night table. Her heart raced when she saw Logan's name. She fumbled for it. "Hey."

"G'Morning Ava, I hope this isn't a bad time."

"No. Not at all."

"I need to speak to you about something important, but I don't want your mother or brothers to know just yet. And I need to speak with you as soon as possible. I have to go into the newsroom today, but I'm wondering if I could stop by the library on my way there. Sometimes, Jackson leaves the back door open for me when we're going to meet up. Maybe you could unlock the back door, and I'll meet you in the executive board room about a quarter to nine. That way, no one will be the wiser, and we can speak privately."

"Sure. I can do that."

"Maybe you should open the door now, so you don't forget."

"Don't worry, I won't forget."

"But I'd feel better knowing you did it now."

She smiled as she teased, "Okay. I'll go down and unlock the back door."

LOGAN STARED AT his watch. He had to time his next call just right and put his acting skills to the test. Taking a deep breath, he pulled out the burner phone he'd purchased first thing that morning at a 24-hour convenience store. He dialed the police emergency line.

"911, what's your emergency?"

Logan used the most frantic voice he could dredge up. "Gas leak. It's bad. Near 7th Street and Faraday. My brother... my brother..."

"Sir, please state your name—"

"Going to the hospital. My brother. He's not breathing!" Logan disconnected the call and took out a second burner phone. Once again, disguising his voice, he called in a report of a gas leak, saying it was in the vicinity of a consignment store near the library. Afterward, he drove to a row of dumpsters behind a strip mall and disposed of both phones. When he was done, he headed toward the library. He could hear sirens in the distance as he got closer. He parked his car a block away and pulled on a baseball cap, sunglasses, and a nondescript sweatshirt. He strapped on a beat-up old backpack, containing his camera. He had to hurry now. He wanted to reach the library before anyone could stop him. Emergency officials were starting to evacuate the area, while other workers searched for the gas leak. He watched a couple of guys poking around outside the library. He fished out his cell phone and called Ava. "Hey, something's come up, I can't make it."

"It's just as well," Ava replied. "We're being evacuated. Talk to you later."

Logan entered the gate leading to the back of the library. He slipped through the unlocked rear door and took out his camera. First, he rushed to the hotel suite and took video of the Eiffel Tower, pulling back and panning the suite as he exited it into the library. Then he rushed up five flights of stairs to the highest level of the library, so he could take pictures of the portals. Finally, he opened several books, one at a time, with the camera running, to illustrate how they came to life.

*

Johanna, Jackson, and her parents transported into the Fantasian vault to pick up the key before materializing in the library's executive board room. Johanna set the Re Transfigurator on the table and placed the key beside it. At first look, the box had appeared to be made out of a misty glass or stone that sat in the middle of finely intertwined spaghetti-like strands of brass, but under the board room lights, it looked oddly opaque. Johanna conjured a soft, wet cloth and wiped it down, going over it several times, until it finally lost layers of Juvenile dust that had built up over the years, or more likely, centuries.

Ryden Simmdry rubbed his hands together. ⌘ *There's no time like the present.*

Johanna examined it more closely, looking for a keyhole. "There appears to be an odd-shaped opening on the bottom, but it's not the same size or shape as the key we found."

⌘ *I believe you're overlooking something.*

"I'm not," Johanna said, turning over the box again.

⌘ *Magic has the power to obfuscate as well as elucidate.*

Jackson rubbed his week-old stubble. "I feel like such a simpleton saying this," he looked at Ryden Simmdry, "but what does that mean?"

⌘ *It means that the key may very well fit in that opening, however, magic is making it look like it doesn't.*

"Oh." He looked at Johanna. "So, try it."

She picked the key up and directed it toward the opening. As it drew close, the air shimmered and the key transformed in size and shape until it slid neatly inside the lock. Johanna turned it, almost dropping the box when the top sprang open. She quickly turned it upright and a figurine, taller than the box itself, rose out of it.

★*Oh, my.*

⌘*Yes.*

The figure of a wizened old man resembled an antiquated overseer, wearing a highly embroidered satin robe. He sported a matching cap attached to a starburst-shaped, embroidery-covered mortarboard, perched at a jaunty angle like a saintly halo. The figurine's eyes appeared to be made of autunite—a yellow-green fluorescent crystal—that made the figure's face appear to glow. And in one hand, he held an intricately carved gold staph with a smooth, perfectly circular crystal orb on top. The figure stood atop an elaborately carved base of clear crystal.

"Is that glass?" Jackson asked, tapping the base with his fingernail.

Ryden Simmdry waved his hand over the object. ⌘*I believe it is Iceland Spar, which can bend light into two separate rays. If my memory serves me correctly, this crystal can cause an image or projection that lines up with the sun—even on cloudy days.*

Jackson leaned in and squinted at the statue. "He's a peculiar looking little guy, yet strangely familiar."

Ryden Simmdry nodded. ⌘*It appears to be Ailill Caomhánach, the first master.*

Jackson perked up. "An overseer?"

Ryden Simmdry nodded.

Pru Tellerence laid her hand on his arm. ★*Wouldn't that make this a very important and powerful artifact?*

⌘*It would, indeed.*

DOZENS OF PEOPLE—expressing emotions from excited to irritated—poured out onto the pavement near the Library of Illumination. The surrounding mixed-use buildings were oddly located in an isolated district, away from the more popularly traveled thoroughfares. The tenants of one three-story office building included accountants, architects, and real estate agents, while a nearby mom-and-pop grocery store just hosted Mr. & Mrs. Englewood. Officials had to nearly drag Mr. Lee out of his dry-cleaning establishment, while a dentist and his assistant supported a patient—who had not quite recovered from the effects of nitrous oxide.

The Roths did not have much opportunity to mingle with library neighbors. Mrs. Roth reminded her children not to reveal too much about the library. "If you have to, just say it's a limited research library for subscribing members. Or that we're filling in for the regular staff who's away." Not that they had much of an opportunity to get into lengthy conversations. The entire disruption was over within an hour. It had taken workers nearly as long to vacate the buildings as to determine there were no indications of a gas leak.

"You can return to your offices," a police officer called out. "The area is secure."

"Did you find the gas leak?" one woman asked.

"You mean aside from the happy gas in Dr. Davis' office?"

The dentist's jaw dropped. "Did I leave the gas on?"

"Don't worry doc, we turned it off for now. But that's the only gas we found. It looks like the whole thing is just a hoax."

"Maybe," one of the other cops said, "but we received reports from more than one person?"

The first cop smirked. "Okay, change that to an *elaborate* hoax."

*

SEVERAL REALMS AWAY, Mal had enlisted the aid of Natalia Dalura to drill the Educons, a non-confrontational race of people, in warfare. Together, they demonstrated different methods of fighting, similar to what Natalia and her Romantican cohorts had taught their militairres before the Terrorian incursion.

"I really must get going soon," Mal stated. "I have a meeting set up with some of the top doctors here, to establish a board that will oversee and track the health and well-being of all Educons." He studied the people who had come for training. "Will you be able to handle them alone?"

"Let's put them to the test." They observed the Educons' skill in each specialization, and Natalia soon realized she would need more help to whip them into fighting shape. "I must return home and enlist the aid of the Jolen sisters. Together, we'll be able to accomplish this task much more efficiently.

"However," she continued, removing a small, parchment envelope from a utility bag, "may I ask if you'll be seeing Johanna anytime soon? I have something I would like you to give to her."

"I can make that happen, and I'd be happy to do your bidding."

Natalia gave him a dazzling smile, handing him the envelope. "Thank you."

LOGAN STARTED DOWN the cupola stairs, noticing a fire truck pulling away. *Shit! I'd better get out of here.* He rushed down the stairs and ran toward the back door, but had to duck behind shelves of books when he heard the front door open.

Ava was the first to speak. "Can you believe they evacuated us for a gas leak, and then said it was a false alarm?"

"An all-out response like that, even on a local level, costs taxpayer dollars," her mother replied. "There better be an investigation."

"Maybe it's a coverup," Chris surmised. "Maybe there *was* a gas leak, but they don't want anyone suing the gas company, so they're calling it a 'false alarm.' Unless it's just a prank."

Mrs. Roth huffed. "If it is a prank, I hope they catch the person responsible and put him or her behind bars. What a waste of time and industry. All those people out on the sidewalk instead of inside their businesses, working."

While the Roths spoke, Logan inched his way toward the back door. He was almost there but needed to cross an open gap to reach the door. Remembering a scene from a recent movie, he fished a coin out of his pocket and threw it across the room. It clattered when it hit the ground on the other side of the main reading room.

"What was that?" Niamh asked.

She and her children moved in the direction of the sound.

Chris rushed ahead of them. "Wouldn't it be something if tomorrow's news had a story about all the places in the neighborhood being robbed?"

"Not this place," Mrs. Roth said. "It's built like Fort Knox."

Ava's eyes widened as she remembered unlocking the back door. She turned and ran to the door, pulling it open. She heard the gate latch in the distance, but missed seeing whomever was there.

"What's the matter?" Chris asked.

Ava jumped, not expecting her brother to be behind her. "I thought I heard something back here, but I don't see anyone."

"Come inside and let's lock this door," Mrs. Roth said. "I think our imaginations are all getting the better of us."

"Then what was that noise we heard inside?" Chris asked.

His mother rolled her eyes. "Probably Johanna's cat, Ophelia, playing with one of her toys."

FOR SEVERAL MINUTES, Johanna, Jackson, Pru Tellerence and Ryden Simmdry quietly stared at the object, allowing their thoughts to coalesce. The quietude was disrupted by pounding feet.

"Chris, no doubt," Jackson muttered.

They ignored the noise until they heard the back door opening and closing.

More footsteps sounded outside the door, and Jackson turned to see what was going on when a bright blue-green beam of light shot around the room, like a pinball seeking its target. Everyone, including Jackson, froze—their eyes becoming fixated on the Re Transfigurator.

The figurine's arm pointed the staph holding the orb around the room, finally resting it on a corner of the base. His eyes lit up—glowing green. It passed through the orb and split into various rays. The conference room melted away, and the overseers and co-curators found themselves standing on a rocky outcrop, surrounded by misty water in an eerie twilight-like dimness.

Johanna took a step forward, then stilled completely.

"I shouldn't have been able to do that."

Jackson reached out and touched her arm. "Do what?"

"Take a step forward. The conference table was right in front of me, but now, there is no conference table."

⌘ *The Re Transfigurator has altered our reality.*

"How do we return to normal?" Johanna asked.

⌘ *You must close the Re Transfigurator.*

Johanna stared at her hands. She had been holding the artifact, but now an intricately scrolled, gold tube rested in her palms. She studied the object for a moment, looking for a way to open or close it. She tried twisting the top and bottom in opposite directions. Nothing happened. "I don't know what this is, or what to do with it."

Jackson reached out his hand. "Here. Let me take a look at it."

Ryden Simmdry pulled Jackson's hand away. ⌘ *No. We must not change anything. It is up to Johanna to find the way.*

Jackson's brows knitted. "Is this some kind of teaching moment?"

⌘ *No. It is a very real dilemma, and the more we change this reality, the more difficult it will be to return to our own.*

SEVENTEEN

Ava shivered. She crossed one hand over the other, each rubbing the opposite arm. She couldn't get the idea out of her mind of someone being in the library during the evacuation. If only she had remembered the unlocked back door a minute sooner. *Maybe it's the person who called in the hoax. Maybe he was looking for a place to hide and found our back door unlocked.* She played with the beads of her bracelet. The idea of someone being in the library worried her. She turned decisively. *I should tell Mom. She'll know what to do.* She froze. *I'd have to tell her I left the back door unlocked for Logan.* She definitely didn't want to do that. *Maybe it* was *Logan.* She shook her head. *It couldn't have been. He would have told me.*

"Ava," her mother called out. "I have some books I need you to pull."

"Coming."

I have to call Logan. She fished her cell out of her

jeans pocket and punched in his number. It rang several times before going to voicemail. "Logan, call me," she said. "I have something important to ask you."

THE WATERS ROILED around the rocky outcrop in Johanna and Jackson's alternate reality.

A black, silken form began to take shape as it rose out of the sea. Jackson stood statue-like, moving only his eyes as they watched the movement of the water. "Something's going on."

Johanna felt her shoulders knotting. Getting everyone back to their own reality was up to her. She continued to study the gold scroll, unfortunately without elucidation. Unwittingly, she dropped her chin to her chest pressing the tube against her forehead, thinking, *all I want to do is get us all back home safely.* A moment later, they were standing in the conference room and Johanna rushed to close the automaton. She pressed the figurine into the box, surprised that it actually fit, and slammed down the cover, hurriedly placing the artifact on the table.

"That was something," Jackson said. "Was it real, or did I imagine it?"

⌘*It was quite real.*

Jackson snaked his arm around Johanna's shoulders and hugged her. "How'd you get us all back here?"

"I thought it."

Her co-curator scratched his head. "Why didn't you think it sooner?"

"I did," she replied, "but nothing happened 'sooner.'"

Jackson turned to Ryden Simmdry. "What do you think was coming out of the water?"

⌘ *What scares you the most?*

"You mean, whatever my answer is, that thing would become it?"

⌘ *It would stand to reason. A Re Transfigurator can create a completely different reality. So can Class V libraries, although they do it in a much more controlled manner, which is probably why the use of artifacts, like this one, has been discontinued.*

Johanna shivered. "But why that outcrop? And what was rising from the waters?

⌘ *Did either of you have any thoughts or ideas this morning that could be tied to what we saw?*

"No. Nothing." Johanna was emphatic.

"Uh…" Jackson had a strange look on his face.

Johanna punched him in the shoulder. "What?"

"Remember when we first studied Lumi and saw those mermen rise out of the water and attack those people?"

⌘ *You were thinking of that?*

"My mind wandered a bit while you were playing with the doll that popped out of that contraption."

⌘ *Well done.*

Johanna placed her hands on either side of her face as she stared at her father. "Well done?"

⌘ *Yes. We learned a very important lesson today. Our thoughts dictate the Re Transfigurator's response, where it will take us, and how we return to our home base. Although, Jackson merely had to think of a location for us to be transported to something similar, while you physically had to touch the alternate artifact to your head, so it could react with your most prominent thought to return home.*

★ *Apparently, it's easier to get into trouble than out of it.*

⌘ *Exactly. It is not an object to be toyed with.*

Johanna sighed. "Now I know why the key and the object were hidden on two different realms.

LOGAN WALKED BACK to his car as quickly as possible and drove straight to work at the mall. It was the last place he wanted to be, but the safest. He couldn't pretend 'something came up' if Ava found him at home, and he didn't want to show up late at GRUNT and have them start asking him questions. At least at work he could keep busy, get paid for his time, and would be seen by people whether he was on the schedule or not.

His manager's eyes widened when Logan walked through the door. "Good. Charlie got ahold of you."

For an instant, Logan didn't know how to reply. He decided to blunder through. "Yeah. What's that all about?"

"He said it may be food poisoning. I'm just glad he was able to get in touch with you to fill in."

"Well, here I am. Glad I can help."

When he had a spare moment, Logan called Charlie, saying he got his message to fill in for him at work. Charlie may not remember ever having called him, but would probably say he did, just to earn points with their boss for doing the right thing.

I just hope this day doesn't drag, Logan said to himself. He couldn't wait to get home to look over the video he shot that morning in the library.

His cell phone vibrated and he saw a call from Ava. He shook his head and stuffed the phone back into his belt case.

*

Johanna locked the Re Transfigurator in the closet of the Executive Board Room.

"Out of sight, out of mind?" Jackson asked.

"Not really. It's just that it's an attractive nuisance. It's too interesting to pass up. Even now, I feel like picking it up and playing with it. I would hate to have a member of your family walk in here and start playing with it and have something happen to one of them.

"As long as you don't leave the key with it, there shouldn't be a problem." Jackson ran his knuckles over his facial scruff. "Should there?"

"I don't think so, but just to be safe, I'm taking it with me." She picked up the key and slipped it into her pocket before pushing Jackson out of the board room.

Ryden Simmdry removed his miter and rubbed his hands through his hair, before turning to Pru Tellerence. ⌘*I wish Johanna had agreed to let us take either the artifact or the key when we left. It's dangerous for her, having them together in such close proximity.*

★*I agree. I'm worried, as well. But Johanna has been on her own for a very long time and has her own way of doing things.*

⌘*She's also very curious. I only hope she thinks everything through before she takes further action with the Re Transfigurator.*

★*What do we know about it that she might not?*

⌘*Not very much. I think I may spend some time with the oracle. Perhaps it can be illuminating.*

★*You should have invited Johanna to accompany you.*

⌘*That is an excellent suggestion. And I can do it with merely a thought.* The worry lines etched in his forehead eased, as his mouth widened in a smile. ⌘*She'll be here in the morning.*

★*Good. I think I'll send her a subliminal message to bring only the key with her.*

⌘*Subliminal?*

★*I wouldn't want her to think I'm interfering.*

Ryden Simmdry walked over to Pru Tellerence and pulled her into a hug. ⌘*I think you are a wonderful mother.*

★*I hope so.*

⌘*I've been thinking, even though it is not a custom on many of the realms, it is on Fantasia, where Johanna lives.*

★*What is?*

⌘*A wedding, of course. I think we should legitimize our daughter's existence—not that she needs it—with a formal ceremony.*

★*What brought this on?*

⌘*I like being able to say she's our daughter. I also want to be able to say you're my wife. You are the love of my life, and a very long life it has been. I think a ritual that celebrates our coupling would send a wonderful message to Johanna. It would also make me feel complete,* he said before kissing his companion. When he stepped away from her, Pru Tellerence said nothing. His brow creased. ⌘*Are you refusing my proposal?*

A tear rolled down Pru Tellerence's cheek. ★*Not at all. I'm just so overwhelmed that you feel that way. I have always loved you beyond reason, but I was never sure you felt exactly the same way about me. You always appeared to be much more pragmatic and undeterred by others' customs or opinions. I have dreamed of a union such as marriage, but never dared hope for it because it seemed beyond who you are and what you believe in. And, of course, it was banned to us as overseers. As I've said, I AM overwhelmed, but it's with happiness. And yes. I do want to be your wife.*

EVEN IN A DARKENED closet, the outside of the Re Transfigurator appeared to glow. Inside the device, a lot more was going on.

We have been awakened, a hazy blue shadow thought aloud, *even though our visitors did not wish to escape into the environ they created.*

The figurine didn't move but its thoughts were crisp and clear. *That is not my concern, Ailill Caomhánach* replied. *It has been more than a millennium since we've been tested. It is time for us to renew our purpose.*

And how will we do that? the shadow asked.

While you have remained stagnant all these years, I have been growing my strengths. Planning for our next infusion of consciousness. The outsiders will not leave us to our rest. They will re-open our world, and when they do we'll be ready for them.

JOHANNA AND JACKSON sat in her office hashing over everything that had happened. She started pounding on the keys of her computer.

"What are you doing?" he asked.

"Research. I'm trying to find out everything I can about automatons in general and *ours* in particular."

He laced his hands behind his head and closed his eyes. "Let me know what you find."

"There's plenty of stuff on automatons, but nothing so far on the Re Transfigurator."

"Do you think it predates time as we know it?"

She looked up. "I don't know, but you've given me an idea."

Jackson grinned. "Great! What idea is that?"

"I'll probably have more luck looking into ancient Luminan texts rather than our own."

"Do we have any of those here?"

"We should. I just need to check downstairs."

The trip down to the sublevel housing Luminan texts intrigued Jackson. He always like checking out the sublevels. Every once in a while, they would find something unexpected, turning the trip into an adventure. He trailed Johanna down the stairs to the old elevator located on sublevel six.

"Oh!" Johanna's eyes had widened briefly.

"What's the matter?"

"My father had asked if I wanted to visit the oracle with him to learn more about the artifact. He's doing that now."

"Can I come too?"

"I don't see why not." She grabbed Jackson's hand and a moment later, they were standing beside her parents in Lumi.

All afternoon, Ava fought the urge to contact Logan and ask him if he'd visited the library that morning. *He already said he couldn't make it. If I push, he's going to think I don't believe him. I'm going to come across as needy and mistrustful. I will not call. I will not call. I will not call.*

The afternoon dragged on in direct contrast to how the excitement of the morning had flown by. Ava re-shelved books and helped her mother pack up deliveries for non-local patrons who had requested specific materials. Still, the minutes ticked by slowly.

"Ava," her mother said, "are you not feeling well?"

"I'm fine," Ava answered.

"You seem quieter than usual."

"I guess after all the excitement this morning, everything dulls in comparison, including me."

Niamh gave her daughter a hug. "You may seem quiet today, but you are never dull."

Ava gave her mother a small smile.

Niamh pushed the last package of books in line with the ones they had previously packed. "What we need is a pick me up. How about a nice cup of cappuccino and a delicious french pastry?"

Ava nodded, smiling again. "Now you're talking." However, the diversion didn't last very long, and she spent the rest of the day continuously talking herself out of calling Logan.

JOHANNA AND JACKSON materialized next to Ryden Simmdry, who was already standing inside the Oracle Chamber. The oracle was not a person but a large ovoid with a smooth surface, often shiny as glass but sometimes rippled like raindrops hitting water, sometimes pulsating with an interior glow, and sometimes hazy with a smoky appearance. On this particular morning, the oracle pulsated light.

Johanna hugged her father, kissing his cheek.

Jackson pointed to the oracle. "Is it supposed to be throbbing like that?"

⌘*It has sensed our inquiry regarding the artifact and is working on it.*

"And it will just spit out an answer?" the teen asked.

⌘*It will illuminate us to possibilities.*

Jackson's eyes narrowed. "What does that mean

exactly?"

Johanna grabbed his arm. "It will spark ideas within each of us that we can then discuss, and which should ultimately lead to answers."

⌘*Johanna is correct. Unlike Greek oracles, which were usually priests or priestesses who would interpret the words of the gods, this oracle is more of a virtual lodestone, an object of unusual properties that helps guide our thoughts into the channels of Illumini history and encourages discussion that could lead to the answers to our questions.*

"That's not right," Jackson said. "It's supposed to show us what we need to know. When Johanna was taken by the Terrorians, I saw it in an image above the oracle."

⌘ *That was something else entirely. It merely allowed us to see beyond the wall that separated us from Johanna. In this case, we are looking into history and not something that is taking place right now. We are trying to determine the history of a particular artifact. The artifact is not here for us to view. The oracle can only guide our thoughts, it cannot provide a window into a past dimension from another world.*

Jackson's shoulders slumped as he shook his head. "How will we even know if it's working?"

⌘ *We will know when we have our answer.*

"Except, it's not doing anything," Jackson complained. "Do you feel it doing anything?"

⌘ *It can sometimes take hours, or days. The first step is to sit quietly and think about the questions we are looking for answers to. The oracle will sense that from us and feel our thoughts and feelings. It requires quiet contemplation.*

"I wish I brought my iPad," Jackson said under his breath.

"Why is that?" Johanna whispered.

"Because I think I'd find out more by just Googling my questions."

LOGAN DROPPED HIS stuff on his bed, glad to be home. He was even happier that his parents had left a message saying they'd gone out to dinner. He didn't want to be interrupted while he went through the video he'd shot in the library that morning.

He wrote down every shot, how long it lasted, and coded it *one*, *two*, or *three* in importance with *one* being the highest. He put an asterisk next to video that would look good slowed down, so he could get more mileage out of what he had. When he was done, he edited some of the video into the next story that he planned to release on the library. But first, he needed to go back to GRUNT and cobble together a couple of regular news stories for *The Elliott Report*.

He didn't want to rush the information that he released about the library. Once he did, he would be forced to sever contact with the Roths and Johanna. He had to make sure he had everything he needed to put together a plausible case against the library first, before blasting the magical world apart.

EIGHTEEN

Johanna and Jackson entered the Grand Illumini Hotel.

"They should give us our own honorary suites here, we've stayed over so often," Jackson said.

"Not nearly enough nights for honorary suites, although it would be nice to have the same rooms again," Johanna mused.

"And maybe be able to keep some stuff here, so I'm not always wishing I had brought my toothbrush."

They stepped on a transportation disk that would bring them to their rooms. Johanna whispered an incantation, fisting one hand and waving her other hand above it. When she finished, a couple of toothbrushes and two tiny tubes of toothpaste were nestled in her fist.

"I want to be able to do that."

"All you need are overseers for parents."

"Yeah. I think it's too late for that."

"Then just smile, tell me you love me, and say, *Thank you, Johanna.*"

"You know I do, but this is the *Land of No,* as in no PDAs, so let this be enough." He gave her a quick peck on the cheek, grabbed a toothbrush and toothpaste, and gave her a two-finger wave goodbye as the disk carried him away.

Before going to bed, Johanna removed the chain she wore around her neck and slipped the key to the Re Transfigurator back on it. *That should keep you safe,* she thought. She had previously worn the key around her neck, so she wasn't prepared for how heavy it had suddenly become. *I'm just tired and my imagination is playing tricks on me.*

She woke up more than once during the night because she felt like the chain was tightening around her neck, choking her. Finally, she jumped out of bed, groaning, and checked the time on her phone. *4:00 a.m. Much too early to start the day.* She yawned.

Before crawling back into bed, she removed the chain from around her neck and placed it on the night table, hoping she'd be able to get at least a few more hours of uninterrupted sleep before she had to get back to work.

AVA ALSO HAD a miserable night. She barely slept, and the few times she did doze off, she dreamt about trying to not call Logan. She finally dragged herself out of bed when the first rays of the sun spilled past edges of the drapery on her bedroom window. She immediately called room service and ordered espresso and pastries so they would arrive by the time she got dressed.

"Mornin'," Ava mumbled when she walked out of her bedroom and saw her mother sitting at the table having toast and tea.

"Good morning, Ava." Her mother studied her

face. "Is anything wrong? It looks like you didn't get a wink of sleep."

Knock. Knock. Instead of answering her mother right away, Ava headed to the door, hoping it was room service. Retrieving her breakfast gave her time to think about how to answer her mother.

"What's wrong?" Niamh asked.

"Nothing, any more. I woke in the middle of the night feeling all achy, and I had a sore throat. It kept me from falling back asleep right away, but it's better now. I think I just need some breakfast. And maybe a nap later. That's all."

"Why didn't you wake me up? We could have ordered some tea with lemon and honey, and doctored it up with a little whisky from the bar. That would have fixed you right up."

Ava grinned. "Irish whisky, right?"

"I'm not condoning drinking, but a little whisky in hot tea with honey would have made you feel better. Even cough medicines have some alcohol in them."

"A license to drink." Ava pretended to cough. "Oh, you know, Mom, I think I need some whisky in my tea." She pushed her cup closer to her mother.

"Absolutely not," her mother replied. "You already told me you're feeling better."

Ava snapped her fingers. "Dang!"

She put off calling Logan until 9:00 a.m. and then berated herself for waiting after he texted back a single word: **GRUNTING.** It was going to be another long day.

LOGAN ARRIVED AT the GRUNT newsroom at about the same time as Jennifer O'Laughlin. "Hey, Jen, I hope there's something juicy going on today."

"A couple of movie stars are in town promoting the release of their new film, but Pam already put in a bid for that one. I heard something about a pileup on the interstate, but I don't have the details on that yet. And the Chalet at the Dunes is apparently on fire but I don't have the details on that, either."

"I'll do the fire. That's a story with legs. It's a popular place. They'll probably rebuild it. It will have a new unveiling. There's more there that lends itself to follow-up stories. I like that."

She dumped her bag, coffee and newspaper on her desk. "Okay, why don't you get on the phone with officials and see what you can find out."

Five minutes later, Logan gave Jennifer a quick salute before heading out for the fire. *I'll be able to repackage this and use updates on The Elliott Report. Plus, I'll borrow the footage from the other two stories and do something with them as well.*

His phone rang. *Ava.* While he waited for a light to change, he quickly sent a text that said, **GRUNTING**, before throwing his phone on the passenger seat. *That should keep her.*

Jackson knocked on Johanna's door as soon as he got dressed. The automatic entryway *whooshed* open and he stepped inside. He stared at Johanna who had dark circles under her eyes. "Rough night?"

"Too little sleep."

"Were you reading?"

"No. The chain I always wear around my neck, and in which I always sleep, turned on me last night and kept trying to choke me."

One side of Jackson's mouth lifted in a half-smirk. "Really. You're going to blame some necklace for your obvious hangover?"

"Very funny."

"What are we doing today?"

"We're going back to continue a dialogue with each other and my father in the presence of the oracle."

"Did you think it helped at all yesterday? Because I sure didn't. It felt like a waste of time to me."

"Patience, Grasshopper."

"Don't go citing *Kung Fu* to me. It was *my* favorite TV show, not yours."

She laughed. "Your favorite TV show is from a quarter century before you were born."

"Mom said I wanted to have a Master Po in my life to take the place of my father."

Johanna grabbed his hand. "I might not be able to take the place of your father, but you can consider me your own personal Master Po."

"Really? And do you have a pithy quote about wasting our time consulting the oracle?"

"Yes, Grasshopper. If you believe you will find illumination, it will brighten your soul. If you condemn the possibility, you will find only darkness."

Jackson's eyebrows shot up. "Did Master Po really say that?"

Johanna laughed. "How do I know? It was your favorite show. Not mine."

"But you said something just like Master Po would say."

"You don't have to be a character on TV to speak with wisdom."

"You just lost him. It was close, but I don't think Master Po had ever heard of TV. It hadn't been invented yet. Besides, he was blind."

"As are you, Grasshopper. As are you. Many people who are visually impaired enjoy television and movies. And it may be even more enjoyable for them because they use their imaginations to fill in the blanks. Plus, people can turn on audio descriptions of the action for some shows, which describes what's going on."

"Okay. I stand corrected. What's for breakfast?"

"Crow, young Grasshopper. Crow."

MANY MILLENNIA AGO, Ailill Caomhánach—a gifted wizard—had been a powerful entity among the realms of the Illumini Constellation. The Ancients appointed him to be the first Master of the Libraries of Illumination, and Ailill Caomhánach created the portal system as his first order of business. The Ancients also tasked him, as the first Master, with creating a board of overseers for the libraries.

Early on, the hierarchy of the libraries and their overseers seemed almost perfect and curators allowed patrons to use the portals to travel to distant realms. It didn't take long before one corrupt curator realized he could reap riches by charging the rich and powerful exorbitant amounts to travel to other realms. Soon, the portals went from being a useful tool for the libraries and the people who frequented them to an elite and expensive system of travel.

The Ancients soon realized their *perfect network* no longer functioned and asked Ailill Caomhánach to remedy the situation. However, by this time, the wizard had turned as corrupt as the system he created.

Ailill Caomhánach, alone, had the power to bend *what is*—into something totally different. It was a talent that commanded a high price, and primaries, kings, rulers, and priests with rich purses often called on the wizard for assistance. He also wielded the ability to mesmerize and dominate others, making them believe his every word. He commanded more power than any one entity had a right to possess.

Instead of succumbing to the desires of The Ancients, Ailill Caomhánach broke away from them and created a new type of portal, one that could easily travel and looked to most like a sophisticated toy. But it was much more than that. The enchanted Re Transfigurator could transform futures, ruin lives, and give the person in possession of it—ultimate control. The Re Transfigurator even transformed Ailill Caomhánach, turning him into a god.

He used the portals to travel among the realms and transform life for those who could afford to pay. And he was revered by many. But he was equally despised by a great number of people who feared his power and wished him vanquished.

The Ancients ultimately regretted the day they had chosen him to become the first master overseer of the Libraries of Illumination. They finally devised a plan to remove the wizard from power, even though they knew it would never be a perfect solution. Their remedy locked the first master inside his device with its key hidden someplace far away. And the remedy sufficed for many millennia.

JOHANNA AND JACKSON arrived at the Library of Origination by mid-morning. Both Pru Tellerence and Ryden Simmdry accompanied them to the Oracle Chamber.

Pru Tellerence sat down beside the oracle. ★ *Your father said the light of illumination remained dim yesterday.*

Johanna sat next to her. "I didn't feel any closer to having answers, just more questions."

⌘ *That is the first step. The oracle is guiding our thoughts in new directions.*

★ *Jackson, do you feel like you have more questions, as well?*

Jackson paced the floor. "Only questions about how the oracle really works. As far as the Re Transfigurator is concerned, I'm in the same muddle I was in before we began."

⌘ *Take a seat and relax. Communing with the oracle is a meditative process. It is best done in a state of tranquility. Not muddlement.*

The teen smirked. "Is 'muddlement' even a word?"

⌘ *It is a descriptor, which is the basis of language. If the term 'muddlement' helps communicate an idea or state of being, then indeed, it is a word.*

Johanna nudged Jackson with her elbow, "It's in the dictionary."

"Right. I should have known you would know that. You always know stuff like that. You must have been teacher's pet in school."

Johanna frowned, reminded of her days growing up and being educated at Peakie's Group Home. She most definitely was not teacher's pet; abused would be more accurate. She dredged up a half smile, "I read a lot. It's the best education."

"You would say that."

Ryden Simmdry held up both hands as if to quiet them. ⌘ *Let's discuss what is uppermost on our minds about the Re Transfigurator.*

Johanna took a deep breath. "I would like to know why it seems so difficult to exit whatever place we might be transported to?"

★*Especially considering the device no longer looked like itself.*

Jackson made a face. "I'd like to know how it read my mind when I wasn't even the person holding it?"

⌘*A very good question, indeed.*

"Really?" Jackson smile.

⌘*I would really like to know why the device changed form. It's almost as if it were trying to trick us.*

"I never did take a good look around," Johanna said." Were we totally surrounded by the alternate reality?"

⌘*Completely. I believe our saving grace is that none of us moved a step off the spot we were standing on. Everything around us changed, but when I thought about this same dilemma yesterday afternoon in the presence of the oracle, I had a vision of the stone floor under our feet only turning into dirt once we had lifted them. I believe we were moored to the library because we did not move.*

"Johanna took a step for—"

She grabbed Jackson's arm, stopping him mid-sentence. "Only with one foot; I left the other one firmly in place."

⌘ *Johanna controlled the power. I believe it would have been more difficult for all of us to return if Johanna had moved much farther, because she held the Re Transfigurator in her hand.*

"Okay," Johanna said, speculating out loud, "If I had stayed in one place, and instead, Jackson had moved to take a look around, would we all still have been able to return here?"

⌘*Another excellent question. I would hope that if you*

wished us all to return here, it would have happened. But I cannot be sure. The story behind the Re Transfigurator is a murky one. It's as if the device has reached out to obfuscate its past.

★ *Or the legacy of Ailill Caomhánach.* Pru Tellerence placed her hand on Ryden Simmdry's arm. ★ *Last night, you said you found very little information about the first master, even though you knew that years ago, the library had contained much more information about him. Could the power of the Re Transfigurator rewrite its own history?*

"That's not good," Jackson blurted out.

⌘ *No. That wouldn't be good at all. But it could be possible.*

Johanna searched her father's eyes. "How can we find out if any of these ideas we're discussing are taking us in the right direction?"

⌘ *Notice the oracle stone. It is glowing with a clear, blue light. Blue is the color of trust and calm.* He paused. ⌘ *Jackson, say something outrageous.*

Jackson closed his eyes for a second. "Johanna, if we don't get married by this weekend, I'm going to kill you."

The light surrounding the oracle faded to a dull rust color with bilious streaks of yellow.

⌘ *The oracle senses a combination of malignant intent and an untrustworthy nature. It is warning us against Jackson's last statement.*

"But it was a lie, you know?" Jackson looked concerned. "The oracle doesn't hate me now, does it? Johanna, I love you and would never hurt you. You believe that, don't you?"

The light emitted by the oracle returned to blue.

Johanna smiled. "How could I not believe you with this giant lie detector telling me it's okay?"

⌘ *It's much more than a lie detector. Our questions are neither truths nor lies, for they are just statements we may not know the answers to. The oracle aligns our words with history, not just the past but the history of the future as well—for time folds upon itself and all is written—even that which has not yet come to pass. The blue light reveals that our thoughts mesh with what has been and what will be.*

NINETEEN

Ailill Caomhánach buzzed with anticipation. He had been dormant for a very long time. Now he wanted to reclaim his position of power within the Illumini Constellation realms. He knew he had weakened over the past millennia. A young woman proved that when she bested him just moments after his release. He needed to restore his strength, but couldn't do that locked up in the automata he had devised. He had believed the Iceland spar would preserve his strength, no matter how long he might lay dormant. An obviously erroneous belief. But even his short time out-of-the-box had reconstituted some of his energy. He needed to decide how to best utilize the few resources he had remaining to rebuild his stamina and influence. He knew the people who recently released him would do so again, if only because they wanted to understand the power of the Re Transfigurator. *I must be ready for them. I must be able to turn the tables.* Ailill Caomhánach put himself in their place to determine what their next move might be before concocting a scheme that would twist their logic in unexpected ways, and allow him to gain his freedom.

JACKSON'S STOMACH GRUMBLED. The sound carried through the quiet Oracle Chamber. "Are we going to break for lunch anytime soon?"

Johanna took a deep breath and relaxed her shoulders. "Food would be good. Being overseers, my parents rarely get hungry, but I could use a pick me up."

★*I'm sorry. I should have considered your needs. You're right about us rarely needing nourishment. But I can certainly understand why you do. Would you like me to conjure a meal?*

Johanna leaned over and patted her mother's hand. "No thank you. I think it would be good for Jackson and I to take a walk outside; get our blood pumping and our lungs expanding. We could use the exercise. We'll probably go to IllumOrangerie. It's his favorite restaurant here, and it's not that far. We won't be gone too long. A couple of hours at the most.

⌘ *We will continue to consult the oracle about the Re Transfigurator in your absence.*

Jackson took Johanna's hand. "Sounds like a plan."

Twenty minutes later, they were seated in the restaurant.

"I'm glad we walked here," Jackson said as he looked around to see what other people were eating. "I was falling asleep."

"I didn't notice," Johanna replied.

"Yeah. Well, I know I did because I had a short but vivid dream. More of a nightmare, actually. We had opened the Re Transfigurator and were brought to a place without gravity, where we couldn't tell up from down. Without anything to hold our feet in place, we floated and lost our ability to return home because we were no longer 'rooted.'" He stopped speaking as his eyes narrowed. "You're staring at me with a weird look on your face. I told you it was a nightmare."

"This happened in the Oracle Chamber just before we left?"

"Yeah."

"I had my eyes on the oracle the entire time we were there—even after your stomach rumbled. The oracle never changed color. If it knew your thoughts, or in this case your dream, and continued to stay blue, I wonder if it means that your dream is going to come true?"

"Why'd you have to say that? Now I'm going to worry."

"Don't. Or perhaps you should. What I'm trying to say is I think it's a good thing it happened. We'll discuss it with my parents when we go back. This may be a sign of the oracle aligning your thoughts in the right direction."

"Yeah? Why my thoughts? Why not your thoughts?"

"Maybe yours are the path of least resistance."

"So, you're saying I'm the most simple-minded."

"No. I'm saying because you were falling asleep, your brainwaves were probably moving in a synchronized pattern that was very welcoming."

"Now you're just finessing it."

"No, Jackson. I'm saying you have a different take on things than I do, and by extension, than my parents do. That doesn't make you simple minded. It makes you a dynamic counterpart and helps us see things we may otherwise miss because we wouldn't have thought of them in the first place."

The middle of the table opened up and a three-tier tray of Fantasian treats rose from the middle. "Well, since you put it that way, I'm glad I could help," Jackson said, before plucking a roast beef sandwich off the middle tier.

JOHANNA PULLED JACKSON into the Oracle Chamber, where her parents were so deep in meditation that their eyes were closed.

Pru Tellerence sensed their arrival. ★*Are you ready for another round?*

"Jackson had something important happen that you need to hear." She nudged his arm. "Go ahead, tell them."

That piqued the interest of both overseers who gave Jackson their undivided attention.

He told them about his dream.

Johanna took over the conversation before Jackson had a chance to take a breath. "The entire time, I had my eye on the oracle, and the color never wavered from blue. Is the oracle saying that Jackson's dream will actually happen?"

Ryden Simmdry's right brow shot up. ⌘*An interesting query.*

Pru Tellerence took his hand. ★ *You think that could be true?*

⌘ *The Re Transfigurator was banished for a reason. It was probably becoming too powerful and dangerous. This may be an indication of its ability to adapt to preserve its own interests.*

Jackson's shoulders slumped. "How do we fight something like that?"

⌘*I have no idea.*

Johanna shook her head. "We don't have to. We

aren't interested in the artifact because of some problem that needs a remedy. We're just looking into it because we randomly found a key. If we just separate the two and bury the Re Transfigurator someplace where it can't easily be found—"

"Like inside a junkpile of toys on Juvenilia!" Jackson exclaimed.

Johanna nodded. "We won't have to deal with whether we can get back home or not. We only have to refuse to play the game."

★ *My ingenious daughter. You must take after me.*

Ryden Simmdry smiled indulgently at the woman he wished to marry before turning his attention back to his daughter. ⌘ *Where is the Re Transfigurator now?*

"Locked in the closet of the Executive Board Room on Fantasia," Johanna replied.

⌘ *And the key?*

"I have it in my pocket."

⌘ *Good. Keeping those two items separate is our best defense.*

★ *Perhaps it would be better if you locked it inside your vault.*

"I'll do that when we get home," Johanna replied.

⌘ *Well, if we're not going to wage war against the Re Transfigurator, then I believe our meditations here are done.*

"That's it?" Jackson asked. "What about my dream?"

⌘ *If I'm not mistaken, your dream and our discussion about it led Johanna to the conclusion that we will refuse to engage with the artifact, thereby solving any problems before they have begun.*

"Oh. So, it helped?"

Johanna linked her arm in his. "Of course it helped.

That's why we're so good together. We bring out the best in each other."

Jackson smiled and gave her a quick kiss before looking at her parents. "May I take your daughter home?"

⌘ *With our blessing.*

★*But please tell me you're not going to kill our daughter if she doesn't marry you by this weekend.*

Jackson held up both hands, palms out. "I'm willing to wait until she's ready."

"Good answer." Johanna kissed her parents goodbye before taking Jackson's hand. "Let's go home."

THE FIRST THING Johanna did when she walked inside her residence was to take the key to the Re Transfigurator and throw it into her night table drawer. *You should be safe in there for now. But first, I need to take care of your more devious partner.* She hung the cashmere top she was wearing in the closet and pulled a tee-shirt over her head. Some of the items in the vault were dusty and she didn't want to worry about what she was wearing. She also removed her boots and slipped on a pair of sneakers. She rubbed her hands together. *Now, I'm ready to wage battle.*

Just as she reached the bottom step, the lights went out and an alarm went off. "What now?" she asked aloud. Backup lights came on but the alarm kept ringing.

Mrs. Roth and Ava came out of the hotel suite. "Do you think the library is on fire?" Mrs. Roth directed her question to Johanna.

"I have no idea. Where's Jackson?"

He came out of the hotel suite. "There doesn't seem to be anything wrong in the suite. I'd better head up to the top level and work my way down."

Johanna sniffed deeply. "I don't smell anything that smells like fire. Could it be the burglar alarm?"

"I'll check," Ava said, running to the back entrance.

Johanna and Mrs. Roth searched the remainder of the first level, looking inside the storerooms and offices.

They all met back near the information desk. "The back door was locked," Ava said.

"There's nothing going on in here as far as I can see," Jackson added.

Johanna grabbed his hand. "I think we should check downstairs. The basement was a maze filled with old furniture and fixtures, oversized equipment and paraphernalia, and old level-0 books that had outlived their usefulness. The co-curators checked the basement the best they could, but it took a while because it was laid out like a huge maze. They met up at the elevator.

Jackson scratched his head. "If we have to search more than a thousand sub levels, this is going to take forever."

Johanna closed her eyes and spoke telepathically with her father. Her eyes popped open a moment later. "I think we can turn off the alarm. My father said all the sub-basements are protected by a safety protocol overseen by the library generator, you know, the big blue orb. He said if we haven't found anything by now, it may just be a short in the electrical system. And he asked if it happened to any other buildings in the neighborhood."

"Good question." Jackson followed her upstairs, and they exited the front of the library. Each slowly turned and surveyed their surroundings. "It doesn't look like much is going on. Weird, huh?"

Johanna nodded. "Let's go back inside and turn off the alarm."

"I'll do that. You'd better alert the police and fire departments."

Chris Roth came in the front door a minute later, carrying pizza boxes from Piccolo Italia. "Why are police and fire trucks here?"

"I told them it was a false alarm," Johanna said.

Two first responders followed Chris inside. "We need to check the premises." A fire fighter and a police officer did a quick walk around the main floor of the library, while their counterparts checked the exterior of the building.

"It does look like a false alarm," the police officer told them. "This is the second strange incident in this neighborhood in as many days. Do you have security cameras mounted outside?"

Johanna and Jackson each looked at the other and shook their heads. "Do you think we need them?" Johanna asked.

"It depends on what you've got here. If you have a lot of rare books and historical documents, then I would say *yes*. If it's just an old lending library, you may not care. But it looks like a pretty nice place from in here; much nicer than it looks from out front. You ought to ask the library board to include a surveillance system in your next budget."

Johanna simply nodded and walked them out.

She remained strangely quiet until they all sat down to eat pizza. "What do you think the police meant by two strange incidents in two days?" Johanna asked Mrs. Roth.

"Didn't Jackson tell you? We were evacuated yesterday morning. They said there was a gas leak in the area but it turned out to be a false alarm."

Johanna blanched. "The library was left unattended?"

"Don't worry. We locked the doors. Everything was fine."

"Maybe not every—" Chris stopped speaking when Ava's foot connected with his ankle.

Johanna punched Jackson's arm. "Did you know about this?"

He shrugged. "Yeah. They mentioned it to me."

Why didn't you tell me?"

"I don't know. It was just a false alarm, and you already had a lot on your mind. I didn't want to clutter it up."

Johanna's shoulders sagged as she leaned back in her chair. "I think we should get a surveillance system. Things have changed since the library was first built. I'll feel better knowing it's protected."

Jackson looked contrite. "Do you want me to do a little research to see what's available?

"Yes, please."

"Consider it done.

THE CHALET FIRE at The Dunes was a combination brush and rubbish fire that merely darkened the rough, exterior wood finish of the building with soot. It apparently did not affect the interior at all. Police told reporters that they suspected teenagers had lit a fire for an impromptu make-out session. Officials surmised the teens used the building to block strong winds, only to have the wind whip the flames over toward dried out beach grasses that had been planted to prevent erosion of the sand dunes. The result looked like a large smoky fire from a distance but a less serious blaze up close.

Logan quickly edited his story, before offering to help edit other reporters. While they filled out paperwork on their news packages, Logan copied their footage onto a disk he had brought with him from home. *This should help beef up* The Elliott Report. *Now, I need to come up with something to get Ava off my back for a few days.*

By the time he climbed into his car and headed home, Logan knew just what he would tell Ava. He pressed a button on the steering wheel. "Call Ava Roth, line two." The hands-free system in his car dialed Ava's cell phone.

"Logan?"

"Hey, Ava, I'm glad I caught you. I have to head out of town for the weekend. There's a college I'm interested in that called and asked if I could come in for an interview. I'm heading out straight away and you probably won't be able to reach me all weekend. I thought I'd just call to let you know, so you wouldn't wonder where I am."

"Oh. Okay."

"Good. I'll talk to you after I get back."

"Wait! Logan?"

He tried not to sound impatient. "Yes?"

"Were you in the library yesterday morning? I know you said you couldn't make it. But then, someone *was* in the library and ran out the back door. Was it you?"

Logan felt the hairs on the back of his neck tingling and unconsciously rubbed his hand over them. "Nope. Wasn't me."

"It's just that—"

A car horn blared. "Look, Ava, I gotta go. It wasn't me. I'll talk to you next week." And before she could say another word, Logan disconnected the call.

That was close. Hopefully she'll forget all about it by the next time we speak.

When he got home, he parked his car in the garage rather than his usual spot in the driveway. He entered the house and found a note from his mother saying she and his father were having dinner at their country club, and he could join them if he liked.

I don't like. He ordered food delivery and bought extra, so he would have plenty for the weekend. He wanted to put together at least two generic shows for *The Elliott Report,* and a third one that would blow the roof off the Library of Illumination.

TWENTY

Ava felt the blood rushing up to her face as she listened to the conversation between Johanna and Jackson and then felt her blood drain back out when Chris started to mention the back door. She pushed her plate away. "Can I be excused? I'm not all that hungry."

Her mother stared at her for a moment. "Go ahead."

Guilt weighed heavily on Ava. She decided she'd feel better if she worked it off doing something for the library. She went into the broom closet and grabbed some furniture polish and dust clothes. She looked around the massive main floor. *I guess I'll start in the back corner and work my way to the front.* She walked toward the back entrance, eyeballing the automatic lock on the door to make sure it was engaged. She looked at the entrance to the Executive Board Room. *This is as good a place to start as any.*

She fished her earbuds out of her pocket, and a

half-eaten package of licorice fell out. *Forgot about this.* She popped a piece in her mouth before plugging the earbuds into her ears. She turned up the music on her phone and started waxing in time to it, all the while worrying about whether someone had actually broken into the library because she left the back door unlocked.

EVERYONE INSIDE THE Library of Illumination was too involved in what they were doing to notice a subtle vibration. It appeared to be less strong than it really was, and less noisy than a similar event would be. This vibration was centered around the key Johanna had thrown in her night table drawer. As the vibration grew, the drawer slowly worked itself open—just a sliver—allowing the key to the Re Transfigurator to escape its confinement and float away. It rounded the corner through Johanna's living room and dove to nearly floor level before disappearing under the door. The seemingly self-propelled key slowly followed the circular pattern of the curator's stairs to the main floor. From there it made a bee-line to the Executive Board Room unobserved.

Ava had her back to the door as she polished a bookcase that stood between two windows. She never noticed the key entering the room or sliding under the door of the attached storage closet. Nor did she hear the Re Transfigurator levitating as the key slipped into the artifact. If she hadn't been so preoccupied while facing in the wrong direction, she might have noticed the strange orange luminescence escaping from around the door's perimeter. The glow permeated the room, creating a perfect carbon copy of the Executive Board Room behind her. However, the duplicate did not lead to the rest of her world. By the time she turned and took a step, it was too late.

*

POLISHING SHELVES COULD be boring; however, the repetitious movement created the perfect atmosphere for daydreaming. Ava imagined herself standing on a stormy beach.

"It's beautiful isn't it?" Logan slipped his arm around her shoulders and she leaned into him.

"Fancy seeing you here."

"I've been here all along, just waiting for you."

She smiled. "Were you now?"

"Yes. I know how much you love walking along the shore."

"What else do you know about me?"

"I know you love books. Tell me more about the books at the library, Ava. What makes them so special?"

Something nudged Ava's consciousness. "You're not real. You can't be."

Logan's shoulder's slumped. "You were so excited the first time we came here together. Now, you're acting like you don't even want to be with me."

"I remember coming here with you. It was nice. And warm. Now, it isn't. It looks like it's going to rain. What are we doing here?"

"This is what you've been hoping for, Ava. You and I alone on the beach."

"In. The. Summer."
*"I'm going. If you need me, I'll be inside
the Chalet."*

Ava shuddered. *That was weird.* She popped the last piece of licorice in her mouth and threw the empty package in the waste basket. It wasn't enough to stop her stomach from growling. Tired of polishing shelves, she decided it was time for a donut and hot cocoa. She opened the door to leave the Executive Board Room but stopped on a dime, realizing her world had drastically changed. The hairs on her arms tingled as she watched waves roll onto the beach at The Dunes, again. She looked down. They nearly touched her feet. She searched the shoreline for Logan but didn't see him.

The wind howled and a sudden crack of thunder made Ava shiver. She noticed the Chalet Restaurant not too far away. A large piece of hail smacked her in the head. *Great.* She dropped the polish and rags in the sand as she ran for the building, hail pelting her the entire way. She felt relieved and grateful when she finally pulled the restaurant door open, but those feelings quickly faded when she stepped inside and found a totally different environment than expected. The lobby was dark, however an open doorway at the other end displayed a brightly lit room. Ava walked into the room, half-expecting to find Logan, but instead found she was entirely surrounded by working automata. Instead of feeling engaged, she felt her skin crawl. *Gotta go.* She turned to leave but the door had disappeared. *Am I dreaming? This is too weird to be real.*

Believing it was a dream, she finally relaxed and took her time, inspecting the fascinating mechanisms on display. *It's like an old-fashioned museum.* Everywhere she looked, she found figures in motion. Dancing girls from several different eras and countries, dressed in all manner of costumes from simple muslin aprons to richly embroidered satin kimonos, were featured in several of the displays. Acrobats. Musicians. A 17th century aristocratic lady sitting at a dressing table, powdering her nose. Everywhere Ava looked, she noticed something unique and intriguing. The animation filled her with wonder. A life-size artist, standing in front of an easel, raised and lowered his hand from a palette to his canvas, as if brushing on strokes. A judge dressed in black robes and a white powdered wig stood behind his courtroom bench, pounding a gavel with one hand while moving papers up and down in the other. A *tableau mécanique* featured a tower with a working clock. It overlooked a river that had boats moving among the tin waves. Ava turned again, spotting puppeteers maneuvering marionettes. She walked along a narrow aisle separating the objects. Nearby, an old man with a spinning wheel turned straw into gold. In another display, her eyes widened, as she spotted a colorful clown balancing a juggler on his shoulders. The juggler had his head tilted back, and a small boy performed a one-armed handstand, his hand firmly clasped around the juggler's nose. Ava turned toward the largest automated display in the room, a life-size cyclist riding on a path through a park. The wheels of the bicycle spun around, as a girl dressed in a pleated satin blouse, a black skirt and buttoned boots, appeared to peddle along the cobblestone path amid shrubbery and flowers. Ava took a step closer. The cyclist was very compelling. *Something about her is so familiar.*

*

Niamh looked up from her book. The clock on the wall said it was after 11:00 pm. *Where is Ava? She didn't say anything about going out, although it is Friday night.* She got up and walked around the library, calling out Ava's name.

Jackson emerged from Johanna's residence and called down to his mother. "What's up?"

"I can't find Ava," she answered. "Did she say anything to you about going out tonight?"

"Nope."

"I'd better keep looking. She must be around here somewhere."

Johanna came out of the residence, walking over to Jackson.

"What's going on?"

"Ava's missing. I'm going to go help mom look."

Johanna closed the door to the residence. "I will, too."

"Where's Chris?" Jackson asked.

His mother picked at her cuticle. "He said he was going out with his friends."

Jackson pulled out his cell phone and called his brother. "Is Ava with you? ... She seems to be missing. ... Right. Bye." He looked at his mother, shaking his head. "He said the last time he saw Ava was when he was leaving. She'd just come out of the supply closet with a bottle of polish and some rags."

"Then she must be around here somewhere."

They divided the areas of the library among the three of them and searched. An hour later, Johanna and Jackson met up in the back hall by the Executive Board Room.

"Last room," Jackson said as he grabbed the doorknob.

"Wait," Johanna said, grabbing his arm. She banged on the door with her fist. "Ava are you in there?"

Jackson grimaced. "Wouldn't it have been easier to just open the door and see if she's inside?"

Johanna pointed to the bottom of the door. In the semi-darkness of the back hallway, a subtle, orange light was noticeable. "We're waiting here."

Mrs. Roth caught up with them. "Anything?"

"Could be. We need my father." Johanna closed her eyes for a second, and a minute later Ryden Simmdry appeared. ⌘*Your mother is exhausted. I thought it best to leave her behind to rest.*

"Of course. I wouldn't have bothered you except Ava is missing. There's an odd light coming from the Executive Board Room and the Re Transfigurator is inside, locked in the closet."

⌘*I thought you moved it to the vault.*

"I meant to, but then we had a problem with our alarm system, and the police and fire departments came, and then we ate dinner, and by then I'd forgotten all about it."

⌘*Where is the key?*

"Upstairs," she said before disappearing. She materialized a moment later, her face white. "The key is missing. The drawer where I placed it was open."

Mrs. Roth turned as white as Johanna. "And you think Ava took it." It was more of a statement than a question.

Johanna shook her head. "I don't see why she would. She wouldn't have known it was there."

⌘*There's something else at work here. Something we will face together. But I would advise you, Niamh, to return to your suite and wait there, just in case Ava is not mixed up with the forces creating the energy behind this door. The less people exposed to the malevolence of Ailill Caomhánach, the better.* He took off a ring and handed it to her. ⌘*If you do not hear from us within the hour, rub this ring and say,* Pru Tellerence, *out loud. She will come immediately.*

NIAMH COULD NOT sit still. Her impulse was to keep moving, regardless of whether that meant pacing the floor or vacuuming it. One of her children was missing. *Why does it have to be Ava? At least the boys can take care of themselves.* She shuddered. Deep down, she knew it wouldn't really matter which of her children was missing. She was an equal opportunity mom and a major worrier.

Forty-five minutes later Chris stormed in, demanding to know what was being done to find his sister.

His mother burst into tears.

Chris grimaced before pulling her into a hug. "Sorry, Mom, I guess I got ahead of myself. Are the police here? Are they looking for her?"

"No. Jackson, Johanna, and her father are looking for her."

Chris moved his hand in a rolling motion. "In the neighborhood? Here in the library? Why didn't you call the police?"

"They think a malevolent force may have taken her. Something about a strange orange glow under the door. They didn't want me to come with them. They wanted me to be here in case Ava returned."

"Where are they?"

"I left them outside the Executive Board Room."

"How long ago was that?"

She looked at her watch. "About fifty minutes."

"That's pretty precise."

She held up Ryden Simmdry's ring. "If they're not back in another ten minutes, I'm supposed to rub this and say 'Pru Tellerence.'"

Chris took the ring and rubbed the carnelian intaglio stone. "Pru Tellerence."

The overseer didn't appear instantaneously, but she did arrive within minutes. Pru Tellerence wore a pale, shimmery robe that looked nothing like the overseers' usual mode of dress. Nor did she wear her miter. Her hair hung loose about her shoulders. She carried the insert from her miter, which allowed overseers to transport at will, in her pocket. ★ *What has happened?*

Niamh squared her shoulders. "Nothing. They've been gone close to an hour and we're still waiting to hear from them.

Pru Tellerence dropped her gaze as she telepathically communicated with her future husband. Her eyes suddenly opened, as did her mouth. ★ *They are in the library—*

Chris shook his head. "The Executive Board Room."

★ *Not exactly. It would appear to be this library but they are in another dimension.*

Mrs. Roth dropped into a chair and stared at the overseer. "Another dimension?"

Chris shook his head. "What does that even mean?"

★ *They are in this space, in a different time, perhaps. Or in this time in a different space, when this space is physically in a different position in relation to your sun and its position in the universe. It's difficult to say. Every moment has different parameters than the moment before.*

Niamh whispered, "Will they be able to return? To us? To our time?"

★ *They are the three smartest people I know. If anyone can figure this out, they can.*

"Yeah," Chris replied, "but what if nobody can figure this out?"

★ *They will. I will stay here and serve as their control.*

Mrs. Roth wiped a tear from her face. "How will you do that?"

★*Regardless of where they are, we can communicate telepathically. They will use my thought waves as a beacon, so they can eventually travel back to me here—in this space and time—rather than a different version of me in another dimension.*

Ryden Simmdry held out one hand, palm facing up and the other hand two inches above it, palm facing down, and moved them in opposing circles. He closed one palm, and when he opened it a wide black band appeared. He uttered a chant, and the band separated into three narrow ones. He placed one on his wrist before handing off the other two. ⌘ *These will keep us connected to each other. Do not take it off, no matter what happens.* He watched as Johanna and Jackson slipped on the wrist bands. ⌘*Are we ready?*

They nodded.

⌘*Let's join hands. For the first few seconds, Jackson, I would like you to remain in this hallway while I enter the room. Johanna will keep us joined together.*

Jackson squinted. "I thought that's what the bands are for?"

⌘*It is, but it never hurts to take extra precautions. I first want to see if I can notice any obvious anomalies.*

"Right."

Ryden Simmdry pulled open the door and looked inside. Aside from the slight orange tint around the periphery of the room, everything looked normal.

⌘We have no choice but to all enter and close the door behind us.

A moment later, the appearance of the boardroom changed, and they were on the beach at The Dunes. The sky looked threatening and a stiff breeze chilled them. The waves appeared to be almost navy in color and broke into white bands of foam on the darkened sand.

⌘Do either of you know why Ava would have been thinking about this place before she disappeared?

"Maybe she likes it here," Jackson said. "Most everyone does."

⌘Does it have a special meaning that you know of?

"No," Jackson answered.

"Logan," Johanna replied.

Jackson's head jerked. "Logan? What has he got to do with anything?"

"He took Ava to the beach and they walked along the sand. She said it was very romantic."

"Romantic! She's not supposed to be thinking about him like that. He's my friend."

"Calm down, Cowboy. When you start crushing on someone, you don't really have control over your feelings. They're just there. And Logan taking Ava to the beach—for whatever reason—felt romantic to her."

"How do you even know this?"

"Because she confided in me."

"And you didn't tell me?"

"It's girl talk, Jackson. All girls have crushes and

they want to talk about them. Ava talked about hers with me—in confidence."

"So, you think she's around here with Logan?"

"I don't think she's with Logan from our dimension, but she might have been thinking about him when the artifact cast its spell." Jackson went to pull his hand away, but Johanna held it tightly, saying, "We need to stay connected."

He scrubbed at his face with his other hand. "Do you think she's in there?" He stopped rubbing long enough to point to the chalet.

"Could be."

Ryden Simmdry searched the shoreline, finding no one. ⌘It is, most likely, our best bet. Shall we go?

Pru Tellerence paused for a moment, before placing her hand on Mrs. Roth's shoulder. ★They are on a beach. It looks like a storm is coming in. No sight of Ava yet. They think she was brought there by the Re Transfigurator because she previously spent time there with a boy named Logan.

Mrs. Roth straightened. "Logan is with her?"

Pru Tellerence hesitated for a moment before saying ★They don't think so, at least not Logan from this world. They believe she was daydreaming about Logan when the artifact activated.

"They haven't found her yet?"

★No, but they haven't been there long. They need some time.

Niamh nodded as tears slid down her face.

"Don't cry, Mom." Chris slid his arm around her shoulders and gave her a hug. "They'll find her."

His mother wiped the tears from her face. "Yes. But in what condition?"

TWENTY-ONE

Logan spent hours squaring away two regular episodes of *The Elliott Report.* He made several phone calls to get the latest facts on the video and stories he already had copies of and re-edited updated reports for his internet show. *I need something else.* He played mindlessly with the Newton's Cradle on his desk, while he thought about what else he could do to flesh out his show. By the fifth time the end ball sent its energy through the stationary spheres in the middle, causing the ball on the other end to propel upward, he had his answer. *I'll play to everyone's lowest common denominator. Celebrity news.* He also created reports on trending videos on YouTube and put together separate montages of political new and business happenings. *This will make it more like a regular newscast.* He worked late into the night until he felt satisfied with the content for the two shows. He anchored one newscast right away before preparing the remaining content for another show.

Afterward, he slipped on his headphones and relaxed, listening to his favorite music, while he planned the rest of his attack against the library.

AVA FOUND THE automaton of the girl on the bicycle to be hypnotic. She drew closer as she stared at the girl's face. When she was merely inches away, the figure's pale porcelain complexion changed its hue. It became more golden tan with a sprinkling of freckles. The cyclist's hair grew from short, dark curls to long blond waves. As the girl's cheekbones lifted, Ava gasped. The figurine was adopting Ava's appearance.

She tried to step away, but found herself glued to that spot. As she fought to retreat, her strength slowly left her body. She couldn't stop herself from being pulled into the figurine, even though she wanted to move as far away as she could. She felt her body dissolving, like pixels on a TV. Suddenly, her entire torso shifted into a new position. She froze as her hands grasped the handlebars of the bicycle. She felt her legs pumping the pedals. She tried to get away, but found the rest of her body frozen in place.

Ava had become the girl on the bicycle.

THE SAME POWERFUL storm that Ava had encountered, pommeled Johanna, Jackson, and Ryden Simmdry with all the ferocity of an impending hurricane. The trio literally fought their way to the Chalet, however, for every step they moved forward, they appeared to be that much farther away from their destination.

"What's going on?" Jackson shouted, his voice nearly drowned out by the wind.

⌘*Johanna, follow my lead.* Ryden Simmdry began

to chant, and Johanna repeated his words, concentrating telepathically and focusing on what her father was trying to achieve.

Johanna's words grew louder as her conviction grew stronger. Father and daughter continued to fight the storm, slowly moving forward. The major difference was they now made headway in their journey. As they neared the Chalet door, it sprung open, leaving the inclement weather behind them. They all stepped inside, and as suddenly as it had opened, the door slammed shut and disappeared.

"Now what?" Jackson asked.

"We stay together," Johanna answered.

⌘ *Or at least close. Ailill Caomhánach has us where he wants us.*

"Why?" asked Jackson.

⌘ *He needs to reinvigorate.*

The teen stared at Ryden Simmdry for a moment, then narrowed his eyes. "Define 'reinvigorate.'"

"He wants to suck our lifeforce out of us," Johanna replied, "and use it himself. So, I suggest you stay on your toes."

Jackson turned to Ryden Simmdry. "Is that true?"

⌘ *In a manner of speaking. I suggest we remain alert but not too close.*

Ryden Simmdry let go of Johanna's hand. Jackson did the same.

They followed the light into the main exhibition hall and focused their attention on the mechanical exhibits surrounding them.

"Some of these are so lovely," Johanna said, taking a step closer to examine an old woman making lace at a pedestal table.

⌘*Do not get too close, Johanna. We do not know Ailill Caomhánach's modus operandi.*

"It's just so mesmerizing." Johanna reached out to touch the lace. "Ouch."

She suddenly turned on Jackson who had slapped her hand away from the automaton. "What do you think you're doing?"

"Keeping you safe," he replied. "For all we know, that stuff has some kind of poison on it that's absorbed through the skin to paralyze you. I don't think we should touch anything."

Johanna craned her neck from side to side. "You're right. I don't know what I was thinking. It was almost like being under a spell. I *had* to touch it."

⌘*That could happen to any one of us at any time. I doubt the artifact is strong enough to command all of us at once, so we should be all right as long as we keep watch over each other and not touch anything that could, in turn, take over our life force.*

Both teens nodded their agreement.

★*OH DEAR!* PRU TELLERENCE had not expected Ryden Simmdry's latest message.

Niamh's eyes widened. "What is it? What's happened."

★*They appear to have encountered a very strong storm. But they're alright now. They found their way into a place called the Chalet.*

"They're at the Chalet? What are they doing there? Is Ava with them?"

★*No. Johanna says it's not the Chalet as they know it. It's a manifestation of a place Ava must have thought about.*

"It's not that far from here. I can't imagine how there can be a storm there, when it's so nice outside."

★*It is an alternate reality in an alternate universe.*

Niamh felt her resolve crumbling as a tear slid down her face. "But how did Ava get there?"

Pru Tellerence grew very serious. ★*Niamh, do you believe in magic?*

"I didn't, until I encountered this place. But Jackson and Johanna never refer to anything that happens here as magic. Johanna usually refers to it as, 'special properties.'"

Pru Tellerence managed to suppress her smile. ★*That's an excellent explanation for it. The word 'magic' conjures up the idea of tricks. But what Ava has encountered isn't a simple trick. It's a malevolent force, creating a problem, albeit, in another dimension. I realize this seemingly unbelievable malicious intent goes against everything you believe to be real and normal, but it does actually exist. That's why there are overseers like Ryden Simmdry and myself. We do our best to protect the realms against evil anomalies like this. I know you're worried, but try to stay positive. Johanna's growing powers are even stronger than her father's, and I'm sure Jackson would do anything to protect his sister. We have to believe they'll be able to sort things out and bring Ava home.*

JOHANNA, JACKSON, AND Ryden Simmdry, walked among the automata in single file, always within steps of one another. Johanna kept reminding herself not to be taken in by the intriguing design of each display, but to look only for signs that Ava might be there. It wasn't an easy task. *Who would have ever imagined that this many different and very complex automata existed?*

Her father read her thoughts. ⌘*They may not. Many*

may be projections of what we have already seen, making the task seem more daunting and tiresome, as well as obfuscating any clues that might be here.

As they proceeded forward, Jackson yelled, "Stop."

"What is it?" Johanna asked.

"We need to turn right. We *have* to turn right, here. I feel a pull in this direction. My spidey sense tells me Ava is over there." He waved his right arm in the direction he wanted them to go in.

⌘ *It may be a trick.*

"Or even worse, Johanna added, "a trap."

"I have to," Jackson said, breaking away.

Johanna changed direction, following him, and Ryden Simmdry took up the rear.

To his credit, Jackson proceeded slowly, trying to take everything in before taking another step forward. "Did either of you notice where we turned, so we don't get lost? I know the door had been right behind us before it disappeared. And we went straight for a while. But I forgot to take note of where we deviated from our original course."

⌘ *When we turned, I was studying a pair of 18ᵗʰ century Fantasian nobles dueling with swords.*

Jackson hesitated for a second. "I didn't see that. Do you think it's some kind of scam? Are we each seeing something different?"

⌘ *That would take an enormous amount of energy, and I don't think Ailill Caomhánach has that much power yet.*

Johanna grabbed Jackson's hand. "My father saw the swordsmen, but I was behind my father and I watched as an archer drew back an arrow. It was right after the narrow aisle you turned down. You didn't see the swordsmen because you hadn't reached it yet."

"Okay. I just wanted to make sure I'm not going crazy. Or being tricked."

⌘ *We are being tricked, but not on that grand a scale.*

They continued forward in the new direction.

"Jackson stopped again, and Johanna almost bumped into him. "Do you hear humming?" he asked.

"I hear a lot of whirring and clicking, coming from the movements of each of these displays." Johanna looked around. She pointed to a particular automaton. "Maybe that's what you heard. The turning of those wheels."

Logan and Ava walked along the shore at the Dunes. He slipped his arm around her shoulders, pulling her close. "What's the oddest thing you've ever seen in the library?"

"That has to be the thingy-ma-bob that absorbs people, taking over their bodies."

"There's no such thing."

"Yes, there is. Here, I'll show you." She led him to the Chalet and pulled open the front door. Inside, stood the Library of Illumination. They walked into the main reading room, which was filled with odd looking devices. "This is our latest exhibit," Ava said, leading him past a row of mechanical contraptions, describing each one as they walked past.

At the end of the display stood a life-size statue of Mephistopheles. "Who's this bad boy?" Logan asked, touching the statue.

"You shouldn't have done that," Ava said.

Logan tried to pull his hand away but couldn't. Instead, he watched in horror as his hand melted into the sculpture.

"Mephistopheles doesn't like to be handled," Ava continued. "Now he's going to have to teach you a lesson. You really shouldn't touch anything in the library. Everything here is special, but unforgiving, and will do anything to protect itself."

Logan's entire arm had now been absorbed into the statue. "You have to stop this, Ava. Help me."

"There's nothing I can do. I warned you that the library was unusual. I told you it held secrets that have to be protected. But you insist on worming your way in. Now you've taken it a step too far."

Logan could feel his torso being pulled into the figure. "What is this thing?" he cried.

"He's an evil spirit and it looks like he's decided to devour your soul. Bye-bye, Logan. I'll miss you."

Logan sat up with a start, his head pounding along with his heart. He was covered in sweat. He looked around the room. *His* room. *That was weird.*

The front door *slammed.* "Logan, are you home?" he heard his mother shout.

He was about to answer when he saw the hallway light illuminate the small space under his bedroom door.

"I told you he wasn't home," his father yelled from right outside his room, "or else his car would have been in the driveway. Besides, it's Friday night. Did you honestly expect him to be home rather than out with his friends?"

Logan decided not to answer them. He didn't mind his parents thinking he was out. But it meant he would have to be extra quiet. He could hear his father thumping back down the stairs.

He flipped off the light in his room, so his parents wouldn't see it. *I may as well get some rest.* He shrugged off his clothes in the dark and got back into bed. It was still early for a Friday night—or a Saturday morning—just after midnight—but he was exhausted from all the mental activity he had invested in producing two episodes of *The Elliott Report.* He laid in bed, thinking about what he would tell his parents about his car not being in the driveway. He could always say he had some drinks with friends from his internship, and didn't feel well afterward, so one of them dropped him off. He'd say his car would be fine in his friend's driveway.

Hmmm… maybe I should say I felt ill. And that I parked the car in the garage so my friends wouldn't bother me. That's even better. He closed his eyes to go back to sleep but it eluded him. The nightmare he'd had felt so real, it haunted his thoughts and ruined the remainder of his night.

OH NO, WHAT'S happening? I can't move, except for my legs, which feel like they're pumping. All I can see are the handlebars of a bicycle. But why can't I turn my head? Ava tried to call out for help. A muffled sound was audible, but she couldn't say anything clearly. *What is happening to me?* Her mind raced as she tried to force herself to wake up from this nightmare. *It has to be a nightmare, right?* But try as she might, she remained in the same spot unable to move anything but her legs, which seemed to peddle for hours. "My legs ache.

I'm tired. I want to go home," she tried to say aloud. Her words were lost but not completely. Instead, an incoherent hum replaced them. She felt her eyes prickle with unshed tears. *Why me?*

AILILL CAOMHÁNACH FORCED himself to put a lid on his fury. This girl who should provide some much-needed life force, had eaten the one thing that would prevent him from taking it. *Eiulqar.* Similar to licorice, *eiulqar* prevented the easy absorption of energy. *It will pass out of her system if she burns enough energy, but then there will be less for me.* Who knew how long it would take? Just thinking about it increased his fury tenfold.

Like most overseers, his thoughts could be heard by others, if he so desired. In this case, he was so angry, he did not shield his thoughts, instead allowing everything around him to know the full force of his wrath.

NIAMH FELT HER eyelids drooping. "I need coffee," she told Pru Tellerence. "Would you like some?"

★*It's an oddly bitter drink that I was unfamiliar with until I stayed here for a time with Johanna. Cream and a sweetener of some kind made it more appetizing. Would you have those items on hand?*

Niamh felt herself smile, if only momentarily, for the first time that evening. "I believe that can be arranged."

Niamh led the overseer inside the hotel suite. Pru Tellerence stopped and stared. ★*This is very unusual to find inside a Library of Illumination that is not class V.*

"Hmmm. I guess this is some of that magic you were talking about. Although, again, Johanna said it's possible because of the 'special properties,'" Niamh made air quotes, "of the travel guide that makes it possible. This suite of rooms and services only exist as long as the travel guide remains open."

★ *Yes. It is a special property. But magical in its own right.*

It was a mild evening and the doors to the balcony were open. While Niamh ordered room service, Pru Tellerence walked outside, smiling when she saw the twinkling lights of Paris, shining in the distance.

"It's special, isn't it?" Niamh said, joining her.

★*Indeed. Does this go away, as well, when the book is closed?*

"Yes. The city exists, but it's thousands of miles away."

They chatted about Paris until room service arrived. Niamh poured their coffee while Pru Tellerence telepathically checked in with Ryden Simmdry and the teens. The overseer had done an excellent job of controlling her facial expressions to show no emotion, but it betrayed her at the exact moment Niamh turned to hand her a cup of coffee.

The cup began clattering against the saucer as Niamh's hand shook in anticipation of whatever dread she saw on the overseer's face. "You have news." Her voice quavered but she had to know, "What is it?"

RYDEN SIMMDRY ANALYZED the animated diorama featuring a grist mill with a water wheel. Through the openings, he could see a 2-D miller moving a bag of wheat over a hopper. The water wheel for the grinding stone definitely rotated, but it did not produce a hum; it sounded more like a subtle *whir.* Through another opening in the diorama, he watched a man's arms move as he appeared to pass a bag of flour to a woman. ⌘*I cannot see any relation between this particular device and your sister's disappearance.*

"I don't think that's what I heard," Jackson said. He took a few tentative steps forward, slowly turning his head from side to side, narrowing his eyes as he strained to listen, again.

Johanna and her father moved forward as well, always wanting to remain within reach of Jackson in case anything happened.

"Maybe I—" Jackson's eyes widened. "There it is again."

Ryden Simmdry tensed. ⌘*I believe I just heard Jackson's hum.* The overseer closed his eyes. He inhaled deeply before opening them again. He pointed to the automaton at the end of the aisle. I believe it's coming from down there.

Jackson walked quickly, Johanna and her father rushing to keep up with him.

"Not so fast," Johanna said. "You could be rushing straight into danger."

Jackson stopped abruptly in front of the automaton. "It's life-size. It's one of only a few here that are that big."

Johanna pointed. "Are those wheels creating the hum you hear?"

Jackson looked down. "I don't think so."

"No!" Johanna gasped.

"Right. That's not what I hear."

Johanna grabbed Jackson's arm.

He turned to witness a look of dread on her face. "What?" He followed her line of sight and saw the problem. The automaton looked exactly like his sister, and the hum came directly from within it.

TWENTY-TWO

Johanna grabbed her father's hand. "Do you think that could be Ava?"

Ryden Simmdry closed his eyes for a moment. When he opened them, he nodded once. ⌘*I'm quite sure of it.*

"How do we get her back?" she asked.

"Without hurting her," Jackson added.

⌘ *This is very dark magic, indeed. I'm not sure how we will reverse it. Then, there is the larger problem.*

"What's that?" Jackson asked.

⌘ *How do we go about avoiding becoming automatons ourselves? We mustn't get too close. And we must remain on guard.*

"There must be some kind of a spell we can perform together," Johanna said. "We're really strong when we combine our abilities."

⌘ *Yes. Yet we must be careful not to overpower this*

version of Ava, lest it shatter. We do not want to lose her in the process.

Jackson frowned. "How can we tell if Ailill Caomhánach already sucked her lifeforce out of her?"

⌘*I don't think he has. Not completely. I believe the humming is Ava, screaming for help.*

"Don't worry, Squirt," Jackson reached for her arm, "we'll get you out of there."

Johanna grabbed his arm before he made contact. "What part of don't touch anything, don't you understand?"

Jackson scowled. "Are you allowed to do that?"

"What, stop you from becoming a victim?"

"No. Using 'don't'—twice like that—in a sentence."

Johanna narrowed her eyes before realization dawned. She pulled him in for a hug. "Look, I know you're worried about Ava, but my father and I will do everything we can. I just don't want you to rush into anything without thinking."

"I wish I had your powers," Jackson said quietly, his eyes glistening with unshed tears.

Ryden Simmdry placed a hand on Jackson's shoulder. ⌘*When all is said and done here, and Ava is safely back at home, we'll start working on that.*

"Working on it? You mean I can develop powers like Johanna's?"

⌘*Of course. Only a few of the overseers were born with powers. The others had to work hard to develop them. Ask Pru Tellerence. She devoted several millennia to improving her abilities. We shall teach you. It may take time, but we shall prepare you to be better-able to respond to threats. However, right now, we need your strength. And your natural capacity to think innovatively. And we must work quickly. I think time may be of the essence, where Ava is concerned.*

"Do you have something specific in mind?" Johanna asked.

⌘ *We need to find Ailill Caomhánach's original automaton. It may be disguised in some way, but it has to be here. He could not have yet absorbed enough energy to break free from it.*

Jackson nodded. "So, we just have to find that little box."

⌘ *It may no longer appear to be as small as it was. Or the color may have changed. It could very well be hidden behind something else, or among other things.*

"But its magical signature shouldn't have changed," Johanna reasoned. "The same signature that led us to it in the first place must still be there. Right?"

For the first time all evening, Ryden Simmdry smiled. ⌘ *Yes. Just remember, everything else in this room was created with the same magic and will bear the same signature, albeit, a weaker one.*

Ava concentrated. *I can hear Johanna and Jackson. And Ryden Simmdry.* She tried making her voice louder. "Help!" It remained an inarticulate gentle hum. *I hope they find a way to get me out of this thing. My legs ache. I don't know how much longer I can peddle. I feel like the girl Hans Christian Andersen wrote about in,* "The Red Shoes." She imagined herself pedaling until someone chopped off her legs. If she could shudder, she would. She stopped daydreaming long enough to hear Johanna talk about a magic signature. *I hope that works. Please let it work,* she prayed.

*

Logan awakened to the sound of the front door slamming. He dragged himself over to a window and saw his parents loading their golf bags into his father's SUV. For a split-second, he wondered why his own car wasn't in the driveway, then remembered he had parked it in the garage. That moment of uncertainty jolted him awake. He slipped into the shower, ready to jumpstart his day. *I should go to a library and do a little research into the Library of Illumination. Get some background from sources other than Jackson and his family. Maybe there's a little history that doesn't paint the library in a wonderful light.*

Rather than stay local, he drove over to Gainsford to use the Graydon Ransom University Library, which was linked to university libraries across the country. If there was anything to find out, he planned to ferret it out. He arrived just as the assistant librarian unlocked the main door to the building.

"You're here early," she said with a smile. "Big paper due?"

"No. I'm looking for information on an obscure library not too far from here, one that doesn't appear to be part of any major library system."

"An independent, boutique library?"

Logan lifted an eyebrow. "What do you mean by 'boutique'?"

"A library that's unique. One that only houses books on a single topic, or is aimed at a particular segment of society; like a library just for engineers or one that is specifically for children. Would you say this library has a very specific purpose?"

"Definitely."

"How would you sum it up?"

"Surreal. Supernatural. Weird." Logan shrugged. "Regular people don't go there. Apparently, you have to be invited to become a member."

"That definitely fits the bill. What exactly do you need to know?"

"Anything," he paused, "and everything."

"I'm Aubrey, by the way," she said as she led him to the main desk and pinned on her name tag. She pushed a blank index card in his direction. "Write down the name of the library, and I'll launch a search."

JOHANNA, JACKSON, AND Ryden Simmdry faced each other. "Can we join hands?" Johanna asked. "I feel stronger when I'm connected to both of you."

"Of course," her father replied.

Jackson intertwined his fingers with hers.

Johanna concentrated on the magical signature she had followed all along her quest to find the automaton. After a few seconds, she could feel it tugging at the perimeter of her consciousness. With eyes closed, she pictured the room and searched for anomalies as she allowed Ailill Caomhánach to tease her consciousness. Everything within the room seemed to pulse. Her thoughts were pulled from one exhibit to another as if each one commanded her to choose it. Her mind's eye darted from exhibit to exhibit, as energy poured off each one in waves like a throbbing white light. The only exhibit appearing to be stagnant, was the very one they believed Ava to be trapped inside. *Interesting. He doesn't want that exhibit to attract attention. But that's not him.*

Ryden Simmdry had apparently read her thoughts. She could hear him in her head. ⌘*Concentrate, Johanna.*

Look for something that is a little off.

I'm doing my best, she answered, *but I'm getting a malevolent vibe from something that feels like it's trying to absorb our energy.*

"Me, too," Jackson mumbled.

Johanna squeezed his hand. *Talk with your mind. I'll hear you.*

I can never be sure, Jackson said telepathically.

Johanna squeezed his hand again. *You can always be sure. We're connected. 'Amalgamated.' Remember?*

RYDEN SIMMDRY INITIATED a search of his own, however, instead of searching for the original automaton, he probed the *humming* exhibit, looking for a weakness. Releasing Ava would be a risky maneuver. If she was already being absorbed by the automaton, trying to separate her from it could kill her. Yet, allowing it to absorb her being would also kill her. They would have to think it through carefully, and make the best possible decision.

As he used his mind to examine the exhibit, he discovered fluctuations in the amount of energy being emitted by different parts of the automaton. The bicycle and the surrounding scenery gave off a steady flow of energy, while the energy of the actual rider fluctuated wildly. *We must separate the figurine of the girl from the rest of the exhibit.* He cast his mind back to long forgotten sorceries. Perhaps, if they concentrated on focusing a single musical note at the delicate connections between the figure of the girl where it connected to the bicycle, the automaton's brittle outer casing would shatter, leaving the living, breathing life inside, intact.

*

JOHANNA'S MIND SWEPT the room again. Nothing seemed to stand out except the girl on the bicycle. Johanna looked for the point in the room located the furthest from Ava. An Organ Grinder in a feathered red hat slowly turned the handle of a dark wooden box. She dismissed it. She didn't feel the signature.

She returned her attention to the girl pedaling a bicycle. She felt an odd pull. She tried to push it away, until she noticed an empty table behind it, draped with a pink, green, and gold striped tablecloth that appeared to be made out of ribbons. It pulsated like everything else, even though it contained no automata. And it appeared to cast a faint aura. She concentrated on it, and the more she probed, the more it seemed to fight her, until the repellant force broke her concentration and made her drop Jackson and her father's hands.

Without speaking, Ryden Simmdry nodded.

Johanna turned her head toward him, her eyebrows raised. *Now what?*

JACKSON HATED STANDING still when something important needed to be done, but for Ava, he knew staying put and helping Johanna concentrate was his best course of action. So, why did he feel wrenched in the opposite direction? Whenever he tried to still his mind so Johanna could connect to his strength, he felt hazy fingers of smoke trying to grab onto him. It occurred to him that he was using more energy to *fight the freaking fingers* than he had available to share with Johanna.

RYDEN SIMMDRY SENSED Jackson's dilemma. He tried to shield Johanna from it, knowing she needed all her strength to overpower the source of evil, controlling the room. If living for thousands of years had taught him anything, the overseer had definitely learned how to compartmentalize his thoughts. So, while part of his psyche sought a way to free Ava, another part shielded Johanna from Jackson's dilemma, while the rest of his power fought a growing malevolence. Suddenly, Jackson went rigid. Ryden Simmdry redirected a beam of consciousness to determine Jackson's problem and narrowly managed to deflect an evil surge of energy targeting the teen. He stepped away, yanking Jackson toward him—just as a spear of dark energy flashed through the space where Jackson was standing.

Jackson's eyes shot open. He took a deep breath and looked at Ryden Simmdry, nodding once to acknowledge the overseer's assistance.

Jackson's breath shuddered. Beads of perspiration broke out on his forehead. "It's getting hot in here." He removed his sweatshirt and tied it around his waist.

⌘ *We are stronger holding hands.* Ryden Simmdry quickly grabbed Johanna and Jackson's hands. ⌘*It's trying to separate us because we are individually weaker. We must stay connected.*

JOHANNA HAD MISSED the drama unfolding in the room. She was too busy trying to determine their best course of action. *Hurry,* she said telepathically, leading them to the table behind the girl on the bicycle. *We must all concentrate on levitating the cloth, masking what hides beneath this table.*

They took a collective breath before putting their telekinetic powers to use. Slowly the cloth lifted, all the while fighting their attempts to remove it. In a burst of determination, Johanna yanked her head to the side, and the tablecloth flew across the room, landing in a heap on the floor.

While the cloth melted into a bilious pinkish green piece of sludge, a throbbing green box hidden beneath it appeared to grow bigger with palpitations from within.

⌘*It is growing stronger. We must act quickly to disarm it.*

Yes, Johanna agreed, *but how?*

LOGAN WANDERED AROUND the Graydon Ransom University Library, pulling books off the shelves at random. He was bored. Every minute or so, he would look over at the main desk to see if Aubrey was there, and every time he looked, he saw no sign of her.

He circuited the library again, searching for her, but it was as if she had disappeared.

He sighed. *Why did I think this was going to be easy?*

He watched a student approach the desk and saw a door open behind it. A woman his mother's age walked out to assist the student. *I bet that woman knows where Aubrey is.* He approached the desk and waited impatiently for the student to finish explaining what she needed. He kept looking at his watch, hoping she'd see him and get the hint, but she was too absorbed in explaining her research to the librarian.

He wanted to applaud when the door opened again and Aubrey walked out with a stack of books. She nodded toward a table and headed in that direction.

"I thought you forgot about me," Logan half-joked. "It's been a while."

"This Library of Illumination is pretty obscure. There are few references to its actual existence, and many more stating it is the extension of someone's fantasy. However, there are two credible citations that lead me to believe it's real." She pulled out an old book with a worn cover. "I'm amazed this book, which came from the science section, is still on the shelves because by all rights, it's outdated. However, it has relevant information by Albert Einstein that is still pertinent. The author apparently interviewed the physicist about his work. Einstein told him just because you can't see something, it doesn't mean it doesn't exist, famously saying, 'Nature shows us only the tail of the lion. But there is no doubt in my mind that the lion belongs with it even if he cannot reveal himself to the eye all at once because of his huge dimension.' He went on to talk about his membership in a library that defied physical properties, one which many people were oblivious to; one they could not see. However, Einstein said, even though few people knew about the library, it did not mean it didn't exist, in fact, he said it held many wonders, viewed differently through various peoples' eyes, even though each *wonder* was supported by the written word. He said, 'Imagination is more important than knowledge. Knowledge is limited. Imagination encircles the world.'"

"And what is the second credible citation?" Logan asked.

"Benjamin Franklin."

His jaw dropped. "Ben Franklin knew about the Library of Illumination?"

"Yes. He was a founder of the Junto, a club which he and his friends established for the betterment of Philadelphia. The Junto established a library comprised of the groups' own books, kept together in a single space, so they would all have access to them when they met.

"He later stumbled upon the Library of Illumination, which he both criticized and praised. He said he stood in awe of such a place where words could come to life, yet mocked the establishment's doctrine to only allow a select few members to examine its books, thereby depriving the public of the vast wealth of knowledge the Library of Illumination held. He said that edict surpassed the burning of the Library of Alexandria in depravity, because even though it had been decided long ago, it was allowed to stand without update."

Logan pointed at the armful of books Aubrey held. "What's all this other stuff?"

"They mention the Library of Illumination as well, however the statements are not attributed to anyone of note and are not verifiable. But your library appears to be very… colorful. Even if it were not a fact, it would make a remarkable fiction."

TWENTY-THREE

JACKSON STUDIED THE pulsating box that sat in close proximity to his sister, or at least, what he believed to be Ava. "So, we think that's the Re Transfigurator, right?"

Johanna nodded.

⌘ *Yes.*

"Can't we open it like we opened it when we first found it?"

⌘ *We opened it with the key you and Johanna found in the puzzle box.*

Jackson scratched his head as he stared at the floor. Slowly he faced Johanna. "You don't have the key any more, do you?" It was more of a statement than a question.

"It disappeared when Ava disappeared," she answered.

Jackson looked from Johanna to her father to the Re Transfigurator. "Do you think it's in there?"

⌘ *I believe the box opens and remains open when the*

key is inside the lock. Considering the box is closed, I surmise the key is elsewhere.

"Right," Jackson said, but *where* elsewhere? On some other realm, or right here in this room?"

⌘*It would be close. Ailill Caomhánach would want easy access to it.*

"Okay," Jackson sighed. We've identified Ava—"

Johanna cocked her head, narrowing her eyes as she stared at him.

"—we think." Jackson continued. "We think we've identified Ava."

She nodded.

"We've identified Ailill Caomhánach, pretty much, I think." Jackson looked to Johanna for assurance.

She nodded again.

"And now, all we have to do is identify the location of the key."

JOHANNA GRABBED JACKSON and Ryden Simmdry's hands. "We can do that the same way we originally located it." She closed her eyes and concentrated on finding its magical signature. She had the same problem she previously encountered; everything pulsated. It took a while before she sensed an inconsistency in a far corner of the room. "Come." She tugged them away from the girl on a bicycle and the Re Transfigurator.

The trio approached a heavy velvet drape. Instead of releasing her father's hand to pull the drape aside, Johanna mover her chin left to right in a quick motion. The drape swept to one side. Behind it lay a large pile of keys. Not just hundreds of keys, but thousands of them—fitting every description—were piled into a giant heap. Small keys, large ones, some simple, others complex, each one different from the next. "This may take a while."

"A while is too long." Jackson sighed. "Can't you identify the key in question with you mind?"

⌘*Perhaps if we spread them out.* Ryden Simmdry waved his hand over the keys but they resisted his command to move. ⌘*Give me your hand,* he said to his daughter. Together they concentrated on scattering the keys.

LOGAN PUSHED THE last reference book aside. He had a binder filled with notes about the library. It had a colorful, if secretive, history and apparently had been around since time immemorial. One book hypothesized that the Library of Illumination may have been planted on earth by alien intelligence before the time of Adam and Eve, although the author admitted he couldn't fathom it predating the dinosaurs.

Logan pushed his chair back and laced his hands behind his head as he slouched down to think. *If I repeat this information, I'm going to need video behind it. I can probably buy stock footage showing animatronic dinosaurs, Guttenberg's Bible, Ben Franklin and Albert Einstein. Maybe do some fancy graphics of the two men's quotes. And I already have a shot of a book coming to life. That takes care of a lot of it. I just wish I had images of prom night that weren't whitewashed.* He thought back, trying to recall if Jackson had ever mentioned putting security cameras in the library. *I doubt it. No one would want video to get out of what exactly goes on in there.*

He stacked the books, taking them to Aubrey who stood behind the main desk.

"Thank you, Logan. I hope you found what you needed."

"There's a lot here, but I think I was hoping for more visuals."

"I doubt you would find much, even if the library is as old as they say. You said yourself it's private. What blows my mind is that they found cave paintings depicting it."

Logan blinked. "Cave paintings? I didn't see any cave paintings."

"Sure." She took one of the books and paged through it. "Here," she said pushing the book toward him. "Look at the caption."

He stared at a picture he had previously rushed past. It was a rusty looking depiction of a human form standing in front of a crude box with circles in it. Another hazy figure in the painting resembled a man reading a scroll. He glanced down to the caption. *Pre-historic cave painting from the Americas, believed to predate ancient Egyptian scrolls and text, clearly portraying a man reading. Some scholars believe it to be an early depiction of what may be the first collection of accumulated knowledge, known as the Library of Illumination.*

Logan hadn't realized his mouth had dropped open until he snapped it shut—his teeth audibly clicking together. He looked at Aubrey. "Can I interview you?"

Aubrey's eyes widened. "Why would you want to interview me? I just pulled the reference material that matched your search criteria. I don't know anything about it."

"I just want you to tell me on camera how you felt when you first saw this particular reference, and the citations from Einstein and Ben Franklin. You said yourself that you'd never heard of the Library of Illumination. You must have formed some kind of opinion seeing this, even if it's only to repeat that you'd never heard of the library before and are surprised to see cave paintings of it."

"It's an unusual request, and it's not my place to comment."

"Please," Logan begged. "You'd really be helping me out with," he paused for a microsecond, "a project I'm working on." He couldn't tell her it was for a newscast. She'd certainly balk at that.

She looked around him. "Where's your camera?"

He thought of grabbing his camera equipment from the back of his car but that might scare her off. He reached into his pocket and pulled out his cell phone. "This is all I need."

The corners of her mouth turned up a little as she let out the breath she had been holding. "All right. What do you want me to do?"

He positioned her, holding the book open—with the cave painting facing out toward him and asked her to point to it and paraphrase the caption. Then he interviewed her about Einstein and Franklin and took video of her pointing to the pages where their quotes about the library appeared. He took shots of the book covers and close ups of the text. When they were done, he broke into a huge smile. "That was great. Can I buy you lunch for being so helpful?"

Aubrey blushed. "Thank you, but I need to work straight through until 2:00 pm. It's only 11:30."

"I can come back. Okay? I'll see you later?"

She smiled. "Okay."

"Great. Two o'clock, then. I'll pick you up out front." Logan headed for his car. He wanted to get home and check his video. And just in case he needed to re-shoot anything, he'd be having lunch with Aubrey. *I'm a freaking genius.*

JACKSON LOOKED DOWN at his hands, turning them palm side up. *I guess they don't need me for this.* He took a few steps away and stared down the aisle at the girl on a bicycle. He could see a corner of the Re Transfigurator sticking out behind it, its green glow—distinctive. He looked back at Johanna and her father. Working together, they appeared to be having some success, moving the keys.

Jackson sighed. He turned back to look down the aisle again. As he stared, his eyes narrowed until he squinted. *Is the Re Transfigurator growing smaller?* As he watched, it seemed to shrink out of sight.

AVA FELT HER consciousness slipping. *No. No. No. I cannot let whomever did this to me win. I have to stay alert. I have to fight him.* She paused. *Where are Jackson and Johanna? They were here before, but now I don't hear them. I hope they didn't leave.* "Help!" she screamed. "Don't leave me here!" But like before, her words only sounded like a faint hum, drowned out by the sound of the bicycle pedaling and the wheels turning.

GOTCHA! JOHANNA CONCENTRATED on lifting one key away from the others, slowly pulling it toward her. As it came closer, she felt renewed strength and knew her father was assisting. A moment later she reached out and grasped it from the air.

"You've got to see this," she heard Jackson say and turned to see him standing several feet away.

She approached her co-curator in time to see him scowl.

He turned to her. "It's back. For a while there, the Re Transfigurator thingy was shrinking, but it just grew back to nearly the same size. It was like a balloon that deflated, then re-inflated." His shoulders sagged. "Just for a moment there, I thought our luck had changed."

She smiled at him. "It did change. First of all, we now have this." She held up a nondescript key. "And I'm willing to bet the reason why the automaton holding Ailill Caomhánach shrank, is because he was draining his power to fight us off while we searched for the key."

Jackson's eyes lit up. "So, we're good to go."

⌘ *Not quite,* Ryden Simmdry interjected. ⌘ *There are several considerations we must all remain aware off. First, Ava is in a very fragile state, and we must not do anything to weaken her condition. Second, we may have the key, however, Ailill Caomhánach will ensure inserting it into the Re Transfigurator is as difficult as he can make it. And third, we have no idea what dimension we are in, so we have to make sure we do nothing to compromise it, lest we destroy our ability to return home.*

Jackson stood speechless, his face forlorn.

Johanna sympathized with him. "We will have to do our very best then, to be careful."

⌘ *Indeed.*

Johanna and Jackson split up from Ryden Simmdry. The teens approached the Re Transfigurator from one side while the overseer drew near from the opposite direction.

⌘ *Wait.* The master of the overseers removed a small drawstring pouch from his pocket and held it in his hand as he began chanting. Ever since Pru Tellerence lost her arm in a battle against Terroria, the overseers had begun carrying protective crystals and salts with them at all times. The gems worked their magic to protect the carrier without having to be removed from the pouch. The contents' power was even stronger when used in conjunction with an incantation. Ryden Simmdry opened the pouch and pinched some of the yellow salt between his fingertips, removing it from the bag. As he continued to chant, he sprinkled it on the Re Transfigurator, which caused it to rock violently.

Ryden Simmdry's chanting became louder as he repeated the process. The box began to shrink but continued to quake as the spirit inside fought against the master's power.

THE AUTOMATON NEXT to Johanna and Jackson contained a shepherdess holding a staff. Jackson stared at the staff for a moment, removed his sweatshirt from around his waist, and used it to wrench the staff free. In a lightning fast move, he jammed it into the box immediately dropping the stick. The box tipped over, exposing the keyhole on the bottom.

"Showoff," Johanna said sternly, although Jackson could see the hint of a smile. Then her eyes narrowed. "Did the stick heat up when it touched the box? You dropped it pretty quickly."

"No. I just didn't want to get sucked in like Ava."

She grabbed his hand. "Good thinking. Do you mind if I use your sweatshirt to hold the key while I try to insert it into the box?"

"Be my guest." He swooped down and grabbed it with his free hand, quickly pulling it away from the stick.

"I need you to continue holding my hand for this. I need your strength."

"I'm with you all the way."

Johanna took a deep breath as she inched closer to the box.

Ryden Simmdry's chants grew louder still, and he showered the box with salt a third time.

The box emitted a loud groaning sound, and became smaller still as the light it emitted started to fade.

Johanna lurched forward and jammed the key in the keyhole.

Jackson pulled her back to safety as the box popped open, righting itself in the process, and narrow bolts of lightning shot out of the rapidly expanding figure of Ailill Caomhánach.

TWENTY-FOUR

THE FIGURE OF Ailill Caomhánach grew to about three and a half feet, not the full measure of a man, but larger than the original figurine when first discovered.

⌘*Ailill Caomhánach, you have regained some power.* Ryden Simmdry resumed chanting, sprinkling more salt on the former overseer. The figure shrank several inches. A black cloud tinged with a deep purple light began to build around the automata, causing it to look more menacing even with a reduction in size.

Jackson took a step back, pulling Johanna with him. "That can't be good."

⚡*I will evolve much more before the day is done.*

Ryden Simmdry changed his chant and the salt he sprinkled turned from yellow to cobalt. ⌘*That cannot be allowed. Release the girl.*

⚡*I have not completely drained her life force. Once I do, I will surely capture one of you and do the same thing.*

⌘ *You have no rights here. You gave up the privilege of being an overseer long ago. I cannot allow you to disrupt the Illumini Constellation.*

⇧ *You have no say in the matter.* Ailill Caomhánach's crystal eyes changed color from yellow-green to a violent violet. ⇧ *I am not alone. I have allies.* The dark cloud surrounding him grew.

⌘ *You have no allies here. You are merely using a mirroring spell to make your power look enhanced.*

⇧ *You cannot defeat me, Overseer, I am stronger than you.* The dark cloud sparked a needle-like bolt of lightning, which flew past Ryden Simmdry, narrowly missing him.

The overseer did not allow it to divert his concentration. ⌘ *You were vanquished after you nearly destroyed Lumina. And captured again when you manifested as Attila the Hun. You are an old entity losing your grip on power and sanity. You are still evil; however, your malevolence is not as strong as before. None of your confederates remain in existence.*

⇧ *I will destroy you.*

Johanna felt the hostility mount between her father and the evil first overseer. Neither showed signs of weakening.

⌘ *You will be completely eradicated,* Ryden Simmdry told Ailill Caomhánach as he continued to shower salt on the automaton. The salt color changed to green.

The dark cloud that had previously surrounded the malevolent figure, burst into flames but did not engulf him. Instead, they flared as if to protect him.

Johanna could physically feel Jackson's stress growing. His grip on her hand tightened and she could hear his teeth grate. She leaned over and whispered, "While my father keeps Ailill Caomhánach occupied, let's see what we can do about Ava. Remember, no sudden moves."

Johanna heard a very faint whisper inside her head. ⌘*If Ava has lost more than fifty percent of herself to the automaton, separating her from it may kill her. Proceed cautiously.* She looked at Jackson and saw no change in his demeanor. Her father had apparently spoken only to her.

Very slowly, they shifted position to study the girl pedaling the bicycle. Her eyes gave the only hint that Ava existed within. They were the same bright blue color as Ava's and instead of looking like glass, Johanna could sense fear in them. She concentrated on directing her telepathic voice only to Ava. *Ava, if you can hear me, say something. Scream, shout, sing, make any kind of noise you can.* The automaton gave off an intermittent hum.

Jackson leaned forward, his forehead creasing. "Do you hear that?" he said turning to Johanna. It sounds like Morse Code." He concentrated on the sound. "S-O-S." He sniffed back tears. "We have to get her out of there."

Johanna squeezed Jackson's hand and directed her thoughts to him telepathically. *She's still with us.*

Logan didn't have to wait long before Aubrey emerged from the library. He got out of his car and ran around to open the door for her.

"This car is so cute," she said as she climbed inside.

"Kind of like you," he replied, smiling. He drove to the Meister Burgerie, which wasn't far from campus. It was a popular place that usually had a line out the door. However, it was a Saturday during summer and it was later than two o'clock, so the place was quieter than during a regular week day. The hostess led the pair to a corner table and told them their waiter would be right with them.

Aubrey checked out the people at the nearby tables. "I'm surprised we got seated as soon as we walked in. I rarely come here because it's always so packed."

"Their burgers are the best." Logan put down the skinny menu the hostess had handed him. "And their fries are even better."

"I rarely eat red meat. I'm trying to switch to vegan. But the smell in here makes me want to dig in."

"You can get anything on the menu made with an Impossible Burger. That way, you get all the flavor and none of the meat. And it comes with the fries, which are the best I've ever tasted." He winked at her. "Trust me."

On the opposite side of the Meister Burgerie, Ava's friends Mackenzie and Hailey, as well as her nemesis Keli Gaughren stared at Logan while whispering among themselves.

"I saw Ava holding his hand at the beach—gazing at him longingly. I wonder if she knows she's not his *paramount paramour*?"

Mackenzie frowned. "I'm not going to tell her we saw him with another girl. If there's nothing between them she won't care. But if there is, she'll be crushed. I don't want to be the person who does that to her." She turned toward Hailey.

"Don't look at me," Hailey replied, shaking her head. "I'm not telling her."

"Well, I think she deserves to know," Keli said with the hint of a smile. "And if you two, who claim to be her closest friends, won't tell her, I will, if only to save her from further embarrassment." She pulled out her cell phone. "What's her number?"

Mackenzie choked on a french fry.

"You're going to call her now?" Hailey asked in a squeaky voice.

"Of course. What good is telling her what's going on, after the horse has left the barn. This way, she can be proactive if she wants." *Or embarrassed to death, which would be more likely. Either way, it will be grossly entertaining.*

Mackenzie pushed her dish away. "I'm not giving you her number."

"Neither am I," Hailey chimed in.

Keli scowled, then suddenly smiled. "I guess you forgot how you got here. If you want a ride back home, you'll give me her phone number."

Hailey opened her bag and pulled out money, throwing it on the table. "I'll take the bus home."

"Me, too," Mackenzie said, following her lead.

The two girls walked out of the restaurant together.

A waiter walked over and placed the check on the table. The total amount due was more than covered by the money Mackenzie and Hailey had left. Keli added a couple of bucks for the tip and left, feeling pretty sure she had Ava's cell phone number written down at home.

As she drove past the bus stop, she couldn't help rolling down the window and shouting "LOSERS!" before she burst out laughing.

RYDEN SIMMDRY FELT like he was making progress, reducing Ailill Caomhánach's power. But he could feel his own power waning. *I cannot let Johanna down* he thought to himself. *Or Ava. Or Jackson. Together, we will beat this. I just hope my brilliant daughter has the ability to set Ava free, while I hold off this monster.*

What Ryden Simmdry didn't know was that

Ailill Caomhánach did have an ally—Grynsmiþ—a dark power from the Decahedron System whom he had been conspiring with when they both become trapped. At the first indication of trouble, Grynsmiþ had called on the power of *scinncræft*, rendering himself invisible. It didn't prevent him from becoming trapped, but Grynsmiþ could provide Ailill Caomhánach with unexpected assistance.

LOGAN DROVE AUBREY home after their lunch together, making sure to get her phone number and take note of her address. The lunch had been a pleasant one, and Aubrey had hung onto his every word as he chatted about being a reporter for GRUNT. He told her all about starting *The Elliott Report*, and his plans for the future, at first holding nothing back because he never expected to see her again. However, there was something immensely likeable about Aubrey. She challenged him with questions, rather than rebukes when she didn't agree with something he said. And she laughed easily. So, while he had planned on Aubrey being a means to the end, he now wondered if she might play a part in the long game. *What would Aubrey say if she knew all about the Library of Illumination?*

His thoughts instantly shifted to Ava. *She's cute but she's young. And she's Jackson's sister, so there's no future there. But Aubrey? She's got promise.*

THE GALAXY THAT hosted the Decahedron System existed in the shadows on the far side of the known universe.

Being one of the earliest galaxies, it contained several civilized worlds, however, only the population of one world, Decada, achieved both the technological knowledge for interstellar travel and perfected the extraordinary power of sorcery—it's people so advanced, they quickly became feared by the worlds they conquered.

The system's existence, early in the evolution of the universe, was often marked with upheaval, for one of the more prominent traits of its people was boundless greed. It was a given, like the nose on a human face. And it meant war and tumult, first among the planets in near proximity, and then reaching further out to other galaxies.

Midway during this power-hungry maelstrom, a young man named Grynsmiþ made his mark as one of the most enterprising sorcerers of Decada, if not *the* greatest one alive. Making items appear and disappear was child's play to him. He could move objects of massive size with the flick of a wrist. Casting spells required few words and fewer potions. His magic appeared to stream naturally from his fingertips. He could turn stones into precious metals and water into potent elixirs. And one of his more unique abilities was the mastery he held over the power of *scinncræft*—the ability to become invisible. His powers soon caught the eye of the masters of his planet—the commanders who waged war among the stars.

Many of them recognized the power Grynsmiþ would wield during warfare. However, few were aware of the sorcerer's greatest skill. Indeed, Grynsmiþ himself had not yet become aware of it. His eventual claim to fame, and fury, would be immortality. No one else on Decada had that advantage.

Hints among the Sages' whispers said Grynsmiþ was conceived during a galactic collision, during which gravitational interaction forced the zygote that held the seed of his essence to turn inside out, changing its morphology. His mother had died giving birth, and his father had died taking life during an intergalactic war when Grynsmiþ was still a boy. So, the young sorcerer was raised in a military institution, where his fair to middling intellect was far superseded by his increasing show of powers.

To say Grynsmiþ was ignorant would be incorrect. He had an average level of intelligence, but not the mental capacity and brainpower you might expect from a great leader. However, his propensity for magic launched him to a level of prominence, that his intellectual capacity alone would never have attained. And so, it came to pass that the premier general of Decada was not the smartest man in the military but the one commanding the most supernatural prowess. Other generals used their intellect to try to knock Grynsmiþ from his pedestal, but the sorcerer used his magic to undermine his enemies and create bonds with more like-minded individuals.

One of those like-minded individuals was a wizard named Ailill Caomhánach. Grynsmiþ met him on a world he had just conquered. Unlike the other deposed leaders whom he had sentenced to an early death, there was something about this wizard that the premier general liked. He felt an alliance might be in order, as long as the wizard understood that Grynsmiþ would be in charge.

Ailill Caomhánach recognized Grynsmiþ's strengths and weaknesses immediately. He knew he could implant thoughts in the premier general's brain, bending them until the Decadian sorcerer believed they were his own thoughts and ideas. He also realized that in a test of power alone, he could not come close to Grynsmiþ's abilities. But that didn't bother him. If he could control the general's mind, he could easily make use of his impressive powers to his own advantage. It would be the perfect symbiotic relationship. Grynsmiþ would never grasp that the real reason why he spared Ailill Caomhánach's life was simply because the wizard planted that idea in his brain.

Ailill Caomhánach used some of his power to delve into Grynsmiþ's consciousness and measure his strength. The premier general remained in stasis. His army had been powerful at one time but his light appeared to be diminished, at least for the time being.

It is time to awaken him. However, the first overseer could not be sure what to expect from the sleeping sorcerer. Unfortunately, Ailill Caomhánach didn't have much of a choice. He needed more power, quickly. The spells and incantations being performed by the current master of the overseers prevented him from drawing lifeforce from the girl pedaling the bicycle.

He studied his options while doing his best to hold off *the meddling Ryden Simmdry.* The scheming wizard had little chance against the current Master and the young woman who accompanied him. She literally bristled with power. *I must not underestimate my opponents.* However, he sensed no such power in the young man who stood by her side.

If I plan it right, I can perform a split-second lightning extraction of life force from the one called Jackson before anyone realizes what is happening. He will provide much more power than the girl pedaling the bicycle.

TWENTY-FIVE

J OHANNA CLOSED HER eyes and focused her power on emitting magical pulses toward the girl on the bicycle. Like an ultrasound machine, she examined the pulses as they bounced back from the automaton to map out Ava's living tissue and active neural pathways. The feedback she received exhilarated her. While Ava appeared to be encased inside the mechanical device, her body seemed whole. She found Ava's heartbeat and brain activity more worrisome. *Poor Ava must be on the brink of collapse. I've got to bust her out of there.*

She turned to Jackson. "Stand behind me and hold me as tightly as you can. I need full surface contact."

"You want 'full surface contact?' Here? Why can't you ask me for that at home when we're alone?"

Johanna opened her mouth to reply, but Jackson forestalled her words by grabbing her to his chest and wrapping his arms tightly around her waist. "Just remember how accommodating I am."

She refocused on Ava and began chanting, "*Aheorde! Aheorde! Aheorde! Āscēadest mægden.*" She repeated it over and over, her volume increasing each time. *Set her free! Set her free! Set her free! Release the girl.*

JACKSON SENSED THE tension building in Johanna as he clutched her to his body. Every time she repeated the line, he could feel her pulling forward—away from him—but he held her tightly. *No way these things are gonna get you, babe. You're mine.*

"*Aheorde! Aheorde! Aheorde!*" she chanted more loudly. "*Āscēadest mægden. Aheorde! Aheorde! Aheorde! Āscēadest mægden. Aheorde! Aheorde! Aheorde! Āscēadest mægden.*" Johanna's body pulled harder, but Jackson kept a firm grip. *Have at her!*

Johanna added another command to her chant, her body temperature increasing along with the speed and volume of her chanting. Jackson could feel himself breaking into a sweat as he held her.

"*Aheorde! Aheorde! Aheorde! Āscēadest mægden. Háligest. Aheorde! Aheorde! Aheorde! Āscēadest mægden. Háligest. Aheorde! Aheorde! Aheorde! Āscēadest mægden. Háligest.*" *Set her free! Set her free! Set her free! Release the girl. Heal her.*

Jackson heard Johanna repeat the same words so many times, he began chanting them too, his rich baritone harmonizing with her dulcet, yet demanding tone. "*Aheorde! Aheorde! Aheorde! Āscēadest mægden. Háligest. Aheorde! Aheorde! Aheorde! Āscēadest mægden. Háligest. Aheorde! Aheorde! Aheorde! Āscēadest mægden. Háligest.*" As they chanted in unison, Jackson could feel the pull grow stronger. He dug in his heels. *There's no way this thing is going to beat us!*

RYDEN SIMMDRY FELT weaker than he had in many millennia. Although he used every fiber of his being to defeat Ailill Caomhánach, the malevolent figure shrank much more slowly than before. The one thing that helped was seeing the cloud surrounding the automata dissipate. He could hear his daughter, Johanna, chanting but dared not look her way for fear of losing his battle with the first overseer. *She can fend for herself. She's strong and has Jackson to back her up.* The master of the overseers didn't know how much longer he could last but knew he had to duel to the death for Johanna, Jackson, and especially Ava's sakes.

AILILL CAOMHÁNACH COULD feel his resolve weakening. He could not continue fighting unless he replenished his power, and he could not recharge unless he stopped fighting. He realized he would have to change the dynamics of the battle in order to win. If he employed cunning, he might find time to recharge before the next test of power. *I must let them believe they have beat me. It is the only way I can stop wasting my energy, engaging with this overseer rather than building my strengths. If I play dead, it will both give me time to refocus, as well as awaken Grynsmiþ.*

In the blink of an eye, the wizard allowed himself to shut down completely. He sank back into the Re Transfigurator, dragging the essence of Grynsmiþ with him, allowing the lid to slam shut above them. The rapid reduction of the automata to a miniscule size—smaller than a baby pea—caused a pseudo black hole that momentarily sucked anything loose in the near vicinity toward its point of existence. Suddenly, everything around it crashed to the floor.

A STUNNED RYDEN SIMMDRY felt himself being pulled forward for a moment before a giant weight released him. Rivulets of perspiration rolled down his face as his chanting faded. He looked for the Re Transfigurator but did not see it among the debris, cluttering the area where it once stood. He turned to Johanna and Jackson, watching their attempt to extricate Ava from an automaton. Walking over, he grasped Jackson from behind and joined the chant, concentrating on making Ava whole.

The added power of Ryden Simmdry—even in his diminished capacity—added exponentially to the spell Johanna was performing.

LOGAN SPENT THE rest of the afternoon writing his exposé about the Library of Illumination. He had already put together a lot, but now that he was armed with the third-party information he had learned in the GRU library, he wanted to rethink each segment.

He re-edited the first package—the one Jennifer had asked him to take down. He added new visuals of a book coming to life inside the library, as well as a soundbite by Ava and information about membership in the library attributed to Albert Einstein that backed up its uniqueness. He used graphics of Einstein's own words blending into a picture of the physicist. As he watched the playback, he smiled. *Slick!* The re-edited story far surpassed the original one in content and design and made Logan eager to edit the other four segments he planned to use.

So, that introduces the library and the debacle of

prom night. What I need are the pictures that Jackson's mom took. He wondered if they were still on her camera, or if the overseers had erased them? There was only one way to check. *I'll have to stop by for a visit, preferably when Ava is in school, that way I don't have to deal with her as well.* His brow crinkled. *It would be good if Jackson and Johanna were away at school as well, although that might be tougher to pull off.* The fact that it was a weekend didn't help.

He stood up and grabbed a jacket off the back of his chair. *Chris. It's a Saturday night. I'll bet anything he's at Piccolo Italia right now with his friends.* He stopped short. *What if Ava is with him?* His mind ceased to work. He didn't want Ava to see him, although he was pretty sure he could lie his way out of being home by saying he *didn't like* the school he had visited and returned early. It wasn't that he liked Ava in a romantic kind of way. But he didn't dislike her. And he might need her to back up what she said if things got ugly when he aired his *exposé. I'll just lie to Ava. It's never failed me in the past. People are so gullible.* He grabbed his car keys and headed out the door.

Boom! Johanna, Jackson, and Ryden Simmdry were showered with debris. Standing in front, Johanna took the brunt of the force, finding her right forearm slashed and her nose bloodied. It took a moment for her to return to her senses.

The girl pedaling the bicycle no longer existed. Detritus from the mechanism and shreds of the figurine's costume littered the area. Johanna felt a tear roll down her cheek before she noticed something move under the wreckage where the automaton once stood.

"Ava!" she called out as she elbowed Jackson in the gut and broke away from him and her father. She rushed to the moving form and lowered herself to the floor.

"I knew you'd save me," Ava whispered, before passing out.

"We have to get her out of here," Johanna told the others.

⌘ *That may not be as easy as it sounds.*

"No. No. No!" Jackson shouted, tears rolling down his face.

Johanna reached out to him, "We'll find a way."

But Jackson just stood there, obviously overwhelmed.

"She's alive, Jackson. It's okay."

Jackson shook his head and sucked in a sob. "She not whole." He pointed toward his sister's leg. "Her foot is gone."

Johanna gasped.

Ryden Simmdry quickly crouched down, checking for further signs of injury. ⌘ *That seems to be all.* The overseer stared at Jackson, demanding the teen make eye contact with him. ⌘ *We can fix this, Jackson. Like we did with Pru Tellerence's arm. We will make Ava whole again.*

"Can you make her mind whole again?" Jackson asked. "She's been through hell. What if she suffers from something like PTSD? Or becomes scared of her own shadow? Or suicidal?"

⌘ *One step at a time, son. Ava is alive. We can ask the Adventurans to replace her foot. We can work with her to restore her courage and rebuild her sense of safety. But it will take time and we must proceed slowly.*

Jackson picked up his sister, cradling her in his arms as he touched his forehead to hers.

Johanna felt more tears prickling her eyes and blinked them away before turning to her father. "What did you mean when you said leaving may not be as easy as it sounds?"

⌘ *It depends on what dimension we are in. This place could be anywhere.*

"Yet we were able to find it without too much trouble. Can't it be on Fantasia?"

⌘ *The exterior was on Fantasia. The interior might not be. However, there is wisdom in your belief that we are close to home. Ailill Caomhánach could not have had more than minimal strength when he transported Ava here, and creating all of this would have taken much of his power. In retrospect, I must concur with your extrapolation.*

Johanna placed a hand on Jackson's back and steered him toward the door where they had made their entrance. Instead of a door, they found a wall of heavy draping. Johanna pulled back each panel, exposing nothing but bare wall. For several minutes, she and Ryden Simmdry searched for the door.

The longer they looked, the angrier Johanna became, finally shaking her head. "Enough of this." She clapped her hands and the room flashed white.

The blinding light caused Jackson to bury his face against his sister's neck and groan. "Was that necessary?"

When the intensity of the light faded, the heavy drapery had fallen away from the walls and all that remained was a faint outline where the door should be.

⌘ *Of course.* Ryden Simmdry reached for the edge of it and appeared to grab something invisible in his hand, pulling it toward him. Suddenly, the sounds of gulls surrounded them, and they could smell the ocean.

The storm had abated, and the shoreline was bathed in moonlight. ⌘ *Outside, quickly.*

They exited the building and walked across the parking lot before the overseer placed his hands on Johanna and Jackson's shoulders and transported them back to the Library of Illumination.

PRU TELLERENCE PUSHED up from her perch on the loveseat in the living room of the hotel suite. Niamh twisted around and jumped in front of her, rushing toward Jackson and Ava.

"You found her," Niamh said. "Is she all right? Is she hungry? Why is she sleeping? She is sleeping, isn't she? Ava," she said gently, placing her hand on her daughter's arm. "Ava," she repeated more loudly, shaking the girl's shoulder.

Niamh felt compelled to look at Ryden Simmdry. ⌘ *She has had a rough time of it. She needs rest.*

"But she's okay, right?" She quickly turned away to look at Jackson, spotting the tear tracks on his face. Slowly, the color drained from her face. The volume of her questions and her urgency faded. Her voice came out as barely a whisper, "What is it you're not telling me?"

Jackson laid Ava on the sofa.

"Remove her shoes, Jackson, or they'll dirty—" She never finished the sentence. How could she, after noticing her daughter's missing foot. "Has a doctor…" She couldn't finish what she wanted to say. Visions of Ava running down the stairs; dancing across the room; trying to trip one of her brothers when she was angry, flooded her mother's brain. Like her son, tears soon tracked down Niamh's face.

TWENTY-SIX

JACKSON LOOKED AROUND the room. "Where's Chris?"

"He was wound tighter than a watch spring. I told him to go out with his friends. I said you'd call his cell with news of Ava as soon as you got back."

Jackson pulled out his phone and punched in Chris's number.

Chris answered almost immediately. "Jax, did you find her?"

"Yeah."

"Is she okay?"

"Can you come home? Now?"

"What do you mean? Is. She. Okay?"

Jackson paused. He didn't want to tell Chris about Ava's missing foot over the phone. "Just come home," he said, before disconnecting.

*

Ava felt like she was floating on a cloud. *I'm not pedaling. Finally. Now I can sleep.* She stiffened. *What if I'm dead. I don't want to be dead!* She tried forcing her eyes to open. It was harder than she expected. She was so very tired her eyelids wouldn't obey her command. She could hear faint murmuring around her. *People. I have to open my eyes and tell these people I'm not dead.* She struggled in her climb to wakefulness. *I can do this. I HAVE to do this.*

Logan walked into Piccolo Italia and had no trouble spotting Chris slamming his hand against the top of the table. He watched as Chris jumped up and fished car keys out of his jeans pocket.

"Leaving so soon?" Logan threw an arm around Chris's shoulder. "I thought we could talk. I'm buying."

"Can't. Something's going on at home. I've got to leave. Now."

Logan was torn as Chris flew out the door. Part of him wanted to go with Chris to see what was going on. *Maybe something juicy happened at the library.* But the last thing he wanted to do was run into one of the other Roth siblings. Still, it might have been an opportunity to send himself the photos from Mrs. Roth's phone. *Damn.*

Chris rushed in the front door of the hotel suite, half worried about Ava, half mad at Jackson for not telling him what was going on over the phone. He caught sight of his sister passed out on the couch, covered by a blanket.

"Well, I guess she's alive," Chris muttered. "Her chest's moving, so she's still breathing."

"Christopher!" His mother's voice sounded sharp. "Don't talk like that."

Pru Tellerence reached for him, pulling him in for an impromptu hug and directed her thoughts at him only. ★*Nerves are a little frayed, right now. Everything should turn out alright, but you may want to think before you speak.*

Chris slumped down into a chair. "It's Jackson's fault. He wouldn't tell me what's going on."

Jackson grabbed his arm and tugged him to a standing positing. "This way, little brother. Let's talk." Jackson dragged him into their bedroom and closed the door. He pushed Chris onto the bed. "Ava is alive. Johanna's parents say she should be fine physically, but she's mentally exhausted. They said we need to let her rest for now without trying to ask her questions."

"So, where was she?"

"Trapped inside a machine that looked like a moving figure of a person."

"Like the animatronics at Disney World?"

"Except these are different. They're much older. Practically ancient. They're called automata but they're different from the ones you might see in a museum, because she was trapped inside something magical. It held her prisoner and was absorbing her life force, making her become part of it. We got her back. Except... not all of her."

Chris's head jerked. "What the hell is that supposed to mean?"

"She doesn't know it yet, but one of her feet is missing." Jackson ran his hands through his hair, making a mess of it. "It already looks like she might suffer some psychological damage from the ordeal, but learning she's lost an appendage might put her over the top."

"So, is she... like... gonna need crutches or something? A wheelchair?"

"Maybe. For a while at least."

"Just for a while?' Chris's mouth gaped for a moment. "It's not like she can grow a new foot."

"Ryden Simmdry says she can get a new prosthetic foot on Adventura."

"Adventura." Chris rubbed his face. "What's that? Another realm?"

"Yeah."

"So, they're going to fit her with one of those metal things like you see in the Paralympics?"

"More like something that we won't be able to tell is fake. Like Pru Tellerence's arm."

"What about her arm?"

"A Terrorian blew it off with a decimator during a battle."

Chris's eyes widened. "I didn't even notice. She touched me with her good arm and I never even notice the other one."

"No, Chris. She grabbed you with her prosthetic hand and arm."

"No way that was fake."

"The Adventurans are very good at what they do. Ryden Simmdry says they'll do the same for Ava and after a while, she'll hardly remember it's fake."

Chris remained silent for a moment, taking it all in. "So, she's going to get to travel off-world. What about me? Am I the only Roth destined to stay shackled to Earth?"

Jackson's face took on the color of a pomegranate. "First of all, she's going because she lost a foot after becoming a victim. Second, in the Illumini System, this world is known as Fantasia, not Earth. And third, I should break your nose for selfishly thinking of yourself and not Ava."

"It could have been me as easily as it was Ava."

"Yeah, but it wasn't, so stop thinking only of yourself."

'Why is everyone picking apart every little thing I say?"

"Probably because you're an idiot."

Jackson opened the bedroom door and walked back into the living room. Chris waited a moment before following.

"What was that all about?" Niamh asked.

"Chris said I wouldn't tell him what was going on," Jackson said. "So, I told him what's going on."

Niamh looked at her younger son, her eyebrow raised expectantly.

"What he said," Chris mumbled. He didn't want to say what he was really thinking. He'd probably get in trouble for whatever he said, so he decided to keep his mouth shut.

That's Jackson… and Chris, I think. I can do this. Once again Ava struggled to open her eyes. This time, she felt her lashes flutter, but the light burned them, so she clamped her lids shut again. *No. No. No. They'll embalm me if they think I'm dead. What if I become a zombie? I have to open my eyes.*

Johanna rushed over to the sofa, sitting on the floor next to Ava. "She's trying to open her eyes. I saw her lashes move." She took Ava's hand.

Niamh joined her on the floor and placed a hand on Ava's shoulder. "Ava, it's Mom. Can you hear me?"

There was no immediate response.

"Come on, Squirt," Jackson said. "Don't keep us all waiting. We want to order room service and you won't get anything if you don't wake up and tell us what you want."

Chris nudged his brother. "Who's being selfish now?"

"I'm not being selfish," Jackson said under his breath. "I'm giving her a reason to wake up."

"You've got to wake up, Ava," Johanna said, "just so you can tell your brothers to stuff it. And I'm not talking about donuts from room service."

Ava's eyelashes fluttered again, but this time they stayed open.

"Paris-Brest," she whispered. "And hot cocoa."

"Hah!" Chris exclaimed. "Johanna may not have been talking 'room service,' but Ava is."

Jackson ruffled his sister's hair. "I always knew you wouldn't let a good snack go uneaten."

Ava sighed. "You'll have to carry me to the table. I can't get there on my own."

The room suddenly became quiet.

JACKSON STIFFENED. *SHE knows.* "Sure, Squirt."

"I'm too tired to walk there myself."

His eyes narrowed. "O-kay," he said, hesitantly.

Ava tried to push herself up to a sitting position. "Can someone help me sit up?"

Jackson scooped her up blanket and all, and carried her to the table where he placed her in her usual chair. "I'm willing to provide full service for my favorite sister," he said, pushing her chair in.

"I'm your only sister," she answered.

"That is not my fault. Take it up with Mom."

"Stop it, the two of you," Mrs. Roth admonished. "We have guests."

"Not guests," Johanna chimed in, "family. And I hope by now they love us all, no matter what we say or how we behave."

OVER PASTRIES, EVERYONE gently questioned Ava about being captured, and she told them everything she could recall. What she didn't remember was breaking free of the automaton. One minute, she said she was so tired she wanted to die, and the next she felt she needed to prove she wasn't dead, so her family wouldn't bury her alive.

CHRIS REACHED FOR the last Paris-Brest donut on the tray. "I don't know how you got yourself into this predicament, Ava. Everyone says you're smarter than me but that didn't stop you from getting into major trouble. Just remember this the next time you want to tell me I'm dumb."

"All I was doing was dusting shelves. I shouldn't have ended up in trouble. I was being productive."

"Where *was* Ava being held?" Niamh asked.

⌘ *Not far from here. According to Johanna and Jackson, you're familiar with the Chalet at the Dunes.*

"That's where I was?" Ava squeaked. "It didn't look like that to me."

⌘ *That's because it was well disguised by magic. And at first, I wasn't sure that was actually where you were being held, because Ailill Caomhánach could have taken you to another dimension. We were lucky he was still in a weakened state because that meant he couldn't take you far.*

"So, I never left Fantasia," Ava sighed. "That's kind of a bummer."

"What are you whining about?" Chris asked. "You're going to get to go to Adventura for a new foot."

Almost everyone at the table gasped.

Ava *tsked* and shook her head. "What are you talking about?"

The color drained from Chris's face. "Uh…"

Johanna leaned forward. "How do you feel, Ava?"

"Tired, I guess."

"Do you have any pain?" Johanna continued.

Ava narrowed her eyes. "No."

"Good. It sounds like—physically—you're feeling okay."

"Yeah." Ava put her fork down. "What's going on?"

Johanna asked Jackson to swap seats, so she could sit next to Ava. She placed her hand on Ava's arm. "You know, that thing was trying to make you part of it?"

Ava shuddered. "Yeah. I remember."

⌘*Johanna, perhaps this isn't the best time.*

"Of course, it is. Chris set it up perfectly. And Ava deserves to know." She turned back toward the younger girl. "Ailill Caomhánach didn't fail entirely. He managed to absorb a part of you."

Ava grinned. "This is a joke, right."

"No, Ava. It's not a joke, but the news isn't all bad. What he took from you will be replaced."

"I have no idea what you're talking about."

"When we finally managed to release you from his control, there was an explosion. We found you under the rubble and you were mostly alright. You even spoke to us. Do you remember that?"

"No. What did I say?"

"You said, 'I knew you'd save me'."

"I did? I remember thinking that while I was trapped. But I don't remember telling you that."

"Okay. I want you to concentrate on hearing me out, and not stop listening when I tell you what the small problem is."

"Fine. Talk."

"Your left foot is missing."

"No." Ava tore off the blanket that Jackson had carried over with her and looked down at her foot. "Oh my god, oh my god, oh my god." She began hyperventilating.

Johanna put her palm on Ava's face and said, "Look at me. You promised to hear me out. "You said you're not in any pain and your leg is not damaged where it was attached to your foot. The Adventurans can create a new foot for you that will work like your own."

"You mean like a wooden foot?"

★*No, Ava, like my arm.*

Ava stared at Pru Tellerence. "Except your arm is real."

★*My arm was created by the Adventurans to replace the one I lost during the war with the Terrorians. I can't tell it from my real arm. It feels real and the Adventurans say unless another enemy shoots it off again, I will have it for life. They will do the same thing for you; replace your foot and put you on a regimen of physical therapy, so that a couple of weeks from now, you won't even know it's not your own.*

Ava squinted. "That's really not your arm?"

★*It's my arm; I just wasn't born with it.*

Ava's face drained of color as her breathing became shallower. "Will I have to stay there. By myself?"

⌘*Perhaps Christopher would like to go with you, so he can help you with your physical therapy after you return home.*

Chris nearly jumped out of his chair. "Sure. I can do that."

★ *And, of course, your mother will want to accompany you.*

"Yes." Niamh blinked back tears.

⌘ *Unfortunately, Johanna and Jackson will have to stay here and hold the fort, as they say.*

"That's fine. It doesn't mean we can't be there in the blink of an eye for a quick visit," Johanna said.

Jackson nodded. "Think of it like a vacation."

Ava tried to smile, but just as quickly as her lip quirked upward, the smile slid off her face. "Do you think it's going to hurt?"

TWENTY-SEVEN

SUNDAY MORNING COULD not be any more picture perfect. The bright blue skies were heralded by birdsong and the air was fresh and invigorating. The sun's reflection on the exterior of the Library of Illumination glowed like honey—bringing with it the feeling of a new beginning.

Conditions were similar outside the George V hotel in Paris. Ava awoke and without thinking, swung her legs off the bed and propelled herself into a standing position. AAAIIIEEE!!! Her scream permeated the air. She crumpled to the floor—suddenly reminded of her loss.

Jackson was the first to rush into her room. "What happened?" he asked, picking her up and placing her on the bed.

Ava took three little breaths in quick succession, trying to get her emotions under control, but tears streamed down her face. "Uh…" Her tears became sobs. She turned away, not wanting to talk about it.

Jackson pushed a lock of her hair behind her ear. "You forgot, didn't you?"

She nodded, saying nothing more.

"Don't fret, Squirt. We're gonna make this better. I promise?"

She didn't really believe him but she nodded.

"Do you want me to help you inside? It's Sunday morning and Mom's probably planning to attend church. I bet she already ordered breakfast."

It took several sniffles and extensive deep breathing before she could choke out an answer. "You… go. I'm… not hungry."

"I can carry you if you'd like?"

Ava cringed. She hated feeling needy. She shook her head and rolled onto her side with her back towards Jackson, pulling the blanket over her head.

"Right," he mumbled.

Johanna walked in as Jackson left. "I'm surprised to see you're up. But then, you're probably used to getting up early on Sundays."

"Mom and Ava are. Me and Chris, not so much." Jackson took one last look at Ava before leaving.

"Hey, Ava, are you awake?"

Ava's shoulders shook as she silently sobbed. Johanna sat on the edge of the bed and placed her hand on Ava's back. "Do you want to talk about what happened and how it's making you feel?"

"No," Ava sobbed.

Johanna rubbed the younger girl's back. "I'll be around if you need someone to talk to. Meanwhile, I heard the doorbell when I walked in, so I think room service must be here with breakfast. Do you want me to save you anything?"

"No."

"Alright then. See you later." Johanna gave Ava's shoulder one last pat before leaving.

LOGAN INTENTIONALLY PARKED a couple of blocks away from the library. He tugged down the visor of his baseball cap and pushed a pair of cheap rubber sunglasses up the bridge of his nose. He wore oily-looking ripped jeans and a baggy sports jersey—the opposite of how he usually dressed. *I'm a natural at being incognito. If anyone comes my way, I can always duck up an alley.* He spotted Niamh's car across the street from the library. Logan ducked down, so the car sat between him and the library. *This is stupid. I should have just taken my mother's car and parked around the corner and watched from inside her car. I'm too exposed out here.*

He leaned his forehead against Niamh's passenger side window.

Suddenly, his eyes bugged open. Mrs. Roth's cell phone sat in plain sight in the cup holder inside her car. *Pay dirt.*

He looked around but the sidewalks were empty. *Why would anybody be out this early on a Sunday?* The sheer absurdity of it (to his mind) made him smile. He pushed in the handle to open the car's passenger door. It was locked. *Who locks their cars in Exeter?* He banged his head against the window. *Oh!* The door he hid behind might have been locked, but he could clearly see the lock button on the driver-side door in the open position. *I just have to walk around the car, open the door, grab the phone, and walk away.*

Once again, he studied the sidewalks. *Quieter than deep space.*

He walked to the other side of the car and opened the door, leaning in to grab the phone.

"Hey, what are you doing there? That's not your car."

Logan's shoulders tightened. He looked up to see a local business owner rounding the corner. Logan had no idea who he was and did not want to hang around to find out. He grabbed the phone, turned and ran. He could hear footsteps behind him and knew he was being chased. He passed the block he had parked on, not wanting to lead anyone to his car. After several blocks, he ducked down an alley—and crossed through to the next block. He looked for yet another alley to disappear into and found one a half block away. He scrambled behind a dumpster and tried to regulate his breathing. After several moments, he held his breath and listened. *Nothing. No footsteps or people yelling or anything.* He took off the baggy jersey and threw it in the dumpster along with the baseball hat and sunglasses. He couldn't do anything about the jeans, but maybe he had changed his appearance enough to avoid detection. He carefully exited the alley and casually strolled to his car. Once inside, he wasted no time starting the engine and heading home.

His parents' car was gone, and he parked in the garage again, hoping they'd never realize he had gone out.

Inside, Logan laughed as he fired up the stolen phone. *Mrs. Roth should really learn to use password protection on this thing.* He found her photo app and scrolled through the images. *Jackpot!* The overseers may have been able to erase memories, but their technology was lacking when it came to erasing non-student cell phone photos.

He sent copies of all the prom night images to

himself, including the ones of his former girlfriend, Cassie, who had recently committed suicide. He broke into a slow smile. *Cassie, you're the best thing that ever happened to me.*

RYDEN SIMMDRY AND Pru Tellerence arrived toward the end of breakfast.

⌘ *Where's Ava?*

"In bed," Jackson said, "crying over the loss of her foot. It seems she had forgotten all about it when she woke up this morning and fell when she jumped out of bed."

"She's inconsolable," Johanna added. "I don't know what we can do but let her cry it out."

★ *There's no time for crying today. We've just come from Adventura.*

⌘ *They're waiting for Ava. They know she is the sister of the curators who saved the Illumini System from being conquered by Terrorians, and that she needs a new foot. They're excited to get started. They apparently have new technology with enhanced feedback that will make getting used to it as easy as learning to dance.*

★ *Perhaps they should have a look at your feet? You never were a very good dancer.*

⌘ *Pru Tellerence, I'm hurt. You have always told me in the past that my inability to dance did not matter.*

★ *We're growing older. I think we should learn to kick up our heels a little before we become one with the elements.*

Niamh folded her napkin before placing it on the table. "If this new foot works out for Ava, I'm sure she will be happy to teach you to dance herself. I only hope she'll give it a chance. When do you think they'll want to do it?

★ *Today, of course.*

Niamh's mouth dropped open. "So soon?"

⌘ *We can leave as soon as she's dressed and ready.*

*

LOGAN ADDED A prom picture to his first segment and then reworked the voiceover tracks for the second package of his library exposé. When he mentioned Emily being dangled over the balcony by a Terrorian, he showed a picture of Emily on the balcony in her prom gown. He followed it with video of a Terrorian coming to life out of a book he had recorded during the library evacuation for the bogus gas leak. He couldn't ask for anything better than the sheer, unanticipated ugliness of a Terrorian played against the grace and beauty of Emily Brent. *Everything is coming together.*

CHRIS FOUND HIS entire family as well as Johanna's, surrounding Ava when he entered her room.

Jackson picked up his sister. "There's no time like the present."

"What are you doing?" Chris asked.

"I'm transporting my little sister to Adventura."

"I though you and Johanna have work to do here at the library?"

Jackson smirked. "I can be back in a matter of minutes."

Chris slipped his arms under Ava's arms and legs and took her from Jackson. "No need. I can take it from here."

⌘ *Don't worry, Jackson. We have everything well in hand. And after everything you and Johanna went through with Ailill Caomhánach, I'm sure you both can use the rest.*

"What about you?" Jackson asked. "Don't you need to rest, too?"

⌘ *Being an overseer, I do not require as much food and relaxation as other human beings. I was able to amply recharge overnight. And the Adventurans have invited me to tour the facilities they've upgraded since their sun nearly destroyed their world.*

⌘ *I'm sure your mother and Christopher will give Ava all the moral support she needs.* He paused. ⌘ *Unless I'm wrong,* he said, looking at Ava. ⌘ *Would you like Jackson and Johanna to accompany you as well?*

"No," Chris answered before Ava had a chance to open her mouth.

Ava sighed. "They don't need to go. I'll use Chris as my slave. I'm sure he'll be happy to fulfill my every wish."

Chris scowled. "I will?"

Niamh smiled. "You will."

JOHANNA SAT CURLED up in a large leather chair in the main reading room of the library.

"A buck-fifty for your thoughts," Jackson said, slumping down onto the chair across from her.

"A buck-fifty?"

"Yeah. What can you do with a penny? I figure a buck-fifty is more in keeping with the times."

"Then you should have offered me twenty dollars, allowing for inflation."

"How do you figure that?"

"The saying originated in the early 1500s. The value of a penny has gone up quite a lot since then."

Jackson scrubbed at his face. "How do you know this stuff?"

"We work in a library. I read."

"I read, too, but I've never seen a comparative report on the value of a penny over the past five centuries."

Johanna smiled. "I was just thinking about the Re

Transfigurator."

"Why? Your father pretty much put it out of its misery."

"Basic physics."

"What are you talking about?"

"Any scientist will tell you that energy cannot be destroyed and it doesn't die. Ailill Caomhánach had an awful lot of energy behind him, yet one minute he was there and the next he was gone. What happened to his energy?"

"It became the force of the explosion."

"And once the explosion settled, where did the energy go?"

"Okay. You've got me. What are you trying to say?"

"I don't think Ailill Caomhánach was destroyed. I think he was scattered about the room until he could regroup and find another way to fight us."

"That's not what I wanted you to say."

Johanna unfurled her legs and stood. "I think we should visit the Dunes and take another look around."

'Without your father?"

"You think we need him?"

"I think three is stronger than two."

"He's busy right now. How about I create an amulet to strengthen and protect us."

"Can you really do that, or are you just trying to pull off some type of Jedi mind game?"

"I can create a charm to help us focus our thoughts. And a second one to protect us from outside influences. One of each for both of us. It's not just to help you. It's to help me, too. And while I create them, I will explain what I'm doing, so you can see the logic behind my thinking and ask questions. How's that?

"Okay. If you really believe it will help?"
"I do. And then we'll go visit the Chalet."
"If you insist."
Johanna smiled. "I love it when you're malleable."

THE DOOR TO the Chalet was not latched and a wind gust blew it open—just enough for an animal to push through. It didn't take long before a pack of wild dogs forced their way inside, sniffing at the automatons that remained and marking their territory with their urine.

The leader of the marauding group growled. Smelling Ava's scent, he latched onto the remains of the costume that had belonged to the *Girl Pedaling a Bicycle*. He ran around the room like a rampant flag bearer, displaying his colors. The other dogs gave chase, trying to snatch away his prize. Suddenly, they all stilled and growled.

Like dust motes rising, a wispy dark cloud formed in the center of the room. Ailill Caomhánach pulled his focus and began absorbing what had once been his. Small bits of debris, nearly unrecognizable, began to grow beneath the rubble and swirl like a slow-motion cyclone. As they did, they changed form, morphing into energy.

The dogs' growls became snarls and barks and they began snapping at the moving bits of debris.

I will rise again, Ailill Caomhánach declared, *and I will build my strength. Then I will taste the sweetness of vengeance.*

The dogs' angry howls became cries for sympathy, as the malevolent entity began absorbing their energy.

TWENTY-EIGHT

HALFWAY ACROSS THE Illumini System, Ava, Chris and Niamh stood mesmerized as Prophet IAN c. explained the procedure Ava would go through to replace her foot. As the Adventuran curator spoke, a medi*bot carried in a container and placed it on a small cart, which he rolled under Ava's legs. "This is Prophet ANDREW r. who is going to take an impression of your right foot."

"No," Ava gasped. "It's my left foot that needs to be replaced. I don't need another right foot!"

"Do not fear," Prophet IAN c. replied. We will reverse engineer the foot to its mirror image."

ANDREW r. lifted Ava's foot and pushed it into the container of cold, green gel. He then turned on a light stick and aimed it at the gel.

Ava could feel the gel warming up as it changed color from green to yellow. She sniffed. "It smells like lemons."

IAN c. nodded once. "Pru Tellerence suggested we add a recognizable scent to make the procedure more pleasant for you. I cannot see a difference, although I am programmed to recognize and catalogue more than 5,475,322 scents. Your new prosthetic foot will not smell like lemons, nor does the addition of an odor add to its integrity. I argued against it, but she said it would make everything appear less foreign to you. Is it correct that the aroma is lessening your discomfort?"

Before Ava could think of an answer, ANDREW r. sharply tugged the container away from her foot, creating a large sucking *thwoop* sound as it broke free. Ava looked down to see the container was still intact and that the only visible opening in the gel was the size of her ankle. "Is it alright?"

"Perfect," IAN c replied. "Prophet CARL a. and some of his medi*bots will have your new prosthetic prepared in no time. While you are waiting, the overseers have been kind enough to provide a luncheon next door."

"A question, first," Mrs. Roth said. "How long will the procedure take?"

"In your time, approximately 2 hours."

Ava's forehead creased. "Will I be knocked out?"

"You will not be knocked out, although you will not feel pain. You will need to answer questions during the operation, so that your new foot is connected correctly."

"Is that necessary?"

"It is. When you wish to rotate your ankle to the left, it is best if your ankle rotates in that direction, rather than having your toes wiggle. Your feedback will make that a reality."

"Huh," Ava replied. "I didn't think I'd be able to

rotate my ankle, much less wiggle my toes."

"When we are done, you will not know the difference between the foot you lost and the one we replace it with. We are very good at creating prosthetics. We probably would no longer exist as a civilization if we weren't. We're hoping to use this new technology to reinvent ourselves, to return our appearance to what it once was many millennia ago. Our desire is to appear to be fully human even if we are not yet ready to replace all our robotic parts."

"Wait." Chris stuck out his arm, stopping IAN c. "You're using something on my sister you've never used before?"

"Technically, that is true. However, the technology is very similar in what we used to replace Pru Tellerence's arm and hand. It will look and feel completely natural. However, what we use on Ava will be more advanced. Pru Tellerence can move naturally, but cannot feel soft impressions, like the tickle of a feather. Your sister will be able to feel everything the way she once did."

JOHANNA SPENT THE morning realm-hopping, gathering the herbs, unctions, and materials she would need for amulets.

When she reappeared in the Fantasian library, she found Jackson pacing the floor.

"Where did you go?" he asked. "One minute we were talking about a certain plant you needed, and the next minute you were gone."

"I took a quick trip to Mysteriose. It's the only place I know of where I could get fermented *eiulqar*. At least, I thought it would be a quick trip. It seems that everyone now knows I'm the offspring of two overseers, and they all want to ask me questions and," she grimaced, "touch me. I wish I had asked you to come with me. You could have been my bodyguard."

Jackson smirked. "Just remember that the next time you want to leave home without me."

"Now there's a saying I haven't heard in a long time."

Both teens swung around to see Johanna's predecessor, standing behind them."

"Mal," Johanna screamed, launching herself into his arms.

"Hey, Mal." Jackson waited for Johanna to step away so he could shake Mal's hand. "What haven't you heard in a long time?"

"You sounded like an American Express commercial from the last century, 'American Express, don't leave home without it.'"

"I should get an American Express card. You, too, Johanna."

"Nope. I have an official Illumini Bank credit card issued especially for the overseers. It's all I need."

Jackson frowned. "How come I don't have one of those?"

Johanna smiled. "I believe yours is being used by Mr. Osbourn-Fitzpatrick of New York to pay his George V hotel bill."

Jackson's mouth pulled to one side as he narrowed his eyes. "You're making that up."

"Am I?" She turned to her predecessor. "So, what brings you here? I'm so glad to see you!"

"I needed a few days off and wanted to stop by to say hello and see what's new."

Jackson's eyebrows crawled up his forehead. "Boy have you missed a lot. Where have you been?"

"I spent a month on Mysteriose helping Hue the Elder redesign their supply system. Then I was asked to go to Educon to establish the foundations for two different agencies that they need very badly."

"More taxes," Jackson asked.

"No. Something along the lines of WHO, the World Health Organization, to oversee their nutrition and health. Educons are among the smartest beings in the Illumini System but they survive on junk food. It's an addiction that's affecting their future. It was all too evident when they were fighting the Terrorians. They were basically useless. I'm working with them to establish training guidelines to get them in shape. Natalia Dalura is there, now, teaching fitness classes.

"I was also tasked with helping them establish a military branch," Mal continued, "so they can defend themselves. They currently have nothing like that and apparently became paranoid after the Terrorian incursion. I've had my hands full and we're just getting started. I don't suppose you two have any free time."

"Not at the moment," Johanna answered.

"Ava was kidnapped by a malevolent force and we managed to save her, but we aren't sure if *Dr. Evil* is still out there."

Mal laughed. "Dr. Evil?"

"His real name is Ailill Caomhánach."

Mal's eyebrows shot up. "The first overseer?"

"Yeah," Jackson answered.

"Apparently he was banished for doing something really diabolical. Unfortunately, Jackson and I managed to find and unleash him and he's demonic all the way through."

"He tried to steal my sister's energy. We got her back, but at a cost."

Mal grew more serious. "What cost?"

"She lost a foot. It's like he absorbed it or something."

"Because decomposing flesh gives off energy," Mal said, his mind going in a million different directions.

"The good news is, the Adventurans said they can fix it. Ava's there now."

Mal nodded. "It sounds like we are all inundated with work. I won't keep you." He immediately transported to Adventura, very much wanting to talk to Ava. *Damn. I forgot to give Johanna the note Natalia asked me to give her.*

OVER THE NEXT hour, Johanna described every step she took in preparing the herbs and minerals for the amulets. She even stopped to gather the different books Jackson could use for reference in the study of potion making.

The charms were made from small crystals like clear quartz and tiger's eye placed in tiny sacs that they could suspend—like the amulets—from leather cords worn around their necks.

Jackson studied her every move. "How'd you learn all this stuff?"

"I must have picked it up from Beck the last time we saw *Eahta Frean fram Drycræft.* I was wearing Myrddin's ring and it brushed against Beck's sigil. We had quite the power exchange, although, I don't know if he received back as much as he gave me. It felt like information overload at the time, but all those bits and pieces are coming in handy when I need them."

"That's the day you changed from my plain old super-smart and beautiful co-curator into an absolutely astounding Athena—goddess of war *and* poetry. Even that doesn't describe you. You're like the female equivalent of *Gandolf the White.* You're big." Jackson held his arms out, palms facing each other and widened the space between them. "BIG."

"And that's the answer to your question."

"Yeah. I guess." He watched as Johanna put tiny pieces of clear quartz and tiger's eye in a miniscule bag with some fluorite and amazonite. Her last addition was blue sapphires. She stitched the bags shut and used a special tool to place a grommet in each bag. She added the crystal charms and herb amulets to leather neck cords and knotted them.

"Here." She handed one of them to Jackson. "Place this under your clothing, so it's close to your heart."

"Will that make it stronger?"

"More than that."

Jackson inhaled sharply. "What do you mean?"

"It will prevent the cord from getting caught on something and choking you to death."

He lowered his lids, focusing on Johanna through narrow slits. "Thank you, I think."

"I'm not joking. Just in case we encounter someone or something, it helps if they're not able to easily see something they can garrote you with."

"So, you're thinking someone, or something, might still be there."

"I'd like to say *no,* but I can't."

*

Ava answered every question Prophet CARL a. asked her. Even though he asked several times if something hurt, she never felt any pain. Yet, she did feel the sensations they asked her about, including something that felt sticky, and something else that was warm and mushy. She giggled, guessing they were ticking her foot before they could even ask her about it. It was like a big game.

CARL a. broke an ampoule under her nose. "Inhale this as deeply as you can."

"What is it?" she asked, inhaling the pleasant scent.

"Something to make you sleepy."

"I don't want to go to sleep. I want to see my new foot."

"In time," the medi*bot answered. "In time."

While Ava was unconscious, they performed the finishing touches to permanently affix the foot. CARL a. meticulously built up Ava's lost muscle with medical grade artificial tissue before grafting on replacement skin. It had been decided it would be better if Ava couldn't smell the burning tissue needed to complete the process.

A while later, she awakened to find her mother and brother by her side. "You missed some tour," Chris said, as soon as she opened her eyes. "Did you know this whole planet nearly died a couple of months ago, when its sun went solar flare crazy?"

"I must have missed it," Ava replied, groggy from whatever anesthetic the Adventurans had given her.

"They said, until then, the whole place looked like a wasteland. But after that, they decided to clean everything up and restore the planet to what it once was before the Two Millennia War, which was ages ago. They must have been up to their necks in cleaning supplies because the place really looks good."

Ava jerked herself up into a sitting position. "My foot," she cried, as she jerked a blanket off her right leg. What she found was a heavily bandaged foot. She tried to wiggle it. It was difficult with all the gauze wrapped around it, but there was no pain. "I want to see it," she whined.

CARL a. walked in from an adjacent room. "How do you feel, Ava?"

"I feel great. I want to see my foot."

"It must remain bandaged for now. We do not want to invite rejection or infection. It will take a few days for your new skin to mesh with your existing skin and for your muscles and tendons to adhere to the mechanism that drives your new appendage. After a short visit with your family, I suggest you rest for the remainder of the day. We will give you something to help you sleep through it. Tomorrow, we will focus on physical therapy, getting you out of bed and making sure that you can walk. The following day, we will remove the bandages and you can return home.

"Are you experiencing any pain?" CARL a. asked.

"No. None."

"Good. I'll be back when your family leaves. They're scheduled to tour our Museum of Robotic History this afternoon and will attend a banquet we are hosting for the overseers this evening.

Ava's shoulders slumped. "Why do I have to miss out on that? I feel fine."

"Your foot will heal better when you are in stasis. But you will miss nothing. We will do it all again just for you when you return for a checkup."

"Okay," she said.

Her mother gave her a hug before tucking Ava's foot back under the blanket.

"See you later, Squirt," Chris said, lightly punching her in the arm.

Ava scowled. "Only Jackson is allowed to call me that."

Chris laughed. "I'll be sure to tell him he now has your permission to call you that. Last I heard, you chewed him out for it. I'm sure he'll be pleased."

CARL a. led her mother and brother away as another medi*bot handed her a glass bowl filled with berries and cream. Ava didn't realize how hungry she was until she devoured it. She would have licked the bowl if the medi*bot wasn't watching. "That was delicious," she said. "What was it?"

"Something to make you sleep," the medi*bot answered, but Ava never heard him. She had fallen asleep almost immediately.

LOGAN USED SOME of his own pictures of Cassie along with the prom pictures he had of her for the third segment on the library for *The Elliott Report*. He portrayed her as scared and tormented, following the prom night attack by the Terrorians. He reported that she became increasingly irrational until she couldn't take it anymore, and ended her own life.

> "While most students you might question now would give you vague answers about prom night at Exeter High School, I can report most assuredly that Cassie Turner, who was already under strain after witnessing a monstrous creature at the Library of Illumination dangling her best

friend over the balcony, snapped when yours truly was selected as Emily Brent's Prom King. Cassie was my date, however, being voted Prom King meant I couldn't spend as much time with her as I would have liked. Unfortunately, I wasn't able to give her the continuous support she obviously needed. No one was more surprised than me when she chose to take her own life rather than relive the memories of terror inside the library, coupled with her ill-conceived feelings of abandonment. My deepest sympathies go out to her friends and family. It is a regret, even though I've been told I'm blameless, that I will bear forever, having been her long-time boyfriend."

Logan lifted his chin, looking up as if toward the heavens.

"Cassie, I loved you. And I only wish you had believed in me enough to have received the help you needed, rather than thinking suicide was the answer. If you are looking down on us now, I hope you realize that all the blame belongs to the Library of Illumination, and not the seniors who didn't choose you as their Prom Queen, or me for escorting Emily that evening after being voted king."

Logan sighed deeply, before looking at the camera.

"Please forgive me. This is a personally emotional topic, and I find I can't continue for now. This concludes today's edition of *The Elliott Report*. I'm Logan Elliott. Goodbye."

He sniffed before looking down at the papers he had on his desk. He straightened them out before turning off the camera. The corners of his mouth lifted into a wide smile. *That should garner the sympathy vote. Who's to say those things didn't kill her? It's my word against a dead girl. No one can prove me wrong.*

TWENTY-NINE

Aɪʟɪʟʟ Cᴀᴏᴍʜᴀ́ɴᴀᴄʜ ɢʟᴏᴡᴇᴅ as his vitality increased. The wild dogs provided enough power for him to not only regain the strength he had depleted fighting Ryden Simmdry but to also increase his drive.

Now that he had faced off against his new enemies, the first overseer formulated a new plan. *I must condense my reserves. It will make me appear diminutive and less powerful, misleading my opponents.* He concentrated on the Re Transfigurator, which stored his essence, using magic to change its properties. The original box reduced in size, its angles smoothing into a rounder shape. The Iceland spar remained as the base, but appeared smaller and more polished. Even the color changed to a marbleized cream and white, making it look non-aggressive.

Then the object itself shapeshifted, becoming a mere whisper of the sheerest paper caught by a breeze. It floated toward the door left open by the dogs but hesitated.

Sensing danger, its trajectory changed, taking it to the back of the room near a kitchen vent.

JACKSON AND JOHANNA stood outside the Chalet as Johanna used her mind to probe the inside for signs of Ailill Caomhánach.

Off in the distance, the joyful squeals of children playing on the public beach mixed with the calls of gulls, passing overhead. The sounds reminded Jackson of years gone by when his mother had brought her children to the beach on weekends. He remembered *living* for those weekends. His mother worked during the week, while he and his brother and sister did odd jobs around the neighborhood; deals their mother had worked out in exchange for bartered items like jars of jelly and bottles of homemade tomato sauce. He remembered cleaning out a seamstress's garage in exchange for her sewing a new dress for Ava and mending Jackson's hand-me-downs for Chris. A distant rumble of thunder coincided with a sudden darkening of the sky and brought him back to the task at hand. "You getting anything?" he asked Johanna.

"I sense movement," she answered, "but nothing specific."

"No flashing, neon sign that says, *Bad Guy Inside?*"

"Wouldn't that make it easy."

"No magic signature?"

"I feel a weak magical signature, but it could be left over from the fight to rescue Ava."

Jackson sighed. "I wonder how she's doing?"

"We can pop up to Adventura later to say hi and make sure she's okay."

His shoulders relaxed. "There's nothing like a plan."

"But first, let's see what's still inside."

Jackson grabbed Johanna's arm before she could enter the building. "What if *His Royal Menace* is still in there, and he's regained his strength? Shouldn't we ask your father to do this with us? Just in case?"

"My father won't always be around to help us. And together, you and I are already pretty tough. We need to man up and do this ourselves."

Jackson tried to hide a smirk. "Don't *man up* just for me. I like you as a woman."

Johanna smiled despite herself. "As man and woman, we have to be self-sufficient. More than self-sufficient. Even though we're already a pretty dynamic team."

Jackson let go of her arm. "Okay. I'm ready."

Inside, it took a moment for Johanna and Jackson's eyes to adjust to the light.

"Something's different," Johanna whispered. "Something's changed." She grabbed Jackson's hand.

Together, they approached the entrance to the main room. As soon as they stepped inside, something dove at them from above.

THE RE TRANSFIGURATOR, disguised as a wisp of paper, broke apart into salt-like particles and floated out of a vent, reuniting behind the building. It became caught up and swirled within a dust devil for several seconds before finally drifting to the ground. It rose to catch the next breeze that passed behind the chalet—free to travel wherever it desired.

"ACK!" REFLEXIVELY, JOHANNA and Jackson ducked in unison.

"What was that?" Johanna asked. She quickly

turned to get eyes on whatever dive-bombed them.

"I'm pretty sure it was a seagull," Jackson answered, looking for a piece of paper or a rag to wipe bird poop off his shirt.

"I'm pretty sure you're right. He's right up there in the rafters." She pointed toward their attacker. "And that means no more Ailill Caomhánach."

"How can you be so certain?"

"If he were still here, that bird would be immobilized, while he sucked out its energy."

"Maybe he can't reach that high."

"Trust me. Besides that, all the automata debris is gone."

Jackson swiveled his head, looking all around. "Huh. Nice of him to clean up after himself."

"All the debris he cleaned up was probably made out of his energy. He just gathered it all together, re-consolidating his power."

"Where do you think he went?"

Johanna's eyes widened as her mouth gaped open. "We've got to get back to the library."

Ava drifted in and out of a deep sleep. At one point, she felt a hand on her shoulder. She struggled to open her eyes. Squinting, she murmured, "Mal?"

"Hi, Ava. Johanna and Jackson told me what happened. I thought I'd drop in and say hello."

"Nice to… see you." Ava struggled to keep her eyes open, fighting the sleeping medication she'd been given.

Mal smiled. "I don't want to keep you from resting. I just wanted you to know I'm thinking about you and hope you feel better soon."

"Thanks, Mal," Ava said, before drifting back to dream land. She moaned, suddenly remembering something. She tried to reach out for Mal but her hand only moved a few inches.

He hadn't left yet and noticed her struggle.

"What is it, Ava. Do you need something?"

"Tell them… that thing… doesn't like… licorice," Ava managed to whisper. "I think… it messes… its ability… to steal… energy. Maybe that's… why it… only got… my foot… and not… the rest… of me. Tell them." Exhausted, her hand flopped onto the bed.

MAL THOUGHT ABOUT Ava's warning as he transported out of the hospital. *Licorice.* It sounded far-fetched, and he wondered if something in the medications the Adventurans used to keep her sedated made her dream it. It was not that he doubted licorice had unusual and sometimes medicinal properties over and above its use as a flavoring, but it was difficult to embrace the notion that candy could prevent an entity from absorbing power. *Then again, just the idea that anything could suck someone's lifeforce out of them is beyond my understanding.* He doubled back to Fantasia to let Johanna and Jackson decide if it was something they wanted to follow up on.

IT DIDN'T TAKE long for the Re Transfigurator to make its way back to the Library of Illumination, carried on a breeze as a wisp of paper. It shapeshifted into a puff of smoke and entered the building through an air vent—in much the same way it had escaped the Chalet.

The library was well lit, however, everyone who worked at the library was someplace else, and the main reading room was empty. The Re Transfigurator solidified into its new smaller, more benign form and settled into a corner of the information desk. To the untrained eye, it could have simply been a decorative box for storing paper clips and rubber bands.

Mal appeared inside the library's main level. It was so quiet, he could have heard a spider spinning its web. "Hello! Is anybody here?" he called out.

Dead silence.

I guess they're out. I'd better leave a note. He walked behind the information desk looking for a pen and paper and wrote a brief summary about the possibility that licorice could reduce Ailill Caomhánach's abilities. He also mentioned that Ava was "out of it" when she gave him that information, so it was questionable. He folded the paper and put it on top of the desk where Johanna and Jackson would see it.

He noticed an open package of Larson's Licorice Lozenges. *Ah, Ava. Now I know why you have licorice on your mind. You were snacking on this, were you?* He picked it up and opened it, slipping a piece in his mouth.

He was about to leave when he remembered the note Natalia Dalura had asked him to give to Johanna. He stuck his hand in his pocket and pulled it out. *I'll just clip this to the top.* He looked around the desk and saw a small box that looked like it might hold paper clips. Mal flipped it open.

Ailill Caomhánach rose out of the Re Transfigurator and wasted no time casting a paralyzing spell to remove Mal's ability to fight back.

This is not a safe place for extraction, the malevolent being reasoned. He attached himself to Mal and transported him to the one other place on Fantasia that the first curator was familiar with—the Chalet. He hated going back there, knowing Ryden Simmdry, Johanna, and Jackson knew of its location. But he was also confident that they believed they had erased him from existence, and they would not return there until after he had taken Mal's life force as his own.

Inside the Chalet, Ailill Caomhánach used some of the power he had stored away to turn it back into a display of automata. It was easier for him than it had been the first time and required less energy. With the incorporation of a full-grown human's force, Ailill Caomhánach felt confident he could win future battles.

MAL'S CONSCIOUSNESS SLOWLY took hold but he found it wasn't easy to regain his faculties. He felt drugged and couldn't recognize where he was, nor did he know why he was there. He found it difficult to move his head or his arms more than an inch or two, although his eyes had enough movement to allow him to look around the room. It took a while for his brain to comprehend what his eyes saw. He was in a room that appeared to be filled entirely with automata. His hand almost continuously moved involuntarily. He looked down to see why it was moving, and realization dawned on him. He appeared to be hovering over an automaton he had once seen in an exhibit of swiss workmanship dating from the 1700s. *What am I doing here? More importantly, why can't I move?*

He closed his eyes and concentrated on transporting himself to Lumina. He was disappointed to find himself still trapped in the strange location.

He watched as his hand continuously dipped a goose quill pen in an inkpot, and slowly penned words across a piece of paper. Oddly enough, the paper was in a brass-bound frame and seemed to move more than his pen did. He could see the fine lace that spilled from his sleeves and jabot and felt oddly overdressed. Yet his legs and feet felt cold. It took Mal several minutes to realize he was inside the automaton. *How can that be? I know the original exhibit was 1:5 scale. How could I possibly be inside it?* It didn't take long for the word "magic" to cross his mind.

His eyes caught sight of a dark shape hovering inside the room. It appeared to have no solid form and moved about, sometimes quite quickly. Mal put his brain to work, trying to determine the intent of the shadow. At first sight, it appeared ominous. After several moments of study, Mal determined it was most definitely ominous.

He chanted under his breath, and he realized he had something in his mouth. *Licorice.* He could taste it. *Thanks, Ava.* He recited a charm to ward off the effects of magic. *I need to hold on to as much of what is real to me as I can, if I'm going to deal with this threat without losing myself in the process.*

JOHANNA AND JACKSON spent the night searching for the Re Transfigurator inside the library. They started with the Executive Board Room where the automaton had originally been placed, then methodically searched every other room, looking for anything unusual.

Jackson squatted down, using his hand to search the shelf where they'd found the puzzle box that initially started their whole quest for the Re Transfigurator.

"Nothing." He looked up at Johanna. "What makes you think Ailill Caomhánach came back here?"

"He still needs power, and this is the one place he's most familiar with. Whether he's here to teach us a lesson, or just came back for your sister to prove we can't outsmart him, it seems the most likely location because he knows what to expect here."

"So, you think he wants to suck the lifeforce out of one of us?"

"I think he wants to suck the lifeforce out of *all* of us. He expended a lot of power fighting Ryden Simmdry, and needs a large supply of energy to get off Fantasia."

"How do you know he isn't already off Fantasia?"

"Because he's still too weak."

They slowly worked their way back to the front of the library, finding nothing.

Johanna sighed, slipping behind the information desk to check messages. She spotted the note Mal left. After reading his message twice, she stared at it for a very long time.

"Are you going to tell me what's in the note, or is it something personal?"

"It's about Ava. She told Jackson about Ailill Caomhánach's possible problem with licorice."

"What?"

Johanna gave Jackson a half smile. "I think Mal had the same reaction. He said Ava was heavily sedated when she said it and mentioned it might be drug-induced."

"That makes more sense. It was nice of Mal to leave a note, although we weren't gone very long. I'm surprised we didn't run into him when we got back here."

"Really." Johanna's brow lowered, then shot up as

her eyes widened. "What if Ailill Caomhánach did come back here and intercepted Mal?"

"Would he have been strong enough?"

"Which one are you talking about?" she asked.

"Good question."

"We have to go back to the Chalet," she said, throwing the note back on the desk.

"You don't think—"

"I do think. Until he grows stronger, it's the easiest place for your favorite malevolent being to siphon unsuspecting prey."

THE LIGHT WAVERED across the room as Ailill Caomhánach drew upon his energy to materialize. His specter was ghost-like, as if he didn't want to waste energy manifesting. *ᛋGrynsmiþ, where are you hiding? I know you must be about. You can't be dead. You're immortal.*

A dark cloud took shape not too far away. Apparently, that was the easy part. It took a quarter of an hour for it to shift into the shape of a man—a very tall, narrow man—wearing sandals with steep platforms, wide trousers, and a long tunic. He had long black curls that fell across his back and shoulders. And his smirk contained a hint of wry amusement. "*Hæsere*, it has been too long since I've taken form. What is your intention? Pray tell the task isn't arduous."

ᛋYou prefer imprisonment?

"I prefer stupefaction. It is so very undemanding."

ᛋSave it for death.

"I cannot, for immortality dogs me."

ᛋMany crave immortality.

"They crave the pain of repetition and exhaustion because they don't know better."

We have the promise of adventure, power, and freedom at hand. I require your involvement.

"Only if my involvement will set me free. Release me from all bonds afterward, and I will involve myself fully for one last adventure."

THIRTY

THE NEWLY CREATED automata in the Chalet looked almost identical to what had previously been there. Even the *Girl Peddling a Bicycle*, which had been destroyed when Ava was liberated, was back in place. However, there were differences. Ailill Caomhánach was now hidden inside a large glass music box where the smaller Re Transfigurator appeared to be part of the interior workings. He had a clear line of sight down a long aisle, to another automaton, in which Mal was now trapped. With any luck, the sorceress and her assistant would return without Ryden Simmdry. *The overseer could prove to be my undoing, but the other two are naive and inexperienced. That plays right into my hands. They're young enough that their energy will be strong, and unseasoned enough that they'll be easy to trick.*

AVA AWOKE ON Adventura the following morning feeling no residual effects of the painkillers or other medications she had been given.

Prophet CARL a. arrived soon afterward and uncovered her foot. "Twist it to the right," he instructed. She did so. "Twist it left." Again, she complied. "Wiggle your toes." Ava moved her toes—marveling to herself how each one felt like it was her own. CARL a. took a feather from his pocket and tickled the bottom of her foot. She quickly pulled her foot away, giggling. "Any pain?" he asked.

"No. It feels fine."

"Let's get you walking around the room."

Ava slid out of bed, allowing the medi*bot to help her. She took a tentative first step. Realizing it didn't hurt, she put more weight on her foot and walked normally across the room.

"Can you hop?" CARL a. asked.

Ava hopped. "Yes," she answered with a huge smile. "I can't believe it. It feels just like my own foot and there's no pain. It's like it's always been there."

CARL a. picked up her chart and studied it. "No fever. No signs of rejection. Get back on the bed, please."

Ava hoisted herself up.

He picked up her foot and studied the raised ring around her lower leg where the prosthetic attachment had been covered with synthetic skin. He rubbed it thumb across it. "Does this hurt or itch?"

"No. Not exactly. There's a funny feeling. The kind you get in your lip when Novocain is wearing off."

CARL a. studied her for a second. "I don't know what that feels like."

"It's like tingling with a little numbness."

"Yes. That would be your natural skin knitting together with its synthetic counterpart. That should go away in another day or so. The raised skin should go down and the pinkness will fade. After that, no one will ever be able to tell that your foot is not your own."

"Will I be able to run faster and jump higher?" Ava joked.

CARL a. remained quiet for a moment. "No one told me you required those abilities. If you need them, we will have to detach the foot and reprogram it. Is that what you would like?"

"No. No. I was just kidding. This foot is fine. Perfect, really. I was just joking."

"Joking. It is something we have long discussed on Adventura, whether to include it in our future programming. We have organic brains, but they are enhanced by artificial intelligence. We are trying to return to our roots and appear more human. Jests have been a long-missing personality trait for many of us. However, a number of Adventurans believe they are quite funny. I do not number among them. Other species have noted it when conferring with us. Thank you for pointing out that you were joking. Right now, it's difficult for some of us to recognize. Although our curator, Prophet IAN c. is noted for his wit. I'm not exactly sure why."

Prophet IAN c. chose that moment to enter the room. "How is the patient doing?"

"She is walking without a limp and says she has no pain. Her foot rotates fully and easily. There is no sign of tissue rejection. All other test results are perfect."

"That is remarkable," IAN c. said, examining Ava's foot. "I can't see any reason to keep her here. As soon as you teach her exercises to strengthen her ankle further, she may return home."

CARL a. turned back to Ava. "I do not believe he's joking."

*

LOGAN ARRIVED BRIGHT and early at Graydon Ransom University. He slipped into the newsroom right behind Luke and quickly scanned local news on the computer, searching for good stories. It looked like a slow news day. The only report that piqued his interest was one about growing complaints of wild dogs roaming the shoreline at the Dunes. *This could work. People are afraid to go to public beaches in fear of being attacked. I like it.*

Jennifer walked in, making a beeline for the assignment desk.

Logan waited a few minutes, giving her time to settle in before approaching her.

"There's not much going on," she said, when he finally made an appearance at her desk.

"I wanted to ask you about a story I saw online. Police are getting complaints about wild dogs at the Dunes. People are apparently scared of being mauled or bitten. It's still summer and it could be a threat to a lot of people. If residents stop going to the Dunes during the busy season, it could even affect the economy. I'd like to run with it. What do you think?

Jennifer looked up with raised eyebrows and a slight smile. "I think it's an excellent choice. Go for it."

"I'm on it," Logan answered with a quick smile. He picked up his gear and headed out the door.

Even with the threat of wild dogs, the beach was already half-full early on a Monday morning.

Logan swapped out his shoes for a pair of sandals he kept in the car and grabbed his camera, switching it on. He took several establishing shots of the area, before looking for people he could interview.

*

Ava was overjoyed to return to the library a day earlier than anticipated. It wasn't home, but it was comfortable. And she felt content to be surrounded by family.

Ryden Simmdry and Pru Tellerence, who had transported the Roths back to Fantasia, said their goodbyes in preparation for their return to Lumina. ⌘ *Tell Johanna to contact us if anyone needs our help. We will not hesitate to assist.*

Once the overseers were gone, Ava relaxed into the cushions of the couch. "I think I'd like filet mignon with mashed potatoes and those little baby carrots steamed in sweet vinaigrette."

"For breakfast?" Chris asked. "It's barely ten o'clock."

Ava glared at him through half closed eyes. "I've been through a grueling ordeal. Two grueling ordeals. And if I want steak for breakfast, why shouldn't I be allowed to have steak for breakfast? Besides, it feels more like lunch time to me."

Her mother picked up the phone to call room service. "First, let's see if the kitchen can even prepare steak this early in the day."

Room service told Niamh they would be happy to comply with the request. *"Mais bein sûr."* They would deliver the order within a half-hour.

"What about the rest of us?" Chris whined after his mother hung up the phone.

"I ordered a selection of your favorite pastries and pots of coffee and tea," his mother answered.

"So, I don't get steak?"

Niamh's smile was tight. "If I recall, you had a

rather large breakfast while your sister was having her foot examined."

"But that was a whole hour ago."

His mother's smile faded entirely. "Zip it, Christopher."

Ava punched her brother in the arm. "Yeah. Zip it, Christopher."

AILILL CAOMHÁNACH HATED when Grynsmiþ wandered off on his own. Not having the sorcerer's power in extremely close proximity made him feel weak. The immortal being hadn't traveled that far away, yet the small distance between them reduced the impact of the Re Transfigurator.

He watched as Grynsmiþ played with his shadow. *There's no accounting for power, especially in one with so little intelligence.*

AT THE DUNES, Logan spotted a woman holding the hands of two small children near the water's edge. He smiled disarmingly before shoving a microphone in her face. "Do you feel safe bringing your children here even though there are reports of wild dogs running around the beach?"

The woman's jaw dropped. "What do you mean? I haven't heard anything about wild dogs."

"Police are reporting packs of wild dogs have been annoying beach-goers. Do you feel safe?"

"Has anyone been bitten?"

"That could happen at any time. How would you feel if your child was the first one attacked?"

The woman yanked her kids away from the gently lapping water. "Who'd like ice cream? Come with Mommy." She dragged her kids back to the blanket, quickly packing up and leading them back to the car.

Logan shot as much of it as he could. Her reaction was perfect. Too bad she hadn't given him a good comment to go with it.

"What was that all about?" an older man asked. He and his wife had witnessed most of Logan's interaction with the young family.

"Wild dogs on the beach," Logan answered.

"Could you say that again," the elderly woman asked. "I don't have my hearing aids."

"Wild dogs on the beach," he shouted. "Have you seen any attacking people?"

Almost everyone in the near vicinity heard what he said, and began packing up, *en masse.*

"I haven't seen any wild dogs today," the old man said into the microphone, "but I did hear someone say they saw some last week—pulling over garbage pails and growling at young children."

"Did they say how they felt about that?" he asked.

"They were scared. Real scared. And they said they're not coming back here."

"But you came," Logan noted.

"Cause it's hot. And I forgot. But I'm going now. The last thing I want is to be mauled by a bunch of rabid dogs."

He and his wife packed up as Logan shot additional footage of what was now becoming a mass exodus.

I should head over to the mayor's office and get a statement.

As he walked along the sand, he realized there was another key element missing from his story. He didn't have any video of wild dogs.

*

JOHANNA AND JACKSON materialized outside the Chalet. Unlike the last time they'd been here, the door was locked. Johanna took a quick look around. She paused and pointed down the shoreline. "Is that Logan?"

Jackson followed her finger, and saw Logan interview an elderly couple. As soon as he did, they seemed to flee. "I don't know what he's doing but he seems to be upsetting people."

"We can't talk to him now. We have to find Mal. Come on." She transported them inside the vestibule.

"Did you notice what was happening out on the beach?"

"No," she whispered. "Why?"

"It looked like people couldn't get away fast enough. All of them."

"Could be anything," she said, approaching the inner door.

"Like Ailill Caomhánach?" Jackson held her back.

"Like jelly fish. Rip tide. Shark sighting. Thunderstorm warning—"

He pulled his hand away from her and held it up, palm out. "Okay, okay, okay. Forget I mentioned it."

Johanna snuck a peek inside the main room and gasped.

"What is it?" Jackson asked.

She grabbed his hand. "It's all back. All the automata. That means Ailill Caomhánach is here, too."

"Let me see." Jackson poked his head in the door. The first thing that caught his eye was the automaton of the Girl Peddling a Bicycle. *Would he trap Mal in the same automaton?* He continued surveying the mechanisms near it. Suddenly, he withdrew his head so quickly, he'd be surprised if he didn't get whiplash. "Did you see that huge, dark shadow flickering on the far wall?"

"I didn't notice it. There was too much other stuff commanding my attention."

"How could you miss it?" he asked, his eyes growing wide. "Take a look."

Johanna poked her head back into the main room, looking for Jackson's shadow. Suddenly it crawled up the wall, looming over everything. "Right," she said, suddenly pulling back inside the vestibule. "It definitely doesn't look friendly, although, I don't think it's Ailill Caomhánach."

"Then, what do you think it is?"

"I don't know," she said.

"Yeah. Well, I can tell you what it looks like," he whispered. "It looks like the freakin' shadow of death."

THIRTY-ONE

GRYNSMIþ INSTILLED FEAR in his enemies. His dark, shadowy figure, befouled the air around him with the stench of decay, and unknowingly added an unnatural heaviness to the atmosphere. He appeared monstrous and was used—by those who sought to control him—for nefarious purposes. Evil might not be all he was, but it was all he knew. And though naturally skilled in sorcery, he harbored no innately malicious intentions. Quite simply, he lacked the greed-driven, self-involvement at the core of most villains.

Grynsmiþ could easily be befriended through benign gestures like showing an interest in him or giving him small trinkets. Anyone who took the time to look past the darkness covering him like a cloak, would soon realize that beneath his malevolent appearance lay the eager-to-please innocence of a playful five-year-old with a spirit of adventure.

Performing magic gave him joy, and if it also pleased the people around him, that was a bonus. Unfortunately, it led him to use his talents for *other* people's evil intent because he thought it made them happy.

Animals sparked his joy, as well. He smiled, remembering how much fun he had playing with the dogs that had entered the Chalet a few days ago. It made him feel energized to fly around—dodging and weaving among them—as they howled. It was only when their howls had turned to growls, and then yelps as they withered and died, that he sensed there was a problem.

Now, he soothed himself by making shadows on the wall, and wondering if any other visitors would come to play games.

THE ALARMING SILHOUETTE that Jackson had witnessed growing to immense proportions inside the Chalet, bore all the earmarks of evil. It looked like death, it smelled like death, and Jackson was sure if he could take a bite out of it, it would taste like death. *Ugh.* Going inside the main area of the Chalet was the last thing he wanted to do, but he knew if Mal was in there, they had to save him. Johanna showed no reluctance in storming the automaton exhibit, or did she? She seemed to be taking more time, thinking things out this morning, although he doubted it was because she was having second thoughts. More likely, she was trying to come up with a fool-proof plan. "So, what do you think?" he asked.

"I wish I knew which automaton Mal is trapped in."

"You definitely think he's trapped inside one of those things?"

"I do. How else is Ailill Caomhánach going to keep him here? It would be like someone locking you in a coffin so they could rob the mortuary."

"Why do I have to be the one locked in a coffin? Why not you?"

"Because all I have to do to transport myself someplace else is think about it."

"Can't Mal do that, too?"

"Yes, but we can't assume he did. Ailill Caomhánach may be preventing him from doing that. We still have to investigate.

"So how are we gonna find Mal?"

"We're going to have to go in there and look around to see what's different."

"Begging for trouble," Jackson said in a sing-song voice.

"We have amulets, protective crystals, and each other. We merely have to hold hands to combine our energy. And like last time, I'll scan the individual mechanisms."

"That was handy for finding Ailill Caomhánach, but will Mal give off a magical signature?"

"Yes. And with luck, Mal's will be stronger."

"I hope you're right."

"You ready?"

Jackson glanced at the wall where he had seen the shadow, but it was gone. He pulled Johanna inside, and slowly they walked down the widest aisle as Johanna searched for distinct magical signatures. Since all the automata were created by magic, it was not an easy task. Most of the mechanisms looked familiar and Jackson racked his brain, trying to recall if any of them were different. As he approached one particular exhibit, he unconsciously began singing under his breath:

> "Come on and hear, come on and hear
> Alexander's Ragtime Band
> Come on and hear, come on and hear 'bout
> the best band in the land"

Johanna stopped walking, looked around and spotted a military drummer. About all it had in common with a band musician was its regimental jacket with epaulettes. "I think that's a Revolutionary War drummer, and he predates ragtime by about a hundred years."

Jackson twisted his head to look at her as if he were coming out of a dream. After a long hesitation, he muttered, "Right. No ragtime." He took a step forward and pulled her, but Johanna didn't budge.

Instead, she turned 180 degrees and walked toward a mechanism stuck in a niche in the back. They had both bypassed it on their journey down the main aisle because the back walkway ended in a blind alley. She was forced to stop when Jackson didn't let go of her hand. "Come this way," she told him.

"No," he answered. "We have to keep moving forward. Not going back."

JOHANNA THOUGHT JACKSON'S voice sounded oddly hollow. Almost automated. She pulled on his hand but he neither moved toward her nor let go.

Something's going on here. She imagined them naked in her bed and used telepathy to plant the image in Jackson's mind. *"Sex,"* she said forcefully.

Jackson stopped pulling against her and blinked. "What?"

As she stared at him, a slow blush crept up his face.

"I thought that might get your attention. Where were you just now?"

"What do you mean?"

"I'm trying to get a closer look at the automaton in the back of the room and you're trying to pull me away from it. Why?"

Jackson shook his head. "I don't know."

She tugged his hand again, "Come with me."

This time he followed.

MAL HEARD VOICES, even though he couldn't see where they were coming from. His movement was very limited and even though he could turn his head a little, it was not enough to allow him to see the speakers. However, he thought he recognized the voices of Johanna and Jackson and prayed he was right. *I hope they brought reinforcements. I would hate to see them trapped like me.*

"That doesn't look familiar." Jackson motioned with his head toward an exhibit labeled *The Draughtsman*. "I think I would have remembered something like that."

JOHANNA SIMPLY SHOOK her head in agreement. She didn't want to speak out loud in fear of tipping off Ailill Caomhánach with her sudden excitement.

She felt a definite vibration coming from this particular automaton. More so than the other mechanisms, although it didn't have the type of magical signature she'd expected.

Jackson leaned in as close as he dared. "He's drawing a dog. That is so cool."

No. The word planted itself in Johanna's brain. *Not a dog. Words.*

Johanna looked closer. This automaton was definitely into drawing. "We need to find something like this with words."

Jackson didn't answer. His eyes had glazed over.

Johanna immediately imagined a tight curl of water off a Hawaiian beach and stood Jackson on a surfboard in the middle of it before projecting the image into his mind. "Watch out," she shouted.

Jackson gasped for air and immediately crouched. A moment later, he stood up. "What the hell…?"

"Ailill Caomhánach keeps trying to pull you away from me. He's really powerful and his energy is all coming from the front of the room. I need to find Mal, but I need you to stay behind me. I don't want to lose you, too."

"Aargh," Jackson squealed, his eyes bulging.

"What?" Johanna asked.

He pointed to the front wall and Johanna turned in time to watch a huge shadow crawl up the front wall like a savage behemoth. "Do you see it?" he asked.

"It's a shadow."

"Yeah. But what's making the shadow?"

"We need to find Mal," she said, pulling him further into the dead end. "We need his energy."

"Yeah. But the *Sultan of Sinister* is probably saying the exact same thing."

LOGAN LOOKED AT the people fleeing the beach. It appeared to take families with small children much longer to pack up their belongings. He took some video of one of those families, so he could mention how especially vulnerable they would be. As he held the shot, he realized that even though some groups were slower than others, the mass panic might be enough to keep the dogs away. He looked down the beach toward the Chalet. *I wonder if there have been any workers there lately, and if they've left lunch scraps laying around? That might attract wild animals.* He turned off his camera and headed down the beach. Perhaps he would be more likely to find what he needed at the Chalet.

★*Do you think it is odd that we haven't spoken to Johanna since she rescued Ava?*

⌘*Not at all. I'm sure she and Jackson have a lot to catch up on at the library after all the time they spent tracking down the Re Transfigurator and rescuing Ava. That was quite an ordeal. The two of them are probably also craving some much-needed rest.*

★*And time together. Alone.*

⌘ *They have plenty of time for that in the future.*

Pru Tellerence smiled. ★*Spoken like a true father.*

⌘*Besides, Johanna and Jackson are very industrious. I'm sure they have everything in hand.*

Ava awoke from her steak-induced stupor several hours later, when her cell phone rang. After speaking with her friends, she found her mother at the information desk packing books. "Where are Johanna and Jackson?"

"I'm not sure," her mother answered. I haven't seen them since before we traveled to that place to have them work on your foot."

"It's called Adventura, Mom, and it's not just a place, it's another realm."

"What does that mean exactly? Another realm?"

"Tonight, look at the stars in the sky and pick one far, far away. That might very well be Adventura. It's a different world, a different planet, whatever you want to call it. It's a place most people on Fantasia, or Earth as you keep calling it, will never get to see because they probably don't even know it exists."

"We traveled there in seconds." Her mother gave her a puzzled look. "How is that even possible?"

"How is it possible that we're staying in a French hotel suite with a view of the Eiffel Tower, even though we're in the middle of Exeter?"

Niamh shook her head. "If all that is possible, perhaps leprechauns do exist."

Ava laughed, leaving her mother alone. She returned several minutes later with the book *How to Catch a Leprechaun.* She opened it up to the middle and a little man is a bright green suit with a top hat scurried away.

Niamh's mouth opened, silently, as she watched him scurry inside the hotel suite. "Ava! Go catch him before he causes any trouble."

"You want to know how to catch a leprechaun, Mom?" She slammed the book closed. "Like that."

"You'd better go check."

"I will, but he won't be there. This is only a level one book."

"Why are you looking for Johanna and Jackson?"

"I want to talk with them about Logan."

Her mother's shoulders sagged. "Ava, I really think he's too old for you."

"He's also a cheater."

"What?"

"One of my friends texted me that she saw him at the Burger Meister in Lowell with some older girl and she said they looked very cozy."

"Not that I want to contradict myself," her mother said, "but you can't believe everything, everyone else says. Especially someone like Keli Gaughren, whom you've complained about in the past. However, I still think he's too old for you."

"Yeah. Maybe." She sighed.

JOHANNA DIDN'T SEE any automata writing words, and pulled Jackson off the aisle, choosing instead to walk through the exhibits crammed closer together. It was slower going, because there was more to look at. After a while, she nudged Jackson in the side with her elbow.

"What did you do that for?" he asked, rubbing the area where her elbow connected with his rib cage.

"Just making sure you're still with me."

"I'm keeping you between me and that big glass box in the front that seems to be casting the shadow on the wall."

"What makes you think it's coming from there?"

"I don't know. It had a kind of eerie glow that darkens when the shadow is there."

"Perhaps the shadow is what's causing it to darken?"

"Don't do that," Jackson said, stopping suddenly. "You're messing with my spontaneity."

Johanna didn't respond.

"Johanna?"

She pulled Jackson through the automata, looking for something similar to *The Draughtsman*. As they searched, the building began to creak. Johanna looked up at the rafters, and thought she saw them moving. Growing. *Ailill Caomhánach is trying to scare us off.* Rather than take another step, she used telepathy. *Mal, can you hear me?*

¢Johanna!
We're trying to locate you. I'll do my best to get you out.
¢Do you have reinforcements?
Jackson is with me.
¢Where is your father?

Johanna took a minute to focus on telepathically speaking with Ryden Simmdry. She could not make a connection.

Eeerrichhh. The rafters squeaked again, breaking her concentration.

I can't reach him, Mal. There's too much interference from Ailill Caomhánach. Jackson and I have to hope we can do this on our own.

THIRTY-TWO

"THE LAST TIME we approached an automaton—the one Ava was stuck in—we did it from two different sides," Jackson whispered. "Do you want to split up?"

"The last time my father was with us. We don't have his added assistance, now."

Jackson rubbed his chin. "How are we supposed to rescue Mal if there's no one to neutralize Ailill Caomhánach?"

Johanna didn't move or say anything.

"Johanna? You still with me?"

She shielded her thoughts, so only Jackson would hear them. *I think you need to do what you do best.*

"What's that?"

Use that magnificent brain of yours to create mass confusion.

"How am I supposed to do that?"

I don't know, but you'll think of something. You always do.

Above them, the rafters creaked and a nail popped out, *pinging* loudly seconds later as it crashed against the floor.

Jackson flinched. "I don't think it's safe in here."

We're not leaving without Mal.

"Okay. So, let's find him."

AILILL CAOMHÁNACH FELT a mixture of anger and frustration. He had failed to receive the energy boost he needed from Mal. *What is it about this being? He is a nobody. Just some visitor to a library. Yet he wards off my advances.*

Grynsmiþ, where are you? What are you doing? I require your assistance. I want you to tap into the power of those young people, while I concentrate on breaking this rather perplexing conquest. He is proving to be more formidable than expected. Immobilize the couple, so we can drain them quickly and move to a safer location; one where we won't be detected.

GRYNSMIþ'S BLUBBERY LIPS stuck out in a pout as he sulked. He didn't want to help Ailill Caomhánach. He was still angry with him for killing the dogs that had brought the Decadian so much joy. However, not wanting to help, and not helping, were two different concepts. Grynsmiþ had no more control over being at Ailill Caomhánach's beck and call than Mal did. Besides, he knew if he didn't help, his usefulness would be over, and he would end up locked away in a small, dark box for all eternity. Ailill Caomhánach currently commanded every fiber of his existence, and whether the Grynsmiþ wanted to acknowledge it or not, he was currently a puppet.

Maybe it won't be so bad, he thought. *Ailill Caomhánach may be millions of years old, but he is not immortal. I'll be free when he dies. Even if it's not be for a very long time.*

Grynsmiþ's shadow appeared on the far wall. "What is it you want me to do?"

ᚲ*Capture them and tie them down.*

"Why don't you just trap them inside more of your toys?"

ᚲ*Because they're not normal beings. I don't know what ever happened to plain, old-fashioned people. It seems like everyone we encounter has some kind of superior power. I don't care what you have to do to secure them. Just make sure that you do.*

Grynsmiþ felt his skin crawl. He had never hated anyone before but was now developing a distaste for Ailill Caomhánach.

A FAST-MOVING VESSEL carrying rogue treasure hunters approached the outskirts of the Fantasian atmosphere. They had stolen the latest advancement in interstellar vehicles, and added their own technology to its system. It could jump through space at hyper speeds, without the need for wormholes, but more importantly, it could now detect supernatural anomalies.

The thieves, known as Helions, had received alerts that bursts of magic were seeking out a parallel supernatural signal. While the Helion race did not possess magical qualities of their own, they believed in its power and knew anything magical commanded a high price on the interstellar market. Unfortunately, every time they approached the coordinates of the mystical burst, their equipment registered only trace amounts, indicating the source was no longer in range.

MAL SWALLOWED THE extract from the licorice in his mouth. He knew it wouldn't last much longer and had no idea how long its effects would continue. He needed to be proactive starting now.

What will thwart Ailill Caomhánach? he asked himself. Mal's main concern was protecting his energy. *I need to cocoon my internal reserves, yet repel any advances.* He had never been one for chants and charms. Fantasia was not a magic-based realm, even if there were magical communities scattered about the earth. However, having recently spent time on Mysteriose, Mal couldn't help but learn some of their spells, including one he knew parents used to lull their babies to sleep. It was an overpowering hypnotic that he hoped would work on Ailill Caomhánach.

LOGAN SHIELDED HIS eyes as he eyed the Chalet. Something about the building seemed desolate. He hadn't been here since the fire, and although the building hadn't sustained much damage, it now appeared eerily abandoned. *It's like it's giving off waves of despair to keep people away.* He took a shot of the outside of the building and the empty beach before pulling the door handle, expecting it to be locked. He was surprised when the door creaked open. It felt creepy walking into the vestibule of the building. The hairs on the back of his neck tingled as he caught the reflection of lights coming from the entrance to the main room. The ceiling rafters creaked, doubling his anxiety. *What am I doing here? This is not a risk I need to take.*

Then he thought about *The Elliott Report.* He

sighed. *I work for myself, now. Nothing ventured, nothing gained.*

Niamh looked over the edge of her teacup when Ava entered the suite. She quickly lowered it to the matching saucer. "Do you know where Jackson and Johanna are?" she asked her daughter.

"Nope. Haven't seen them since they rescued me."

Niamh cocked her head, thinking about what Ava just said, realizing she hadn't seen them since then, either. "I have no idea where they are. Or if they're in trouble."

"Johanna's parents probably know where she is."

"Yes, but there's no way for me to get in touch with them. Johanna usually takes care of that."

"I guess we'll just have to wait for someone to turn up, either Jackson or Johanna or her parents."

"That doesn't make me any less worried about what could be going on with them."

Disregarding the automata around them, Jackson dug into his pocket with his free hand and pulled out his phone.

Johanna's eyes narrowed. "You're making a call, now?"

"I have an idea, but we need to move to the area reserved for DJs and pray there's some way to hook up my phone to the Chalet's inhouse speaker system."

"What are you planning?"

"Something I hope is unexpected." He motioned with his chin. "Over there."

She grabbed his hand as they made their way over to a raised platform surrounded by a short wall.

He looked at their joined hands. "I need to use both my hands."

Johanna moved her hand up his arm to his shoulder. "As long as we stay connected, we should maintain strength. Will this work for you?"

He nodded and began searching through his playlist. "You asked for mass confusion, and I just thought of one way I might achieve that."

"With music?"

"Not just any music," he said, smiling.

Johanna looked down at his song choice. "*Layers of Time?* Our brains are going to melt if we listen to that."

"Yeah. But maybe his will, too. Besides, my brain is immune to it. I'm hoping it creates enough confusion to send the *Maester of Malice* over the edge."

Jackson pulled out part of the sound system looking at the connectors on the back. He picked up a cable and waved it at Johanna. "Bingo!" He plugged one end into the system, and he connected the adapter hanging off the other end into his phone.

Johanna pursed her lips to stop from smiling. "That was incredibly lucky."

"Not really. All the kids in school have been talking about coming here and using their own playlists to dance to." He pressed play. "Let Operation Mal begin."

THE REPETITIVE MOVEMENT of writing a few words over and over did not take much of Mal's energy, leaving his mind clear to think about the swirling potion he once saw in a huge cauldron behind Hue the Elder's home in Mysteriose. At first, Mal had kidded the Mysterian about brewing moonshine. However, he stopped when Hue explained that the viscous liquid, *blæc cwēade,* had supernatural properties that could be manipulated by thought waves to induce physical magic.

"We used this the first time the Terrorians paid our realm a visit. It was their first incursion, and they had only taken two people hostage when I discovered them near the library. Using my mind, alone, I imagined becoming stuck in blæc cwēade, unable to move my feet. I envisioned myself reaching down to find a way to liberate them, only to see my hands become stuck in the thick liquid. In my mind's eye, it was too difficult to move. I projected these thoughts on the Terrorians. And as I continued to think about being stuck, their movements slowed, until they were hardly moving at all. It was easy after that to incarcerate them and release our countrymen."

Mal secured the image in his mind and imagined endlessly stirring the cauldron with a large, flat paddle until he believed it the most boring task he ever had to do. The tar-like thickness of the potion in his imagination was extremely difficult to turn—exhausting him. In his mind, he inhaled deeply and found he could barely move—finding the fumes of the mixture hypnotically sleep inducing. Mal kept imagining how drained he felt, while making sure a separate segment of his mind stayed sharp, lest he put himself to sleep instead of Ailill Caomhánach.

With the sound system in the Chalet now blasting heavy metal music, Johanna and Jackson carefully made their way back down the aisles, looking for an automaton that could write.

Johanna tried splitting her internal resources, trying to recognize *The Writer* while simultaneously attempting to re-connect with Mal. It left her feeling nervous. Ever since

Jackson had hooked up the music, she seemed to have lost track of Mal. She became more worried with each passing moment. *Mal, I don't know why you're not answering me, but I hope it's for a good reason.*

Eeerrichhh. Eeerrichhh. Ping. Ping. Ping. The rafters squeaked again as a few more nails popped out.

Jackson squeezed Johanna's hand, but she wasn't sure if it was to reassure her or to signal his uneasiness.

THE HEAVY METAL music hadn't registered on Ailill Caomhánach's consciousness. The dark entity was so focused on getting around Mal's defenses, he had shut off his mind to everything else.

But trying to breach Mal's self-protective sheath was exhausting him. Ailill Caomhánach hadn't experienced physical pain or tired muscles for many millennia, yet those sensations were all too quickly coming back to him.

Little did he know that rather than a simple source of energy, he had captured someone with the powers of an overseer.

EVEN IF AILILL Caomhánach remained unaware of Jackson's choice of music, the gothic metal song had a profound effect on Grynsmiþ. He *loved* it.

Instead of thinking of ways to subdue Johanna and Jackson, Grynsmiþ allowed himself to be swallowed up by the driving beat and felt it pulsating throughout his being. It made him feel alive. It made him want to dance. And it made him feel kindly toward the young couple who played it, for it reminded Grynsmiþ of home and the music of Decada.

*

JACKSON CONCENTRATED ON the clash of the music while Johanna continued searching for the correct automaton.

"We've searched up and down every aisle," she said, "but none of these exhibits have a figure writing words." She half-closed her eyes to rest her brain, but partially opened them when she sensed Jackson moving next to her. That's when she noticed light leaking in around the edges of a doorway. Yet when she opened her eyes fully, the same space appeared to be a solid wall. She tugged Jackson's arm. "Come with me."

Even up close, the wall appeared solid until she laid her palms against it. In an instant, the outline of painted cement blocks disappeared and a door appeared. Johanna motioned at the door with her free hand and it flew open. *Finally.*

Standing alone in the center of a small office, an automaton known as *The Writer* moved with precision, forming his words perfectly every time. This mechanism appeared larger than its counterpart, *The Draughtsman.* Indeed, it was larger than life, and if Jackson wasn't mistaken, it was growing.

"That thing is huge," he exclaimed. "Did it come from a museum?"

It came from Ailill Caomhánach's mind, except I don't know how he could have become so familiar with it. This looks 18ᵗʰ century, and we both know he predates that era by eons.

"Maybe the *Diabolical Devil* scanned some books in the library before snatching Ava," Jackson said, posing a possibility.

There you go again. I'm willing to bet you didn't give that much thought before you said it, yet it's probably true because it seems like the most plausible thing that might have happened.

"So, now what?"

Logan froze when music began blasting from the sound system. He tried not to move when the ceiling creaked, spewing nails to the floor like projectiles. And yet, some strange magnetic energy drew him toward the inner entrance, where the chaos appeared to be centered.

He felt his sandals scraping against the floor as they pulled him into the mayhem. And before he knew it, he stood at the brink of bedlam: the music pulsating, countless automata operating at accelerated speed, waves of unnatural energy washing over him, and a hypnotic vibe making him feel like putty. He stared at one of the automatons. It was just like the one in his dream.

Logan fought his fear, beads of sweat forming on his forehead and upper lip. He managed to turn on his camera, shooting as much video as possible while describing his feelings.

His voice cracked when an unearthly shadow danced up the wall. A HUGE shadow. Yet, even as his body tensed, he still shot video. *If anything happens to me, I want the world to know what caused it.*

Let's get to work. Johanna said, taking a deep breath, clearing her mind, and chanting. "*Aheorde! Aheorde! Aheorde!*" She pulled a pouch out of her pocket, removing pieces of black tourmaline. She tossed them, one at a time, onto the automaton.

"What is that stuff?"

Black Tourmaline. It changes negative energy into positive energy.

Jackson half-listened as Johanna chanted again,

fully intending to join in. However, his attention was diverted by the dark shadow crawling up the wall of the room they were now in. The room felt colder. "Johanna," he whispered, "do you feel that?"

Instead of answering him, she continued chanting, "*Aheorde! Aheorde! Aheorde!*"

Jackson tried to think of a way to foil an attack by the huge shadow but his nerves prevented his brain from kicking into gear. Regardless of the chill, he felt beads of sweat rolling down his forehead and used the back of his hand to wipe them away.

Johanna's chants became more frenzied, and the song blasting from the speakers grew in volume.

Creeeaaak. Ping. Ping. Ping. Ping. Nails bounced off the floor around them with alarming frequency.

THIRTY-THREE

A FRUSTRATED JOHANNA redirected her thoughts. *Come on, Mal, use your powers to force your release from Ailill Caomhánach. Help me.*

However, Mal was more intent on preventing the malevolent being from draining Johanna and Jackson's life force. He concentrated on being encumbered in Mysterian *blæc cwēade*, which continued to have a profound effect on his predator.

"*Aheorde! Aheorde! Aheorde!*" Johanna chanted in earnest. "*Onlíese hīe!*" *Release him.* She took pieces of black obsidian and hematite and hurled them at the automaton.

The music grew louder, even though Jackson had not adjusted it, and everything in the room shook.

Johanna lit a pair of sage bundles, waving their smoke toward the automata that held Mal hostage. A wispy wreath settled over it.

What is that?" Jackson asked, wrinkling his nose.

Sage. Its smoke drives away negative energy.
"Then why does everything seem to be getting worse?"

JACKSON DREW HIS head back as *The Writer* increased in size to fill the entire room it had been hidden in.

He listened as Johanna continued to chant, *"Aheorde! Aheorde! Aheorde! Onlíese híe!"* and added his voice to hers, chanting as well, while disregarding the blasting music. He kept a firm grip on Johanna's waist as he lent his energy to the fray. They had done it before with Ava. *Why wouldn't it work for Mal, as well?*

BLÆC CWĒADE HIT its mark. Ailill Caomhánach felt himself weakening, his fatigue so profound, he wanted to crawl back into the Re Transfigurator and sleep forever. The feeling overwhelmed him, however, he knew if he gave up the battle, his future would be lost. He would not live to fight another day. And so, he hung on, using every last ounce of strength, if not to steal Mal's energy, to fight to stay alive.

A FLASH OF white-hot light penetrated the entire space, and three beings materialized in the room. They resembled stick figures swathed in select places in cotton candy, which appeared benign enough, except they carried weapons with unknown power. Their attention settled on Johanna.

They emitted a series of discordant musical notes, not unlike the music blasting through the speakers, yet distinct enough to be heard clearly.

Johanna's arm waved to enact a translation charm, although she never appeared to take her attention away from the spell she was casting.

The new intruders aimed their weapons at Johanna. "*Gesylelgesell scinncræft.*"

"Yeah, that was a big help," Jackson surmised.

The building groaned louder, raining splinters and nails upon everyone inside. One of the infiltrators slowly reduced in size, eventually melting into nothing.

"Did you see that?" Jackson asked. "Where did he go?"

A second being began to melt.

Johanna looked away for a fraction of a second. "I think Ailill Caomhánach is having them for dinner. But not as guests."

Jackson shouted, "Two down!"

Johanna ignored everything going on around her, working desperately to free Mal.

MAL FELT A SUDDEN reduction of tension when Ailill Caomhánach began absorbing someone else's life force. *It's now or never.* He switched everything in his being from fighting the first overseer to freeing himself. As long as his predator was preoccupied, Mal had a slim chance of success.

He switched his emphasis from being stuck in *blæc cwēade* to chanting along with Johanna and Jackson.

THE TREASURE HUNTERS proved to be a boon to Ailill Caomhánach. The evil entity felt his energy surge. *Just a little more and I'll be done with these unexpected but not unwanted miscreants. Then I can get back to the ones from the library, who will restore me to full power.*

*

JOHANNA MAY HAVE not liked Jackson's choice of music, however, Grynsmiþ fed off it, absorbing it like a sponge. It made him feel free. And powerful. He had sensed Ailill Caomhánach's weakening power and realized he could finally be free of the nasty entity that treated him like an errand boy. Now, he felt his nemesis growing stronger.

Grynsmiþ switched his attention on Johanna and Jackson, listening to their words and absorbing the intent of their spell. He felt the magic emanating from Johanna and knew, she would not give up until she put an end to Ailill Caomhánach.

"*Aheorde! Aheorde! Aheorde! Onlíese hīe!*" Grynsmiþ recited, his barely used voice a deep rumble, no smoother than sandpaper. "*Aheorde! Aheorde! Aheorde! Onlíese hīe!*" he said again, wanting to free himself from Ailill Caomhánach forever.

"DO YOU HEAR that?" Jackson whispered in Johanna's ear. "Someone else in here is chanting!"

Don't worry about that. Just keep concentrating.

"Whoever or whatever it is, sounds terrible."

"*Aheorde! Aheorde! Aheorde! Onlíese hīe!*" a gruff voice repeated, gaining speed and volume with each exhortation.

"Oh. My. God. Are you seeing what I'm seeing? Jackson watched as Grynsmiþ's shadow took over the entire room.

The appearance of the air surrounding them wavered.

Eeeaaarrrk. Ping. Ping. Ping.

"I think it's time to get out of here." He tugged on Johanna's waist.

No! Aheorde! Aheorde! Aheorde! Onlíese hīe!

*

GRYNSMIþ WAS THE most powerful sorcerer Decada had ever produced. The addition of his strength to the chant made the walls in the Chateau throb. Coupled together, the music and chanting gave off enough sound waves to increase the temperature in the room, changing it from frosty to fever-inducing in just seconds. The audio vibration manifested itself as a visible color glow, producing giant bubbles of light that pulsated—changing from violet to blue to yellow to red. As the intensity of the quivering in the building increased, so did the bubbles, crowding together until everything exploded with a sonic *BOOM!* creating another brilliant flash of light, followed by total silence.

JOHANNA RUBBED HER eyes. The ultra-bright flash had robbed her of her sight, and she wondered if she was blind, or if she were even still alive? *Just breathe* she told herself. And then she realized, she *was* breathing. *Dead people don't breathe.* She opened her eyes to determine if she could see.

Everything was out of focus. It was all light and shadow, without detail. She realized Jackson no longer held onto her waist and whipped around, wondering if he were still with her. *That was a mistake,* she thought, as her head began to pound.

"*Oof!* What are you doing? It's bad enough I can't see or hear and now I hurt, too."

Johanna grabbed the shadow in front of her. "Jackson, you're here! Are you okay?"

"No. I thought I made that clear in my last statement."

"Can you see?"

"Not really. You're just a big silvery blob in an otherwise white world of nothingness."

"Whatever just happened has apparently turned you into a poet."

He sniffed. "If we're in heaven, they burnt the toast."

"That's the sage I burned to free Mal." She gasped. "Mal!"

"I have never been happier to hear your voices," a faint voice replied.

"Where are you?" Johanna pushed away from Jackson, turning in a circle to look for another shadow.

"I think I'm lying on the ground. I'll try standing as soon as my muscles remember how to function. I've been concentrating on a Mysterian spell to thwart Ailill Caomhánach and it affected me as much as I had hoped it would affect him."

"Is he here?" Jackson asked.

"No," a deep voice grumbled.

"Uh-oh. That doesn't sound good," Jackson whispered to Johanna. "He sounds just like the giant in *The Princess Bride*."

Who's speaking?" she asked in her most forceful voice.

"I am called Grynsmiþ."

"Grin-smith," Jackson repeated.

"Where are you from, Grynsmiþ?" Mal asked.

"Decada. Far away."

"How did you get here?" Johanna demanded.

"Ailill Caomhánach."

"Where is he now?" Jackson asked.

"He has expired. This is good. His was a dark

power. He had evil inside him."

"We can't disagree with that," Mal said, slowly pushing himself into a sitting position.

GRYNSMIþ USED HIS powers to restore the balance of energy in the room to normal.

All that remained inside the Chalet, was Johanna, Jackson, Mal, Grynsmiþ, and Logan, who stood off in a corner, recording video on his camera. The automata had all disappeared. Unlike the time Johanna and Jackson had freed Ava, no debris remained. It had all been magically created and had now disappeared. The only reminder of what had just gone on, was Grynsmiþ.

In reality, the Decadian was not as huge or scary as his voice and shadow had led everyone to believe. He may have been immortal, but was born at a time and place where people did not exceed five feet in height. His skin, which had an unnatural greenish-purple tint, was almost translucent, and his voice rattled from disuse. However, while he was unusual in appearance, his slightly bulging, watery blue eyes made him look non-threatening in a pathetic sort of way.

Grynsmiþ turned toward Logan and pointed. "Why is he holding that little black house? Does another dark entity live inside?"

Johanna, Jackson, and Mal finally noticed Logan and his camera.

Johanna's chin lifted a bit as she steeled her voice. "What are you doing here, Logan?"

"I might ask you the same question," he replied.

"You shouldn't be in here, Bud," Jackson said in a friendlier voice.

"I'm shooting a follow-up to the fire they had here last week as well as a story about wild dogs bothering people on the beach. Why are you here?"

Jackson helped Mal up from the floor. "Just showing Mal the Chalet. We're always talking about it and he wanted to see it."

"There was a lot more going on in here a little while ago than just you showing Mal the Chalet. Come to think of it, I didn't see Mal at all. Care to elaborate?"

Jackson took a couple of steps toward Logan. "I'll need your camera."

Logan stepped back. "Freedom of the press, 'Bud.' You don't want to go up against the Constitution, now, do you?"

Behind the building, sounds of a pack of barking dogs grew louder.

"Friends," Grynsmiþ shouted.

While everyone automatically turned to look at him, Logan slipped the SD card out of the camera and pocketed it.

The Decadian ran to the back door and opened it, letting the dogs inside.

Johanna, Jackson, and Mal all took a step back, when the overly-energized dogs began growling at them.

Grynsmiþ noticed their distress.

Logan slipped a blank SD card in the camera and began shooting the dogs.

"Aaowooh!!" Grynsmiþ howled, running toward the far side of the room, leading the dogs away.

Logan began backing out of the room. He didn't want to tangle with Johanna and Jackson, nor did he want to come face to face with the weird little man and the dogs.

"Logan. Stop." Johanna's voice was forceful.

"What is your problem?" Logan replied in turn.

"Give me your camera," she said.

"Like hell," he answered.

Johanna's head jerked in a quick nod and the camera flew from Logan's hands into hers.

"What the—. There's nothing on there but a pack of dogs."

"We'll see about that," she said, viewing the footage.

Jackson looked at it over her shoulder. "There's nothing on there but a pack of dogs," he noted, mimicking Logan.

Johanna tried to navigate to earlier footage, but saw nothing else there. "Where's the rest of it?"

"I don't know what you're talking about," Logan complained. "I just got here. GRUNT sent me to do a story about complaints people are making about wild dogs on the beach."

"Sorry," Johanna mumbled, handing him back his camera.

"You two are pathetic. I'm out of here." Logan turned and left abruptly.

THIRTY-FOUR

BEFORE LEAVING THE beach, Logan called Graydon Ransom University News Tonight, telling Jennifer he wasn't able to finish the story because he had become extremely dizzy at the Dunes and had to return home.

He hung up, looking down at his notes. *This is it.*

He returned home, sat down at his computer, and finished editing all the video about the Library of Illumination that he planned to run on *The Elliott Report*.

THE SILENCE INSIDE the Chalet was stunning.

"Can we go home now?" Jackson asked.

"That depends," Johanna answered. Where's Grynsmiþ?"

Jackson smirked. "Running with the dogs?"

Mal moved toward the door. "We'd better find him before the police do. I wonder if I can transport him as far as Decada? I may have to take him to Lumina with me and seek Ryden Simmdry's assistance."

No sooner had Mal mentioned Ryden Simmdry, than the master of the overseers appeared in front of them.

⌘ *I've been thinking about you, Malcolm Trees.*

Mal laughed. "Using my whole name, now, are you? Does this mean I'm in trouble?"

⌘ *Hardly. You had better get used to hearing your full name. As an overseer, everyone will call you by both your given name and your surname.*

Jackson's face lit up. "Is there going to be another Overseers Competition?"

⌘ *Not quite. We have two positions to fill, however, both Malcolm Trees and Dame Erato have proved themselves in previous competitions, moving them to the top of the list. The College of Overseers has unanimously agreed to induct you both formally into our ranks. We wish to conduct a ceremony tomorrow.*

"WILL ALL THE curators be invited?" Johanna asked.

⌘ *Of course, as it will be a full day of festivities. We will celebrate the bestowal of the Majorious Longevicus Blessings in the morning, and then, at sundown, Pru Tellerence and I will be joined in matrimony.*

Johanna stared at her father. The inside of her nose prickled. She appeared frozen, except for the tears that threatened to spill from her eyes. She had so much she suddenly wanted to say, but was too overwhelmed and tongue-tied to form the words.

Pru Tellerence put in a sudden appearance. ★ *You told her without me!*

⌘ *I merely said it would be a full day and explained why.*

She nodded vehemently. ★ *You told her without me,* she repeated.

The tears finally escaped down Johanna's cheeks. "I'm so happy for you." She pulled her mother close, hugging her fiercely.

⌘ *But you're not happy for me.*

"Of course, I am." Johanna laughed and let out a small sob at the same time. She and her mother widened the hug to include Ryden Simmdry.

Jackson took Mal's hand and pulled him in for a man-hug. "We're happy for you, too, Mal, even if it is hard for us mere mortals to compete with a family of superpowers."

When everyone broke apart they found themselves under observation.

"Grynsmiþ," Jackson said. "There you are! Now we can all go home."

"Decada?" The sorcerer's face lit up.

"Mal?" Jackson inquired.

"Ryden Simmdry?" Mal asked. "Do you think it's possible for us to return… uh… Grynsmiþ? To his place of birth?"

⌘ *We would need the combined power of three overseers to travel outside the Illumini Constellation, however, Malcolm Trees, many of the powers befitting an overseer were bestowed upon you when you became Chancellor of the Exchequer. Not to mention the power Johanna seems to have developed as her birthright. I believe if we all join hands, we should be able to accompany this traveler home.*

"Can I go, too?" Jackson asked.

★ *Of course, Jackson.* Pru Tellerence extended her hand to him.

Jackson grabbed Johanna's hand, and she and her father reached out for Grynsmiþ. Mal closed the circle.

⌘ *Concentrate on your home world.*

Grynsmiþ closed his eyes and a smile grew across his face. Suddenly, a strong wind buffeted the group, almost knocking them off their feet. When they opened their eyes, they found themselves on a darkened, grassy plain between two peaks.

Grynsmiþ nodded enthusiastically. "Home!" He knelt down and rubbed his hands in the grass, touching his forehead to the ground.

"Am I imagining it, or is the grass purple?" Jackson asked.

"Maybe it just looks that way because it's twilight," Mal answered. "A very bright twilight, I might add." He raised both arms toward the heavens. "That is quite an abundance of stars."

★ *Look at the profusion of colors in the sky!*

Jackson crouched down and pulled out his camera, more interested in what lay below his feet than above his head. He switched on the flashlight app. "Yep, the grass is purple."

⌘ *That is not what is unusual about this place.*

Jackson stood. "Being from Lumina, I can see how you might not be impressed by all the strange colors. What is it you find unusual?"

⌘ *The position of the night sky is off. We didn't only travel in distance. We traveled in time.*

"No way!" Jackson said. "How can you tell?

"Look up," Johanna answered. "Mal noticed it, too."

Her co-curator shrugged. "The sky looks different

because we're in a different constellation."

⌘ *The sky looks different because what Fantasians refer to as the* Big Bang Theory *happened much more recently, here. The proliferation of star formations above us may even contain your very own solar system before it expanded out into the universe. I imagine when Grynsmiþ thought about home to facilitate our traveling here, he thought about home in his own time. We may be standing here, but I'm willing to bet that none of us, including myself, have been born yet, and I've been around for many millennia. Soak it in. You're witnessing something that no one else in the Illumini System has ever seen before.*

"It's really beautiful, when you think about it," Johanna commented. "Look at how clear everything is. Don't you feel like the stars are so close you can reach out and touch them?"

"Maybe," Jackson said, "but the real question is, how do we get back to our own time?"

GRYNSMIÞ POKED AROUND between the blades of Decadian grass until he found a sliver of stone. It almost looked like a cross section of the sky, containing brilliant blues, deep reds and swirls of yellow, interspersed by small bits that looked like diamonds. He held the stone between his palms and chanted, bowing down to the ground beneath his feet, then rising to extend his hands toward the skies.

He handed it to Jackson. "This will take you home." He looked at everyone. "Hold hands." He positioned Jackson between Johanna and Ryden Simmdry and inserted the stone between Jackson and Johanna's grasped palms. "Think of home."

⌘ *Wait.* Ryden Simmdry let go of Jackson's other

hand, breaking the strength of the circle. ⌘ *We must all think of the same realm in the early twenty-first century. Let me suggest that we all think of the main lobby in the Fantasian library, even if Lumina is now home for some of us. I wouldn't want our individual thoughts of home to dilute the effect of the stone, placing us somewhere we don't desire or belong.*

"Library of Illumination. Main lobby. Today. Got it," Jackson said.

Mal smiled. "Me, too."

Before thinking thoughts of home, Jackson nodded at their new acquaintance. "Grynsmiþ, thank you. You're the best."

Their journey back to Fantasia felt as bumpy as their initial trip to Decada. Indeed, when they appeared inside the library, it was difficult for any of them to land on their feet. Ryden Simmdry managed to hold Pru Tellerence upright by grabbing onto the information desk, and Jackson and Johanna stabilized each other, however, Mal ended up on the floor, hitting his head upon landing.

Niamh screamed when they all suddenly appeared. "Oh my gosh, I hope everyone is alright. You all look off-balance.

"Mal isn't alright," Jackson said, kneeling on the floor.

Johanna squatted on Mal's other side. "Mal?" She lifted his hand and patted it. When he didn't respond she lowered her face to see if she could feel him exhaling. "He's breathing."

⌘ *We should move him to the couch.*

Without hesitation, Jackson picked the former curator up and carried him inside the reading room.

Ryden Simmdry telepathically probed the future

overseer's mind.

A moment later, Mal's eyelids flickered as he endeavored to regain full consciousness. "What happened?"

"Our trip home from Decada was a little rough," Johanna said.

"But all's well that ends well, Jackson quipped.

Mal rubbed his forehead for several seconds. "What's Decada?"

THIRTY-FIVE

"I WISH MY PARENTS hadn't whisked Mal away so quickly last night. I'm still worried about him," Johanna said over an early breakfast.

"It not like you can't telepathically ask how Mal's doing, and know the answer in two seconds."

"I already know he's doing fine. I checked. But him saying, 'what's Decada,' haunted me in my sleep. I had a nightmare that Mal really got hurt quite badly."

"That sucks," Jackson commented. "But it really was pretty funny. The look on everyone's face was priceless."

"You had the same look on your face."

"Only until Mal started laughing. You gotta love a guy who still has a sense of humor after being knocked out during a crash landing."

"I'm glad we'll get to see him again today." She looked at her watch. "And soon. I'd better get ready." Johanna swallowed the last dregs of coffee and rushed away.

"Me, too," Jackson said to the now-empty room.

Ryden Simmdry and Pru Tellerence had invited all the Roths to their wedding, as well as the overseer induction.

Upstairs, Johanna looked for the white shirt her mother had made especially for her. She had been saving it for a special occasion, and this was it. She paired it with full, silvery-blue pants and matching sandals. She carefully styled her hair in a loose French roll and added simple blue diamond jewelry Pru Tellerence had given her after learning Johanna was her daughter.

The sounds of the Roths gathering downstairs by the information desk and chatting about the trip to Lumina told her it was time to leave. She grabbed a small handbag and made her way down the curator's staircase.

Chris wolf-whistled.

Jackson took a step toward her. "You look beautiful." He leaned in and kissed her lightly on the lips.

"Are we all ready to go?" she asked.

"Yep."

An instant later, they were in the courtyard outside the Library of Origination.

Jackson cleared his throat. "Aren't we supposed to be at the amphitheater?"

"No," Johanna answered. "This isn't the competition, it's the induction. And it happens here at the University of Lumi."

"The sky is purple," Chris said.

"Just like the grass on Decada," Jackson remarked.

Ava pointed at evenly spaced stanchions to which dozens of balloons were tethered. "I would have thought the people here are too high brow for balloons."

Jackson grabbed her in a one-armed hug. "Let's just say the Luminans like to celebrate with a bang."

"What are they going to do, pop all the balloons?" Chris asked.

"In a manner of speaking," Jackson answered.

Ava turned in a full-circle. "I love the way the buildings sparkle."

"They're made out of diamond," Johanna explained.

Niamh raised an eyebrow. "Not real diamond, something industrial, right?"

Johanna shook her head. "Real diamond. This whole world is made of it. It's as plentiful as our rocks back home.

Chris bent down and picked a diamond stone out of a flower bed.

"Put that back, now." Jackson's voice was stern.

"Why, they're not going to miss it and this might buy me a new car."

"It'll buy you certain death."

Niamh tsked. "Jackson, don't talk that way to your brother."

"I'm not going to kill him," he said defensively. "Diamonds from Lumina explode if anyone tries to remove them. They only exist within this world's atmosphere. And if Chris has that on him when we all try to go home— together—we're all going to be killed. So, put that down." He grabbed his brother's wrist and banged it against his hand—forcing the diamond to fly out of it. "That's better," he said sweetly, letting go of Chris.

Jackson and Johanna advised the Roth's on which foods to stay away from, and finally, as lunch wound down, the induction ceremony began.

Pru Tellerence introduced Dame Erato first. The overseer discussed the unique attributes that Dame Erato would bring to the position, while moving images of her appeared in the sky overhead, illustrating everything Pru Tellerence said. There was polite laughter as Bel saw her *great aunt* in the sky and started screaming, "Dama! Dama!" her name for Dame Erato.

The same was done for Mal, with Bel screaming, "Malalalal!"

Afterward, several songs were sung, while the new overseers were transported to a special room under the amphitheater where their special blessings were bestowed. For Mal, it was more of a formality, however, Dame Erato received the full treatment all at once, which left her breathless.

They returned to the College of Overseers, where the music was just wrapping up and were brought up before the crowd once again. There, they were handed their miters, which were fitted with the apparatus that allowed them to transport, and presented with a special medal that all overseers wore on special occasions. These were placed around their necks and they were congratulated by Ryden Simmdry and their fellow overseers with the approving roll of their forefingers. As a *finalé*, hundreds of balloons were released into the air.

"That's so festive," Niamh said, just before cringing at the first explosion. As each balloon reached the inner edge of the atmosphere, the diamonds inside exploded, raining diamond dust on everything below.

"And that's why you can't take any of the diamonds you see home with you," Jackson said, nudging his brother.

*

Pʀᴜ Tᴇʟʟᴇʀᴇɴᴄᴇ ᴀᴘᴘʀᴏᴀᴄʜᴇᴅ her daughter to tell her she and the Roths could wait inside the College of Overseers' Keeping Room, until it was time for the wedding ceremony. ★ *You look beautiful in that blouse. I knew you would.*

Johanna tugged at the hem. "It feels scratchier than I remember when I first tried it on."

★ *Did you launder it with something harsh?*

"No. I've never worn it before."

Ava's face turned pink.

"Ava," Niamh asked, "Do you think the dry cleaners used something caustic on Johanna's shirt?"

Johanna's brow wrinkled in confusion. "Why was my shirt at the dry cleaners?"

"I borrowed it," Ava said softly.

Pru Tellerence's eyes nearly bugged out as she looked from Ava to her daughter. ★ *You should have never lent out this shirt, Johanna. It could have been dangerous.*

Johanna rested her hand on her mother's arm. "I assure you, I didn't."

"I'm sorry," Ava cried. A tear clung to her lower eyelash.

Niamh turned just as pink as Ava. "You told me you had Johanna's permission!"

Ava looked at Johanna imploringly. "I didn't think you'd mind."

"I do mind, Ava," Johanna said quietly. "This is a very special shirt. I'm more than happy to share most of my clothing with you, but you have to ask me first."

★ *At least you weren't hurt.*

"How could a dumb shirt hurt me?" Ava muttered.

★ *This shirt has special properties. I had it designed specifically for Johanna because she's sometimes involved in dangerous confrontations. If you had been accosted while wearing it, you might have been hurt. It reflects malicious intent—including the intent of the wearer. If someone had wished you ill, it would have reflected that wish back on them. However, if you wished harm on someone else, even in jest— like saying 'I wish you were dead'—it would have reflected back on you, and you would have died.*

Ava and her mother both turned white.

Jackson looked pointedly at Johanna. "Is that shirt even safe for you to wear?"

"Of course. I'm well-aware of its properties and intend to wear it wisely. It's more for protection than anything else. Besides, it's a little dressy, so there aren't that many occasions where I would wear it."

"That's a relief. It's kind of scary when you think about it."

"Although, I was thinking of asking my mother for a similar shirt," Johanna continued, "in a more utilitarian design."

"Great. Something new to worry about."

She leaned over and kissed him. "You'll be safe, as long as you harbor no ill will against me."

Jackson took a step back. "This is the Land of No." He shook a finger at her. "No kissing. No public PDAs of any kind."

"What do you mean?" Chris asked.

"It's against the law here to show public displays of affection. Also, to litter, loiter, sing, skip, dance, and a whole host of other stuff."

"They just sang in the ceremony," Chris stated. "I didn't see anyone getting hauled off for singing in public."

"We're inside the College of Overseers. This is

private property, not a public building. So, it's alright here. Just don't start belting something from *Those Damn Crows* outside.

THE OTHER-WORLDLY sounds of dozens of lutes playing in symphonic harmony set a mood in keeping with the ultra-luminescent glow of millions of diamond dust particles floating in Lumi's twilight fog. They reflected the fairy lights strung throughout the gardens behind the Library of Origination as well as the hundreds of tiny candles, resting in small nooks and crannies, which added to the enchantment. There were no chairs, no center aisle, no altar—none of the trappings of a Fantasian wedding, Romantican Sisterhood ceremony, or Mysterian Binding Ritual. Pru Tellerence and Ryden Simmdry preferred an uncomplicated statement of vows proclaiming their love for each other and their commitment to maintaining their relationship for eternity.

When it came time for the actual ceremony, the pair of overseers simply appeared beneath the arbor in the center of the garden, surrounded by their fellow overseers in a circle. Johanna and Jackson would act as witnesses to the ceremony and were perfectly placed nearby. Their participation gave the Roths the advantage of having a front row position from which to observe the declaration of marriage.

The music lasted longer than the ceremony. Pru Tellerence and Ryden Simmdry had already been together for a very long time, and didn't see the need to make much ado about it. What they did wish to make a special note of was their daughter. While word-of-mouth had spread like wildfire, Johanna had never been formally introduced as the overseers' daughter and they both wanted everyone to know not only why they had chosen this time to pledge their troth, but also how special the product of their union was and what this meant to the future of the College of Overseers.

Johanna blushed prettily but ignored the stares and whispers aimed her way. This was her parents' special day and she turned a blind eye to all references to herself and the abilities she suddenly possessed.

Afterward, the assembled well-wishers celebrated with a toast of Herg wine before the newly-married couple disappeared on a short honeymoon to an idyllic beach in an unknown location.

Johanna and Jackson left imprints of their left palms in the Luminan marriage register, and then gathered all the Roths together for the return trip home.

Back at the library, the Roths said goodbye, leaving Johanna and Jackson to their own devices.

Jackson sighed meaningfully. "I guess this means I can marry you without giving a second thought to your previous illegitimacy."

"Excuse me?" Johanna said.

"I'm not saying you're any less of a person. Even Jon Snow was believed to be a bastard. But now, you're just as legitimate as he turned out to be.

He watched as Johanna quietly stared at him. "I'm not endearing myself to you, am I?"

"Not at all."

"It doesn't mean I don't love you. I love you as much as I possibly can without busting a gut."

"Still not endearing yourself..."

"Let's talk in the morning, after you've had your beauty sleep."

She shook her head. "Still not feeling the love."

"I'm going to go sit in the corner of my bedroom by myself until I'm duly chastened."

"Good plan," she said before disappearing up the curator's staircase.

THERE HAD BEEN a lot less pomp and circumstance in Exeter, although, in Logan's eyes, the day was every bit as eventful as what was taking place in Lumi.

He jumped out of bed that morning, feeling refreshed. After grabbing a cup of coffee and a scone for breakfast, he put on a light blue shirt, red tie and navy-blue jacket, along with a pair of khaki cargo shorts. *What the hell, no one's gonna see me from the waist down.* He had made a decision. Instead of stringing out his exposé of the Library of Illumination over five different shows, he would produce one comprehensive report. Today. Right now, for that matter.

"Hello everyone, I'm Logan Elliott and this is *The Elliott Report.*

"For some time, our village has played host to a very unusual library, not well known among local residents. I'm not talking about the Exeter Memorial Library on Piedmont Street. That library has served the general public well. I'm referring to the private Library of Illumination, located on a small square that, apparently, I can't seem to find on any map. But it's there. Believe me. My best friend works there and we had our prom pictures taken there."

Logan continued, introducing each successive package in turn, slowly building a case against the Library of Illumination. From books opening and objects appearing, to a luxury hotel suite in the middle of the library with views of the Eiffel Tower, he spun a web of magical mystery. In between each segment, he recalled anecdotes Jackson had told him, including the doubloons he had found left behind by the pirates in Treasure Island. He recalled how his friend, a teenager, had purchased a gun to protect the library against Terrorians.

Logan's pièce de résistance, however, was the final package, showing the nearly unedited video he had taken in the Chalet the previous afternoon. From the creaking rafters, to the massive variety of automata gone wild, to the blasting heavy metal music, he had captured it all. He built up to the frenzied chanting and subsequent light show in the office where *The Writer* had been hidden and how it all erupted—so suddenly. It was a damning piece against the library, but a career-making report for Logan and he wanted to upload it as quickly as possible. *This is big. Really big.*

He no longer cared about the GRUNT newsroom or what they thought of his webcast.

Nor did he care about the overseers of the library. *What are they going to do? Cast a memory spell on everyone in the world who has access to a computer?*

He didn't give a second thought as to how it might affect Johanna and Jackson, or the Roth family.

However, he did care about how it would impact the Library of Illumination.

And it had just the effect he was seeking.

The impact was huge.
No. More than huge.
Colossal.

·•·

Indie writers rely on our readers' feedback, so we can continue creating the books you want to read. If you enjoyed reading *Fifth Chronicles of Illumination*, please help others discover it as well.

Review it: Most readers rely on reviews to decide what to read next. Help them out by describing what you liked or didn't like about this book.

Recommend it: Tell your friends or book club about it. Ask your local library to carry it.

Lend it: This book is lending enabled. Share it with your friends.

Join my Inner Circle: Receive information about all my forthcoming books and giveaways. Sign up at:
http://www.artiquapress.com/inner-circle/

I love to hear what my readers have to say about my books, good and bad. But especially good. Write to me at:
c.a.pack@libraryofillumination.com.

• • •

Turn the page for a sneak preview of:

Sixth Chronicles of Illumination

The Story of the Century

ONE

"IN CLOSING, I CAN'T stress too much that the Library of Illumination is a danger to us all. The very idea that a facility exists, where someone can open a book about Hiroshima, literally setting off a nuclear disaster, is beyond belief. This library, located near our homes and children, claims to have portals to other dimensions where who knows what can gain entrance to our world, threatening our very existence.

"This is not a depository for books. It's an arsenal filled with potential weapons. I am asking each and every individual living or working within 50 miles of Exeter to contact your public officials and request— NO—demand that the Library of Illumination be shut down immediately. We cannot allow this devastatingly dangerous place to continue to operate. And once it's shuttered, please call for an investigation of curators Johanna Charette and Jackson Roth. Ask *yourself, why are two teenagers allowed to operate such a hazardous facility? Then ask for a more in-depth look into the administrators they call 'overseers,' supposedly older and wiser beings who are responsible for a chain of these libraries— Oh yes, more of them exist! Notice I called the overseers 'beings' because, according to the Roths, they're not from Earth! Please, pull the plug on the Library of Illumination before it 'illuminates' us out of existence. I'm begging you. I've seen what it can do, firsthand.*

"And that's it for this special edition of The Elliott Report. I'm Logan Elliott. Thank you for watching.

Logan stuck out his arm and pointed directly at the camera.

"Now that you've been illuminated, do what's right. Join the fight. Goodnight."

Logan hit the upload button before walking over to his bed. He dropped on top of the covers still wearing a suit jacket and tie. Within seconds, his breathing evened out and he was fast asleep.

THE FIRST CALLS started moments later. Cell phones, land lines and switchboards at police and fire departments, political offices, and media newsrooms lit up. People called anywhere and everywhere they thought might shed some light on a library they had not previously known existed.

The next morning, the phones at the Exeter Village Hall rang off the hook; every caller wanted either the address of the Library of Illumination or directions to it. Most people couldn't fathom the reports they had seen on the internet and television news stations about an ancient library where books sprang to life.

Some didn't believe it and wanted to see it for themselves. Others believed it and wanted to open the library's books about treasure and wealth, so they could fill their pockets. Then there were those who wanted to take the place over and dissect its workings, so they could franchise and monetize it.

The Library of Illumination was a menace, a rare gem, and an amusement park all rolled into one.

One particular moving image seen on *The Elliott Report*— of Icarus flying out of the pages of a book and soaring toward the sun, only to plummet moments later into the sea—was quite visual and almost immediately went viral. It received much more attention than the recording of Terrorians received. And that small fact underscored the one saving grace for the library, which was the rapid advancement of technology. While many people trusted what they heard on the news, they didn't necessarily believe the images they saw. Too many blockbuster films filled with special effects had inured them to spectacular visuals and unusual aliens.

Still, everyone wanted to go to the library and witness its wonders first-hand. *Maybe it was true.*

Oddly enough, no one at Village Hall, or Town Hall for that matter, could find any mention of the Library of Illumination on record, so for the general public, its location remained a mystery. However, that wouldn't last forever because enough people, like Logan Elliott, the entrepreneurial college student who had created the current uproar, knew of the building's location, even if most other people found it a difficult place to pinpoint.

Meanwhile, even though no digital or printed directory listed the library, Logan's report had named names. Plenty of people knew co-curators Johanna Charette and Jackson Roth's cell phone numbers and gave them out freely to reporters in return for a quick shot of personal television fame.

Library patrons also knew how to get in touch with the library's staff, but they had signed non-disclosure agreements, warning them away from talking about the facility's unusual properties. So, there were some images of people pressing their palms toward the camera lens in an attempt to stop the recording. However, a knowing nod or lack of an outright dismissal of the many outrageous claims being made public, only fueled the story, even if they did not disclose an exact address.

Regardless, with every network and cable news station latching onto the story, the huge revelation made by *The Elliott Report* was now being called *the story of the century.*

JOHANNA AND JACKSON glared at each other. She felt anger over Logan's apparent betrayal of their friendship, and considering he was Jackson's best friend, she held her co-curator responsible. Logan certainly hadn't gathered his impressive collection of knowledge about the inner workings of the library from her. Indeed, the wayward reporter attributed a lot of his information to Jackson's younger sister, Ava. How else could he have video of books opening inside the library, as well as one long tracking shot of the camera moving from between library shelves into the front door of a luxury hotel suite, out onto a balcony that overlooked the Eiffel Tower.

Jackson's return glare was fueled by guilt. He knew his family was partially responsible for what had happened and had let Johanna down, but his siblings would have never knowingly leaked information about the library if they knew Logan planned to go public with it. Besides, Chris and Ava were *kids.*

Johanna took a deep breath and closed her eyes. *Dad, we need you.*

In less than a minute, Ryden Simmdry and Pru Tellerence appeared inside the library. Johanna's parents were overseers, members of a board of deans who guided the Illumini System, a constellation made up of the thirteen worlds on which Libraries of Illumination and the Library of Origination were located. Overseers had special attributes and blessings, that allowed them to grow very old, very slowly, and gave them supernatural and magical powers.

⌘*Johanna, you sound distraught.*

★*Is something wrong?*

Their daughter's eyes glassed over with tears. "Everything is wrong. We've failed the library."

Ryden Simmdry's eyebrows shot up. ⌘*Failed is a very strong sentiment. What do you mean exactly?*

"It's my friend, Logan, Sir," Jackson said deferentially. "He's made public claims about the library's… unique properties. And now the world knows what goes on here."

⌘*The world is a very large number of people.*

★*How could your friend have possibly told so many about the library, so quickly.*

"The internet," Johanna replied.

"It went viral," Jackson continued. "People took clips of it and posted it on social media. It's on YouTube. SiriusXM. All the TV stations are following the story. It's everywhere."

⌘*Can you be more specific about what happened exactly?*

Johanna turned on the monitor standing behind the Information Desk. "Better yet, we can show you," she said as she walked over to the computer and clicked on Logan's website. *The Elliott Report* began playing.

After Logan signed off, Johanna navigated to several of the different news sites on the internet. Each one said it had *exclusive* information about the "phenomenon" called the Library of Illumination. The "exclusives" ranged from conspiracy theorists declaring, "We're only just hearing about the transgressions of the Library of Illumination now, due to a massive government coverup," to members of covens discussing the growing use of magic in our world, to filmmakers talking about the integrity of the video Logan used and whether it depicted actual scenes.

⌘*Who else has access to what you are showing us? This* Elliott Report?

"Everyone," Johanna and Jackson said in unison.

★*And I thought the Oracle was efficient. All the realms should have this ability. It's a wonderful way to make information known quickly.*

⌘ *That would be a mistake. It's easy to see how disinformation can be spread almost instantaneously to a wide audience. The only realm that has something similar is Adventura, but they apparently have had the foresight to use it wisely.* Fantasia's current dilemma illustrates why information needs to be disseminated only by knowledgeable experts after the ramifications of its release have been thoroughly vetted.

LOGAN THREW OFF his blankets and stretched before getting up from bed. He had spent so much energy over the past few weeks, gathering and editing information about the Library of Illumination, it had exhausted him. He'd slept nearly fourteen hours after uploading last night's special edition, getting up only once to remove his suit and tie before falling back in bed.

Now he felt renewed. He walked over to his computer to see if anyone had shared his post or left comments.

Server not available.

He squinted his eyes as he read the screen. Other sites were available, why not his. He tried to view his website several time before navigating over to a local news channel to see if there was a power outage or something like it affecting his web server.

His eyes widened as he caught sight of his video playing on the news. From the way they were reporting it sounded like a big story. He switched to another news site. They reported on it as well. As he switched from newscast to newscast, all he saw were clips of his video playing and experts weighing in on the validity of what might be going on at the library.

"Not might be, what *is* going on," he shouted at the computer.

"Logan, is that you?" his mother called out from down the hall. She followed it up with a knock on his door.

He grabbed a robe and unlocked the door. "What's up, Mom?" he said, rubbing his day-old face stubble.

"I heard you yell. I thought maybe you saw the stories about Jackson's library."

"I just woke up. I must have had a bad dream."

"I can understand why. Whatever possessed you to release those stories about your friends?"

TALK ABOUT A RUDE awakening, Ava Roth couldn't believe her eyes. Her brother Chris woke her from a sound sleep to show her what was trending on social media. She was stunned to learn it was her—talking about the library. "How am I ever going to show my face again? Johanna and Jackson are going to kill me."

"And according to Christopher Roth, Jackson's younger brother, both curators received some blessing that slows down their aging so they'll live for hundreds of years."

"Aargh! Did he just use my name?"

For the first time that morning, Ava smiled. "Yes, he did, brother dear. It looks like you and I are in this together." She paused as she gathered her thoughts. "You know, I have no idea when he could have taken video of the hotel room and the Eiffel Tower. That would have been blatant. Did you let him do that?"

"No. Uh… maybe. I mean, not the really long shot we saw that went from the shelves to the Tower. But I kind of showed him the tower, and then I saw him with his phone in his hand. But he said it was a call from his mother."

"Ugh! I remember that. It was when he came over for dinner."

"He used us."

Ava covered her face with both hands. "I feel like such a fool."

Chris placed his hand on Ava's arm. "Don't worry. We're going to make him pay for this."

"How?"

"Well, first we have to live through this without being banished to some prison realm, or maybe even put to death. But if we survive, I'll think of something."

Tears streamed down Ava's face.

"Hey," Chris continued, "I was just kidding. I don't think it will come to that. At least, I hope it won't."

"My life is ruined," she said, before unleashing a barrage of sobs and tears.

•●•

ABOUT THE AUTHOR

C. A. Pack is an award-winning former journalist, who gave up fact for fiction. She was inspired to write the Library of Illumination series after a discussion about what the perfect library would look like. *Fifth Chronicles of Illumination* is the eleventh book in the series. The book that gave birth to the series, *Chronicles: The Library of Illumination*, contains Johanna and Jackson's first five adventures and was named one of the "Best Indie Books of 2014" by Kirkus Reviews.

The author is also the creator of the *Evangeline's Ghost* series—historical thrillers about a WWII spy who seeks to avenge her murder.

In addition, she is the co-author (under the name Carol Pack) of non-fiction, self-help books on aging, including, *Over-Sixty: Shades of Gray*, a lighthearted yet informative journey through life's later years (on the road to fossilization), along with its companion puzzle/coloring book, *Mind Games & Soporifics*, and her all-too-real look at the COVID-19 pandemic in, *Our Coronavirus Diary*.

C. A. lives on Long Island with her husband, and a picky little parrot who loves to play peek-a-boo.

You can learn more about the author on her website:

www.carolpack.com